THE BABY'S GUARDIAN

BY
DELORES FOSSEN

First published in Great Britain 2011
Harlequin Mills & Boon Limited,
Eton House, 18-24 Paradise Road, Richmond, Surrey TW9 1SR

THE BABY'S GUARDIAN © Delores Fossen 2010

ISBN: 978 0 263 88506 4

46-0211

Harlequin Mills & Boon policy is to use papers that are natural, renewable and recyclable products and made from wood grown in sustainable forests. The logging and manufacturing processes conform to the legal environmental regulations of the country of origin.

Printed and bound in Spain
by Litografia Rosés S.A., Barcelona

Welcome to the first book
in Delores Fossen's fantastic new
TEXAS MATERNITY: HOSTAGES mini-series.

Don't forget to look out for the final instalment
The Mummy Mystery
in April 2011

Chapter One

The sound of the gunshot sent Captain Shaw Tolbert's heart to his knees.

Hell. This couldn't happen. He couldn't lose a single one of those hostages.

"Hold your fire!" Shaw shouted to the nearly three dozen officers and SWAT team members he had positioned all around the San Antonio Maternity Hospital.

For a split second everything and everyone around him froze. No more frantic orders and chatter from his men. Even the reporters and photographers who were pressed against the barricades nearly a block away went still, their cameras no longer flashing the bursts of light that knifed through the night.

The stunned silence didn't last. The officers and the SWAT team already had their weapons ready, and they adjusted, taking aim in the direction of that shot.

But the shot hadn't come from any of them.

It'd come from the fourth floor where a group of pregnant women, newborns and hospital staff were all being held at gunpoint. Hostages that included Nadine Duggan, the wife of one of Shaw's own men, Lieutenant Bo Duggan.

That shot meant Nadine or one of the others could have been killed.

Shaw didn't know all the hostages' names. Heck, he wasn't even sure he had an accurate head count. Basically, anyone unlucky enough to have been on the fourth floor at 3:00 p.m. had been taken captive by at least two gunmen wearing ski masks and carrying assault weapons. Shaw had managed to get that meager bit of information from a nurse who'd made a hysterical nine-one-one call during the first minutes of the attack. Since then, neither the nurse nor any of the other known hostages had answered their cells or the hospital phones.

Using the back of his hand to swipe the slick sweat from his forehead, Shaw maneuvered his way through his men and the equipment and hurried from his command center vehicle to the hostage negotiator. It was Texas hot, and the unforgiving August heat was still brutal despite the sun having set hours earlier.

He spotted the negotiator, Sergeant Harris McCoy, in the passenger seat of a patrol car that several officers were using as cover. The blond-haired, blue-eyed officer might look as if he'd just stepped off a glossy recruitment poster, but he was the best that San Antonio PD had. In the past four years, Harris had successfully negotiated nearly twenty hostage situations. Shaw desperately needed him to add one more gold star to his résumé.

"What happened?" Shaw asked.

Harris shook his head. "I'm not sure. I was talking to one of the gunmen on his cell—trying to get the guy to give us his demands. Then he shouted 'she's getting away' and he hung up. About five seconds later, someone fired the shot."

Shaw cursed. He prayed that shot had been fired as a warning and not deadly force. Because if a hostage had been killed, he'd have to seriously consider storming the place ASAP. He couldn't sit back and let all those people die. But the SWAT team and police forcing their way onto the ward would almost certainly cause its own set of casualties.

"Try to get one of the gunmen back on the line," Shaw told Harris.

While Harris pressed redial and waited for the gunman to answer, Shaw held his breath and paced. Not that he could go far. The scene was a logjam of law enforcement officers who'd initially responded, and more had arrived as this ordeal had dragged on. Nine hours. God knew what kind of havoc the gunmen could have created in that much time.

"What happened?" Harris demanded the moment he had one of the gunmen on the phone. Like the other calls throughout the afternoon and evening, this one was on speaker.

"Everything's under control," the gunman assured him. Which was no assurance at all.

After nine hours, Shaw was familiar with that voice, though the guy had refused to identify himself. But it was a voice Shaw would remember, and when he had everyone safely out of this, he was going after this SOB and his accomplice. That wasn't his normal role as a captain. These days, he was pretty much a supervisor working from his desk, but for this, he'd make an exception and do some field duty.

"Is anyone hurt?" Harris asked the gunman.

"No. It was a misunderstanding, that's all. It won't happen again. Will it?"

"No," someone said. A woman. And her voice created an uneasy feeling inside Shaw.

No way.

It couldn't be *her*.

Shaw jerked his phone from his pocket and scrolled through the numbers until he found Sabrina Carr's. He jabbed the call button. Waited. And cursed when he heard the ringing. Not just on his own phone, but the sound was also coming through Harris's cell. Each ring went unanswered, and each ring confirmed that this nightmare had just gotten a lot worse. Sabrina's phone was on the fourth floor of that hospital.

And so was she.

"That was Sabrina Carr's voice," Shaw managed to say to Harris in a whisper.

Harris's head whipped up, and he pinned his alarmed gaze to Shaw's. "You mean…" Harris mouthed, but he didn't finish.

Shaw didn't finish it for him, either, but they both knew what this meant. Sabrina Carr was the surrogate carrying Shaw's child. She was eight months pregnant.

And Sabrina was a hostage.

Shaw resisted the urge to lean against the patrol car that was just inches away, and he choked back the profanity. This was a complication he didn't need, and the situation had just gotten a lot more personal.

"Are you certain the hostage is all right?" Harris demanded from the gunman.

"See for yourself," the man answered.

Shaw looked up at the row of eight-foot-tall windows that encircled the entire fourth floor. The building was about thirty yards away, but he still saw the movement behind the thick glass.

Someone pushed a woman into view.

The height and build were right for it to be Sabrina. About five-six and average. So was the pregnant belly that her tan cargo shorts and bulky green top couldn't hide. Ditto for that mop of shoulder-length red hair— Sabrina had hair like that. But praying he was wrong, Shaw grabbed a pair of binoculars from the officer next to him and took a closer look.

Hell.

It was Sabrina all right.

She was shades past being pale, and he could tell from her expression that she was terrified. Probably because she'd just come close to dying. That shot had no doubt been fired at her.

Even though there was no love lost between Sabrina and him, Shaw wasn't immune to the terror he saw on her face and in her eyes. After all, she was carrying his child.

Their child, he silently amended.

The image of his late wife flashed through his head. The baby Sabrina was carrying should have been his wife's. His and Fay's. Sabrina should have been just a surrogate, that's all, but that had changed when none of Fay's eggs had been viable. Sabrina had become the egg donor then, too. Sabrina's DNA, not Fay's. More than a mere surrogate. But that was an old wound that he didn't have time to nurse right now.

"Did you know Sabrina was in there?" Harris asked, placing his hand over the receiver so the gunman wouldn't be able to hear the question.

Shaw shook his head. Sabrina had her regular pre-natal checkups at a clinic in the hospital, but she wasn't scheduled for anything this week. Shaw knew that because she always sent him the dates and times of her appointments. Not that he'd ever gone with her to any of them. But he knew she wasn't scheduled for anything until the day after tomorrow.

So, why was she there?

"Ask to speak to her," Shaw instructed.

Harris nodded. "I want to talk to the hostage to make sure she's okay," he relayed to the gunman.

The gunman didn't respond right away, and with the binoculars pressed to his eyes, Shaw watched. Waited.

The seconds crawled by.

Then, much to his surprise, he saw the gloved hand jut out and give Sabrina the cell phone.

Because Shaw was watching her so closely, he saw her look in the direction of that hand. The gunman's hand. Shaw could hear the man give her whispered instructions, but he couldn't make out what the guy was saying. It was almost certainly some kind of threat.

"Captain Shaw Tolbert?" she said.

That sent another hush around him. Inside, Shaw was having a much stronger reaction than a hush. Why the devil was she asking for him? If the gunmen knew her association with the captain of the SAPD, things could get even worse for her.

And the baby.

"Yes?" Shaw answered, trying to sound official and

detached. Judging from the sound of her voice, the call was on speaker at Sabrina's end, which meant the gunmen were listening to his every word. He certainly didn't want to let them know that he knew her name, just in case he could salvage this situation.

"They read my medical records," Sabrina explained. She swallowed hard. "They know you're my emergency contact."

Shaw choked back a groan. By knowing that bit of information, the gunmen had already guessed that Sabrina and he had some kind of relationship. Heck, her records might even say that he was the baby's father. If so, the gunmen had some serious leverage.

Both Sabrina and the baby.

"Are you…all right?" Shaw asked.

"She is, for now," the gunman answered for her. "You'll need to do some things to make it stay that way."

Even though he could clearly hear the man, Shaw took Harris's phone and brought it closer to his mouth. "What things?"

The gunman grabbed Sabrina's phone as well, but she stayed in the window, staring down at the crowd. He saw her pick through the faces until she spotted him. Shaw looked away. He needed to focus, and he couldn't do that if he was looking at her. Because looking at Sabrina only brought on those haunting images of his wife.

A man didn't forget watching his wife die in his arms.

"My partner and I are ready to get out of here," the gunman announced.

Shaw didn't celebrate either silently or aloud because

he knew this was just the first step to ending this, and every step afterward would be even more dangerous than the present situation.

"We're coming out through the front entrance," the gunman continued. "And we'll have a hostage with us."

They were probably planning to take Sabrina, unless Shaw could get them to change their minds.

"So, no tricks," the gunman warned. "Have your officers back way off and have a car waiting for us out front. We'll give the driver instructions as to where we need to go."

Shaw sandwiched the phone between his shoulder and his ear so he could motion for one of his men to spring into action. They'd anticipated the car request and had one ready. A vehicle with not one but two hidden GPS trackers that would allow them to find the guys.

Well, maybe.

There was something not quite right about all of this.

The gunmen hadn't requested money or any other form of ransom. That wasn't just unusual, it was downright unsettling. After all, the men had just spent hours holding the hostages, and they'd done that without saying why this situation had started in the first place. A hospital maternity ward wasn't the setting for many hostage standoffs, especially since this didn't seem to be personal.

At least it hadn't been until now.

Had the gunmen gone after Sabrina in the first place, or had that happened only after they'd learned about her connection to an SAPD police captain? Maybe the plan was to take her to a secondary location and ask for ransom?

That theory would have held some merit if Shaw had been a rich man. He wasn't.

So, what did the men want?

Drugs, maybe. That was always a possibility when it came to hospital robberies. Maybe that was all there was to it. They'd wanted drugs and now they had them and needed to get away. That didn't lessen the danger, but it would make the investigation a little simpler.

The officer parked the car in front of the hospital, and Shaw motioned for everyone to move away. He would pull all his men back onto the sidewalk of the building across the four lanes of St. Mary's Street. The SWAT team would stay in place on the rooftops. Because the surrounding buildings were taller than the hospital, Shaw didn't think the gunmen had actually seen the SWAT team. But still, they must have known they were there. This hostage situation was all over the news, and the world was watching. The gunmen must have realized that every conceivable measure would have been taken to apprehend them.

"The car's in place," Shaw told the gunman over the cell.

"Good. We're coming out. Remember, no tricks."

"My advice? Don't take one of the new mothers or pregnant women hostage. Too much trouble, and too many things can go wrong. Take me instead."

"No, thanks. I got my own ideas about how to handle a hostage." And the gunman hung up.

Shaw didn't have time to react to that bold threat because movement caught his eye. A gloved hand reached out and grabbed on to Sabrina's arms. She snagged Shaw's gaze then. For just a second. And the gunman yanked her out of sight.

It sickened Shaw to think of the stress this was creating for the baby. And the danger. No unborn child or pregnant woman should have to go through this, and Shaw had to make sure this ended now.

Shaw relayed the information he'd just learned to one of the uniforms who would pass it on to the other officers posted at various points around the building. He handed the phone back to Harris, and he drew his gun while he moved back across the street with his men. He kept his attention fastened to the front of the building. Watching. Bracing himself for whatever was about to go down.

When the gunmen came out, it was possible the SWAT team would have clean shots, but if that didn't happen, the plan was to let the gunmen drive away and have plainclothes officers in unmarked cars follow in pursuit. Then, he could get his men inside the building to assess the damage. It was entirely possible they would have dead bodies or injuries on their hands. Ambulances were waiting just up the street since the hospital itself had already been evacuated, and the staff inside might need medical attention of their own.

Shaw wouldn't be able to hold back the lieutenant whose wife was inside, so he hoped this departure ended with the gunmen being killed.

If not, well, the night was just starting.

"Smoke!" Harris shouted.

Shaw looked in the direction of Harris's pointing finger. Oh, mercy.

What now?

It was smoke all right, and it was coming from a window on the fourth floor where the hostages were.

There was a fire engine standing by, and Shaw motioned for it to get in place. It was a huge risk. The gunmen might not come down to the car if they saw the fire department responding, but Shaw couldn't take the chance of leaving those hostages trapped on the floor with a raging fire.

"The hospital has an overhead sprinkler system," Harris reminded him.

But no one needed to remind Shaw that the gunmen could have disabled it. God knows what smoke and fire would do to all those babies in the newborn unit. He had to get them help immediately, even if it meant the gunmen might get away.

"Where are they?" Shaw mumbled, watching the front door.

The fire engine darted across the street and stopped at the side of the building. They immediately retrieved the ladder so they could scurry up the four floors. It was a start, but Shaw needed to get others inside so he could speed up the evacuation. In addition to the babies, there might be patients who couldn't get out on their own.

The passing seconds pounded in his head, and at least a minute went by with no sign of the gunmen or the hostage that they claimed they would have with them.

Gray coils of smoke made their way down to them. Soon, very soon, it would obstruct their view. And maybe that's what the gunmen had intended.

Shaw grabbed the binoculars again and checked out the front windows on the fourth floor. He could see the overhead sprinklers spewing out water. He could also see people running. Women. Some of them pregnant. Some of them carrying babies bundled in blankets.

He couldn't delay this any longer. He had to move now.

Shaw was about to give the signal when he heard the voice on the hand-sized scanner clipped to his belt. It was Lieutenant Bo Duggan, the officer who was positioned on the west side of the building.

"The fire's a smokescreen!" Bo shouted. "The gunmen just left through the side door and got into a white SUV with heavy tint on the windows. I can't see the license plate number—it had mud or something covering it—and they're moving out of the parking lot now."

Hell.

"Shaw?" Bo said. "We couldn't shoot at them because they have a hostage. It's Sabrina Carr."

Shaw's stomach knotted, but he forced back the avalanche of emotion and dread. "Take over the evacuation," he ordered Bo. "Get everyone out of there." He turned to Harris. "You get in there, too. Take every available man." Shaw turned to run toward his squad car.

"Where are you going?" Harris shouted.

"After the gunmen."

And every second counted.

Shaw had already lost his wife, and by God he wasn't going to let the same thing happen to his baby.

Chapter Two

Sabrina forced herself to stay calm.

It was nearly impossible to do that because there was a gun jammed against her head, and one of the ski-mask-wearing kidnappers shoved her into the backseat of an SUV. The other got behind the wheel and sped out of the parking lot.

There were plenty of officers nearby, all with guns aimed, but none of them fired a shot. Probably because they hadn't wanted to risk wounding her and the baby. Sabrina was thankful for that, but she wondered if she'd just gone from the frying pan into the fire.

Her heart was racing, and it was so loud in her ears that it was hard for her to hear, but she thought she might have heard one of the officers shout. Maybe that meant someone would follow them because she wasn't sure she'd be able to get herself out of this without help.

She glanced behind her at the hospital. The building was engulfed in milky gray smoke, but she could still see even more cops. Some armed with rifles were on top of the surrounding buildings.

Shaw was out there, too.

Sabrina had seen him from the window. He'd been

standing among all the officers assembled to respond to the hostage situation. And even though Shaw had been so far away when she stepped into view, she had been able to make out his expression when he realized she was a hostage. That wasn't fear on his face. More like anger.

Or even disgust.

He was probably thinking she'd screwed up again.

And in a way, she had.

The gunman-driver made a sharp left turn and sent her sliding toward the door. Her captor hauled her right back so he could keep her in a close, firm grip against his side. She wanted to punch him for what he was doing.

For what he'd done back at the hospital.

Sabrina had seen him shoot an unarmed lab tech who was hardly more than a kid. He'd used a gun rigged with a silencer for that deadly assault, and the shot had hardly made a sound. It made her wonder how many others had been killed in a silent hush.

And why?

Why would be the biggest question of all.

Was it connected to the call from the nurse, Michael Frost, that she'd gotten earlier? The call that sent her to the hospital in the first place?

Maybe.

But for now, her focus had to be on survival. The cops were no doubt following them, and she had to believe they would launch a rescue. She also had to believe they would succeed. Sabrina couldn't even consider an alterative, not with her baby's safety at stake.

She looked up at the street signs, trying to memorize

them just in case she got the opportunity to tell someone where she was, but the gunman must have noticed what she was doing because he shoved her down onto the seat.

"Curiosity killed the cat," he snarled. He stank of sweat, onion chips from the hospital vending machine and the peppermint breath mints that he'd sucked on throughout the standoff.

Sabrina would remember that sickening scent. That raspy voice. Those dull brown eyes that were flat, like a man on the job rather than one on a personal mission.

He was almost certainly a hired killer.

And when this was over, she would make sure he and his partner were punished for this havoc they had caused. All those women and babies had been put through a nightmare, and it wasn't over. Not for her, not for them. They would have to deal with the terrifying memories forever.

Something that Sabrina already knew too much about.

"We lost the cops," the driver announced.

That didn't help with the fear or the dread. But he could be wrong. *He had to be wrong.*

The driver slowed to a crawl, and several seconds later, the car came to a stop. In a dark alley.

Oh, God.

Sabrina tried not to think of what could happen here. She didn't think these men had rape or assault on their minds, but they wouldn't hesitate to use her as a human shield when the cops arrived.

"Move fast," the gunman ordered, and he threw open the door and pushed her out into the alley.

"Right," she grumbled. Fast wasn't possible for her these days.

She didn't see any other cars or people. Definitely no cops. And her heartbeat grew significantly harder and faster. God. Had the driver been right about SAPD not being able to follow her? Had the gunmen made a clean getaway?

The gunman latched on to her arm and dragged her into the adjacent building. It was dark, musky and hot. No AC. Not even a trickle of fresh air. No furniture, either. From what Sabrina could see in the shadows, it was an abandoned office building, and judging from the distance they'd driven, they were somewhere in the downtown area of San Antonio. Not a good part, either.

"Lock the door," the gunman told his partner. "I'll tie her up. But don't make the call until you're out of her earshot. No sense broadcasting what's going on."

The man didn't take her to a room near the door but to one about midway down the long tiled corridor. He shoved his gun into the back waist of his pants so he could use both hands to snag her wrists.

Sabrina knew what was coming.

She'd already seen him tie up members of the hospital staff and some of the patients. He took two thin plastic handcuffs from his pocket and looped one around her wrists. The other, he hooked through the first so that it chained her to the doorknob. The plastic cuffs might be cheap, but they were extremely effective. They would hold her in place until…but Sabrina didn't want to think beyond that.

She would get out of this before they managed to take her out of the city and to God knows where.

She needed a miracle.

The man reached down and pulled off her sandals. "In case you figure out how to get out of those cuffs, there's broken glass on the floor. It'll slice your feet to shreds," he snarled and went down the hall with her shoes dangling in his hand.

Being shoeless wouldn't stop her, either. Sabrina looked around the dark room, praying there was something she could use to cut the tough plastic. Maybe a piece of the glass he'd mentioned. It was there, all right. Beer bottles had been shattered, but none of the pieces was close enough for her to reach.

There were only threads of light coming from the single window on the center wall. The glass panes were coated with grime and taped yellowing newspapers that practically blocked off illumination from the nearby streetlights. But it allowed her to see just enough to realize there was nothing she could use as a cutter. With the exception of the broken glass and some trash on the floor, the room was empty.

Inside her, the baby began to kick, hard. Probably to protest her cramped sitting position. Sabrina shifted, trying to get more comfortable, but that was impossible on a hard tile floor.

Up the hall, she heard the peppermint-popping gunman say something, and she wiggled closer to the doorway in the hopes that she could hear and see what was going on. The men had apparently stepped into one of the other rooms because they were nowhere in sight, but she did get bits and pieces of their softly spoken conversation.

"Tolbert," one of them said.

That grabbed her attention. They were talking about Shaw. Sabrina tried to wriggle even closer though the plastic cuffs were digging into her wrists.

"It'll work." That was from the gunman who'd driven them away from the hospital. He was whispering as if he wanted to ensure she didn't hear what he was saying, but the empty building carried the sound. "We can use her to get Tolbert to cooperate in case something else turns up."

Oh, God. They were going to use her to force Shaw to do something. But cooperate with what?

All of this had to be connected to the hostage mess that'd just gone on in the hospital, but Sabrina was clueless as to why she and the others had been terrorized all those hours.

What did any of this have to do with Shaw?

The men didn't know she was carrying Shaw's child. Or did they? It certainly wasn't in her medical records, but they had seen that she had listed Shaw as the person to contact in case there was an emergency. Maybe the men thought she and Shaw were lovers.

As if.

Shaw hated her with a passion. And this situation was only going to make him hate her more. Once again, she'd brought danger to someone he loved. This time, the danger was aimed at his unborn child. He would never forgive her for placing the baby at risk.

Of course, Sabrina wouldn't forgive herself, either.

Had that call she'd received all been a hoax? Something designed to get her into the hospital?

If so, then her abduction wasn't a spur of the minute thing as she'd originally believed. She might have been their target all along, and she hadn't even questioned the call. She'd blindly responded to the request and had walked right into a hornet's nest.

The minute she'd stepped off that fourth floor elevator, one of the men had aimed a gun at her and then corralled her into the hall where they were already holding several dozen hostages. Sabrina wouldn't forget their faces. The fear. The overwhelming feeling of doom.

"The car'll be here in ten minutes," she heard one of her captors say. "Go ahead, give her back the shoes. I want us to be ready to roll."

Ten minutes. Not much time at all. And judging from their other conversation, they'd be taking her with them. If that happened, they might kill her once they had what they wanted. Because of the ski masks, she hadn't seen their faces, but she did know details about them. She was a loose end and a dangerous one.

The man appeared again, his ski mask still in place, and he carefully placed the shoes on the floor beside her. When she didn't move to slip them on, he cursed at her, shoved them on her feet and walked away.

She waited until he was out of sight before she fought with the plastic cuffs again. No luck. So, she decided to try to chew her way through them, though she knew that would be next to impossible. The cuffs were designed to prevent such an escape. Still, she had to try. Those ten minutes were already ticking off.

There was a sound. Just a slight bump. It didn't come from the men up the hall but from the window.

Someone was outside.

Sabrina chewed even harder on the cuff, while she kept watch up the hall and at the shadowy figure on the other side of that murky glass.

There was a soft pop. And the window eased open. She got a good look at the dark-haired man then.

It was Shaw.

Relief flooded through her entire body. He'd come for her. Well, he'd come for the baby anyway. Now the question was, could he get them safely out of there?

Shaw glanced around the room and put his index finger to his mouth in a stay-quiet gesture. Sabrina quit struggling with the plastic cuffs and tipped her head toward the men up the hall.

"There are two of them," she mouthed, and in case Shaw hadn't heard, she held up two fingers.

Shaw nodded, climbed through the window, swung his legs over the sill and quietly placed his feet on the floor. He had his standard-issue Glock ready in his right hand, and he lifted it, aiming it at the door. If her captors heard Shaw's entrance, they would no doubt come running.

But they didn't.

The men continued to talk, and Shaw used the sound of their muffled voices to cover his footsteps as he made his way across the dusty floor toward her. Shattered glass crunched softly under his feet. He spared her a glance.

Barely.

That was normal. Shaw never looked in her eyes,

which was probably a good thing. Even something as simple as eye contact between them brought back the painful memories of Fay's death. But Sabrina knew that his eyes were multiple shades of blue. Cool and piercing when he was in a good mood. Dark and stormy when he was wasn't.

She didn't have to guess the intensity level tonight.

With his attention fastened to the hall and doorway, Shaw reached in his pocket, brought out a small knife and used it to slice through the plastic. He didn't waste a second; he took her arm, got her to her feet and eased her behind him. His hand brushed against her stomach. An accident for sure.

Like eye contact, touching was out, too.

Shaw motioned toward the window. "You think you can climb out?" he whispered.

Sabrina glanced down at her megapregnant belly and then at the window. It'd be a tight squeeze, but the alternative was going out into the hall and then trying to make their way through a locked door at the end. That was far riskier than the window.

She nodded, and he maneuvered her behind him while he continued to face the door.

Shaw leaned closer and put his mouth to her ear. No peppermint and sweat smell for him. She took in the scent of his starched white shirt, the leather of his boots and the woodsy aftershave he favored. Not that he would have shaved recently. He had dark desperado stubble on his chin, but a hint of the aftershave was still there.

"Once we're outside and away from the scene, SWAT will storm the building," Shaw whispered.

Good. This had to end, and she didn't want those gunmen to be able to hurt anyone else.

Thankful that she was wearing shorts so she could maneuver better, Sabrina somehow managed to get her leg onto the sill. But then, she heard the footsteps in the hall.

Oh, no. One of the gunmen was coming.

Sabrina tried to hurry, but Shaw clamped on to her arm to stop her from moving. Without the sound of her rustling, the room fell silent.

So did the footsteps.

They waited there. Listening. Sabrina prayed the men wouldn't come closer. The last thing she wanted was a gun battle where the baby could be hurt. Obviously, Shaw felt the same because he moved protectively in front of her. Close. With his back right against her front.

As a cop, he'd perhaps been in situations similar to this where his life was on the line, but this whole ordeal was a first for her, and Sabrina hoped she didn't lose it. Falling apart wouldn't get them out of there, and it wouldn't help the baby.

"Call him back," the gunman finally said. It was the peppermint guy. "I'm getting a weird feeling about being here. We need to get out now."

With her breath stalled in her lungs, Sabrina stayed still, and she finally heard what she prayed she would hear. The gunman went back down the hall away from them. At least she hoped that's what he'd done.

Shaw nudged her to get moving, and Sabrina didn't waste any time. She climbed through the window, trying to protect her belly from scraping against the sill. Her feet finally touched down onto the ground. Shaw was right behind her. While continuing to face the direction of the gunmen, he shimmied out the window and landed right next to her.

"Come on," he ordered. Using his left hand, he grabbed her arm and started to move as fast as she could.

The baby kicked even harder, and her stomach started to cramp. Sabrina silently cursed the Braxton Hicks contraction.

False labor.

Her body was merely practicing for the real thing, but she didn't need the distraction now. She had to keep moving and get to safety.

She saw the SWAT team then, on the building across the street. There were other officers crouched down behind a Dumpster and the gunmen's SUV.

The baby and she were safe.

Or so she thought.

But then, the shots rang out.

Chapter Three

Shaw cursed and hooked his arm around Sabrina.

Despite the urgency that the deadly gunfire created, he tried to be careful with her, and he took the brunt of the fall when he pulled her to the ground. His shoulder hit hard, but he held on tight to his gun so that it wouldn't be jarred from his hand.

Shaw didn't stop there. He crawled over Sabrina, sheltering her with his body, and he came up ready to return fire.

This was obviously a situation he'd wanted to avoid at all costs. He didn't want his baby in the middle of a fight with these armed fugitives, but when they fired that shot, they'd left him no choice. Now, the trick was to get Sabrina safely out of there.

There was another shot. It slammed into the rough brick wall just inches from Shaw's head. Not close, a good foot away, but the sound and the impact allowed him to pinpoint the origin of the shot. It was coming from the window where Sabrina and he had escaped.

"Get down," someone on the SWAT team yelled from the roof of the adjacent building.

Shaw did. He dropped lower, covering Sabrina as best he could.

She was breathing way too hard and fast, and he hoped like the devil that she didn't hyperventilate. While he was hoping, he added that the baby hadn't been harmed in all of this. Sabrina didn't appear to have any physical injuries, but the stress couldn't be good. She needed to get to a doctor so she could be checked out.

There was another shot, but this one came from a rifleman on the SWAT team. Shaw didn't look up, but he heard the sound of glass being blown apart.

Good!

That would stop the gunmen from aiming any more shots at Sabrina and him. At least from that window. That didn't mean they wouldn't go elsewhere to return fire. The abandoned building was large, at least five thousand square feet, and there were a lot of places for someone to hide or get into a position to kill.

The shots continued, all coming from his men, which meant it might be time to try to get Sabrina to better cover. Shaw glanced at the front of the building. Hell.

Too many windows.

And a set of double doors with glass fronts.

The gunmen could use any of those points of attack to fire again. That meant staying put until the officers and SWAT had apprehended the suspects. The one advantage that his officers did have was that the building was only one floor. The gunmen wouldn't be able to move upstairs and launch an assault there. They were going to have to face the SWAT team and other cops head-on.

So that Sabrina's pregnant belly wouldn't be smashed against the ground, Shaw eased off her and moved her to a sitting position so that her back was against the brick wall. They were close. Too close. And face-to-face.

He found himself staring right into those sea-green eyes.

Shaw quickly looked away. Then he turned around so he was facing outward. This would make it easier for him to cover all sides. It was a solid strategic move, he assured himself. And it was far better than staring at her.

With the gunmen no longer firing at them, Shaw's men started to close in around the building. One of the SWAT members bashed in the double front doors, and officers began to pour inside. It shouldn't be long now before he could get Sabrina out of there.

Once he had her in an ambulance and on the way to a hospital, he could return to the original crime scene and try to mop up things. He'd left Lieutenant Bo Duggan in charge, but that was strictly temporary. Since Bo's own wife was a hostage, Shaw needed to get back on scene so that Bo could be with his wife. If their situations had been reversed, Shaw would have certainly wanted to be with Fay.

"The gunmen said they were going to use me," Sabrina muttered, her voice a shaky whisper. But it was loud enough to cut through his thoughts and snare his attention. "To get *you* to cooperate."

"What?" Shaw said that a little louder than he'd intended and glanced at her over his shoulder.

Sabrina shook her head, sending a curl of that wild

red hair flinging over her cheek. "I don't know what they meant by that. Do you?"

"No." But he could guess. "I'm a police captain." A lot of people might want him to *cooperate*, especially when it came to helping with a plea bargain or reduced charges.

That wouldn't happen in this case.

Shaw turned his head away from her so he could keep watch of all the areas around them. "What else did they say?"

"Not much. They were careful not to talk in front of me or the others. But I think they knew I'd be at the hospital this afternoon. They were waiting for me."

Oh, man. That didn't sound good at all. "Why the heck were you even there?"

Sabrina took a deep breath. "Someone from the hospital phoned me. A male nurse named Michael Frost, and he said Nadine Duggan had called an urgent meeting of the moms' support group. So, I went."

Shaw cursed and didn't bother to keep the profanity to himself. Sabrina knew how he felt about that group. It was headed by Nadine Duggan, the wife of one of his lieutenants and a woman who'd also become a hostage. Bo's wife. Nadine was a psychologist and probably bound to keep secret whatever she was told in that support group, but Shaw didn't want Sabrina baring her soul to someone who might share those soul-baring secrets with her husband, a man whom Shaw worked side by side with. Bo and all the other officers knew about Shaw's late wife, of course.

Everyone also knew about the baby.

But Shaw hadn't wanted Sabrina to talk about the

problems that he'd had adjusting to her pregnancy. About all the appointments he'd missed for her checkups. All the calls from her that he hadn't returned.

Their arrangement was complicated since, after all, he'd ultimately given her approval to get pregnant. Hell, he'd provided the semen for the procedure, but he and Sabrina both knew he wasn't really on board. Not emotionally.

And it was those emotions Shaw wanted to keep to himself.

Best not to let his men know the mental turmoil he was going through right now. Something like that could perhaps water down his authority, and as their leader, the last thing he wanted in a dangerous situation was to have his authority questioned or undermined.

That's why Shaw had offered to pay for Sabrina to attend another support group. But she'd refused.

What else was new?

They didn't see eye to eye on, well, anything.

"Is that why Nadine Duggan was there at the hospital, too?" Shaw asked, still keeping watch. Another wave of officers went into the building.

"No. She was actually in labor. I saw her when I first arrived, but then she disappeared when the gunmen starting shouting. A lot of people did. It was chaos, and some of the women ran and hid."

Shaw had to take a deep breath. He hoped that didn't mean anything bad had happened to the lieutenant's wife or any of the patients, staff or babies.

"What about this Michael Frost who called you?" he asked. "Did you see him after you arrived at the hospital?"

"No." She paused. "Why?"

"No reason." Not yet anyway. He'd make a call in a minute or two to have a background check run on the male nurse. Everything and everyone would be checked.

"The gunmen killed someone," Sabrina added.

That caused Shaw to glance at her again, and this time those green eyes were filled with tears. "Who?"

"A lab tech. I don't know his name. They shot him. Right in front of me."

This time Shaw added a groan to the profanity. Sabrina had witnessed a murder, and in addition to the emotional trauma that created, it could mean that she was now a target. If those gunmen thought for one minute that she could identify them, they wouldn't want her around, so that's why it was critical for this to end now.

"Did the men shoot at you, too?" Shaw asked.

She didn't answer right away. "Yes. But not when they killed the tech. It was later. I could tell they were getting ready to leave, and I had a gut feeling they'd take me with them. So, I tried to sneak away."

Unfortunately, he could picture that scene all too well.

"The gunman didn't shoot at me, not really," she added. "The bullet went in the ceiling."

Which confirmed the gunmen wanted her alive. After all, the gunmen had already killed others, so that meant they had a reason for allowing Sabrina to live.

Was he that reason?

"I'm sorry, Shaw. I'm so sorry," Sabrina said. But he

knew she wasn't talking about this situation alone. She was dredging up the past.

Something he wouldn't discuss with her.

"Don't," he warned.

He didn't add more because his phone buzzed. He glanced at the caller ID and saw it was from the SWAT team commander, Lieutenant José Rivera. "Tolbert," Shaw answered.

"Captain, we need you to stay put for a couple more minutes. We're trying to secure the building now, but we don't want Ms. Carr or you out in the open just yet."

"Yeah. Make it as fast as you can," Shaw insisted. Because he didn't want to stay there with Sabrina any longer than necessary, and he was anxious to get back to the primary crime scene.

Shaw ended the call and waited with the sounds of the search going on in the building behind them. He didn't stop watching the place. Definitely didn't lower his gun. Because he didn't want those men, those killers, coming back outside to grab Sabrina.

"Think hard," Shaw said. If he had to wait there with her, he might as well start the interrogation that had to happen for the reports and the cleanup. "What did these men want?"

"I don't know."

Sabrina was crying. He could hear the tears in her voice. Part of him wanted to comfort her, but Shaw resisted. He couldn't open up his heart to that kind of intimacy with her. The only way he had survived Fay's death was to shut himself off, and he would continue to do just that.

Shaw tried again with the questions. He wanted to

keep this conversation on the business at hand. "Other than you and the lab tech they killed, did it seem as if the gunmen were after anyone specific?"

"They kept calling out for someone named Bailey. I don't think they found her though because they kept shouting her name. And then they had a group of us sit in the hall. One of them held us at gunpoint while the other gunman took this one pregnant woman. I don't know where they took her, but she was gone for several hours. Then, she tried to escape, but she fell and hit her head. She was bleeding."

Each new thing he learned disgusted him even more, and it was just starting. All kinds of details would no doubt be brought out when the other hostages were questioned. He'd definitely need to speak to this woman whom the gunmen had yelled at.

If she was still alive, that is.

"What else did the gunmen do?" he asked. "Did they appear to be searching for anything specific?"

"Other than the person named Bailey, I don't think so." She paused, shook her head. "Wait. One of them went into the lab and the records room. The lab door wouldn't open so he shot the lock, and he stayed in there a long time. He also had one of the hostages with him a lot of time."

Okay. That was a start. He'd have every inch of those rooms processed and review the surveillance camera footage to see what the men had been after.

"How about a drug cabinet or something like that?" Shaw didn't enjoy forcing her to go over all the details, but with her memory still fresh, this was the time to do it. Later, the shock and the adrenaline crash might rob her of critical details.

"No drugs. At least, I didn't see them take or use any." Behind him, Sabrina shifted her position, probably because she was trying to get comfortable. But with the shift, her belly pressed against his back.

Shaw felt it then.

The soft bumps.

He glanced back at the contact and realized what he was feeling was the baby.

"The baby's kicking," Sabrina explained, moving away again so that she wasn't touching him.

Shaw immediately felt the loss. It was the first time he'd felt his child move. The timing was lousy, but he couldn't totally stop himself from reacting.

In a month, maybe less, he'd be a father.

His phone buzzed again. Thank God. He needed something to slap him back to the moment. It was Rivera, the SWAT team commander.

"Captain, we have a patrol car ready to get you and Ms. Carr out of here. It's pulling up to the curb right now."

Well, that was good news. "And the situation with the search?"

"We have all points of the building secure. But no sign of the gunmen yet. We're still looking."

"Find them!" Shaw ordered after he got his teeth unclenched.

He pulled Sabrina to her feet so he could get her moving. The sooner he had her away from the building, the better.

Even though she was obviously slowed because of

the pregnancy, she hurried, keeping up right along with him, but she was breathing hard again by the time he got her into the backseat of the cruiser. The driver, a uniformed officer, drove away.

"Ms. Carr will need to go to a hospital," Shaw instructed the driver.

She didn't protest. Which wasn't a good sign. Since Sabrina often protested any- and everything he suggested.

Did that mean she was hurt?

While the driver meandered his way through the deserted downtown streets, Shaw called Harris, the hostage negotiator, for a situation report from the maternity hospital. It took a while—four rings—before Harris answered, and the moment Shaw heard the strain in the man's voice, he knew this conversation wasn't going to be good.

"The fire's out," Harris started. "It wasn't much of one. The gunmen lit some damp papers, and that created more smoke than fire."

And they'd used that smoke to escape. "Casualties?" Shaw asked, dreading the answer.

"Four so far."

Shaw cursed. "Not one of the babies?"

"No, they all seem to be fine, but we have doctors on the way to check them all out," Harris answered quickly, and then hesitated. "Three of the dead were on the medical staff here. The other was a patient. She died just a few minutes ago." Another pause. "It was Nadine Duggan."

Ah, hell.

The lieutenant's wife. *A cop's wife.* Shaw had to

take a deep breath, but that didn't stop the jolt from the memories of the night his wife had died.

"Nadine was nine months pregnant," Shaw said. He didn't dare look at Sabrina, but he was aware that she was sobbing now. She'd obviously heard what Harris had said. "What happened to her child?"

"They're alive. Twins, a boy and a girl," Harris added in a hoarse whisper. "Bo's taking this pretty hard."

Of course he was. Bo loved his wife, and what was supposed to be one of the happiest days of their lives—the birth of their children—had turned into a nightmare.

"We have another patient clinging to life," Harris continued. "I don't think she's going to make it so we have someone tracking down her next of kin. Another woman is in critical condition. Both of them delivered babies during the standoff."

And this might be just the tip of the iceberg. His men had been in that building less than forty-five minutes. God knew what they would find when they searched every nook and cranny. The death and injury toll might skyrocket.

"Sabrina said some of the women hid," Shaw told Harris. "Some might be too scared to come out. You'll need to look for them."

"Of course. We'll go through the place room by room. How is Sabrina? Did you find her?"

Shaw had to clear his throat before he could speak. "I found her. She's safe." And because he needed to focus on the job, he checked his watch. "I'm dropping her off with a uniformed officer at the hospital on San Pedro, and then I can join you on scene."

"Good. Because we can use all the help we can get."

"Nadine's dead?" Sabrina asked the moment Shaw ended the call.

He settled for a nod.

She pressed her fingers to her mouth, but he still heard the sob. Shaw wasn't sure how well she knew Nadine, but they'd obviously met and chatted in that hospital support group. Plus, Sabrina was no doubt thinking that it could have been her who'd ended up dead.

Shaw was certainly thinking it.

Because Sabrina's sobs were getting louder, he felt he had to do something. Anything. Even if he wasn't sure he wanted to do it.

Shaw slipped his arm around her, and she dropped her head onto his shoulder. He expected the contact to feel foreign and uncomfortable. It did.

It also felt comforting.

She was soft and warm and practically melted against him so Shaw just sat there and let her cry it out. By the time the driver stopped in front of the hospital, he felt raw and drained, and figured that was minor compared to what Sabrina was feeling.

His phone buzzed again, and he flipped it open. Not Harris with reports of more deaths or injuries. This call was from Rivera, the SWAT commander.

"Tell me you have good news," Shaw greeted the man.

But there was only a long heavy moment of silence. "Sorry. We've gone through the abandoned office building, every inch of it, and the gunmen aren't here."

"What?" Shaw snarled. Beside him, Sabrina practically snapped to attention.

"We think they escaped through the basement. We didn't even know there was a basement because there are no marked stairs leading into that area. When we got down there, we found a single small window. Open."

"And no one saw two armed men coming out through that window?"

"No, sir. It was on the south side of the building where there are heavy shrubs, and they might have slipped into those and used them as cover so they could get away."

Hell! This was not supposed to happen. "Those men are killers. We have four DBs on our hands back at the hospital, and two more might soon join the list."

"I understand. These are very dangerous men. We're searching the area now, and I'm bringing in more officers."

"Do that. Do whatever it takes." Shaw slammed his phone shut and cursed.

"They got away," Sabrina mumbled. "They got away." And she continued to repeat it. The more she said it, the closer she sounded to getting hysterical.

And Shaw knew why.

"Drive to the precinct now," Shaw ordered the driver. "Ms. Carr can see the doctor there."

He had to get Sabrina to safety and put her in protective custody. Because those gunmen would try to eliminate any and all witnesses.

And that meant they would come after Sabrina to finish what they had started.

Chapter Four

"You can wait in my office," Shaw said to her the moment Sabrina came out of the ladies' room.

He motioned for her to follow him down the glossy tiled corridor that was lined with fallen officers' photos and department commendations.

His voice sounded so professional. So detached. And Sabrina couldn't help but notice that he didn't touch her. He hadn't since they were in the car driving away from that building where Shaw had rescued her. From the moment they'd stepped out of the vehicle and into SAPD headquarters, he'd kept at least several inches of distance between them.

"Thank you, for everything," she managed to say, though she didn't know how. Her mouth was trembling, and the words came out shaky, as well.

When Shaw finally stopped walking and pointed to the open room, Sabrina stepped into the large office with an ornate desk nameplate that had Captain Shaw Tolbert scrolled on it. The nameplate and the office were reminders that Shaw was an important man in SAPD. A leader.

And he had better things to do than babysit her.

"While you were in the bathroom, I had some food brought in for you," Shaw explained. He tipped his head to the bottle of water and wrapped sandwich that had come from a vending machine. "Yeah, I know it's not very appetizing, but I figured you'd be hungry and dehydrated."

"The gunmen gave us water," she mumbled.

No food, though. Despite not having eaten for about ten hours, she wasn't hungry, but she sat in the leather chair next to his desk and opened the water and sandwich anyway. Both tasted like dust. But she continued to eat because the baby needed this.

"Did the gunmen hurt you, physically?" he asked.

She lifted her wrist so he could see the marks. "Just a bruise or two from where one of them grabbed me. That was the peppermint guy who did that. He chewed on breath mints during most of the standoff, and he threw some of the wrappers on the floor."

Shaw took out a notepad from his desk and jotted that down.

"Do you need to bag my clothes so you can check for fibers or anything?" she asked.

"I'll get them later. For now, just eat." Shaw took out his phone and asked whomever he called for a situation report.

While he listened to that report, Shaw stood there so stoically. He looked the ultimate professional. And for just a second, she was reminded of the first time she'd seen him at a fundraiser dinner nearly eight years ago. She and Fay had gone with dates, but the minute they'd spotted the "hot cop" as Fay had called him, they'd both flirted with him.

Shaw had flirted back.

He truly had been a hot cop. Still was, she reluc-tantly admitted. With his classic good looks all mixed together with a touch of bad boy, he was every woman's fantasy.

More than a little tipsy that night eight years ago, Fay and she had drawn cocktails straws for dibs on who would go after him. Fay had won. But even after all this time, Sabrina couldn't help but wonder what her life would be like if she hadn't drawn the short straw that night.

"Your doctor's on the way," Shaw let her know, ending the call.

He didn't come back into his office. He stood in the doorway but fired glances all around. Probably because the headquarters building was buzzing with activity from the hostage situation, and he was trying to keep abreast of what was going on. Or maybe because he didn't want to be too close to her. Nadine Duggan's death was likely bringing back memories. Bad memories. Of Fay.

And of Sabrina.

"Go ahead. You can leave." Sabrina tried to make it sound like an order. She took another bite of the sand-wich. "I'll be fine."

That was a lie. He knew it. So did she. But Shaw still turned and walked away.

"I have to see someone for a minute," he said from over his shoulder.

Sabrina soon saw the reason for his quick exit. Along with several other officers, Lieutenant Bo Duggan was just up the hall, and Shaw went to them.

She watched them through the open doorway, but she couldn't hear their conversation. She didn't need to. Shaw laid his hand on Bo's arm and no doubt offered words of sympathy, something that Shaw knew all about. He was almost certainly remembering Fay's death.

Sabrina remembered it, too.

Bo's wife had died under perhaps violent circumstances, or at least terrifying ones while being a hostage by those gunmen. Fay had chosen her own death. Well, her depression had chosen it for her anyway. Still, the final result was the death of a loved one.

"You shouldn't have gone off your antidepressants," Sabrina mumbled to Fay, who, of course, could no longer hear her.

Sabrina had said the same words to her while Fay had been alive. Fay hadn't listened—because the antidepressants couldn't be taken with the meds necessary for Fay to harvest her eggs for the in vitro procedure for the surrogate. And that surrogate was none other than Sabrina since Fay couldn't carry a child.

A baby at any cost, Fay had said.

Sabrina had argued with her, had even considered telling her best friend that the surrogacy offer was off the table so that Fay would go back on her meds. But Fay hadn't listened to that, either. Sabrina had lost the argument.

Fay had gone through with the harvesting, only to learn that none of her eggs was viable. That's when Sabrina had volunteered to use her own eggs. Shaw had agreed, reluctantly, and only to appease Fay, but there hadn't been time to finish what they started. Because of the long-term effect of going without her meds, Fay had taken her own life before Sabrina could get pregnant.

Some women would have stopped there. Some women wouldn't have continued to press to carry a baby for a dead friend. But she owed Fay. She owed Shaw. And that's why three months after Fay's death, Sabrina had pressured Shaw for her to use the embryos that Shaw and she had created. It hadn't been an easy fight—especially since the embryos were her DNA, not Fay's. However, in the end Shaw had agreed, probably because he'd been too beaten down by Fay's death to realize the full impact of having a baby with Sabrina.

Well, he no doubt knew the full impact now.

Sabrina certainly did. Yes, she'd owed Shaw and Fay. She'd owed them this child, but there were consequences for delivering on a promise to a dying friend.

One of those consequences was headed her way. Shaw was walking back toward her. Alone. Bo was going in the other direction, no doubt so he could start handling the aftermath of his wife's death.

"How's Bo doing?" she asked the moment Shaw returned.

"How do you think he's doing?" Shaw snapped, then he cursed under his breath and mumbled something that sounded like an apology.

He still didn't come in the room with her. But she got his visual attention. Shaw bracketed his hands on both sides of the doorway and stared at her. "Your doctor's in the building, and she'll be here any minute."

"There's no hurry. I wasn't injured. I'm not having any cramps or anything."

"That's good." A moment later, he repeated it. "I just

got a situation report from one of my sergeants. Still no sign of the gunmen, but we'll find them." He was back to sounding professional, as if giving her a briefing.

"Do you need to take my statement now?"

"It can wait until morning. All the interview rooms are already being used."

Yes. Because there were so many witnesses.

So many victims.

"On the drive over, one of those calls I made was to start the process to get background checks on all the hospital employees, including Michael Frost, the person who phoned you about the emergency meeting," Shaw continued. "We've also gathered all the hostages' cell phones we can find. They'd been tossed behind the desk in the nurses' station."

"Yes. The gunmen took them from us within the first few minutes of the standoff."

"I figured they had. We'll check to see if the gunmen used any of them."

"They had their own phones," she remembered. "I don't think they used any of ours. And they didn't use the hospital phones, either."

He nodded. "Is it possible one of the hostages was able to use their cell to take a picture of either of the men?"

Sabrina thought about that a moment, forcing herself to mentally return to the chaos that'd happened on that fourth floor. "It's possible, but I didn't see it happen. Besides, they wore ski masks the entire time."

He opened his mouth, no doubt to continue this cop-like questioning, but he stopped when his phone buzzed again. No call this time, but a text message. When he read it, Shaw cursed and scrubbed his hand over his face.

Despite the wobbly legs, Sabrina stood. "What's wrong?"

Shaw put the phone away, and his grip tightened on the doorjamb. "Another of the hostages died—a woman who'd given birth. And one of the newborns is missing. We just issued an Amber Alert."

"Missing? How? There were only two gunmen, and when they took me from the hospital and to that other building, they didn't have a baby with them."

"Maybe they moved the child before they took you. Maybe the baby was already in the vehicle." The briefing was over, and the raw emotion was coming through his voice. "We don't have any suspects in custody, and we don't even have a motive for the crime."

Maybe it was his stark frustration or maybe it was her exhaustion, but Sabrina was sorry she'd stood. She nearly lost her balance and caught on to the desk to steady herself.

That got Shaw moving. He hurried to her, took her by the arm and put her back in the chair. But he did more than that. He put his hand on her arm, much as he'd done to Bo. And then he looked down at her. However, he didn't get much further than that look.

There was a knock at the door, and Shaw spun around, obviously grateful for the interruption. Sabrina suddenly felt grateful as well because it was her OB, Dr. Claire Nicholson.

"Sabrina," the doctor greeted. "I came as quickly as I could."

"I need to make some calls," Shaw volunteered, and he headed out after giving the doctor a brief nod.

Dr. Nicholson watched Shaw leave and then eased the door shut. While she opened her medical bag, she studied Sabrina's face.

"He's the baby's father," the doctor commented. Dr. Nicholson knew that, of course, because she had also been the one to implant the embryos in Sabrina. "He's worried about you."

Sabrina nearly laughed. "He's worried about the baby, that's all."

"At this point, it's nearly impossible to separate mom from the baby. He's worried about *you*," the doctor confirmed and took out the fetoscope, something Sabrina was familiar with. It was a modified stethoscope used to listen to the baby's heartbeat. The doctor positioned it on her own forehead and motioned for Sabrina to lift her top.

"Any contractions or spotting?" the doctor asked.

"No. Just some Braxton Hicks." Thank God. Other than the practice contractions and being jittery and exhausted, she truly was okay. Now, mentally, well, that was a different story.

Sabrina winced a little when the cool plastic-coated metal touched her belly. The doctor moved it around, paused several moments and then smiled.

"That's a good strong heartbeat." She pulled off the fetoscope and put it back into the bag. "Of course, I'd like to do an ultrasound, but that can wait a day or two." She took out a manual blood pressure kit and used it on Sabrina's arm. "It's slightly high but considering the circumstances, I'm not surprised. Do you have someone to stay with tonight?"

No. She didn't. But Sabrina nodded anyway. "I'll be fine." It was her standard response, one she'd been saying her entire life, she realized.

Tonight it wasn't true. She wouldn't be fine because those gunmen were still out there.

There was a quick knock at the door, and it opened, slowly. Shaw peeked inside. "Everything okay?" Shaw's attention went right to her and stayed there.

The doctor looked at Sabrina before she answered. "Sabrina and the baby are both *fine*. In about four weeks, you'll both have a healthy newborn. But for now, Sabrina needs rest. You can make sure that happens?"

Sabrina got to her feet, to protest Dr. Nicholson dumping this on Shaw, but that's when she noticed why Shaw was staring at her. Her top was still bunched up, and her pregnant belly was bare. She quickly righted her top.

"Rest," the doctor ordered Sabrina, and she stepped around Shaw so she could leave.

"You don't need to keep checking on me," Sabrina insisted.

"I've already arranged a hotel room for you," Shaw let her know. He glanced again at her now-covered belly and swallowed hard. "Does it hurt?"

Sabrina shook her head. "Does what hurt?"

"The baby, when it kicks."

"Oh. No. Not really." She shrugged, puzzled by the abrupt change of subject. "Well, unless she connects with my kidney or something."

Shaw's left eyebrow shot up. *"She?"*

Sabrina shook her head even harder. "I don't know the baby's sex. I wanted to keep it a surprise. *She* just sounds better than *it*."

"Right." He stepped to the side. "Come on. I'll get you to the hotel."

Since this was already more than awkward, Sabrina didn't argue, but as soon as Shaw had her stashed away at the hotel, she would insist that he leave. If he felt forced to spend time with her, it would only make him hate her more.

"Thank you," she told him. She walked out of the office ahead of him, but there was someone waiting outside the door. It was a lanky built cop wearing a crisp blue uniform.

Shaw groaned softly, probably because there was a look of concern on the man's face. "More bad news, Officer Newell?"

He handed Shaw several sheets of paper that had been stapled together. "That's the preliminary background checks you asked for on the hospital employees. Oh, and a guy keeps calling here, asking to speak to Ms. Carr. He said his name is Gavin Cunningham."

Shaw looked up from the papers he'd just received and turned to Sabrina, obviously wanting an explanation. Was it her imagination or did he seem a little jealous that another man would be phoning her? But she rethought that.

Shaw could never be jealous of her.

"Gavin Cunningham's a client," she explained to the other officer. "And yes, he's persistent. I'm head of an organization called Rootsfind that helps adopted and foster kids locate their biological families, and he wants me to help him find his father. Please tell him I'll call him in a day or two."

"I already told him you weren't available, but he said it was a matter of life or death."

Sabrina and Shaw had already started to walk away, but that stopped them. Shaw stared at her, apparently waiting for an answer.

But Sabrina didn't have one. "Gavin called yesterday and sounded frantic and stressed. He said that he needed me to find his father immediately. He wanted to meet with me right then, but I had other appointments. I told him I'd see him today. That obviously didn't happen because I was taken hostage."

"Well, he asked me to give you his number, just in case you'd forgotten it." The officer reached in his pocket and extracted a notepad-sized piece of paper with the number on it.

"Thanks. I'll call him on the way to the hotel."

"You think it's that critical to call him back tonight? Because it can wait," Shaw added, not giving her a chance to answer. He nudged her to get her moving and continued to read the papers the officer had given him. "Unless you think it's possible this client is suicidal?"

Sabrina gave that some thought. "I didn't see any warning signs that he's contemplating suicide."

"Right," he mumbled.

She didn't miss the accusing tone. Shaw seemed to be saying—*as if you'd recognize those warning signs*. She certainly hadn't with Fay. "He's just a little more obsessed than most about finding his father."

Sabrina knew something about that, as well. Since she'd been adopted at birth, she'd spent most of her life looking for her biological parents. She'd failed. And it was the reason she had created Rootsfind. Sometimes, the desire to find those DNA roots just burned hotter in some people.

Shaw folded the papers that Officer Newell had given him, and he led her out of the building and into the open parking garage where there were dozens of police vehicles. "I know you're tired, but I need you to think back to the person who called you about that moms' support group meeting?"

"Michael Frost," she supplied.

"You're sure that's who called you?"

"Positive. Why?"

"Because according to hospital records, they don't have an employee by that name."

Oh, mercy. Had this man been in on it? Had he lured her to the hospital? "I thought something was strange about that call. I mean, he made the meeting sound like an emergency, as if Nadine were in some kind of trouble."

"You didn't phone Nadine first to try to verify what was wrong?"

"No." And she suddenly felt stupid for not doing just that. "Shaw, I'm sorry. Because I didn't follow my instincts about that call, I put the baby in danger."

Other than a sound in his throat that could have meant anything, or nothing, he didn't react. "This Michael Frost called you on your cell phone?"

"No. The office line."

"Then I'll have it checked for all incoming calls. We might get lucky." He got her inside one of the vehicles and drove away. "Stay low in the seat," he instructed.

That got her heart pounding again. "What if the gunmen are lurking around out here, watching us? What if they try to follow us?"

"I'll make sure that doesn't happen. That's why I'll have to drive around for a while even though the hotel is just up the street."

She had no idea how long *a while* would be, but maybe she could get some things done. Important things. She'd ignored her instincts about the call from Michael Frost, but she wouldn't do that with Cunningham.

"Could I use your phone to call Gavin?" she asked Shaw. "Just in case he does have suicide on his mind."

Shaw took out his phone and passed it to her, her fingers grazing his. For some reason, that tiny touch packed a wallop, and it took Sabrina a moment to gather her breath.

"Or maybe I shouldn't use your cell because your name will show up on Cunningham's caller ID," she reconsidered.

"That phone is clean, only the number will show up, and he won't be able to trace it back to me or SAPD," Shaw explained. He took a turn and kept his attention fastened to the rearview mirror.

Sabrina nodded again and pressed in the numbers. Gavin Cunningham answered on the first ring. "This is Sabrina Carr," she greeted. She, too, checked the mirrors to make sure no one was following them.

"Thank God you're all right," Gavin said immediately. "When I saw the hostages on the news, I thought of you. And I tried to call you, but there was no answer at your office or your home. You must have been scared to death."

She debated how much she should say and settled for, "I was rescued."

"Good. That's good." He paused. "Can we meet?"

She didn't have to debate that. "No. I'm still tied up with police business. I called because you told Officer Newell it was a matter of life and death, that you had to speak to me. Gavin, what's going on?"

He paused so long, but she could hear his breathing. It was fast and uneven. Maybe Shaw had been right about Gavin being suicidal, and just in case he was, she pressed the speaker function so that Shaw would be able to hear the rest of the conversation. "I can't talk about this over the phone," he finally answered. "I just need to see you."

Sabrina ignored that request. "Where are you right now?"

"At my house," he whispered. "You can't come?"

"No."

"All right, then. Sorry I bothered you. I'm sorry about everything."

And he hung up.

Shaw cursed, took the phone and punched in some numbers. "Officer Newell," Shaw said to the person he'd called. "I need someone to do a welfare check on that Gavin Cunningham, the man who kept calling Ms. Carr. He's at his residence, and I want someone over there immediately. Let me know what you find out."

Shaw brought the car to a stop beneath the canopied entrance of the Riverfront Hotel. There was a man dressed in a suit in front, apparently waiting for them, and he got into the car and drove away after Shaw and she exited. Shaw ushered her inside the lobby where another person, probably a plainclothes officer, handed Shaw a room key.

"I'm still not safe, am I?" she asked as they got on the elevator.

"You are now." Shaw didn't say another word until the elevator stopped. He didn't waste any time. He hurried her to the room and got her inside.

"Get some sleep," he said, pointing to the only bed in the small room. He closed the door.

Sabrina glanced at the bed, at the small no-frills standard hotel room, and then at him. "Will the officer in the lobby be able to stand guard outside my door?" Suddenly, the thought of being alone—and unprotected—was terrifying. She slid her hand over her belly.

"No." And Shaw didn't add anything to that for several long moments. Then he reached back and set both locks on the door. "The officer is arranging to have some clothes and toiletries sent up, and then he'll report back to headquarters. We're short staffed on the investigation. There are a lot of witnesses to interview. A lot of women who'll need protection."

"Including me," she mumbled.

He nodded. "I'll be staying with you. Until we catch the gunmen, you'll be in my protective custody."

Sabrina's mouth dropped open. "You're going to stay here, with me, *alone?*"

The muscles stirred in his jaw. "Yeah. Now get some rest."

Fat chance of that. "But you must have a ton of work to do. Surely someone else can do this."

Even though she wanted Shaw to be the one. Well, sort of. She knew he'd do anything to protect the baby, and that was a huge plus, but being in such close quarters with Shaw would only make her remember that he was indeed a *hot cop*.

Sabrina cursed herself. Damn hormones. Through much of this pregnancy, she'd been thinking about Shaw, and she hadn't thought of him as her baby's father, either. But as a lover.

As if that would ever happen.

Still, her hormones had persisted.

Like now, for instance.

Yes, she was so tired she could hardly stand, but she felt the trickle of heat go through her, and she wished they were friendly or intimate enough for him to hold her.

"What's wrong?" he asked. "You're breathing hard."

"Am I?" Sabrina tried to fix that, but she didn't think she was successful. "I have to go to the bathroom."

And she got away from him as fast as she could. She used the facilities and went to the sink to wash her hands and toss some cold water on her face.

"He's Fay's husband," she reminded herself. But her body only reminded her that Fay was dead, and her friend would have been the last person to want Shaw and her to stay apart.

Take care of Shaw for me.

That was the message Fay had left on Sabrina's answering machine. The moment Sabrina had come in from work and heard the weakened voice and the slurred words, she'd known something was horribly wrong. She'd tried to call Fay, of course, but it was already too late. Shaw had answered the phone to say that Fay had just died in his arms.

She blinked back the tears, and the old memories. Shaw had been so angry. So hurt. Heck, he was still angry and hurt after all these months.

The baby kicked, a flurry of flutters, and she smiled in spite of the mess she'd made of her life. Then, she braced herself and went back into the room.

Shaw glanced at her, but he didn't have time to say anything because his phone buzzed. "Captain Tolbert," he answered.

Since this would likely be the first of many calls about the investigation, Sabrina went ahead and kicked off her shoes and pulled back the cover. She was so tired she could fall asleep despite the circumstances.

Shaw's expression had her rethinking that.

"Repeat that," Shaw insisted. Several moments went by before he barked, "Find him."

"What's wrong?" Sabrina asked, but she was afraid to hear the answer. There'd already been so much bad news.

Shaw shoved his phone back into his pocket. "A unit arrived at Gavin Cunningham's place a few minutes ago. The door was wide open, so the officer went inside."

Sabrina held her breath. "Is Gavin dead?"

"No. He wasn't there. Neither was his car, and the neighbor said he sped away about a half hour ago. He was going so fast that he knocked down the neighbor's mailbox, and he didn't even stop."

Even though that didn't sound good, many things could have caused him to do that. A family emergency.

Or a sudden illness. But judging from Shaw's expression, it was neither of those things.

"He left a note," Shaw added, "for you." He walked closer and eased down on the bed beside her. He met her eye to eye. "Sabrina, just how well do you know this man?"

She shook her head and held her breath. "Not well at all, only what I've already told you. Why? What did the note say?"

"Gavin Cunningham said he was sorry, that it was his fault you were taken hostage."

Chapter Five

The sound woke Shaw.

His eyes flew open, and he sat up from his slumping position in the chair. In the same motion he reached for his gun, which he'd placed on the nightstand. His training and experience caused him to expect the worst.

An intruder.

Or the gunmen who'd escaped.

The lamp was still on in the far corner of the room, so he had no trouble seeing that there were no intruders or gunmen. Sabrina and he were very much alone, but she was no longer sound asleep as she had been that last time he'd checked on her. She was fighting with the comforter and sheets.

"Owwww!" She got out from beneath the covers and tried to stand.

"What's wrong?" Shaw jumped up from the chair. "Are you in labor?"

She shook her head, but her face was twisted with pain. "Foot cramp."

He glanced down and saw that the toes on her left foot were rigid. "Put some pressure on it," he suggested, and he looped his arm around her waist so he could help her keep her balance.

Shaw forced himself to calm down, but it wasn't easy. He'd braced himself for a fight, and even though he was glad there wasn't one, it would still take him a while to absorb the jolt of adrenaline.

Sabrina adjusted her weight, so she could press her foot to the floor, and all the while she continued to say "owww."

"Pregnancy," she grumbled. "I get these stupid things every night."

Every night? Sheez. Shaw actually felt sorry for her.

And guilty.

He had no idea she'd been going through this. He'd read about possible pregnancy symptoms, of course, but he just hadn't made the personal connection between Sabrina and those symptoms. With her squirming and groaning in pain, it was an eye opener.

So was Sabrina, for that matter.

The clothes she'd worn while a hostage were now bagged and in the corner ready for pickup. She was dressed in a white cotton gown that the department had scrounged up for her.

Thin, white cotton.

Not at all meant to be provocative, but on her pregnant body, it hugged every inch of her, including her fuller breasts and bottom. Yes, she was pregnant, but that didn't stop him from responding to her.

And that made him feel even guiltier.

Sabrina was hands-off in every sense of the word.

"Thanks," she mumbled, her face relaxing a little.

They were hip to hip, with his arm slung around her, and she glanced down at the physical contact between them.

"Sorry." Shaw moved away. "I didn't want you to fall."

"I wasn't complaining. Actually, I was savoring the moment." But then her eyes widened. "I didn't mean it like that. Uh, I'm not really sure what I meant. It's just been a while since I've had a man's arm around me, that's all."

Since Shaw didn't know what to say to that, he settled for, "Yeah."

Her cheeks flushed, and she splayed her hands on her belly. "You're probably thinking it would be impossible for a man to get his arms around me, right?" She chuckled, but the humor was just an attempt to diffuse the situation.

Shaw needed it diffused. He could see the outline of her nipples, and he felt that tug below the belt. It was a basic male reaction, he assured himself, and he told that tug to get lost.

Sabrina sat back down on the bed and shook her head. "Yeah, I know. I look disgusting."

"No. You don't." Shaw decided to leave it at that.

She seemed relieved, or something. Her face relaxed anyway. "I have stretch marks. Three of them. Four," she added after a shrug. "Sometimes, I don't think my body will ever go back to normal."

"It will." Shaw wanted to hit himself. He didn't know much about this pregnancy stuff and should just shut up.

So that he'd do just that, he looked back at the laptop

he had sitting next to his chair. It'd been delivered along with Sabrina's gown and toiletries, and Shaw had been using it to get updates throughout the night. It was nearly 6:00 a.m. so a new update should be arriving shortly.

"Don't get me wrong. I'm so happy to be pregnant," she continued. "I mean, this baby is a miracle as far as I'm concerned. And trust me, I'm a big believer in miracles."

She groaned again, and that drew Shaw's attention right back to her. Sabrina was looking down at her belly.

"My miracle is awake," she mumbled. "And playing soccer with my kidneys."

Shaw looked at her belly, too, and saw the movement. He shifted to the edge of his chair for a better look. "I can actually see the kicks."

"Oh, yes. You can see them." She laughed. It was rich and thick as if she was sharing his amazement, though she no doubt experienced this many times a day.

Sabrina reached out, latched on to his hand and pressed it against her stomach.

Shaw almost pulled back. It was an automatic response when it came to Sabrina. But the baby moves stopped him. That was his baby inside her. A miracle, indeed. And he or she was kicking like crazy.

Amazed, Shaw looked up at Sabrina. Their gazes connected. She was smiling, and Shaw realized he was, too.

Her smile hit him harder than a heavy weight could have.

He drew back his hand. He drew himself back as well and moved deeper into the chair so there'd be some distance between them. This was such an incredible moment, and it was a moment he should have been sharing with his late wife.

Not Sabrina.

"Right," Sabrina mumbled. Her smile vanished, and she didn't roll her eyes, but it was close. "This is about Fay."

"Don't," he warned, certain there wasn't a trace of his smile left, either.

"Don't," she repeated. She got up, started for the bathroom, but then stopped. She kept her back to him. "I miss Fay, too. I miss her every minute of every day. And every one of those minutes I hate myself for not cramming those antidepressants in her mouth. Or for not being there when she overdosed and took her life. I don't need you to punish me, Shaw, because I swear to you, I've done a pretty good job of punishing myself."

She didn't give him a chance to respond. She went into the bathroom and shut the door.

Hell.

Shaw felt lower than dirt. Yes, he was still angry with Sabrina. Always would be. And he would always put some of the blame for Fay's death on her shoulders. But after what Sabrina had been through in the past fifteen hours, she didn't need him adding to her stress.

He went to the bathroom door and knocked. "I'm sorry."

The words seemed foreign to him, and he realized why. It was the first time he'd ever said those two words to Sabrina. It had been so easy to hang on to his anger and hurt when she'd been out of sight, but with her right on the other side of that door, and probably crying, Shaw knew he was soon going to have to come to terms with her and the baby.

But how?

How did he come to terms with having Sabrina in his life when having her there felt as if he were betraying Fay?

He heard the water running in the sink, and several moments later, the door opened. She ducked around him, dodging his gaze, but he saw the red eyes.

Yep, he'd made her cry.

Maybe he should just hit himself in the head with a rock. It might make him feel better.

"What's the latest on the case?" she asked.

Shaw didn't really want to have the conversation he was about to launch into, but it was time to clear the air. Well, partly. He just needed to get Sabrina and him to a place where…where…

But he couldn't finish that.

He just didn't want all this emotion eating up the air between them.

Shaw caught her arm and turned her around to face him. "This baby is a miracle for me, too," he told her. "I want to be a father. Always have. And it doesn't matter that we're not…friends…or whatever, we'll make this work." He frowned, not liking the sound of that.

And why the hell was he hemming and hawing?

He wasn't the hemming and hawing type.

"We'll make the *shared custody* work," he amended.

She nodded, and her chin came up. He recognized that gesture and knew it was all for show. He also saw the tears that still watered her eyes.

"Pregnancy hormones," she complained and swiped away the tears.

Shaw mumbled another, "Hell." And before he could talk himself out of it, he pulled her into his arms much as he'd done in the car after he'd rescued her from that abandoned building.

But this was way different.

In the car, they'd been side by side. Now, they were face-to-face. The baby was between them, of course, but it was still body to body contact. That contact got even closer when her head dropped to his shoulder. She whispered something he couldn't understand, didn't *want* to understand, and her hot breath hit against his neck.

That tug below his belt became a strong pull.

Oh, man.

It'd been months since he'd had a woman, and his body was reminding him of that.

Sabrina slid her arms around him, drawing him closer. He gritted his teeth but didn't back away. He owed her a little TLC. But it wasn't TLC that kept going through his mind.

Was traditional sex even possible when a woman was eight months pregnant? Heck. He didn't care if it was traditional. His body was starting to suggest other possibilities.

"Yes," he heard Sabrina say, and for one heart-stopping moment, he thought he'd asked that traditional sex question aloud.

Shaw pulled back and looked at her.

She looked up at him. Frowned. Then, cursed. "Yes, I'm aroused," she whispered as if confessing to a murder. She glanced down at her nipples, and with the thin, snug cotton, he could see those nipples were puckered. "Sorry about that."

Again, he was speechless. But not numb. Hell, he was aroused, too.

"It's the pregnancy hormones again. Foot cramps, crying spells and the libido of a teenage boy. A libido I haven't acted on, by the way." She turned away from him again and groaned. "And I'm so sorry for telling you that. Don't worry. I'm not asking you to do anything about it."

Too bad. His body was ready to help her out, even though his mind was pulling him back. But Shaw knew from experience that a man's mind rarely won out in situations like this. If this had been any woman other than Sabrina, he would have tested the logistics of having sex during the last trimester of pregnancy.

"What's happening with the case?" she repeated.

He just stared at her. Or rather he stared at her backside. And the air continued to stir, hot and thick, around them. And hot and thick was exactly how he felt.

"Any news about my client, Gavin Cunningham?" Sabrina pressed, obviously determined to have a *normal* conversation. She took her replacement shirt from off the end of the bed and put it on over her gown.

Shaw shook off the effects of his own suddenly raging libido so he could get his mind on anything but the thought of what it would feel like to be deep inside Sabrina.

"We still haven't been able to find Gavin," Shaw finally managed to say. "Have you come up with any possible reason why he would think it was his fault that you were taken hostage?"

She downed some water from the bottle on the nightstand. "This is a stretch, but maybe he knew the gunmen. He said nothing to me to indicate that, but I can't come up with a connection between a Rootsfind client and what went on at the hospital."

Shaw thought about that a moment. "What exactly did Gavin want you to do for him?"

She shrugged as if the answer were obvious. The shrug caused her shirt to shift, and he got another peek at her nipples.

Shaw looked away.

"He wanted me to find his birth father," Sabrina explained, "and he gave me all the normal details—his place and date of birth. His mother's name. She was a single mom and died young without revealing who his father was."

"You said Gavin was persistent, more obsessed than most about finding his parent. Why? Had something changed recently in his life? Like maybe he needed bone marrow or something?"

She shook her head. "He didn't mention that, but I suppose it's possible. Still…" She paused. "I got the feeling this was more personal than medical. He seemed angry that his father hadn't made himself known."

Interesting. It might not be connected to the case, but Shaw would dig deeper. He wanted to learn why Gavin felt responsible for Sabrina being taken hostage. That might be the key to solving all of this.

"I've been getting updates throughout the night," Shaw explained. "That nurse, Michael Frost, called at least two of the other hostages, Willa Marks and Bailey Hodges. Neither was part of the moms' support group, but he told them their doctors had gotten back critical lab results and that they needed to come to the hospital immediately."

Sabrina made a sharp intake of breath. "So, it was a trick. And I fell for it."

Shaw didn't want her to go back to beating herself up. Hell, he probably would have fallen for it, too. "Is it possible that Michael Frost was one of the gunmen?"

She stayed quiet a moment. "The breath mint guy did most of the talking, and he didn't sound like Frost. Of course, he could have disguised his voice."

Absolutely. Shaw was looking into that, too, but it might be a dead end since none of the messages had been recorded.

Shaw sat in the chair across from her so they could be eye to eye. And wouldn't be touching. "Do you know if you had anything in common with Willa Marks or Bailey Hodges, the other two women that Frost called? Maybe you met them before the hostage situation."

Again, she paused, and her forehead bunched up while she stayed deep in thought. "I don't think so. I heard the gunmen calling out for someone named Bailey, of course, but this is the first I've heard of Willa Marks. I'm pretty sure I've never met either of them."

There might still be a connection that could come out later. For now, he needed as many solid leads and facts as possible.

He took some paper from the briefcase that'd been delivered with the laptop, and handed it and a pen to Sabrina. "Why don't you start writing down your statement? I'll arrange to have us some breakfast delivered."

The sun had barely come up, but his body was already screaming for caffeine. And sex. It wasn't going to get the sex, but he could do something about the coffee.

He used his cell to call headquarters and request breakfast. The hotel had room service, but it was too big of a risk to use it. Sabrina's face had been plastered all over the news by now, and he didn't want a hotel employee recognizing her and blabbing to his friends. News like that could get back to the gunmen.

Sabrina was already busy writing her statement when he finished the call so Shaw settled back into the chair to check the messages on his secure laptop. He'd barely made it through the first one when his phone buzzed.

"It's Officer Newell," the caller identified himself. "We caught a break on the surveillance cameras we took from the hospital. Most had been disabled. Nothing sophisticated. The gunmen had smashed them, but they missed a newly installed one at the end of the hall near the lab."

Shaw wanted to cheer. Finally, some good news. "What do we have?"

"Neither of the men took off their ski masks so we don't have images to put through the facial recognition software, but we do have some of their movements. One of them went into the lab, just as several of the witnesses said. And he took one of the hostages with him. A computer tech named Willa Marks. He appears to have forced her to help him look for something. They were going through the files."

"Any fingerprints on the keyboards?"

"Plenty. But both of the gunmen wore surgical gloves.

And even though there's a lot of trace on the computer and the surrounding area, it'll take us a while to rule out what belongs to the staff or the hostage Willa Marks, and what might belong to the gunmen."

Newell was right. That type of sorting might take days or even weeks, especially when dozens of people would have to be excluded. "What's Ms. Marks saying? Does she know why the gunman had her in there with him?"

"She's, uh, not able to talk. She received a head injury when the gunman shoved her down as she was trying to escape. She doesn't remember anything."

Hell. The more he heard, the more his stomach clenched. And this was just the beginning. How many more sickening details were there?

Since Willa Marks might not be able to tell them what had happened, at least for a while, Shaw needed to piece together as much as he could. "What files did the gunman search?"

Sabrina stopped writing and stared at him, obviously waiting for an update.

"We're trying to sort that out now," Officer Newell verified. "They accessed at least four dozen files, but we don't know why. I can tell you that all the files they accessed dealt with DNA."

"DNA?" Shaw questioned. "What kind of DNA?"

"Some were from the babies, some from the parents. We're talking court-ordered DNA tests. Others were apparently done for medical reasons, like for a baby needing a transplant. A few more are for a database for umbilical storage. There were even a few samples that SAPD had outsourced to the lab for processing."

Shaw went still. "Were any for paternity?" he questioned.

"Yes, sir. There were several of those. One of them court ordered, as well. Why, what are you thinking?"

He was thinking the gunmen might have wanted to confirm that Sabrina's baby was his. So the baby could be used as *leverage*.

But leverage for what?

Because if he could figure that out, he could figure out who was behind all of this.

"Let me call you back," Shaw told the officer. "I need to ask Sabrina a few questions. In the meantime, find out if the gunmen tampered with any of those files or if they got access to the DNA samples themselves. Specifically, look for any files that were removed or deleted. The tech should be able to do that in just a couple of minutes."

"I'll tell him," Newell assured him.

"What about paternity?" Sabrina asked the moment Shaw ended the call.

She already looked worried, and he didn't want to make that worry worse, but he couldn't shield her from this. Sabrina might very well have information they could put together with what the police knew, and then they might have the big picture.

That big picture could lead them to make an arrest.

"The gunmen were going through the DNA files," Shaw told her. "Is it possible our baby's DNA was there?"

"Maybe." She swallowed hard. "I had to have an amniocentesis done. That's a test where they draw some fluid from around the baby and test it for abnormalities."

"Why did you have that done?" He felt stupid for not knowing.

"Because I got really sick with pneumonia during my second month of pregnancy. I didn't tell you because I didn't want you to worry. You already had a lot on your mind what with adjusting to being a father, and I didn't want to add to it. Anyway, my OB wanted to make sure the baby hadn't been harmed from all the meds. She wasn't," she quickly added. "The doctor said everything was fine. But the amniotic fluid would contain DNA, and it's probably on file at the hospital."

And if the gunmen had that file, that was likely the reason they had taken Sabrina with them when they fled the hospital. They'd wanted Sabrina and the proof that the baby she was carrying was his.

Well, they didn't have Sabrina. He did. But that didn't mean they wouldn't try to get her again so they could force him to do something.

His phone buzzed again, and when he saw Newell's name on the screen, Shaw answered it as quickly as he could.

"You were right," Newell said, "the tech didn't have any trouble finding the files that'd been deleted. There were three of them. One wasn't labeled, but you'll recognize both names of the two we could identify. One was for Sabrina Carr."

Shaw silently cursed. "And the other?"

"Her client, Gavin Cunningham."

"Cunningham?" Shaw repeated. He didn't like the way the man's name kept popping up in this investigation. "Why was his DNA at the hospital?"

"We're not sure. There was no code to indicate why the file was even there. It wasn't even logged in properly through official channels. But it was his name on the file itself."

Another dead end, except this dead end could be reopened once they had Cunningham. "Put every agency in the state on alert. I want Cunningham found *immediately*."

He glanced at Sabrina who was looking very concerned again. Shaw knew how she felt. He had to question Cunningham.

"Breakfast will be here soon," he said, checking his watch. "I need to wash up before it arrives. Why don't you go ahead and work on your statement? We can go through it after we eat."

She nodded but didn't look at all convinced that she'd be able to concentrate. Again, Shaw knew exactly how she felt, but he had to clear his head before more evidence started pouring in.

He went into the bathroom, but he'd no sooner stepped inside when he heard the noise.

It was a crashing sound.

The sounds of wood and metal being bashed.

Shaw turned, ready to react, but the bathroom door slammed shut when the hotel room door smacked into it.

Someone had broken in.

He shoved at the door, but it was blocked. Shaw rammed his shoulder against it, hard. It still didn't budge.

"Sabrina?" he called out while he tried again.

She didn't answer, but the sound she made tore right through him.

Sabrina screamed.

Chapter Six

Sabrina didn't have any warning of the danger. Just seconds earlier, Shaw had gone into the bathroom to the right of the room entrance. Mere seconds. And then the hotel room door flew open.

The man who came rushing through was wearing a ski mask.

He was also armed.

Worse, he was literally using the hotel door and his body to block Shaw from coming out of the bathroom. She could hear Shaw cursing, calling out her name, and he was bashing against the door, but the gunman wasn't budging.

Sabrina automatically turned, ready to run, but there was no place for her to escape. Behind her were two windows, but they were on the third floor. Even if she could get the windows open before the gunman grabbed her, she couldn't risk jumping and hurting the baby. So, she did the only thing she could think to do.

She screamed again.

The man lifted his gun, something small and sleek and rigged with a silencer. "Come with me," he ordered. "Or I'll shoot."

The terror inside her went up a significant notch. Sabrina recognized that voice. It was the same peppermint-popping man who'd taken her hostage at the hospital. And he'd obviously come back for her.

The fear had her on the verge of panic, but Sabrina forced herself to think. Shaw's Glock was on the nightstand, and she glanced at it.

"I wouldn't do that if I were you," the man snarled. He calmly aimed his gun. Not at her.

But at the bathroom door that Shaw was battering himself against.

And he fired.

It wasn't a deafening blast, the silencer had muffled the sound to a swish, but it was a deadly sound for Sabrina.

Because the bullet could have hit Shaw.

Her heart was pounding now, and it was so loud in her ears that she couldn't tell what was going on behind that bathroom door. Shaw was still struggling, that much she could tell, but she had no idea if he was injured.

The gunman took aim at the door again. "Come here now, or I keep firing until he dies."

"Don't shoot," Sabrina practically shouted. Maybe if she was loud enough, someone would come to help. Her scream had certainly alerted the other guests. Maybe they'd already called nine-one-one. "I'll come with you."

"To hell you will," she heard Shaw yell.

Shaw rammed against the door again. The gunman aimed his weapon, no doubt with plans to shoot a second bullet at Shaw, but this time he didn't get the chance.

With a sound that was more animal than human tearing from his throat, Shaw kicked the door with a fierce jolt. The gunman flew backward and slammed into the wall.

Shaw came out after him.

The gunman had managed to keep hold of his weapon, and he tried to aim, but Shaw's fist connected with his jaw. The blow didn't disarm him, but it prevented him from firing another shot.

Shaw got off another punch, but the gunman fought back. He certainly wasn't trying to run. He bashed his gun against the side of Shaw's head.

Sabrina grabbed Shaw's Glock from the nightstand and pointed it. Not that she could fire. She didn't want to risk hitting Shaw instead.

"Captain Tolbert?" someone called out.

A moment later, the cop she'd seen at headquarters appeared in the doorway. It was Officer Newell. And he had his weapon drawn.

"Get down, Sabrina!" Shaw yelled.

Somehow, she managed to drop to her knees, and then she ducked behind the bed.

The shot blasted through the room.

"Oh, God," she prayed.

But before the last syllable had left her mouth, she heard the heavy thud of someone falling hard onto the floor.

Because it could endanger the baby, she didn't dare lift her head and see what had happened, though that's what she wanted to do. She needed to make sure Shaw hadn't been hurt.

"Are you okay?" she asked with her voice trembling.

No one answered for several long moments.

"Yeah," Shaw finally said.

That got her to her feet, and she saw the officer with his gun still aimed. He had it pointing at the masked gunman who was now sprawled out in front of the bathroom door.

Shaw leaned down and put his fingers against the man's neck and then shook his head. The officer mumbled something under his breath and slowly lowered his gun.

"He's dead?" Sabrina asked.

Shaw nodded.

The relief was instant. Yes, there was a dead man only a few yards away from her, but the alternative could have been much worse.

But then Sabrina saw the blood trickling down the side of Shaw's head.

She hurried to him, even though he motioned for her to stay back.

"You're hurt," she let him know, and she pointed to the wound just above his left eye. No doubt where the gunman had pistol-whipped him.

"It's just a scratch." Shaw reached out, took his Glock from her and then moved her away from the body.

Behind them, Officer Newell pulled out his phone and called for assistance. And she could hear others, guests probably and maybe hotel employees, who were scurrying around in the hall. No doubt trying to get out of there and away in case there were more gunshots.

Shaw slid his arm around her waist and moved her even farther away until they were against the wall near the windows. But not directly in front of them. He closed the tiny gap in the curtains and then angled Sabrina so she wouldn't be facing the dead man.

"It's not a scratch," she said, touching her fingertips to the bruise and cut on his forehead. God knew how many other bruises he had after the multiple attempts to bash his way through the door.

"I'm fine. But I'm worried about you. About the baby," he quickly added. "Did he touch you?"

Sabrina shook her head. "It's the gunman from the hospital," she managed to say.

"You're sure?"

"Positive. I recognized his voice. He's the one who killed the hospital employee right in front of me." Her breath caught just remembering what he'd put the other women and her through. "How did he find us?"

Shaw's jaw tightened, and maybe because she was starting to shake, he eased her closer to him. Not quite a hug but close. "I don't know. But I'll figure it out." Shaw looked at Newell, who was still just outside the door and obviously standing guard. "Check and see if he has any ID on him."

Sabrina wanted to know the name of her attacker, and she only hoped the name would lead them to a motive.

"He could have just shot me," she said more to herself than Shaw. "I wasn't armed when he broke through the door."

"He didn't want you dead. Or me."

"But he shot at you," she pointed out.

"If he'd wanted me dead, he would have aimed higher. That bullet went into the floor. Yes, it still could have been deadly, but I don't think he had killing on his mind. It's my guess he intended to kidnap you again, and then use you and the baby to get me to cooperate with something."

Yes, because that's exactly what they'd wanted when they were holding her before at the abandoned building. Some kind of leverage over Shaw. But that led her to her next question.

"Where's his partner?" she asked. Sabrina suddenly felt on the verge of panicking. "He could be in the hall, ready to strike."

Shaw used his left hand to gently take hold of her arm, and he forced her to look him in the eye. "If his partner had been here, he would have taken out Officer Newell. And he would have come in to assist with the kidnapping."

"According to his driver's license, his name is Burney Monroe," Officer Newell informed them.

"You recognize the name?" Shaw asked her.

"No."

"How about his face?" Newell continued.

She glanced past Shaw and saw that Newell had peeled back the ski mask. There was no blood on the dead man's face so she could clearly see the features. The thin nose, the square jaw, the light brown hair. In death, he certainly didn't seem menacing. He looked average.

Again she shook her head. "I don't know him."

"Probably a hired gun," Shaw provided.

That was even more chilling because the person who hired him was still out there. Or maybe his partner was the boss. She hadn't had much contact with him during the hostage situation or the kidnapping. She wasn't even sure she would recognize his voice as she had Burney Monroe's.

There was a flurry of footsteps in the hall, and Sabrina saw the second uniformed officer. "The medical examiner is on the way. CSI, too," he told Newell, and then looked at Shaw. "Sir, a squad car should be here any minute to take you and Ms. Carr to headquarters."

Good. Because it was the only place where she'd finally feel semi-safe. Of course, they had to get there first, and she certainly wouldn't breathe easy while they were out in the open.

Shaw thanked the officer, but he aimed his question at Newell. "Who made the arrangements for this hotel?"

Newell stood and shrugged. "I'm not sure, sir, but it was probably someone in Special Investigations. They're handling the security detail for the hostages."

"Find out who put us in this hotel," Shaw ordered. "I want to know the names of any officers who would have had access or direct knowledge of that information."

Newell stayed quiet a moment. "You think we have a leak or a mole in the department?" But his tone wasn't that of a question. Newell didn't believe that a breach in security was possible.

"Burney Monroe knew we were here somehow," Shaw countered. It was obvious from his expression that he didn't want to believe it, either.

Newell stooped again and patted his hands over the dead man's black windbreaker. He was looking for something, maybe a proverbial smoking gun such as written instructions from the person who had hired him and sent him here.

The person who might also be a cop.

Suddenly, being at SAPD headquarters didn't seem as appealing as it had just minutes earlier. The baby must have sensed her apprehension because she started to kick like crazy, and the muscles in Sabrina's stomach contracted. It was slightly painful, nothing she hadn't felt before, but it wasn't a good time for a bout of Braxton Hicks contractions.

Another round of contractions hit her, and Sabrina stopped so she could place her hand over her belly. She gave her baby some hopefully reassuring rubs.

Shaw cursed again, but he wasn't looking at the dead body. He was looking around the room. "Someone might have planted a bug in here. That's how the gunman could have known that it'd be a good time to strike while I was in the bathroom."

Sabrina started to search as well, but she had no idea what to look for. It sickened her to think that the second gunman could still be listening to all of this. Heck, he might have even heard of Shaw's plan to take her to headquarters.

"What's wrong?" she heard Shaw ask. But he didn't just ask. He hurried to her.

Sabrina realized then that she had her hand splayed over her belly. The pain was no longer mild. The contractions were harder.

"I'm not sure," she answered. She wanted to dismiss it, to say it would all go away. But she couldn't. Oh, God.

Was there something wrong with her baby?

There couldn't be. This couldn't be happening. Not after all they'd managed to survive.

"Hold on," Shaw warned her a split second before he scooped her up in his arms and stormed toward the door. What he didn't do was holster his gun. He kept it gripped in his hand as if he expected there might be another attack.

"Get me a cruiser, a car, anything!" Shaw ordered the uniformed officer. "And back me up because I'm taking Sabrina to the hospital."

Chapter Seven

This nightmare just wouldn't end.

Shaw scrubbed his hand over his face and mumbled another prayer. The baby had to be okay.

So far, everything had gone well at the clinic where the doctor had told Shaw to bring Sabrina when he'd made a frantic call to her after carrying Sabrina out of the hotel. But they were far from out of the woods.

"You know the drill," Dr. Claire Nicholson said to Sabrina as the doctor helped her onto the small padded bed next to the ultrasound machine. This particular room was just up the hall from the doctor's office, so they hadn't had to leave the building to have the procedure done. Thankfully, Sabrina had even managed to get a bite to eat while they were waiting for the room to be prepared.

Sabrina apparently did know the drill. She used a drab green cotton sheet to cover the lower part of her body, and she lifted her gown to expose her belly. Dr. Nicholson took a bottle of some kind of clear goo and smeared it over the exposed skin.

"Should I leave?" Shaw asked, hitching his thumb

to the door where the doctor had entered just seconds earlier.

The doctor looked at Sabrina for the answer.

"Stay," Sabrina said. "Please."

She was scared. Shaw could see that in her pale color and constant lip nibbling. Hell, the doctor looked worried, too. He certainly was. So, he stood there, praying that this test would show that the baby was all right.

"How are the contractions?" the doctor asked Sabrina.

"Gone. Well, almost. I get Braxton Hicks every now and then, but they aren't at regular intervals." She paused, swallowed hard. "They are Braxton Hicks, right? I'm not in labor?"

The doctor began to move the tiny probe over Sabrina's gel-coated belly. "You don't appear to be. And you certainly haven't dilated. That's the first thing I checked when I examined you after Captain Tolbert brought you in."

Yes, Shaw had definitely waited outside for that part of the exam. It had seemed to take hours, but he figured it was less than fifteen minutes before Dr. Nicolson had come out and said that the preliminary results were good, that Sabrina wasn't in the full throes of premature labor. But the doctor had still wanted to do an ultrasound before she declared the baby safe and sound.

"If all checks out well here, will Sabrina be able to leave?" Shaw asked. Because if the doctor planned to admit her to the hospital, that would require some serious security arrangements. The San Antonio Maternity Hospital was closed and being processed as a massive crime scene, and the other nearby hospitals had had to absorb the patients.

"I think under the circumstances, a hospital might be more stressful, and unnecessary," Dr. Nicholson concluded. "These false labors are fairly common in the last trimester. I seriously doubt the recent events had anything to do with it."

Maybe, but still Shaw didn't intend to let Sabrina out of his sight. Which, of course, would cause a whole set of problems of their own.

"We don't know why some women have false labor," the doctor continued, talking to Sabrina now. "But understand that it isn't your fault. Just relax and try to lead as normal a life as possible. That includes sex if…" She shrugged. "Well, if that applies to you two. I know Sabrina is a surrogate, but I sense something more going on between you two. Or maybe the potential for something more."

Shaw didn't look at Sabrina.

Sabrina didn't look at him.

"Forgive me if this sounds like a medical lecture," the doctor went on, "but recent studies show that sex, specifically a woman's climax, doesn't trigger premature labor. If the labor's going to start, it will with or without an orgasm."

Sheez. Shaw was trying to remember the last time he'd felt this uncomfortable.

"Oh, and sex doesn't hurt the baby, either, in case you were wondering," the doctor mumbled, and stared at the screen.

"Shaw and I aren't having sex," Sabrina interrupted. "Never have."

She seemed to imply *never will*.

"Right," the doctor added. She moved the monitor around. "The heartbeat's still good."

Finally, she was changing the subject. And it was a good change. Shaw stared, too, and saw the baby's images appear on the screen.

Oh, man.

He hadn't expected it to be so clear. He could actually see a baby.

His baby.

Shaw moved closer. Too close. His thigh bumped right into Sabrina's hand. Her fingers brushed against his fly, giving him an uncomfortable jolt.

"Sorry," he grumbled, easing back just slightly. But he couldn't take his eyes off the baby.

"The baby's sucking its thumb," the doctor said, and she chuckled.

Shaw couldn't believe it. "They do that in there?"

"They do a lot of things in there," Dr. Nicholson confirmed.

Sabrina chuckled, too. "In the last ultrasound, she was grabbing her toes. Between that and the daily soccer practice, she knows how to keep herself amused."

It nearly took Shaw's breath away. Seeing that would have been a miracle, and here he'd missed it because he hadn't come to the appointments.

Where the hell had his head been for the past eight months?

But he knew the answer. His head had been in the only place that his heart would allow it to be. With Fay. Her death was a wound that would not heal.

"You still want me to stay mum about the baby's sex?" the doctor asked. "Or do you want to know?"

Shaw looked at Sabrina. No more lip nibbling or signs of fear. She was smiling, and it was dazzling. Man, she was attractive no matter what the circumstances, but with that smile, she was drop-dead gorgeous.

And pregnant, he reminded himself, when he felt that damn tug of attraction.

Sabrina's eyebrow lifted just a fraction. She was obviously waiting for an answer as to whether he wanted to know if they would soon have a son or a daughter.

Too bad he didn't know what to say. "I'll get back to you on that, okay?" He hated that he sounded so removed from this. So angry. Hated even more all the conflicting feelings that were slamming into him at once.

What was wrong with him?

He could certainly go about bonding with this child without bonding with the mother. But that wasn't happening. Every minute he spent with Sabrina, he felt further removed from Fay. And he couldn't let go of her. He couldn't just forget all that had happened. Because if he did that…

He'd have to forgive Sabrina.

And himself.

He didn't deserve forgiveness. Here, all the months he'd blamed Sabrina, but the truth was that the blame was squarely on his own shoulders. His wife had been suicidal, and he hadn't realized it.

He hadn't stopped her.

"I have to go," he heard himself say. He went to the door, with part of him yelling at himself to turn around and accept what was on that examining table: Sabrina and his baby.

But he couldn't.

Shaw walked out and closed the door between them.

SABRINA FOLLOWED SHAW through SAPD Headquarters. She lagged a few steps behind him, on purpose, because she didn't want to look at him just yet.

The passing officers glanced at them. Probably because they knew of the latest attempt to kidnap her. Their glances could have also had something to do with the fact that she was wearing a loaner sundress from the doctor that was bright red and much too tight.

Of course, the glances could have been because she was hurdling silent daggers at Shaw.

She was riled to the core. And hurt. They were a month away from being parents, and he was still shutting her out. She'd expected it, of course, but for some reason it hurt more now than it had weeks ago. Maybe because she thought that she and Shaw had developed some kind of weird camaraderie after running for their lives and fighting off hired killers.

Apparently, she'd thought wrong.

He opened the door to a room that was across the hall from his office. "It isn't much," he mumbled, and he ushered her inside.

Shaw was certainly right. It wasn't much. It was a small room crammed with two sets of bunk beds, a coffee table, a sofa, a tiny fridge, microwave on a metal stand and an adjoining bathroom that was equally sparse. A toilet, sink and tub equipped with a shower head attached to the wall. There were no windows, and the only light came from the florescent fixture overhead, which was humming.

"The guys call this the flop room," he explained. "It comes in handy sometimes when you've pulled back-to-back shifts and are too tired to drive home. Don't worry. I had them change the sheets and put in some fresh towels."

Sabrina settled for a "Hmm" and walked past him. She made sure no part of her touched any part of him. Unlike at the doctor's office where she'd gotten a cheap thrill from their accidental contact.

Shaw shut the door. "You can stay here until I've made other arrangements."

"This is fine," she practically snapped. But it was more than fine. It was safe. Well, hopefully. There was still that issue of a possible leak in the department.

"The door has a lock," he added, probably sensing her concern about that leak and security in general. To prove it, he flipped the switch, and she heard the click. "And you won't ever be in here alone. I'll stay with you until I can arrange for something safer."

Ironic, because this should be the safest place on earth. However, with a gunman still on the loose, no place was without risks.

She stood there. He stood there. And the silence closed in around them. Sabrina had never noticed before just how unnerving quiet could be.

"I'm sorry," Shaw finally said.

"Don't," she immediately answered. She started to walk away, but he caught her arm and eased her back around.

"I shouldn't have left you in the ultrasound room," he added.

She shook off his grip so she could fold her arms over her chest, and she stared at him, waiting for a more thorough explanation.

It didn't come.

"You have to learn to put this baby first," Sabrina clarified. "You hate me because I didn't talk Fay into giving up her dreams for a baby so she could stay alive. Yep, I got that. You've made it perfectly clear, but I'm sick and tired of you using that hatred as an excuse not to love this child." She unfolded her arms and aimed her index finger at him. "If this is the way you intend to act after she's born, then by God, I won't share custody with you. I won't expose this innocent little baby to all this negativity."

There. She'd wanted to say that to him for weeks. But now that she had said it, Sabrina instantly regretted it. She regretted it even more when Shaw looked as if she'd slapped him.

"I love this baby," he said, his words slow and deliberate. "And I don't hate you."

Confused, she shook her head. "You don't have to lie about your feelings for me. As long as you love the child, that's enough—"

"I don't hate you," he repeated.

Sabrina was about to challenge that again, but he took her by the arm and pulled her to him. In the same motion, before she could even catch her breath, his mouth went to hers.

And he kissed her.

He actually kissed her!

The jolt of surprise was instant. But there was another jolt, too. His mouth was gentle. The kiss, clever. With just the right amount of pressure to please her, and make her want more. It was a sensation that went all the way from her mouth to the center of her body.

He slid his hand around the back of her neck and eased her even closer. As close as her pregnant stomach would allow them to get. He angled her head, controlling her completely, and deepened the kiss. His tongue touched hers, and that jolt went through her again.

He made a sound deep within his throat. Not a sound of confusion. But of pleasure. It was all male. And totally designed to make her respond in the most basic female kind of way.

She felt herself go all damp, her body obviously preparing for something it'd wanted for a long time.

Shaw.

Specifically, Shaw naked and inside her. Sabrina no longer felt hugely pregnant and awkward. She felt she could fly as long as Shaw was there to fly along with her.

He slid his hand down her back. So slowly. His fingers caressed her along the way, lighting new fires wherever he touched. Not that she needed more. She was already too hot as it was. But Shaw managed to up the heat by cupping her bottom and adjusting their positions so that his sex actually managed to touch hers.

Sabrina nearly lost it right there.

It'd been so long since she'd been touched intimately that she felt close to a climax. And all from a simple touch and kiss.

Shaw took his mouth from her. But he didn't move

the rest of his body. He stayed there, touching her and driving her crazy.

"I don't hate you," he repeated, his voice as strained as the muscles in his jaw. "I want to…" He kissed her again, and it was as hard as his sex was against her. "I want to, well, let me just settle for saying I want to have sex with you."

Sabrina didn't know who looked more surprised, him or her. "Really?" And she proved her shock by repeating that one word several times. "I figured I look disgusting to you."

"You look amazing," he corrected. He slid his thumb over her bottom lip, collecting the moisture that had gathered there from the kiss. He put his thumb to his mouth and ran his tongue over it. "You taste amazing."

But then he groaned, shook his head and stepped back.

Despite the loss of him touching her, the fire stayed with her, because she had a very good view of his incredible body, including that bulge behind the zipper of his pants. Sabrina was hot enough to want to ask if she could help him take care of that. She didn't know how. She hadn't experienced the logistics of pregnancy sex, but she was betting they could figure out a way.

"You had contractions earlier," he reminded her. "I shouldn't have kissed you."

"It was false labor," she reminded him, "and yes, you should have kissed me."

The corner of his mouth lifted. Almost a smile. Before he got serious again. "We have a lot to work out. Because I'm a man and because I want you, a certain part of me is suggesting we can work it out on that bunk bed."

Sabrina smiled, too. Then she got serious, as well. "But?"

"But while sex would be a good release, it won't help us." He cursed and mumbled something about *I can't believe I just said that*. "I need to work out what's going on in my head before I work out what's going on in my pants. Understand?"

"Yes, I do." And Sabrina was being honest. A hot sexual attraction didn't mean they had gotten beyond the past. But maybe it was a start.

"Plus, I have to keep you safe. That has to be my priority. If I have you on that bed, safety won't be on my mind."

"Well, I should hope not," she said because she thought they could use a lighter moment.

He stared at her and reached out, as if he were about to pull her into another round of kissing. But there was a knock at the door.

"Captain Shaw, it's Officer Newell. I need to speak to you."

Newell, again. He certainly got around. And the thought of that made her uncomfortable. Sabrina shook it off and blamed it on paranoia. Being under attack had made her not want to trust anyone. Except Shaw, of course. She had no trouble trusting him. Or falling hard for him.

That kiss and these close quarters were going to complicate things beyond belief.

Shaw wiped his mouth with the back of his hand, took a deep breath and opened the door. "What is it?"

But Newell looked past Shaw and at Sabrina. "Gavin Cunningham is here at headquarters. Says he hired you and your company, Rootsfind, to locate someone for him. He's demanding to see you now."

"Good," Shaw informed him. "Because I want to see him. He obviously didn't commit suicide and wasn't murdered."

"No. But he is creating a scene."

"Where is he?" Sabrina asked. She walked closer to the door, but Shaw grabbed her to ease her behind him.

"You should be resting," he reminded her.

"And I will. But we both know this conversation could be critical. Gavin said he was responsible for me being taken hostage, and I want to know why he believes that."

"I can question him," Shaw insisted.

She gave him a flat look. "I'm betting you won't get far with him."

"He did say he wouldn't talk to anyone but her," Newell interjected.

Shaw still didn't seem ready to budge, so Sabrina added, "I can sit down while I talk to him. And if I can get him to confess any part he might have had in all of this, then you can arrest him."

It took several more moments before Shaw finally nodded, and they followed Newell down the hall and into another wing of the building. She found Gavin pacing in an interrogation room.

He was just as she'd last seen him, dressed to perfection in a tailored suit. His blond hair was perfectly groomed, as well. He looked the part of a young and upcoming attorney at the prestigious law firm where he worked.

Sabrina had run a background check on him after his first call to her, and she'd learned that even though he had been an attorney for only two years, he appeared to have a solid future and was well on his way to earning a seven-figure income.

"You're here," Gavin said. He didn't try to come any closer, but without taking his eyes off her, he slowly sank into the chair on the opposite side of the table from where Shaw and she stood.

Shaw had her sit as well, but he stood and glared at Gavin.

"For the record, this is being recorded." Shaw pointed to the camera mounted in the corner. "You have a problem with that?"

Gavin gave the camera wary look and then shrugged. "No problem with it. I want the truth to be heard."

"Then we want the same thing," Shaw assured him. "So, why are you responsible for Sabrina being taken hostage?"

Gavin fired some uncomfortable glances among Shaw, Sabrina and the camera before his gaze settled on her. "I guess I should tell you this in front of him. After all, the police will have to get involved."

"The police are already involved," Shaw warned. "*I'm* involved. Now, start talking. Did you arrange for the women to be taken hostage?"

"God, no." He couldn't have sounded more outraged, but it was short-lived. Gavin huffed out several bursts of air and continued, "But I think I know who did. I think it was Wilson Rouse."

Now, that was a name she recognized. "The wealthy businessman who owns a chain of family style restaurants?" Sabrina clarified.

"The very one. I believe he might be my biological father. That's what I wanted you to try to confirm by using your resources at Rootsfind. I figured you had all kinds of databases and such that you could tap into and get me quick results. And by the way, he knows I'm here talking to you because I called him before I came over. I want all our dirty little secrets out in the open."

When Gavin didn't continue, Shaw made an impatient circling motion with his finger. "Keep going."

Gavin cleared his throat. "My mother died when I was six and never told me the identity of my father, but I recently found a letter where she mentioned Wilson Rouse. She implied they had an affair at the very time I would have been conceived. He was married and successful. Already a pillar in the conservative community. She was a waitress in one of his restaurants. So, I believe he dumped her when he found out she was pregnant."

"What does this have to do with the hostages?" Sabrina asked.

"Maybe everything. I wanted proof that Rouse was my father, so day before yesterday, I arranged to meet him by telling him I represented a potential investor. We met over coffee, and I confronted him. He denied everything and said he'd never fathered any bastard children. So, after he left, I took the cup he'd used and gave it to the lab tech at the San Antonio Maternity Hospital. I also gave him a sample of my DNA so he could compare the two."

So, that's how the DNA file had gotten there. Well, that was one mystery solved.

"Why take the DNA samples to the hospital?" Shaw asked.

"The lab tech was an old friend, and I thought he'd keep this between him and me. He didn't." Gavin closed his eyes a moment. "He called me before he ran the test and said even if the results didn't match, he could fake them, and that way we could get hush money from Rouse." He paused again. "Rouse wouldn't want his squeaky clean image tarnished. I told the tech, no blackmail, but I believe he called Rouse anyway and threatened him with the DNA tests he was running for me."

"So, what are you saying?" Shaw pressed. "That Wilson Rouse set up the hostage incident so he'd have a cover for his DNA and yours to be stolen?"

"That's exactly what I'm saying. Was the DNA stolen?" Gavin challenged.

Sabrina thought of the deleted file. Yes, it was possible that it had been.

Shaw didn't answer Gavin's question but went with one of his own. "What's the tech's name who had the sample?"

"Edward Reyes."

"The one who was killed early in the hostage standoff," Shaw provided.

Oh, mercy. So, the one person who could have cleared this up was dead. But they might finally have a motive for why this had happened. Of course, something still didn't make sense. If the DNA had been destroyed, then why would Wilson Rouse still want to kidnap her?

Sabrina had a lot of questions and doubts about what Gavin had just told them, but why would he lie?

Shaw turned and went to the door. He motioned for someone, and a moment later, Newell appeared.

"Two things," Shaw said, his voice low. Sabrina got up so she could hear what he was about to tell the officer. "What's the status of that list of people who knew about the hotel arrangements for Sabrina and me?"

"I'm working on it." Newell dodged Shaw's gaze and looked at Gavin. "Learn anything from him?"

"Yeah. That's the second thing I need. I have to speak to Wilson Rouse. Call him and get him down here. If he won't come, arrest him."

"No need for that. He showed up about five minutes ago because he said Cunningham called him," Newell said, tipping his head to Gavin. "Mr. Rouse is waiting in your office. Should I bring him down here?"

"Absolutely. And get me that list. Within the hour, I want to know the names of everyone who might have put Sabrina and my baby in danger."

Newell walked away. Shaw glanced at Sabrina. Then at Gavin, and he motioned for Sabrina to step into the hall with him. He closed the interrogation room door.

"What's wrong?" she asked and went on the defensive. "Please don't say you don't want me here when you question Wilson Rouse because I want to hear what he has to say. If he's responsible for what happened to me, I have to know."

"So do I. You can stay." He looked down the hall where Newell had exited. "But for now, we might have another problem."

She followed his gaze. "Newell?"

"He couldn't look me in the eye."

Sabrina thought about the uncomfortable feeling she'd had about him showing up at the hotel the way he had. "You think he might be the leak?"

Shaw shook his head. "I don't know, but it appears as if someone compromised our location. A cop would be in the best position to do that."

"But Newell is the one who killed the gunman," she pointed out.

"Maybe to keep him quiet," Shaw pointed out just as quickly. He took out his phone and punched in some numbers.

"Who are you calling?"

"Someone I trust. Lieutenant O'Malley," he said to the person he'd called. "I know you're swamped in Homicide, but I really need a favor. A *quiet* favor. Run a check on Keith Newell for me. Dig deep and look for anything suspicious. *Anything*. And I also need you to see who would have known that Sabrina and I were in that hotel where we were attacked."

Sabrina couldn't hear what the lieutenant said, but his response was short and caused Shaw to nod approvingly.

"Yes, actually there is something else I need. Food and toiletries for Sabrina. I might have to keep her in the flop room for the rest of the day. Thanks," Shaw said a moment later, and ended the call.

He touched her arm with his fingers and rubbed gently. "Don't worry. I'll get to the bottom of this."

He would, if he could, but Shaw wasn't a superhero, and the danger was still there, stronger than ever.

"Captain Tolbert," someone called out.

She recognized the tall man with the graying blond hair who was making his way toward them because she had seen his photo in the newspaper. It was Wilson Rouse. Apparently, round two was about to start.

Rouse walked closer. "Could we talk in private?" he asked Shaw.

Shaw shook his head and stepped just a few feet away. "No. This is Sabrina Carr, one of the maternity hostages, and she's in my protective custody. Wherever I go, she goes with me, so private conversations are out."

"Sabrina Carr," the man repeated. She didn't think it was her imagination that he had some disdain for her. "Gavin Cunningham came to you, and you encouraged his lies."

"Hardly." Sabrina lifted her shoulder. "Gavin just filled us in on the details. Before now, I had no idea that the biological father he wanted me to find was you."

"It isn't me. And whatever that slick weasel told you, it's a lie."

"Really?" Shaw said with skepticism dripping from his voice.

"Really. Because he's trying to set me up. You want to know who's responsible for that hostage mess?" He pulled out a small tape recorder from his pocket. "Well, I got the proof of who's guilty right here."

Chapter Eight

Shaw was having second and third thoughts about Sabrina sitting in on this meeting with Rouse and Gavin. He didn't want her more stressed than she already was.

But he also didn't want her out of his sight.

He trusted almost all his men, but those same men he trusted were swamped with the hostage investigation and the normal cases. Besides, it was possible that Gavin would be more open if Sabrina were in the room, and that openness could maybe lead them to the truth—even if this wasn't standard procedure to have a victim in the same room with the possible perpetrators.

"I want you to stay off your feet," Shaw insisted, and he led Sabrina back to the chair in the interview room where she'd sat earlier.

Shaw sat next to her, directly across from Gavin, but Rouse didn't sit. He walked in, slammed the door shut and aimed glares at all of them. He saved the more intense glare for Gavin.

"I have proof of what you've done," Rouse accused the other man.

"And if you hadn't stolen the DNA from the hospital

lab, I would have had proof that you're my father," Gavin accused right back.

"Not a chance. I had your mother checked out, and she might have worked for me, but I didn't play under the sheets with the waitresses. Or with any woman other than my wife," he quickly added.

Rouse held up the miniature tape recorder and clicked the play button. Shaw immediately heard a man's voice.

An angry man.

"I won't let you get away with this, Rouse. So help me, I will make you pay. I'll ruin the only thing you seem to give a damn about—your precious name—and I don't care what I have to do to make that happen."

It was clear that it was Gavin's voice, and the young man jumped to his feet. "That conversation had nothing to do with what happened at the hospital."

Rouse smiled. "Didn't it?"

"You know it didn't. Play the rest of it." But then he shook his head and sank back down into the chair. "Yes, I did threaten him, and it'll sound as if I'm trying to set him up. But I didn't."

Gavin's reaction seemed honest, but Shaw wasn't about to declare him innocent of anything. "Why did you want to make Rouse pay?" Shaw asked. But he thought he already knew the answer—because Rouse wouldn't acknowledge that Gavin was his son.

"Tell him," Rouse prompted when Gavin didn't answer.

Gavin took his time responding. "I sued him on behalf of a client, and I lost."

"He lost because he tried to cut some corners with

depositions, and I caught him in the act. It was his first big case," Rouse happily provided. "And he blew it big-time. That didn't sit well with the partners in his law firm, and since one of them is a golfing buddy of mine, I explained he should rethink his decision about keeping on the boy genius here."

Shaw silently groaned. He glanced at Sabrina, who had her eyes tipped to the ceiling. "So, you faked this whole fatherhood accusation to get back at him?" Sabrina asked Gavin.

"No!" Gavin practically shouted.

"You bet he did," Rouse contradicted, his voice booming over Gavin's. "You have no blood of mine in your body. And you're not getting a penny of my money." He turned to Shaw. "My theory is that genius here decided to get his lab tech friend to help blackmail me. When that didn't work, he hired the gunmen, probably also friends of his, to make it look as if I wanted to steal my DNA."

Shaw shook his head. "That's a lot of trouble to go through to set you up because you tried to get him fired. People died during that hostage standoff. A baby is missing."

"Well, I'm not responsible," Rouse insisted, jamming his thumb to his chest. "Things probably got out of hand, especially if those gunmen were friends of his. They probably just panicked and screwed up."

"I didn't do this!" Gavin shouted.

The two men launched into a loud argument that could probably have gone on for hours, so Shaw stood and put an end to it. "There's one way to settle this. Both of you give me DNA samples, and we'll see who's telling the truth."

Well, the truth about fatherhood anyway. And it might be a start to the truth about why the hostages had been taken, if Rouse was truly Gavin's father.

"You want my DNA sample?" Rouse asked, but he didn't wait for Shaw to answer. "Then get a court order. Oh, and good luck with that. Unlike the incompetent legal eagle here, I have an outstanding team of lawyers who'll fight you every step of the way."

"Thanks," Shaw said sarcastically. He reached out and took the tape recorder. "Now I can confiscate this. As potential evidence in a quadruple murder investigation."

"Keep it. Use it to put that weasel behind bars." Rouse flashed a dry smile at Gavin and walked out.

"I'll give you a DNA sample," Gavin volunteered.

Again, that seemed to imply he was innocent, but without Rouse's DNA for comparison, it was an empty gesture. Still, Shaw wouldn't turn it down. It would come in handy if they managed to get Rouse's.

"Go to the dispatcher at the front desk. He or she will make arrangements for a DNA swab," Shaw told him. He helped Sabrina to her feet. "In the meantime, I'll see about getting the court order for Rouse's sample."

"Do that, because he's my father, and I want him to pay for what he's done."

Shaw left Gavin still fuming in the interview room, and he led Sabrina back toward the flop room. "You think either Rouse or Gavin could be behind this?" she asked.

"Maybe. But I keep going back to that third deleted

file. Taking your DNA test, I understand. Maybe things went wrong, and the gunmen decided you'd make a good hostage to cover their tracks. I can even understand Rouse wanting his DNA file deleted to protect his name. Or Gavin deleting it to make Rouse look guilty. But then what was in that third file?"

Sabrina made a sound of agreement. "Will your computer techs be able to recover it?"

"They're trying. I got an update while we were at the clinic, and I found out that there'd been two recent attempts to break into that lab at the hospital. That's the reason the new security camera was installed. The head of security had also changed the codes to access the DNA storage room."

"Yes. That makes sense. The gunman, not Burney Monroe, but the other one, he was furious when he couldn't open the door. That's when he shot the med tech. And then he shot the lock on the door. That's how he got inside."

So, maybe the Gavin or Rouse theory was right. If the dead med tech had agreed to help either of them, for a price, of course, he would have been a loose end. That could have been the reason he was killed so early on in the standoff. The gunmen no longer had any use for him. That meant Shaw needed to look for a connection between the gunmen and the lab tech.

Shaw opened the flop room and looked around, just to make sure there was no gunman or rogue cop lurking around and ready to attack. After the incident in the hotel, it would be a long time before he stopped looking over his shoulder.

"Sir, here's the takeout you ordered," someone said

from behind him. It was one of O'Malley's men, some-one Shaw trusted. Otherwise, he wouldn't have taken the bag and handed it to Sabrina. "I figured you'd need to eat something," Shaw told her.

She thanked him, Shaw gave the officer some money, and he closed the door and locked it. The toiletries he'd requested were there as well, sitting in a plastic grocery bag. There was even a change of clothes stacked next to the bag. Lieutenant O'Malley certainly worked fast.

"Eat," Shaw insisted. "And then get some rest."

She tipped her head toward the bathroom. "I think I'd like a shower first."

He nodded. The shower might help her relax, and it would give him a few minutes to get some much needed updates about the case. But Sabrina didn't head to the bathroom. She turned, stepped closer and looked up at him.

"I know I've been saying this a lot, but thank you. I'm not sure I would have gotten through this without you."

"You would have." But Shaw was glad he'd been there. For the baby's sake.

Sabrina's sake, too, he reluctantly admitted.

She leaned into him, putting her head against his shoulder. Like the other times they'd touched, he felt the attraction. The heat simmering between them. But he felt something else, too.

An intimacy that went beyond the attraction.

Again, he wanted to think this was all about the baby, but it scared him to realize it wasn't.

"What am I doing?" he asked, aloud. He'd meant to

keep that question inside his brain, but it somehow made it to his mouth.

Sabrina pulled back, studied his face and then gave a heavy sigh. "I ask myself that all the time. I want you, too much," she added with a grimace. "But you're Fay's husband."

"Widower," he corrected, and he hoped that would sink in if he said it often enough.

"Widower." Sabrina repeated it, as well. When her gaze met his again, there were tears in her eyes. "You know what Fay said to me right before she died?"

He knew, though it hurt too much to remember. Fay had phoned Sabrina, after she'd taken a bottle of sleeping pills, and Shaw knew this because it'd been Sabrina who had contacted him, had told him to get to Fay, that she was dying. Shaw had listened to the message that Fay had left on Sabrina's answering machine. It'd been part of the routine investigation to declare Fay's death a suicide.

"We don't have to talk about this," he insisted.

But Sabrina continued as if she hadn't heard him, "Fay told me to take care of you. I swear, I tried to do that."

She had. That's what this baby was all about. At least, it'd started that way. It felt different now. *He* felt different. But the guilt was still there.

"Do you know what Fay said to me when she was in my arms dying?" he asked. Part of him wondered why he was opening this too-raw wound, and the other part knew it had to be done.

Sabrina blinked back tears and shook her head.

"Fay said I should take care of you, that you and I should have the baby that she couldn't give me."

The breath rushed out of her, and Shaw held her because she looked ready to fall. "I'm sorry. So sorry," Sabrina repeated. "I didn't know she said that. She shouldn't have asked that of you."

"Yeah. She should have. Fay had a lot of problems. Old baggage from being abused in her childhood. New baggage from the infertility issues. But she always put me first. Even when she was dying, she knew how important a baby was to me. How much I wanted a family of my own."

That was his old baggage. He hadn't been adopted like Sabrina or abused like Fay, but his parents had been killed in a car accident when he was five years old. He'd been shifted around from one family member to another, never finding a place he could call home.

Yeah, the old baggage had shaped him, too.

Shaw had to take a deep breath. "If I hadn't wanted a child so much, then Fay might be alive today."

Sabrina frantically shook her head. "She desperately wanted a baby, too. You're not at fault here. Fay's depression is what killed her."

"You're not at fault, either," he whispered. He reached out and wiped away the tear that was sliding down her cheek.

She stood there, staring at him and blinked. "Did we just have the air clearing that we'd been avoiding?"

"Yeah. I think we did." And it felt good. Not perfect. But good. Shaw certainly didn't think this would take away the guilt. It would always be there.

But the question was, just how was it going to affect what he was starting to feel for Sabrina?

"Time for that shower," she mumbled, and grabbed the bag of toiletries and stack of clean clothes from the table. She walked toward the bathroom, leaving him to deal with that question he might never be able to answer.

"If you don't mind, I'll leave the door open just a fraction," she called out to him. "That way, I can hear you if you call. Or if I call you. I might have a little trouble getting out of the tub."

That got his attention. "You need help?" And yeah, it sounded a little sexual, but he was serious. He didn't want her falling.

"I should be fine, and I promise if you have to come running to haul me out, I'll cover myself with the towel. I wasn't kidding about those stretch marks."

She grinned and adjusted the door so there was about a two-inch gap.

Shaw smiled as well and then cursed because this wasn't the time to be cheerful. Maybe he'd get a chance to do that when Sabrina and the baby were safe.

He heard her turn on the shower and about a minute later, he caught just a glimpse of a very naked Sabrina stepping into the tub. She slid the shower curtain so that it shielded her, but not completely. He could still see her outline behind the vinyl.

Oh, man.

The raunchy thoughts started, and here only minutes earlier, he'd been a somber widower. Now, he felt more like a sex-starved teenager.

Because he had to do something, anything, to get his

mind off her, he rifled through the takeout bag, took one of the three sandwiches—turkey on wheat—and started to eat. He also forced his eyes away from Sabrina's nude silhouette. Thankfully, he got a little help in the distraction area because his phone buzzed.

"Lieutenant O'Malley," Shaw answered after he saw the officer's name on the ID screen.

"I don't have much info for you, but I figured you'd be anxious for an update."

"I am." He was anxious for a lot of things, including the woman behind the shower curtain. Shaw forced his attention to stay on the conversation. "What did you learn?"

"Still no word on that third file that was deleted, but we've accessed the hospital's online storage. The company that manages it is going through the cache of old files and comparing them to what's in the system now. We might get lucky and find out what was deleted."

"Good, that's a start. What about the officers who might have known where Sabrina and I were staying?"

"Newell's on the list of those who knew, along with about a dozen others in Special Investigations. The location was kept in the department, but we're still looking at hotel employees. One of them could have tipped off the gunmen."

True. Shaw had minimized how much time Sabrina was in the lobby and in front of the hotel, but it was still possible that someone had recognized her. After all, the hostages' photos had been all over the news.

"I'm still running the background check on Newell,"

O'Malley continued. "Nothing immediately sticks out, but I'm getting his financials."

Another good start. "Any idea why he was at the hotel this morning?"

"None. He was off duty, but he does seem obsessed with this investigation. About a year ago, he had a case with a hostage, and it didn't end well. The hostage was killed. Maybe that's all there is to it—he's trying to right an old wrong."

After what he'd been through with Fay, Shaw understood that, but he wasn't about to trust Newell just yet.

"Keep digging," Shaw insisted.

"I will, and I might soon have an update on the evidence we're processing both from the hospital and the hotel room where Burney Monroe was shot and killed. CSI and Trace are working nonstop, and the reports are coming in."

Maybe there'd be something in all that evidence that would break this case wide open.

"I had a conversation with Wilson Rouse and Gavin Cunningham in interview room 2B," Shaw told the lieutenant. "Could you have someone look at the disk? It was recorded. What I need is for someone to review it and get me a court order for Rouse's DNA."

O'Malley hesitated. "That won't be easy."

"No," Shaw agreed. "But it might provide us with a motive. I also want a tail put on Gavin Cunningham. He's probably still in the building giving us some of his own DNA. After you see the interview, you'll know why all of this might turn out to be critical."

"It sounds it. Anything else?"

Shaw went through his long, mental to-do list. "Any word on the second gunman?"

"Not yet. He's still at large."

Yeah. And as long as he was, then Sabrina wouldn't be safe. "Any leads?"

"Maybe. Burney Monroe was a low level computer tech for a supply company. That might have been why he was hired to do this particular job. He definitely had the computer hacking skills. He also has a younger brother, Danny. He has no phone and no listed place of residence, but he works as a data entry clerk, also low level, and his boss said he's due on shift at midnight."

Shaw jumped right on that. "Did this brother miss work during the time of the hostage incident?"

"He wasn't on the schedule so the boss doesn't know where he was. Still, he said Danny's a good worker, and he never had any problems with him."

"But Burney could have talked him into this." Or someone else.

"True," the lieutenant agreed. "If the two learned about Sabrina and you, maybe they thought they could use it somehow. Maybe to gain money, maybe to gain some kind of legal favors?"

Yes. Because the bottom line was that Rouse and Gavin might simply be distractions. This whole mess could have been orchestrated by the two gunmen, Burney Monroe and his partner. And if they found the partner, they might learn there was no need for Rouse, Gavin and their collective DNA.

Still, he couldn't discount that it was Gavin's DNA file that had been deleted and the sample stolen.

"One more thing," Shaw continued. He checked first

to make sure Sabrina was still in the shower. She was, and with the water running she wouldn't be able to hear this. "Have someone run a check on Dr. Claire Nicholson, Sabrina's OB."

O'Malley made a sound of surprise. "You think she might be involved in this?"

"Probably not. But I keep going back to the fact that the gunmen stole Sabrina's DNA. I want to know who told them to do that, and why."

"You think it's connected to you, because you're her baby's father?"

"Could be. When the gunmen took her from the hospital, Sabrina overhead them say they were going to use her to get me to cooperate."

"Well, that could be motive. But a lot of people already knew the child was yours. Newell certainly knew because I heard him talking about whether or not to collect money to buy a baby gift."

Hell. So, they were back to square one—still suspecting Newell but knowing that this could all be circumstantial.

"I'll put together a team I trust to start handling this," O'Malley let him know. "And, Captain, hang in there. We'll get this SOB even if he's one of our own."

Shaw hoped that was true. A dirty cop wasn't always easy to catch. But neither was a dirty community leader or a lawyer.

And speaking of cops… "How's Bo Duggan?" Shaw asked.

O'Malley wasn't quick to answer. Shaw understood. O'Malley was married, the father of three, and he was no doubt thinking of his own wife and family. "Bo's trying to deal with it. It's not easy. Plus, he's got newborn twins to take care of."

That would have been more than enough on one man's plate, but now Bo had to bury his wife. "Make sure Bo gets as much time off as he needs."

"I will."

He thanked the lieutenant and hung up just as Sabrina turned off the shower. Shaw knew it wouldn't be long before she came back into the room, so he quickly composed himself. There wasn't anything he could do to help Nadine Duggan, but he sure as hell could find the people who'd contributed to her death and put them behind bars.

The shower curtain rattled back, and he got up in case she needed help. Just seeing her helped with the blue mood, and he wondered when the hell Sabrina had become his lifeline to getting through this.

Right.

It'd happened when he started lusting after her.

Yeah, he watched her and told himself it was because he wanted to make sure she didn't fall. That was a huge part of it, but that didn't justify the cheap thrill of seeing her naked. He didn't see any stretch marks, probably because he was gawking at her breasts. They were full and looked ready for the taking.

His taking.

He groaned, looked away and walked closer to the door. "You okay?"

"Yes, other than having no clean panties. There weren't any in the stack of clothes. But I'm washing the ones I have and hanging them on the towel rack. As thin as they are, they'll be dry in no time."

There was the sound of more water running, some moving around sounds, and several minutes later, the door fully opened. Sabrina stood there in a loose blue dress the color of the Texas sky on a good day. Barefooted. Her wavy, long auburn hair was damp and clung to her neck and the shoulders of the dress.

She looked and smelled like Christmas and his birthday all rolled into one.

"Did you just admit you're not wearing panties?" he asked. He meant it as a joke, but the joke didn't quite come through in his voice.

The need did, though.

"It was meant as a warning, so you wouldn't be shocked when you see them dangling from the towel rack." Her expression was light, too, but he didn't miss the long, lingering look she gave him.

"You need to eat," he reminded her. And himself. He stepped to the side so she could get past him. "There are some sandwiches, apples, juice and milk."

Sheez, he sounded like a waiter and decided to shut up.

He couldn't turn off his eyes, though. Shaw watched her cross the room. She was light on her feet for being eight months pregnant.

"Join me," she insisted. She took the bag from the table and took it to the sofa, probably because it was more comfortable than the metal chairs at the small table in the kitchen area.

He did join her, after taking a deep breath.

She opened the plastic bottle of milk, took a sip and stared at him from over the top of the bottle.

The air was suddenly scalding hot.

Still, Shaw took his partially eaten turkey sandwich from the table and sat next to her on the sofa. He was hungry. His stomach was growling, but food didn't seem to be his body's top priority.

Sabrina lowered the bottle and licked the milk from her lips. She probably hadn't meant for it to be provocative, but it was.

Hell, at this point her breathing was provocative because it pushed her breasts against the front of her dress.

"What are you thinking?" she asked. She set the milk on the coffee table.

He started to lie, to tell her he was thinking about the investigation. But it would have been such a big lie that it probably would have gotten stuck in his throat.

So, no lie.

Just the truth. And he'd show her what he was thinking.

Shaw tossed his sandwich onto the table, reached out, clasped the back of her neck and hauled her to him. He caught her slight sound of surprise with a kiss.

Oh, he was going to regret this.

He knew it. Sabrina knew it.

But that didn't stop him.

He kissed her, hard, and pulled her onto his lap.

Chapter Nine

Sabrina didn't have time to think. Nor did she want to. The only thing she wanted was Shaw, and apparently she was going to get him.

Finally!

Judging from the heat of the kiss, he didn't intend to stop.

She certainly didn't intend to, either. Sabrina went willingly when Shaw moved her onto his lap. Her belly prevented them from having full body contact, but it didn't stop the fiery kiss that Shaw was delivering.

The fire wasn't just in his kiss. It slid right through her, from her mouth all the way to the part of her that wasn't covered with panties. She got an interesting reminder of that when she felt Shaw's thigh press against her there. Mercy. Here she was again. Barely a touch, and she was ready to have him inside her.

Shaw didn't make a move to unzip his pants and give her what she wanted. Instead, his mouth left hers and went to her neck. He dropped a flurry of kisses around her jaw. On her throat. But when the kissing exploration made it to the base of her ear, Sabrina moaned. He took the cue and gave her a French kiss there that had her moaning for more.

More was difficult to get.

She tried to wiggle closer to him, so that his sex would touch hers, so she could finally have some relief from this burning ache that was too hot to control. But again, her belly got in the way.

Shaw stopped the neck kisses and pulled back so they were eye to eye. For one horrible moment, she thought he was going to say this had to stop. She thought he was going to move away from her.

That didn't happen.

Sabrina sat there, waiting, with her breath gusting and her heart racing out of control.

"Shh," he said. His voice was soothing and slow.

So was his hand. He slid it from her neck to her breasts. And he circled her right nipple with his fingertips while he watched her.

Sabrina had no choice but to watch him as well, even though that touch caused her to moan again, and her eyelids fluttered, threatening to close.

"Shh," he repeated. His hand went lower, sliding against her, and creating little fires wherever his fingers touched.

He stopped for just a moment when his hand reached her thigh, and with the fire blazing in his blue eyes, he pushed up her dress.

His gaze never wavered. He remained focused on her face. And his fingers trailed up her thigh. Then, over.

To just the right place.

The pleasure speared through her. Instant. Hot. Intense. So intense she had to close her eyes, and she angled her hips forward so that his clever fingers would go deeper inside her. They did, and with a few of those well-placed strokes, he had her right at the edge.

Sabrina forced her eyes open, and she shook her head, questioning him. They should do this together, with his sex inside her.

But Shaw shook his head as well, and he leaned forward to kiss her. It was French. And perfect. The kiss from a man who knew exactly what he was doing. And what he was doing was taking her to that edge.

Alone.

Sabrina wanted to fight it. She wanted to pull back and coax him into joining her. But the kiss continued, hard and deep. So did those maddening strokes with his fingers. Each one, faster.

Harder.

Deeper.

Until she couldn't fight the sensations. She couldn't hang on. Her body betrayed her, and she felt the climax ripple through her.

She slumped forward, because she had no choice, but Shaw caught her and buried his face against her neck. They stayed there, pressed together, until Sabrina could gather enough breath and strength to pull back.

The corner of his mouth lifted. Then lowered just as quickly when he apparently saw her expression. "Oh, no. We're not going to have that argument."

Maybe it was the post-climactic fog in her head, but she wasn't sure what he meant. "Argument?"

"The one where you try to convince me that we should have full-blown sex. Or some other form of pleasure that will end in me having what you just had."

Sabrina blinked. Yes, that was the argument she had been about to launch. She decided instead to get her point across without words. He was hard and huge behind his zipper, so she pressed her hand against him.

A hoarse groan rumbled in his throat, and he moved her hand away. "Tempting, but it can't happen. I need to think, and I can't think if we're having sex."

"We could make it fast." And she was only partly joking. She was still punchy from the climax. "I just want to make you feel the way I'm feeling."

"I am," he assured her. It didn't seem like a lie, either. He leaned in and brushed a kiss on her mouth. Then, he eased her off his lap. "Watching you was incredible."

It didn't feel incredible. Sabrina suddenly felt a little awkward. She'd never had sex that particular way, and Sabrina didn't like the idea of her getting something that Shaw was denying himself.

"Don't overanalyze it," he mumbled. "This wasn't about pity. It wasn't about all the old bad feelings between us. I just wanted to watch you."

How could she argue with that?

Besides, she was too mellowed out with the aftershocks still humming through her. And she didn't want to argue. There had already been too many disagreements between her and Shaw to add another one.

"Now eat," he insisted. He got up and walked to the bathroom. "Then, rest."

Sabrina fixed her dress, pulling it back down in place. She fixed her position, too, and moved so she was sitting rather than leaning into the space where Shaw would hopefully soon return. Then, maybe they could talk.

Or not.

Sabrina thought about that. They were light-years ahead of where they'd been just days earlier, and it was probably best if she didn't push things.

He's Fay's husband.

That old label flashed through her head again, and she felt the guilt return. Oh, mercy. When was this going to stop?

"You okay?" Shaw asked.

She glanced up to find him staring at her. "I'm fine," she insisted.

He looked as if he might challenge that, but he didn't. He came back to the sofa and started in on the sandwich that he'd discarded prior to their make out session. He took exactly one bite before his phone buzzed.

Shaw pulled out his cell from his pocket, glanced at the screen and answered it. "Lieutenant O'Malley."

The officer he trusted. Sabrina only hoped he was trustworthy and good at his job. They needed information.

She ate while Shaw listened. She couldn't hear what the lieutenant was saying, but judging from Shaw's suddenly intense expression, this was an important call.

"Where's the baby now?" Shaw asked.

She remembered there was a missing newborn. Shaw had said an Amber Alert had been issued. Maybe this call was to tell him the child had been found. She prayed that was the case anyway. Even after all the hell she'd been through, having her baby disappear would be much, much worse.

"I want that umbilical cord tested ASAP," Shaw continued before he started another long round of listening.

The minutes crawled by, punctuated only by Shaw's occasional question.

"Repeat that," he said. And his expression tightened even more. "No. You go ahead and question him. I think it's safe to say that it'd be a conflict of interest for me to do it. Record the interview, of course. I want to hear every word."

Shaw ended the call, slipped his phone back into his pocket and blew out a long breath.

Sabrina had so many questions, but she started with the obvious one. "You found the missing baby who was taken from the hospital?"

"No. This is a different baby, one not involved with the hostages." He shrugged. "Well, maybe it is. We just don't know at this point. The tech guys were able to retrieve the deleted file and were able to match it to a DNA request that was generated right here in SAPD four days ago."

Just three days before they were all taken hostage. The timing was certainly suspicious. "Whose DNA?"

"The missing baby's. His birth mother was missing as well, but then her body was found. She was murdered. And the baby wasn't with her. None of her friends and relatives know where the child is, but a family member stated that the dead woman had had some problems with the baby's birth father. He'd made threats about taking the child."

"And the father's name?" Sabrina asked.

Shaw shook his head. "We don't know. Neither did the family member because the dead woman had kept the relationship a secret. That's why the DNA test was ordered. The birth mother had had the baby's cord blood stored at the hospital, so we were able to get a good sample to try to identify the father. Because obviously the father is a murder suspect."

Oh, mercy. Another murder. Another missing suspect. Except this might be the same person who'd created all this havoc. "Will the techs be able to recreate the missing file?"

"No. It had been corrupted, probably on purpose. And the baby's cord blood was missing from the hospital storage room." Shaw paused. "This might be the motive for why the hostage situation happened."

Of course. A birth father who didn't want his identity known because he'd murdered the mother of his child. Sabrina prayed he hadn't done the same to the baby.

She eased her hand over her own child and gave him a reassuring rub. "How will you find this monster?"

"We have several ways. We're trying to track down the dead gunman's brother, Danny Monroe. It's possible he was the second masked gunman who took the hostages. Or he at least might know if his brother was the baby's father."

"Or he could have just been the hired gun," Sabrina pointed out.

Shaw nodded, looked at her. He smoothed his fingers over her bunched up forehead. "Don't worry."

"Right." She nearly laughed. "I want this person identified and found so that our baby will be safe."

"I want the same thing," he assured her. He sat there with his own forehead bunched up.

"There's more," she said. "What?"

"Two things." But then he paused again. "I'm having your OB, Dr. Nicholson, checked out. It's just routine," he added quickly. "She had access to your medical records, and I want to make sure she didn't leak that info to anyone." His eyes came to hers. "Did you know that she'd once been romantically involved with Officer Keith Newell?"

"No." Sabrina took a moment to let the surprise settle in. "But then she doesn't talk about her personal life. How involved were they?"

"Involved. They've known each other since high school. Turns out he listed her as one of his references when he applied to the police academy."

Sabrina gave that some thought, as well. She also thought of how supportive the doctor had been. "That doesn't mean Dr. Nicholson has done anything wrong."

"No. It doesn't." Shaw shook his head, cursed under his breath. "But the report I just got from O'Malley could point the guilty finger right at one of my own men."

Chapter Ten

Shaw stood in the shower and let the scalding hot water spray over him. It didn't help unknot the muscles in his back. Probably nothing would except for an arrest.

Thankfully, that might happen soon.

Not so thankfully, he might have to arrest a cop.

Lieutenant O'Malley had gotten back Newell's financials, and there was an unexplained ten thousand dollars that had been deposited into his account the day before the hostage incident. Ten grand wasn't a fortune by some people's standards, but it was a lot to a cop. And it was a red flag since there weren't any other similar deposits over the last few years. It also didn't help that the money had been transferred into his account from an offshore bank.

Shaw was still waiting to hear Newell's explanation, and by God, it'd better be a good one.

He bracketed his hands against the tiled wall and leaned into the shower spray so it'd hit the back of his neck. He didn't stay in that position long. He couldn't. He needed to finish up and get back into the flop room with Sabrina.

She'd been asleep when he turned on the shower.

And the flop room door was locked from the inside. Newell was in Lieutenant O'Malley's office and would stay there until the lieutenant got some answers. So, Newell wasn't running around the building, ready to strike, but Shaw didn't want to leave Sabrina alone too long.

He dressed in the jeans and black T-shirt he'd had brought to him from his locker. They weren't exactly his normal work clothes, but they'd have to do for now. He didn't have time to drop by his house and pick up his usual dark pants and dress shirt.

Shaw quickly brushed his teeth and used his hand to comb his hair. He opened the door, ready to tiptoe back into the room, but Sabrina was there, standing right in front of him, dressed in the paper-thin gown that'd been among the loaner clothes. Her dress was tucked beneath her arm.

"Anything new on Newell?" Sabrina immediately asked.

Shaw shook his head. "Lieutenant O'Malley said he would call as soon as he got to the bottom of this."

She grumbled something under her breath and pushed her hair away from her face. "I fell asleep," she said as if that were the last thing she wanted to do. "Did you?"

"I napped on and off throughout the night." But it felt as if he hadn't slept for days.

She lightly touched her fingers to the bruise above his eye. The injury he'd gotten when Burney Monroe bashed him in the head with his gun. "It's turning purple." The corner of her mouth lifted. "The color goes well with your eyes."

He wanted to smile, wanted to share this softer

moment with her, but he glanced down at the bruises on her wrist. Burney Monroe was responsible for those, too.

Sabrina must have noticed where he had his attention because she shifted the dress, hiding her hands beneath it. "I'm fine," she assured him. "Well, other than having to use the bathroom."

"Oh." He stepped out of the way, but not before brushing against her. As usual, his body started to beg for something it wasn't going to get.

Not now, anyway.

It wasn't a matter of *if* sex with Sabrina would happen, it was now a matter of *when*. It was amazing how much forty-eight hours could change things.

While Sabrina was in the bathroom, Shaw decided to go ahead and call O'Malley. Yes, the lieutenant might be at a crucial point in his interview with Newell, but Shaw didn't want to wait any longer.

"I was about to call you," O'Malley said the moment he answered Shaw's call. "I just finished up with Newell and need to head home for a while so I can take a nap, wash up and change my clothes. Nadine Duggan's memorial service is today. But I can talk while I'm walking to my car."

Nadine. Shaw mentally groaned. He would have liked to go to the service, to pay his respects and give Bo some support, but it was too risky to take Sabrina out like that.

"Where's Newell right now?" Shaw wanted to know.

"He's on his way to the memorial service, too. Or at least that's where he said he was going. I couldn't hold him, Shaw. He said the money came from online poker winnings. Of course, the poker site is offshore and not exactly eager to cooperate with the police in San Antonio. Still, Newell was able to go to the Web site where he won the money."

"But he couldn't prove the money was a poker payout?"

"Not exactly. He showed me a screen name, and that person had indeed won a large sum of money, but I can't be sure Newell and the winner are one and the same. But I haven't given up yet. I'm still working with the poker site to release the financials. In the meantime, I have a uniformed officer tailing Newell."

Good. The uniform would remind Newell that he was under investigation, and the cop could report back any suspicious activity. But that didn't make Shaw feel any better about Sabrina.

"I need a safe place for Sabrina to stay for a while," Shaw explained. "And after what happened in the hotel, I'd rather not use anything put in place by Special Investigations. Newell probably has a lot of buddies in the department who might not understand he could be a dangerous man."

"I have an idea. A good friend owns an apartment on the Riverwalk, and he's out of town. I've been keeping an eye on the place for him, but it's yours if you want to use it."

"Thanks. I'll take you up on that." It would get Sabrina out of headquarters so that she wouldn't run into Newell. It would also free up the flop room. Shaw had dozens of officers pulling double shifts, and he didn't want to tie up the room any longer, especially when there was a safer alternative.

"The address is six-eight-eight Commerce, apartment four-C. I'll put the key in an envelope and leave it with the motor pool dispatcher. You can get it on your way out. Good luck, Captain. Call me if you need me."

Shaw jotted down the address and checked his watch. It was barely 5:00 a.m. and still dark outside. Probably a good time to move Sabrina to the apartment. Shaw was about to tell her that when she stepped from the bathroom, but she spoke before he could say anything.

"You have to feel this." She had a big grin on her face when she walked to him, and she took his hand and plopped it on her belly. She no longer wore the gown. She had on the blue dress she'd worn the day before.

He immediately felt the kicks. Unlike the last time, however, these were nonstop.

"The baby's boxing this morning," she joked.

Shaw leaned down so he could press his ear to those thumps. He couldn't hear them, but he could still feel them. "I think she needs some breakfast."

"She can hear you, you know. So, if there's anything you want to say to her..."

Shaw looked up at her, and his eyebrow slid up. "She can hear me?"

"It's true. I read nursery rhymes to her."

Shaw got a clear image of Sabrina doing just that. While she was wearing that flimsy gown that showed off her breasts. But then, he thought of another image. His baby had heard those gunmen. The shots. All the violence.

And that riled him to the core.

No baby, especially his baby, should have that kind of start in life.

"Hang in there," he whispered against Sabrina's belly. "Daddy's not going to let anything bad happen to you, sweetheart. Promise."

He looked up at Sabrina again, but her smile had faded. Her eyes were shiny as if she were about to cry. "Do you think she's really a she? Or is it a boy?"

He thought about the offer the doctor had made to tell them the baby's sex. "Honestly, it doesn't matter." And it didn't. "The baby's gender has never been part of this dream family I have in my head. I'd be happy with either. I just want him or her to be healthy."

Her eyes watered even more, and Shaw decided to put a stop to that.

"You need to get your things together," he instructed. "We're moving to a safer place this morning."

She nodded, blinked hard and turned to start collecting her toiletries. Shaw was about to help her, but his cell buzzed. It wasn't O'Malley but another of his lieutenants, Joe Rico. Yet someone else Shaw trusted.

"Captain Tolbert, one of my men just brought in Danny Monroe. I thought you'd like to know."

"Danny Monroe," Shaw mumbled. The brother of the man who'd tried to kill him and kidnap Sabrina. Oh, yeah, Shaw wanted to know about this. "Where is he?"

"I had him taken to the interview room just up the hall from you. I also have a preliminary report on him that my lead investigator just handed me. I thought you'd like to see it. I also thought you'd want to be the one to question him."

"You bet I do." But he glanced at Sabrina. He didn't want to leave her alone in the flop room, so she'd have to come with him. "I'll be there in a minute."

"They found Danny Monroe?" Sabrina asked the moment he hung up.

"They did, and I'm about to question him. Are you up to being in the same room with him?"

"Absolutely."

She seemed certain enough, but Shaw wasn't so sure. He didn't want to create more stress for her, so he'd keep the interview short and let Lieutenant Rico dig into the details.

If there were any details to dig into, that is.

He waited for Sabrina to slip on her sandals, and they walked up the hall. Not far. Just a few steps, and he saw Lieutenant Rico waiting outside the interview door. The lieutenant handed Shaw the preliminary report he'd mentioned.

"There's nothing in the report we can use to hold him," Rico explained. "But he doesn't have a solid alibi for the hostage incident. He claims he was at his apartment, sick with the flu."

Shaw glanced through the report. First the biographical details and then the criminal record. Danny had one, all right. Breaking and entering when he was a juvenile. As an adult, there was a drug charge, but he'd pled down and was on parole for two years. There were others, including an assault in a bar fight and resisting arrest.

But the common denominator in all the incidents was that Danny had been with his older brother, Burney.

"Thanks," Shaw told the lieutenant. He left Rico outside and led Sabrina into the room.

Shaw noticed the resemblance right away. Danny was a younger version of the dead man Shaw had seen lying on the floor of the hotel room.

"You're the cop who killed Burney?" Danny immediately accused.

Danny had been sitting behind the metal desk but jumped to his feet. He was visibly upset, with the veins bulging in his neck, and Shaw whispered for Sabrina to stay near the door. He wanted to get her out of the room fast if there was any sign of trouble.

"No. Another police officer shot your brother while he was committing a felony. He tried to kill me, and he tried to kidnap Ms. Carr." Shaw tipped his head to Sabrina.

"So says you."

"So says me and Ms. Carr and the other officer who witnessed it. Burney broke down the door to a hotel room and fired a shot at me." And those were all the details Shaw intended to give him. "Now, where were you yesterday morning and the afternoon before?"

"I already told that other cop—I was home sick in bed." He coughed as if to prove his point.

Shaw wasn't ready to buy the cough or the story. "I don't suppose you have anyone who can verify that?"

"Just Burney. He called me on my cell night before last, right about the time you cops say he was holding all those women hostages."

"Good. Then we can use phone records to verify that." He cracked open the door and asked Lieutenant Rico to run the phone records immediately.

Danny only shrugged. "I could be mistaken. Maybe it wasn't night before last when he called. Maybe it was some other time. Maybe he didn't call me on my cell after all. Like I said, I was sick and in bed. I could have dreamed it."

"Don't worry. Lieutenant Rico will get it straight. He'll learn when your brother called and where he was when any calls were made." Shaw made sure it sounded like a threat, because it was.

Danny opened his mouth. Closed it. Then, opened it again. "Look, I don't want you trying to pin anything on me. I already have to deal with my brother's death, and I don't need you guys breathing down my neck."

"If you're innocent, you have nothing to worry about." Shaw sat down across from him. "Talk to me about your brother. Why would Burney want to take those women hostage?"

"Who said he did?" Danny fired back.

"For argument's sake, let's say he did. Why would he have done that?"

Danny shrugged again and began to fidget with a hangnail on his right thumb. "I don't know. All I know is I had nothing to do with any of this."

Shaw pushed harder. "Then guess why Burney would have gotten involved in a hostage situation."

The fidgeting continued. "It might have had something to do with an old friend who called him last week out of the blue."

Now this sounded promising. "This old friend got a name?"

Danny swallowed hard. "Gavin Cunningham."

Sabrina made a soft gasp. Shaw did some mental cursing. He didn't like that Gavin's name kept coming up in this investigation.

"Keep talking," Shaw ordered.

"Gavin wanted Burney to help him prove the identity of his birth father. Gavin was all worked up about it, said it was really important."

"Did he say why?"

The fidgeting moved from his thumb to his jaw. Danny scrubbed his hand over his day-old stubble. "He didn't say, but Burney thought it might have something to do with money. I mean, it's usually about money, isn't it?"

Not always.

And especially not in this case.

Did Gavin and Burney conspire to tamper with the DNA so it wouldn't prove that the missing child was Gavin's and therefore connect him to the murder of the baby's mother?

Or was there something else going on here?

"I didn't have anything to do with those hostages or with what happened yesterday when you say Burney tried to kill you," Danny insisted. He looked Shaw straight in the eye. "And I think it's time for me to call a lawyer. I know my rights, and that means this chat session is over. If you want to hold me here, you have to arrest me."

Shaw considered it, especially since Danny would perhaps call Gavin. After all Gavin was an attorney, and he wouldn't mind seeing how the men interacted. Still, he didn't have enough to hold Danny.

But that didn't mean he couldn't have Danny followed.

Danny didn't wait for Shaw's approval. He hurried out ahead of them and rushed down the hall. Shaw made a call to dispatch to request that a tail be placed on the possible suspect. Maybe, just maybe, Danny would go to the person responsible for all of this.

Shaw caught Sabrina's arm so he could lead her back into the corridor where Lieutenant Rico was waiting. The lieutenant was holding some papers that had been stapled together.

"These are Burney Monroe's phone records," Rico announced. "We'd already started to run them before Danny Monroe came in." The lieutenant wasn't smiling, but it was close.

Sabrina glanced at the records, then back to the lieutenant. "Please tell me those records put Burney on the fourth floor of the hospital when I was being held hostage."

"Not quite. He probably used a prepaid cell when he was there. He had one in his pocket when he was killed, but it was brand-new. My guess is he threw the old one away just in case he was caught. These records are from his regular cell phone, the one he has an account for."

So, no giant smoking gun.

"But there is a call from Burney to Gavin Cunningham," Rico explained. "He made it three days before the hostages were taken. And the call lasted nearly an hour."

"Interesting," Shaw mumbled.

"Yeah, but not as interesting as these." Rico pointed to the three calls that had been highlighted. They were all the same number.

"Who did Burney call three times?" Shaw wanted to know.

The lieutenant smiled. "One of the richest men in the

city, and the very person Gavin Cunningham claims is his father. Wilson Rouse."

Shaw gave that some thought and then handed Rico back the phone records. It wasn't proof of Rouse's guilt, or Gavin's for that matter, but maybe this could finally bring things to a head.

If Shaw bent the truth a little.

And for Sabrina and his baby's safety, he would bend the truth. He would do whatever it took.

"Use this to get a court order for a sample of Rouse's DNA," he instructed Lieutenant Rico. "I want it compared to Gavin's, just in case that connection turns out to be relevant to this investigation. And then I want you to do one more thing."

Shaw paused, gathered his thoughts and fine-tuned how this could work.

"I want it leaked that we've found some DNA from the missing baby whose mother was murdered," Shaw continued. "Say that we got the DNA from the baby's pacifier that we found near the crime scene, and we've been able to extract enough to do a DNA comparison so we can identify the birth father."

"Comparison to whom?" Rico wanted to know.

"To Wilson Rouse, Gavin Cunningham, Danny Monroe, his brother and Officer Keith Newell. Leak it that whichever one is the father, he'll be arrested for capital murder and about a dozen other charges."

Rico nodded, then paused. "You do know how to stir up a hornet's nest, Captain."

Yeah. Now, Shaw only hoped he and Sabrina weren't the ones who got stung.

Chapter Eleven

Sabrina followed Shaw through the maze of corridors that, according to the signs, led to the parking garage.

She was actually thankful to be on their way out of headquarters because it'd taken nearly three hours for Shaw to tie up some details about the shooting and the hostage investigation before they could finally leave. There'd been one call after another. Several reports to be read. Questions that couldn't wait for answers.

Shaw had taken all those calls, read the reports and listened to the updates while they were in the flop room, again. It hadn't been easy for her to sit there and wait. Waiting only gave her too much time to think about the danger.

"You think Rouse will fight the DNA court order?" she asked as they walked.

"Of course. He won't want his good name linked to any of this, but the more he fights, the more it's linked. I'm hoping that will spur him to confess what took place in those three conversations he had with a dead gunman."

She hugged her spare clothes and the plastic bag of toiletries to her chest. "Could he have hired Burney

Monroe to steal the missing baby's DNA sample and delete the file?"

"Maybe." Shaw shook his head. "Rouse would certainly have had a lot to lose if this dead woman, Misty Martinez, had named him as her baby's father."

"Because it would confirm his extramarital affair?"

"There's that. But let's just say she wasn't exactly in his circle of friends. She was a cocktail waitress at a seedy bar downtown. From all accounts, she was beautiful but with some questionable habits. She also became a criminal informant after she was arrested for drug possession."

This wasn't painting a very pretty picture of the dead woman, but she still didn't deserve to be murdered. "When did you learn all this?"

He lifted his shoulder. "I had the report on her brought to me last night."

Which meant he hadn't gotten much sleep. Those naps he'd mentioned earlier had no doubt been very short with lots of work in between. Maybe when they got to this so-called safer place, she could prod him into resting the same way he'd been doing to her.

"This dead woman, Misty Martinez, was a police informant," Sabrina commented. "Did she also have a connection to Officer Newell?"

Shaw paused at the door that led to the parking garage and glanced around, probably to make sure no one was close enough to hear them. Sabrina checked, too. But she didn't see anyone within earshot.

"It's possible there's a connection," Shaw explained in a whisper. "She had some information about a hostage case that got botched last year. Newell was partly responsible for that botch."

The wild ideas started to fly through her head. "So, maybe Newell blamed her in some way and then killed her." But then she shook her head. "That really isn't much of a motive for murder and stealing a child."

"Unless Newell fathered the woman's baby. He wouldn't have a sterling reputation to tarnish like Rouse, but it wouldn't make him look good in the department's eyes if he was sleeping with a criminal informant."

True. But then, it probably wouldn't look good to Gavin's high-end law partners, either. Of course, that left Sabrina wondering where was the baby now?

Shaw opened the door, and they went into the parking garage. He stopped by the dispatcher who was in a small cubbyhole office attached to the back of the main building, and retrieved an envelope. When he opened it and looked inside, she saw a key.

"It's for the place where we'll be staying," Shaw whispered to her. He put it inside his pocket.

He also got the keys for an unmarked car. Probably because he didn't want to use his own vehicle to drive to the new location. It was yet another security precaution that she hoped would pay off.

Shaw put his hand on the small of her back, and as quickly as she could move, he got them away from the dispatch office and into the open parking lot. He hurried toward a black four-door sedan that was in the center row, amid dozens of cars. Some were cruisers, some designated for SWAT and other special units, and there were other unmarked vehicles, as well.

He unlocked the car with the keypad, and threw open

the door. Sabrina leaned down to get inside when she heard the sound.

A blast tore through the air.

It took her a moment to figure out what the sound was. It was so loud that it was like an explosion. But it wasn't.

Someone had fired a shot.

Shaw shoved her onto the passenger seat, and she dropped the clothes and toiletries onto the ground. In the same motion he drew his gun from his shoulder holster. His gaze rifled all around them. So did Sabrina's. But she couldn't see who'd fired that shot.

"Get in the car," Sabrina insisted. She was partly covered, but Shaw was literally out in the open.

He stayed put, still looking around, but he did crouch lower next to the seat where Sabrina had hunkered down.

"Captain Tolbert, did you fire that shot?" someone called out.

Sabrina peeked over the dash and saw the dispatcher peering out from the covered area. He, too, had his weapon drawn and ready.

"No," Shaw answered. "It wasn't me. Get a visual on the shooter."

The response had no sooner left his mouth when there was another blast. Sabrina hadn't seen where the first bullet had landed, but she saw this one because it tore into the top of the car door just inches above Shaw's head.

She grabbed him to pull him inside with her, but he shoved aside her attempt and dropped even lower to the ground. It still wasn't low enough.

He was a sitting duck.

The gunman fired again, and the bullet shattered the glass in the passenger-side door. Sabrina automatically shielded her eyes, but the safety glass stayed intact. However, another shot sent a chunk of that webbed glass dropping right onto Shaw.

"The shots are coming from the top of one of the buildings," Shaw shouted to the dispatcher.

Oh, mercy.

There were a lot of buildings around them. Headquarters was right in the middle of downtown, and there were tall office buildings and hotels on all four sides. They were surrounded, and the shooter could be up on top of one of them, ready to deliver the fatal blow.

But who was shooting?

She tried to imagine the person behind the trigger. Gavin? Rouse? Newell? Or maybe this was just another hired killer. Someone whose job it was to make sure she and Shaw didn't get out of this parking lot alive.

The next shot blasted through the car and took out the back window. The bullet that followed gashed through the roof. Even though the sun hadn't fully risen, she could still see the light spearing through that slashed metal. It was a vivid reminder of just how little protection the car actually was.

Sabrina got onto the floor space between the dash and the seat. There wasn't much room, but she squeezed in somehow, and she put her hands over her belly in case those shots made it to her.

She was turned so she could still see Shaw, and she watched as he lifted his gun and fired a shot of his own. The blast was even louder, because he was so close, and she pressed her hands even harder over the baby to try to shelter her from the noise.

"He's up there," Shaw called out, pointing toward the building directly behind the car. He scrambled to the other side of the door, away from the gunman.

Good. At least Shaw was semi-protected now, and they knew where this monster was. That meant he could be stopped.

Well, hopefully.

Even though Sabrina couldn't see the building's exit, certainly other officers had responded by now. Maybe even someone with a rifle who would have the firing range to shoot the guy.

Shaw handed her the car keys through the broken window glass. "Without getting up, turn on the engine, put the car in gear and start driving forward. Only tap the accelerator with your hand to get it moving."

Sabrina shook her head. "No."

"Yes!" Shaw insisted, shouting over the next round of shots. "It doesn't matter if you can't see where you're going. When the car rolls forward and gets to the head-quarters building, someone will tell you what to do. They'll pull you out and get you to safety."

That wasn't why she was shaking her head. "And you'll be out here in the open."

"Not for long. I'll run and get in front of one of the other cars."

And while he was doing that, he could be shot.

"Think of the baby," he reminded her.

It was a dirty way to get her to cooperate. But it was also an effective one. Sabrina desperately wanted to do something, anything, to keep Shaw safe, but she couldn't do that at the baby's expense.

Their child had to come first.

She could see Shaw through the crack in the open door. Well, she could see part of him, anyway. That was more than enough for her to see his resolute expression. He wouldn't back down on this.

"Do it," he ordered, his voice booming over the shout of the nonstop barrage of shots. Those shots were literally tearing the car apart.

When the shots made it to the dash, so close to her head, she knew she couldn't wait any longer.

"Stay safe," she told Shaw.

Sabrina reached up, shoved the key into the ignition and started the car. Somehow she managed to put it into drive. There was no need for her to touch the accelerator as Shaw had suggested because the car started to inch forward.

She caught just a glimpse of Shaw before he left the cover of the passenger door and started to run.

Oh, God.

The shots were nonstop. One loud blast after the other. It took her a moment to realize some of the shots were coming from headquarters. Someone was returning fire.

Sabrina couldn't tell if Shaw made it to the cover of another vehicle. She couldn't tell anything, other than that the car was indeed moving, and the gunman was continuing to shoot. She put her head against the seat, squeezing herself into as tight a ball as possible so if there was an impact, the baby wouldn't be hurt.

"Turn the steering wheel to the left," someone

shouted. She recognized the voice. It was Lieutenant Rico, who'd talked to them earlier.

Sabrina did as he instructed.

"Turn it slightly to the right now," Rico added. Like Shaw, he had to shout over the sound of the gunfire. "You're almost here."

She waited for the impact of the car bumping into the building. But there wasn't one. Instead, she felt the car turn to the left, toward the covered area where the dispatcher's office was. And she soon realized why. There were two officers who had hold of her bumper and were guiding the vehicle. The moment the vehicle came to a stop, one of them pulled her from the car and hurried her inside.

There were at least a half dozen cops waiting there, and they didn't allow her to stay close to the door so she could see what was going on. A uniformed cop took her by the arm and put her in an interrogation room about twenty feet away.

"What's happening out there?" she asked him.

But he only shook his head and headed back to the door. "Stay put," he warned.

She did, because she didn't know what else to do. And she prayed while she heard the shots continue. God knew how close those shots were coming to Shaw. Maybe he'd even been hit, but that was too painful to even consider.

Sabrina counted off the seconds, hoping that each count would end the attack. Finally, the shots stopped. She could hear the shouts of officers barking out orders.

What she didn't hear was Shaw.

There was the sound of the dispatch office door opening, and Sabrina peered around the corner, hoping this was someone with good news.

It was Shaw.

And he had blood on his face and the front of his shirt.

Nothing could have held her back at that point. She hurried toward him, catching him in her arms. "You're hurt."

"Not much. Just nicks from the broken glass." He used his arm to wipe away some of the blood and sweat, and he pulled her closer to him. "Are you okay?"

"I'm fine," Sabrina lied.

She didn't have any physical injuries, but it would take her a lifetime or two to forget those images of the bullets coming at them, and Shaw scrambling for his life across the parking lot. "What happened to the shooter?"

He brushed a kiss on her forehead and pulled back so he could look into her eyes. "He might be dead or at least injured. We think one of the sharpshooters from the SWAT was able to take him out because he stopped firing."

That sent her heart pounding again. "You *think?* You mean he could be getting away?" No. This couldn't continue. It had to stop.

"Shh," he whispered and pulled her to him again. "We have a team making their way to the top of the building. It shouldn't be long before we know for sure."

"And if he's not dead?" But Sabrina wasn't sure she wanted to hear the answer.

Especially when she heard another shot.

This one wasn't a thick blast as the others had been, but it still sounded close. "What's happening?" she asked.

Shaw shook his head. "My men will give me an update as soon as they safely can. Don't worry. If the gunman tries to escape, we already have officers assembled at the base of the building. He won't get away. If we can take him alive, even better. Because we might finally learn who's responsible for these attacks."

Sabrina clung to that hope. She also clung to Shaw. It was probably stupid to hand him her heart and well-being this way, but she couldn't stop herself. He'd just saved her life again. A real hero. And she was falling hard and fast for this particular hero.

His cell buzzed, and Shaw jerked it from his pocket. But it obviously wasn't a call he expected because he cursed under his breath.

"Newell," he greeted, but the greeting was more like a growl. He pressed the speaker phone button. "You picked an odd time to call."

"It's important. I want to know why you're having me followed."

"Now isn't a good time to talk."

"Why am I being followed?" Newell pressed.

Shaw took a deep breath. "Because you're under investigation."

Now, Newell cursed. "Because of those poker earnings I had deposited into my account."

"Among other things. Look, someone just fired a couple of dozen shots at Sabrina and me, and I don't have time for this conversation."

"Make time…*sir*." But Newell didn't say the title

with much respect. "This is my career, and it's the most important thing in the world to me. I don't know what you think I did, but I'm innocent. I'm a good cop."

"Then the evidence will prove that." Shaw didn't give the officer a chance to say anything else because he hit the end call button.

The dispatch door flew open. Shaw turned, though he still stayed protectively in front of her. It was Lieutenant Rico who came walking toward them.

"We got him, Captain," Rico announced, looking straight at Shaw. "He's injured, but he's talking. And he wants to talk to you."

Chapter Twelve

Shaw didn't ask the identity of the wounded gunman. He had one goal—to get to the man while he was still alive so he could get some answers.

But he didn't want to do that unless Sabrina was safe.

"Stay with Lieutenant Rico," Shaw told her, knowing he'd get an argument, but he stopped it before it could start with a quick kiss.

Yes, it was a cheap shot, and Sabrina deserved better, but he didn't want to risk her going outside again until he was positive the area was safe. Right now, he wasn't positive of that at all.

Shaw peeled off the grip Sabrina had on his arm and hurried to the dispatch door. "I won't be long," he told her, but he wasn't sure that was true. He wanted to get as much from the shooter as he could and that might take a while.

He ran across the motor pool parking lot and out the side entrance where a uniformed officer was standing guard. There were lots of officers, just as Shaw expected, but the bulk of them were near the back of the building where he'd spotted the gunman. The guy had likely tried to escape using that route, and he'd been shot when he wouldn't surrender.

The sun was up now and already bearing down on him so he worked up a sweat by the time he made it to the crowd of officers. He pushed his way through, wondering just who he'd see lying on the ground.

Gavin, maybe. It could even be Wilson Rouse or someone he'd hired. It was possible Shaw might not recognize the assailant at all.

But he did.

The man was Danny Monroe.

Shaw cursed. He should have held the SOB even if it meant bending the law.

"Captain Tolbert," Danny said, his voice weak. It seemed he was trying to smirk. The front of his shirt was covered with blood, and even though Shaw could hear the ambulance sirens, the man didn't look as if he would last long.

"You wanted to talk to me," Shaw said, once he got his jaw unclenched. He wanted to finish Danny off for endangering Sabrina and the baby. The SOB didn't deserve to take even one more breath, but Shaw knew each breath could give them answers.

"Take notes," Shaw told one of the uniforms who immediately took out a notepad. One of the others took out a mini tape recorder and moved closer. Good. Shaw wanted every word of this taken down so it could be scrutinized.

"It wasn't personal," Danny said, looking right at Shaw. "This was cleanup for my brother. His debts got passed on to me, and I needed to pay them off or die."

"It felt personal," Shaw let him know.

"I figured it did. That's why I have to set things straight with you. I want you to go after who put this plan together. Go after the person who hired Burney, because if Burney hadn't needed the money so bad, he wouldn't have done this."

"Who hired him? I'll be glad to go after him." And Shaw didn't intend to show any mercy. Not to Danny, nor this idiot who'd put this plan together.

Danny shook his head and dragged his tongue over his bottom lip. "I don't know who's responsible. Burney just said we had to get in the hospital lab and get some DNA samples and destroy a file. It was supposed to be easy, but people kept getting in the way."

"What people?" Shaw demanded.

"We thought that woman, Bailey Hodges, had seen us trying to get in the lab the day before we took the hostages. She saw Burney trying to break the new lock, or at least we thought she had. So, we found out who she was. That's why Burney went after her. Burney had been warned not to leave any witnesses who could identify us."

Bailey. Sabrina had said the gunmen were calling out the woman's name. Now, he knew why. The gunmen wanted her dead. It was a good thing they hadn't found her.

Behind them, the ambulance screeched to a stop, and the medics rushed out with a gurney. Shaw knew he didn't have much time.

"Why were you and Burney supposed to get the DNA samples?" Shaw asked.

"I don't know. That's the truth. But the bastard who

hired Burney will know. That's why you have to find him. You have to make him pay for killing us."

That didn't tug at any of Shaw's heartstrings. "Did you ever speak with the man or woman who hired you?"

"Just today for the first time. Burney handled all the other calls. The other details. I was told what to do. I had to pretend to be a nurse, Michael Frost, so I could call the women we needed to get to the hospital that day."

Well, that was another piece of the puzzle that had been solved.

"Whoever the boss is," Danny continued, "he was putting a lot of pressure on Burney. Burney owed money, you see, lots of it, and the loan shark was coming after him. That's why we got desperate and took the hostages so we could get everyone to back off and we could get into the lab. We did what we were supposed to do. We destroyed the DNA file…and took your woman."

Everything inside Shaw went still. A temporary reaction, no doubt, because he felt a strong storm brewing.

The medics moved between Shaw and Danny and began to get him ready to be transferred to the gurney.

"Whose idea was that, to take my *woman?*" Shaw demanded.

Danny shook his head again and drew in a ragged breath. "I don't know. Maybe Burney's. Maybe not. Burney thought if anything went wrong, then you'd make the cops back off if we had her."

Hell, he might have done just that. He wouldn't have been able to sacrifice Sabrina and his baby. Not even for this investigation.

But that didn't mean the boss of this operation had been the one who ordered Sabrina to be taken.

"Were you trying to kidnap her again today?" Shaw asked as the medics hoisted Danny onto the gurney.

"I got a call from the boss, from the SOB I want you to find. He asked if I had a gun, and I told him I did. I keep a hunting rifle in the trunk of my car. So, he told me to get to the nearest rooftop and fire a lot of shots. Not fatal ones. The boss wants you both alive. This was just meant to scare you, to show you what could really happen if you don't cooperate. He was going to make that clear, he said, after you were good and scared."

So, there could still be more contact and more threats from the so-called boss. And that meant Shaw wasn't getting in the ambulance to ride with Danny to the hospital. He didn't dare leave Sabrina alone.

Shaw looked around at the group of officers and spotted Sergeant Harris McCoy, the hostage negotiator he'd worked with when Sabrina and the others had been taken.

"Go to the hospital with him," Shaw ordered. "Get as much from him as you can. And make sure he's got a guard on him around the clock."

Not that Danny was likely to attempt an escape in his condition, but it was possible his boss would try to eliminate him before he could say too much.

"Yes, sir." Sergeant McCoy moved to the head of the gurney and started toward the ambulance.

Shaw waited until the ambulance drove away before he walked back to headquarters. It was a short distance but a long walk, and he knew what he had to tell Sabrina wouldn't do much to put her at ease. The danger was still there, and as long as it was, she had to remain in his protective custody. That was the official label for it anyway, but he didn't intend to let her out of his sight again.

Sabrina was waiting for him in the hall just on the other side of the dispatch door. Rico was there next to her, and he had his phone pressed to his ear. No doubt getting an update as to what had just happened.

"Lieutenant Rico said the shooter was Danny Monroe," Sabrina said, her voice shaking.

"He was. But he said he was just a hired gun and he couldn't or wouldn't finger his boss."

What little color she had drained from her face. "So, his boss could send someone else?"

"In theory. But that person won't be any more successful than Danny and his brother were." Shaw slipped his arm around her and looked at Rico. "I'm taking her away from this. Sergeant Harris is in the ambulance with Danny. When he finishes the interrogation, I want to know what the man said."

"Will do," Lieutenant Rico assured him. He moved closer to Shaw and lowered his voice. "You wanted the false info leaked that we'd found a pacifier from the missing baby and that we'd been able to extract DNA. I took care of that right after we talked. That would have been about two hours or more before the shooting started."

Two or more hours *before*. Maybe that hadn't been enough time for Danny's boss to have gotten the word and order the shooting. Unless the leak had been fast, like from someone in the department. Then, it was possible Newell could have called Danny and told him to fire those shots.

"Someone was supposed to be tailing Danny," Shaw remembered.

Rico nodded. "From what I can tell, Danny practically ran out of the building after he finished talking with you. By the time the dispatcher got someone assigned, Danny was already gone. The officer was on his way to Danny's place to look for him when the shots stared."

Again, Shaw hoped Danny hadn't been able to make a fast getaway because a cop had any part in this.

"I'll call you with an update as soon as I have one," Lieutenant Rico said, and he walked away.

Shaw stood there a moment, volleying glances between Sabrina's troubled eyes and the dispatch door. The last time he'd taken her out that particular route, Danny had fired shots at them. Danny had been adamant that he wasn't trying to kill them, which might be true, but any of those bullets could have ricocheted and hit Sabrina.

"Are we going back to the flop room?" she asked.

Despite the small size, it had its advantages. It was close and safe. Well, except for the fact that Newell might be behind this. He thought of the key to the apartment that O'Malley had offered him. Going there would get Sabrina away from Newell, maybe, but too much could happen between headquarters and the Riverwalk.

Shaw nodded. "Yeah. The flop room again. I'll arrange some food to be delivered since you didn't eat much of your breakfast earlier."

"And you should arrange for some medical attention. You have two new cuts on your face."

He swiped at them to see if they were still bleeding. They were. But since he wasn't gushing blood, he wasn't about to waste time seeing a medic.

They were only a few steps from the flop room when Shaw saw two people that he really didn't want to see right now. Gavin Cunningham and Wilson Rouse. They were scowling at each other and were being escorted by not one but two uniformed officers.

"They demanded to see you, sir," one of the officers said. "They got here a few minutes before the shooting started, and I had them wait in your office."

"Not a good idea," the other officer added. "They nearly got in a fight."

He was a popular man this morning. First, Danny. Now these two.

"You're bleeding," Gavin observed.

"Yeah, so I've been told. I was on my way to clean up, but I'm guessing you two think this is a good time to air some more dirty laundry."

"You bet it's a good time. Tolbert, what you're doing is harassment," Rouse challenged. Unlike Gavin, he didn't even seem to notice Shaw's cut face. "A court order for my DNA? I'm fighting it. It'll be a cold day in you-know-where before I voluntarily give you my DNA. Now, I hear rumors that you think I hired the clowns who took the maternity hostages."

"He did hire them," Gavin insisted.

Sabrina glanced at both men. "Did you two show up here together?" And there was a lot of impatience in her voice. She was probably as fed up with these two as he was. Especially since one of them might have hired Danny to fire those shots.

"No," Rouse and Gavin said in unison.

It was Gavin who continued. "I called him, to tell him I was coming here before I went in to work. I wanted to demand that you arrest him, to get him off the streets, and he decided to come, too."

"So I could stop him from pursuing that *demand*," Rouse snarled. With his eyes narrowed, he looked at Shaw. "You have nothing to connect me to this."

Shaw didn't want to do this now, but since he had the opportunity, he decided to run with it. "Nothing except phone conversations with the dead gunmen who did take the hostages."

Gavin made a sound of triumph. Rouse, however, just looked puzzled.

"The dead man's name is Burney Monroe," Shaw supplied.

"Him." Rouse scowled. "Yes, he called a couple of times. And get this, he called to ask me for a loan, because he said he worked at one of my restaurants when he was a teenager and had now fallen on hard times. He said I owed him some back pay. I had my people check, and he never worked for me. I told him that, too, when he called me back."

Shaw glanced at Sabrina to see if she was buying any of this. She looked as skeptical as Shaw felt. And she looked as tired. It might be early morning, but it had already been a long day.

"He's lying," Gavin insisted, hitching his thumb in Rouse's direction. "Run his DNA, compare it to mine, and you'll see that he's my biological father. And he wanted to cover that up."

"Gavin has a point," Sabrina mumbled, directing her

comment to Rouse. "If you quit fighting the court order for the DNA test, then this will all be cleared up. The test will prove you aren't Gavin's biological father…"

She stopped, and like Shaw she was studying Rouse's reaction.

"Unless you are his father," Sabrina finished.

"I'm not." Rouse's mouth twisted, relaxed and then twisted again. "But what the hell if I was? All that would prove is that thirty years ago, I was a stupid, weak man. That's all. It doesn't mean I committed a crime, and it doesn't mean I deserve to have my family's name dragged through the mud like this."

Gavin, Shaw and Sabrina all stared at Rouse.

"You're Gavin's father," Shaw concluded. This conversation had just taken a very interesting turn.

"That's what I've been saying all along," Gavin interjected. He didn't make that sound of triumph again, but it was in his eyes.

However, there was no triumph for Rouse. It seemed as if the fight had been taken right out of him. "I won't comply with that court order," he mumbled. He then turned and made his way past the uniforms and down the hall.

"You aren't going to arrest him?" Gavin asked. But his voice was practically a whisper. Maybe he'd just realized that having a biological father wasn't the same as having a dad.

It was a lesson Shaw didn't want his own baby to have to learn.

"He's guilty," Gavin insisted, jabbing his index finger in the direction that Rouse had just exited. "If you want to keep Sabrina safe, then you'll put him behind bars."

Shaw had had enough of this. "When there's evidence to prove his guilt, or yours, that's when I'll make an arrest."

Gavin looked as if Shaw had slugged him. "My guilt? You think I've done something wrong?"

Shaw didn't answer. "Go to work, Gavin. Let us do our jobs, and I swear I will learn the truth. It's just a matter of time, and if that truth leads me to Rouse, then I'll personally arrest him."

Gavin stood there, staring, his eyes focused on the floor, his breathing uneven. "I just hope the truth doesn't come too late," he mumbled. Then Gavin, too, turned and left.

"Finally," Sabrina said, glancing at his face again. "Let's get to the flop room so I can clean those cuts."

They walked toward the flop room while he looked down at her stomach. "Any cramps?"

"None."

He hoped she was telling the truth, but he wouldn't put it past her to smooth over how she was really feeling just so there wouldn't be more pressure on him. But the pressure was already there. Sabrina and the baby were his top priority.

And he was afraid that didn't just apply to their safety.

He opened the flop room, and a detective who was lying on the sofa immediately got to his feet. "Captain. I was, uh, just taking a nap. Double shift."

Shaw nodded. "There's a sofa in my office. You can use that."

The detective nodded and didn't waste any time getting out of there. Shaw locked the door behind him.

Sabrina immediately headed for the bathroom, and she returned with a wet washcloth. "Sit," she instructed. She took him by the arm, positioned him on the sofa and sat next to him. "And then convince me why I shouldn't be calling a medic."

"Because I'd rather have you nurse me back to health." He tried to sound cocky, even tried to smile, but he couldn't when he saw her expression.

With her so close, he could see the emotion and the fear in her eyes. They'd come close to dying, again. Even though this was the third hellish event in just as many days, he knew it wasn't old hat. Never could be. That's why her hands were shaking.

She dabbed at the nicks, turned the washcloth to a clean spot and dabbed some more.

"How bad do I look?" he asked.

Shaw touched his fingers to her arm and rubbed gently, hoping it would soothe the raw nerves that were right at the surface. Her bottom lip was trembling now, and her eyes were shiny. Sabrina was on the verge of crying, but she was fighting it.

She pulled back the washcloth and stared at him. It seemed as if she wanted to say something. Probably not related to the nicks she was cleaning. No, this would be something far more important.

But then she shook her head.

"That bad?" Shaw said, still trying to keep things light.

Sabrina looked down at the cloth in her hands. "You're the most attractive man I've ever seen. A few cuts and a bruise won't change that."

Surprised and a little embarrassed by the unexpected compliment, he thought he might have blushed. He put his fingers under her chin and lifted it so they'd have eye contact.

"Shaw," she whispered the moment their gazes met.

He couldn't stand to see her like this, but he didn't have any idea how to make the fear go away. So, he did the first thing that came to mind. He leaned closer and put his mouth on hers. Shaw kept it soft. Gentle.

And, he hoped, reassuring.

While he was hoping, he added that she would agree to get the rest that he was about to suggest. Yes, it was still late morning, but the adrenaline crash was going to leave her bone tired. It was certainly playing a number on his own head and body. But instead of rest, he wanted to hold her. To have her hold him. He needed to believe all of this would turn out with both Sabrina and their baby safe.

She touched his face, keeping everything slow and gentle, and she eased him closer to deepen the contact of the kiss. Shaw continued to keep it reassuring.

Well, he tried.

His attempts went south in a hurry, though. Because Sabrina didn't just deepen the kiss. She touched her tongue to his and slid her hands from his face to his neck. To his chest. And his body went from being interested to being on fire.

Man, he wanted her more than his next breath.

Shaw shook his head, trying to fight through the haze

and the heat. He considered pulling back. It was the smart, responsible thing to do. To pull back and insist she take a nap.

But he didn't.

He continued to kiss her. Continued to ease her closer and closer. Maneuvering her until he had her on his lap. The last time they'd been in this position, things had gotten intimate fast. Maybe too fast.

"Don't think," Sabrina warned.

Don't think?

He was about to laugh that off, but then she slid her hand from his chest to the front of his pants. The fire went to full blaze and was hotter than Texas heat.

Shaw took her advice and didn't think, other than to accept he would probably regret this.

Later.

Much later.

For now, he just went with the need to take Sabrina. She certainly went with it, as well. The intensity of the kissing went up a notch. So did the touching. And she had him seeing stars and cursing when she went after his zipper. Shaw very much intended for that zipper to go down, but he needed to gather a little control of the situation.

And himself.

His body was begging him to take her fast and hard, but his body wouldn't get its way on this. He forced himself to slow down. Not easy to do. Not with Sabrina kissing his neck and pressing herself to him. He wasn't helping much in that department, either, because he continued to kiss her as if his life depended on it.

Maybe it did.

That thought came from deep within, but he pushed it aside. Sabrina was right.

Now wasn't the time for thinking.

Since her dress was loose and stretchy, he shoved it up so he could get to her breasts. Evidently, both of them were past the point of foreplay, but Shaw intended to satisfy a few fantasies. He shoved down the cups of her lacy white bra and put his tongue to good use on her breasts.

She was full and warm. Like silk. But tasted like sin. Apparently, the breasts kisses were a fantasy for her, too, because she made a sound of pleasure that went straight through him. That sound was a primal invitation to take more.

So he did.

While he kissed her neck and that sensitive little spot just below her ear, he was rewarded with more of those silky moans. More pressure from her body against his. Until everything inside him was yelling for more.

Sabrina gave him more.

She caught on to her panties, hooking her fingers around the elastic band and peeling them off. It wasn't easy, and Shaw helped because suddenly getting her naked was the only thing that mattered. He pulled the dress off over her head and sent it flying across the back of the sofa.

He didn't stop. Didn't bother with finesse, though he swore he'd try better if he got this lucky again. Sabrina shoved down his zipper, jerking open his jeans so she could take him from his shorts.

Shaw took things from there.

He turned and dropped back onto the sofa, so that Sabrina was on top and straddling him. It was another fantasy fulfilled. Sabrina with her pregnant belly, her full breasts and that look of pure heat on her beautiful face.

She put her hands on his chest to steady herself and slid her fingers through his chest hair. She eased her hips forward. Slowly. Inch by inch.

Until she took him inside her.

The pleasure was instant. Intense. And Shaw had to close his eyes a moment just to absorb what was happening. Sabrina obviously had something to absorb, too, because she made that incredible sound of pleasure and slid her sex against his.

Shaw caught her hips to help with the thrusts. Not that she needed help. She seemed to know exactly what she was doing and how to get both of them to a fast, hot climax.

Her belly prevented any mouth to mouth contact in this position, but she leaned down and blew on his lips. Almost a kiss. Better in some ways. Her breath was warm, like her, and he took her taste and scent into his mouth.

She kept moving. Her hips thrusting forward, taking him in and then out of her. Creating the friction with that deep slide into her. She moved faster, and faster, each deep move pulling him closer and closer.

She came first. Sabrina threw back her head. Her grip tightened on his chest. She clamped her teeth over her bottom lip, and her eyelids eased down. She made that sound again, deep within her throat.

Maybe it was that sound, or the tremors of her climax that did it for him. Maybe it was just because this was Sabrina. But Shaw didn't fight it.

He let her take him to the only place he wanted to go.

Chapter Thirteen

Don't think, Sabrina reminded herself.

Fortunately, her body was cooperating with that reminder. Sex with Shaw had left her buzzing and feeling, well, incredible. It was hard to think with all the pleasure still milling around inside her.

She took several moments, to settle her breathing and to allow herself time to drift back down to planet earth. It took even longer before she could look down at Shaw.

He was staring at her.

There was no lift in his eyebrow to indicate he was about to question what had just happened. His jaw muscles were relaxed, a rarity for him. But he didn't offer her a smile or romantic words.

He just continued to stare.

Maybe he was shell-shocked that he'd just had sex with her. Perhaps like her, his body was still numb with pleasure. Either way, the silence began to settle uncomfortably around them.

So did the awareness.

She was naked, except for the bra that Shaw had

shoved down. Her breasts were exposed. *She* was exposed. And she suddenly felt the need to cover up.

Sabrina eased off of him, which took some effort. She was about as graceful as a drunk elephant, and there was no good side of her body that she wanted him to stare at. So, she got up from the sofa and began to gather her clothes.

"You're beautiful," Shaw said, sitting up and putting himself back into his shorts and jeans.

That stopped her. Sabrina glanced down at what she could see of her body and decided she obviously didn't see what he did.

"I'm eight months pregnant," she reminded him.

"And you're beautiful," he repeated. Shaw let the words linger between them for several seconds, and then he looked away and got up. "Get dressed. I'll order us some late breakfast."

She started to say something sexual, like she could have him for late breakfast, but Shaw's mind was obviously already on other things. He took out his phone and pressed in some numbers. He was indeed ordering food.

Since she didn't want to be standing around naked when it arrived, Sabrina gathered up her clothes and went into the bathroom so she could freshen up and dress. She didn't rush, hoping that the awkwardness she felt would fade by the time she went back into the main room.

It didn't.

Shaw was sitting on the sofa, his clothes all back in place, and he was talking on the phone. He glanced at her but kept it too brief for her to see what was really going on behind those stormy blue eyes.

Was he thinking about Fay?

No doubt. Sabrina certainly was. The sex had been easy. And incredibly satisfying. But it was clear that sex wasn't going to solve all their issues. It wasn't going to make them forget. Maybe though, just maybe, a sexual relationship could be the start of something else.

"What do you mean?" Shaw asked the caller. His tone was suddenly gruff and angry. "How did that happen?" He paused, and the tight jaw muscles returned. "Find him. And don't let him inside headquarters, understand?"

"What happened?" Sabrina asked the moment he ended the call.

"Newell slipped away from the officer who was tailing him."

"Just like Danny," she mumbled, and groaned.

"Not quite. Danny just got lucky when he got ahead of the tail, but Newell actually sneaked out of his apartment. He apparently went through the back window sometime, and the guard just realized what had happened."

Sneaking out the window didn't sound like something an innocent man would do. "You think he'll come here?"

"He might try, but the word will be out not to let him in."

That didn't mean he couldn't sneak into headquarters, or that he couldn't coax a friend to let him past watchful eyes.

"It'll be all right," Shaw said. It was something he

was saying a lot lately. He tipped his head to her stomach. "How's the baby?"

"Quiet for a change. I hope she slept through all the noise of those loud gunshots."

"Yeah." That was all Shaw said. He reached to put his phone back into his pocket, but it buzzed before he could do that. His eyebrow did shoot up when he saw the name on his caller ID screen.

"It's Dr. Nicholson," he let her know, and he answered the call. "What can I do for you, Doctor?"

Sabrina couldn't hear what Dr. Nicholson was saying, but Shaw apparently didn't care much for it. "You can do that in just a minute, but first I'd like to know if you've heard from an old friend. Keith Newell." He paused. Listened. "So, you don't know where he is?"

Or else the doctor wasn't saying.

Still not looking pleased about this call, Shaw reached out to hand her the phone. "She wants to talk to you."

Sabrina's first thought was a bad one. The doctor had drawn her blood yesterday, and maybe something was wrong. She practically grabbed the phone from Shaw.

"Is this about the blood test?" Sabrina immediately asked.

"No. All your tests were fine. But I just found out from my business manager that the police are investigating me."

Until this call, Sabrina had forgotten that the investigation had extended to her OB.

Sabrina clicked on the speakerphone function of Shaw's phone. "They're not really investigating you." She stopped, looked at Shaw, and he nodded for her to continue. "It's because of your friendship with a possible suspect."

"Officer Keith Newell," the doctor supplied. "Yes, as I just told the captain, Keith called me last night and said he's being railroaded, that Captain Tolbert is so anxious to make an arrest for the hostage crisis, that he's willing to ruin an innocent man's career."

"If Newell's innocent, that'll come out in the evidence." She hoped.

"Well, whatever comes out, I haven't done anything wrong. Keith and I are old friends. Nothing more." The doctor mumbled something that Sabrina couldn't understand, but she sounded frustrated. "If, and that's a big if, he's a dirty cop, he wouldn't have come to me." She paused. "What exactly do the police think I could have done to help him?"

"There's a DNA file and the DNA itself that was destroyed during the hostage standoff. It belonged to a newborn that's missing. His mother was murdered."

"And you think Keith did that?" the doctor snapped.

"He's just a possible suspect," Sabrina corrected. Then she paused. "Is he capable of that?"

"No."

"Even if it meant this dead woman could have hurt his career?" Sabrina pressed.

Dr. Nicholson wasn't so quick to answer this time. The seconds crawled by. "I don't think he would murder anyone." But she didn't sound convinced.

Neither was Sabrina.

"You should get another OB," Dr. Nicholson said. "You should be in the care of someone you trust completely. Obviously, I'm not that person."

Sabrina wanted to assure her that she did trust her. But it wasn't true.

The doubt was there.

"I'll contact some colleagues," the doctor continued. "I'll get some names of available OBs and call you back. I'll also send over some prenatal vitamins. With everything going on, I'm sure you haven't been taking them."

"I've missed a few days," Sabrina admitted. And she had no idea when she'd be able to go home and get them.

"Not to worry. I always have a supply here at the clinic, but I forgot to offer them to you yesterday. Should I send them to Captain Tolbert's office, since Keith said you'd been staying with the captain at the precinct?"

The question caused Sabrina to hesitate. It didn't sound like a fishing-expedition type of question, but she wasn't exactly eager to volunteer her exact location. "Just phone the script into the pharmacy on St. Mary's, and I'll have someone pick it up for me."

Now, it was the doctor's turn to hesitate. "Of course. Good luck with this pregnancy, Sabrina. I wish you the best."

The doctor hung up, leaving Sabrina feeling frustrated and uncertain. Mercy. If the doctor was truly innocent, she was going to owe her a huge apology. But if Dr. Nicholson did have some part in this, even a small one, Sabrina didn't want to take any chances.

"I'm sorry," Shaw said.

Sabrina shrugged. "Couldn't be helped." Though she did hate the idea of having to find a new doctor this close to her delivery date.

"I'll call Lieutenant Rico in a few minutes and make arrangements for someone to pick up your prenatal vitamins," Shaw offered, just as there was a knock at the door. "Who is it?"

"Detective Luke Hennessey. I have your food and a report that Lieutenant Rico asked me to give you. I also have a message. The lieutenant said the report was important and that you'd want to read it right away."

Shaw stood and went to the door. He eased it open and peered out at the young officer who was in the hall. He handed Shaw a brown delivery bag, the report and a large cup of coffee.

"Lieutenant Rico wanted you to know that Danny Monroe died during surgery."

Sabrina hadn't expected the news to hit her so hard, but it did. Part of her had hoped that Danny would pull through and be able to help them identify his boss. There was no chance of that happening now.

Shaw cursed, but then thanked the detective, and closed the door.

He immediately reset the lock.

It seemed absurd to take these kinds of security measures in police headquarters, but it had to be done.

"I didn't think Danny would make it," Shaw mumbled. But there was still disappointment that he hadn't.

Sabrina took out the food while Shaw read the report. There were several sandwiches, a fruit salad, two bottles of juice and one of milk, and she placed everything on the table. And waited. Whatever was in that report had captured Shaw's complete attention.

"At any point during the hostage standoff did one of the gunmen take your sandals?" he asked.

"No." But then she shook her head. "Wait a minute. When they were holding me at the office building, one of them, Burney, took them. He said it was so I wouldn't escape. There was broken glass on the floor, and he warned that it would cut my feet to shreds. But then, about ten minutes later, he brought the shoes back to me."

Shaw rubbed his fingers over his forehead and winced when he connected with one of the nicks. "Because evidence and trace just got around to examining them, and they found a tiny device that'd been affixed adjacent to the heel of your left shoe. It's a transmitter with eavesdropping capabilities. The heel was just high enough so that the receiver wouldn't hit the ground when you were walking."

Oh, mercy. So, the gunmen could have listened in on everything she and Shaw said from the moment he rescued her. "Did they put the device on me and then let me escape when you arrived at the abandoned building?"

"I don't think they *let* you do anything," Shaw said, staring at the report again. "I think this was their insurance policy. If you did manage to run, they would have been able to track you down."

Yes. And they'd tracked her down to the hotel room where they'd planned to take her hostage again. They'd probably also listened in to determine when the best time was to attack.

"So maybe Newell didn't leak our location," she suggested.

"Not necessarily. He could have followed the transmission to the hotel. Or he could have put it there after the fact so it would give us a reasonable doubt not to suspect him."

Yes. After all, they'd left Newell in the hotel room when she'd started cramping. Her bagged clothes and shoes had been there, and Newell would have had ample time to put a transmitter in place.

Shaw downed some of his coffee and motioned for her to eat, but he continued to read the report from Lieutenant Rico.

"The leak about the fake pacifier and the missing baby's DNA is making the rounds. Rico's already gotten some calls about it. A couple of reporters want to know if it was true, and it'll be the lead story on the noon news."

So, the word was out, and that meant the person responsible might be desperate to keep the information hidden. "What about the baby?"

Shaw shook his head. "He's still missing, but the FBI's involved now. They have a deep cover agent near the border, and he has connections to several black market baby brokers. He's been alerted in case the birth father is trying to sell the child."

Sabrina nearly choked on the sip of milk she'd just taken.

"It takes all kinds," Shaw mumbled.

There was a sound. Like a loud blast. And it brought Sabrina to her feet.

"A gunshot?" she asked Shaw.

He shook his head. "It was more like an explosion." Shaw took out his phone, but it buzzed before he could make a call. He checked the caller ID screen.

"It's Gavin," he relayed to her.

Sabrina groaned. She didn't want to go another round with Gavin, or any of the others. She wanted to know what had caused that sound. Mercy, they might have to evacuate. She only prayed this wasn't some other form of an attack.

Shaw put it on speaker. "How did you get this number?"

"From dispatch. I told them it was an emergency and I had to speak to you."

Shaw rolled his eyes. "What do you want?"

"You have to help me," Gavin said. It was clear from the man's tone that this wasn't one of his usual complaints. "Someone just tried to kill me."

Sabrina put her hand over her heart to steady it and moved closer to the phone.

"I'd parked my car in the lot across the street, and when I started toward it, the damn thing blew up." Gavin's voice got even louder. "Rouse is behind this. I know he is. I told you to arrest him."

"Where are you?" Shaw asked. Unlike Gavin, his voice was calm, but his expression wasn't.

"In the parking lot across from the headquarters building."

"You need to take cover in case the blast is just the beginning." Shaw hung up and made another call. "Lieutenant Rico, what's going on?"

"I'm not sure. It appears someone set a car bomb—"

There was a second blast, a loud crashing sound. Sabrina looked around, wondering if she should take cover.

What was happening?

"Lock down the place," Shaw ordered. "And get some men out there to see what's going on. I just got a call from Gavin Cunningham, and he said someone's trying to kill him."

But Sabrina wasn't sure Lieutenant Rico heard the last part of Shaw's order because there was a third blast. Louder than the others.

This one shook the entire building.

And Sabrina got a whiff of something that caused her heart to pound even harder.

Smoke.

Chapter Fourteen

"What now?" Shaw cursed.

The building's fire alarm started, the shrill noise filling the flop room. The sound didn't do much to steady Shaw's nerves, which were already on full alert. His body was primed for a fight, but he hoped it wouldn't come down to that. There'd already been enough battles to last him a lifetime.

Shaw drew his gun and tried to finish the call with Lieutenant Rico. Whatever was going on out there, it couldn't be good, but maybe Rico already had everything under control. However, Shaw knew that wasn't the case when the lieutenant came back on the line.

"We have a big problem," Rico yelled over the piercing alarm. "In addition to the car bombs, someone set a fire in the men's bathroom. The fire department's on the way, and I have men responding with fire extinguishers. But I'm short-staffed because a lot of officers are at the memorial service."

Well, that explained the smoke and the blasts. "How bad's the damage?"

"We're just now assessing the situation. But I can tell you the car bombs have broken windows and damaged other vehicles. We probably have some injuries. There were three blasts, two from the parking lot across the street and one from a car parked illegally curbside. We're closing off the area until the bomb squad can give us an all clear, but Captain, you should evacuate. We don't know if there are any other explosives or fires."

Hell, this was not what he wanted to hear.

"Keep me posted," Shaw ordered the lieutenant, and he put his phone away so his hands would be free.

There were no windows or secondary doors that he could use for evacuation, so he would have to get Sabrina out through the main hall. And he probably shouldn't delay. The smoke wouldn't be good for her or the baby, and that was especially true if the fire wasn't limited to the men's room.

"What's happening?" Sabrina asked.

He shook his head. "I'm not sure, but we have to get out of here now."

Her eyes widened, and her hands dropped from her belly to her side. "Is it safe to do that?"

She looked terrified and likely was, but this was something he couldn't sugarcoat. "It should be safe, but just in case I want you to stay next to me, and if anything goes wrong, keep down."

Sabrina nodded. Then, she nodded again when he motioned for her to walk with him toward the door. She certainly didn't look confident about this, but then neither was Shaw. He couldn't wait though because if the fire spread, then they could be trapped in a burning building.

As if the building had heard him, the overhead sprinklers came on and began spraying water all over the room. And on them. Shaw tightened his grip on his weapon, disengaged the lock and cracked the door just a fraction so he could peer out into the hall.

He held his breath and braced himself for an attack.

Thankfully, there wasn't one. There were some officers scurrying toward the front of the building, but his end of the hall was empty.

Well, other than the spray from the sprinklers and a few wispy threads of smoke.

"Smoke," he mumbled under his breath. He remembered the fire at the hospital. The gunmen had used it as a literal smokescreen to help them escape.

Was this a smokescreen, too?

Was it meant to cover up something else that was going on?

If so, Shaw had to trust that his officers would put an end to it before it became a bigger threat. Right now, he had to focus all his energy on saving Sabrina.

"This way," he instructed her.

Sabrina moved directly behind him, but he could sense her hesitation when she realized the direction where they were headed. "We're going out through the dispatch exit?" she asked, her voice practically a shout over the fire alarms.

"Yeah." And Shaw was well aware that the last time he'd taken her through that door, Danny had fired shots at them. But Danny was dead, and he couldn't do a repeat attack. "The parking area off dispatch is secure. Guarded at all times. A person wouldn't have been able to get in there and plant a bomb."

He hoped. He also hoped another gunman wasn't perched on a rooftop.

Shaw continued to lead her down the hall, but he stopped when he reached an open office door to his left. No one appeared to be lurking there, ready to strike. But just in case, he checked that room and then over his shoulder.

Hell.

There were open doors behind them, too. At least a dozen of them. He hadn't considered open doors and empty rooms a threat before, but he certainly did now. He needed to hurry and get Sabrina out of there because he was getting a bad feeling about all of this.

"Why is this happening?" she asked.

Shaw heard her, but he didn't answer. He kept his attention on their surroundings. When they were outside and away from the blare of the alarms, he'd give her his theories. Maybe it was a terrorist attack. Or maybe it was an attack of the ordinary variety. If there was such a thing.

But he also had to consider that this was linked to everything that had been going on for the past two days. The hostages. Sabrina's kidnappings. The subsequent attacks. That's why he couldn't let down his guard. Nor could he hang around and take control of this new crime scene. He had to get Sabrina far away and to a safe house.

The tile floor was slick from the overhead sprinklers. Shaw slowed so Sabrina wouldn't slip. It seemed to take forever, but they finally made it to the door, and Shaw placed his hand on the push handle. He wouldn't just shove it wide open, though the smoke and the need to get

Sabrina out of there made him want to do just that. But he couldn't. He had to make sure the area was indeed secure.

He didn't hear any sounds, other than the fire alarm, but Shaw felt the movement behind him. He turned, and in that split-second glimpse, he saw Sabrina.

Her eyes wide with fear. The gloved hand over her mouth.

And her attacker pressing a gun to her head.

SABRINA'S HEART SLAMMED against her chest.

Her breath froze.

She couldn't see the person who grabbed her from behind, but she felt his viselike grip on her shoulder. She felt it more when he hooked his arm around her neck and crushed her back against his chest.

In that same split second, he jammed the gun to her head.

She tried to call out to Shaw, but the person loosened his grip on her throat so he could slap his hand over her mouth. Not that Shaw would have heard her anyway over the noise.

But then Shaw looked back.

And no doubt saw that things had just gone from bad to worse.

Shaw automatically lifted his gun to aim it at her attacker, but the man's only response was to jam his own weapon even harder against her right temple. He didn't have to issue a verbal threat because Sabrina had no doubt that he would shoot her or Shaw.

The man shoved her forward to get her moving. Shaw moved, too. Without lowering his gun, he backed up until he ran into the door. Her attacker used the barrel of his weapon to motion for Shaw to open it.

Oh, God.

He was going to get them outside so he could kidnap her. But who was this, and why was he doing this to her again?

She tried to glance over her shoulder, but the man rammed his chest into her back and propelled her forward, almost into Shaw. The motion sent Shaw into the door again, and he must have hit the push handle, because it opened.

Sunlight spewed into the corridor, and she felt the fresh air reach her lungs. She still couldn't draw a full breath because her chest was tight with fear. She wasn't afraid for herself but for the baby and for Shaw.

Shaw continued to back up while he shot volleying glances behind him, at her, and at her attacker. Could Shaw see the man's face? Did he know who was holding the gun on her?

Despite all the fear and the adrenaline, Sabrina tried to cut through the panic and figure out who was doing this. Rouse? Gavin? Maybe even Newell? It certainly wasn't Dr. Nicholson, but then maybe it was no one she even knew.

This could be yet another hired gun.

At the gunman's urging, Sabrina stepped from the building. So did he, and he kicked the door shut behind them. He also maneuvered her so that she was turned toward the dispatch officer, who drew his weapon the moment he spotted them. The gunman was using her as a human shield.

What should she do?

The adrenaline was knifing through her now, and it was hard to keep control of her breathing. Much more of this, and she'd hyperventilate. The only thing that kept her from totally losing it was Shaw. Even though his gaze was fastened on the gunman, Shaw was right there, and she believed with all her heart he would do whatever it took to get her out of this.

But she needed to help.

How?

She glanced around, looking for a weapon or something she could possibly grab if she got the chance.

There wasn't anything.

Sabrina considered dropping to the ground. Yes, the fall would be risky, but it wasn't as risky as having that gun pointed at her head. Even if the man's immediate plan wasn't to shoot her, something could still go wrong.

The dispatch officer reached for something on the desk just below the keys. A phone. But the gunman obviously saw what was happening.

He turned his gun and fired.

Sabrina braced herself for the gunshot blast, but it was merely a swooshing sound, barely audible over the noise of the fire alarms. That's when she realized he was using a gun rigged with a silencer.

The dispatch officer collapsed onto the ground, and his gun fell from his hand, landing on the concrete next to him. She wasn't sure if he was dead, but he certainly wasn't moving, and there was blood.

Too much.

The gunman positioned her again, moving her closer to the man he'd just shot, and he kicked the gun out of reach. He didn't waste any time, and he shoved her forward again. He pulled a set of keys and some kind of remote control from the hooks above the table, and he pressed the button on the keypad so the car's security system made a loud beep. The lights flashed, and in doing so it identified which car went with the keys he'd taken.

He pushed her in that direction.

Her stomach clenched. He was planning to put her in that car and make a getaway, and unless something happened soon in their favor, Shaw wasn't going to have a clear shot to stop this monster.

She stared at Shaw, hoping he'd be able to convey to her what she should do. But he only focused on the gunman while they made their way to the car.

When they reached the vehicle, the gunman motioned for Shaw to drop his weapon. "Now!" he growled when Shaw didn't comply. He moved his gun from her temple to her stomach.

To the baby.

The fear slammed through her. The threat had been horrible enough when it'd been directed at her, but this SOB was threatening to hurt her baby.

Sabrina tried to figure out who'd spoken that threat and launched them into this nightmare, but it was obvious he was trying to disguise his voice. Still, Shaw could no doubt see his face, and unless he was wearing a mask, Shaw knew who they were up against.

Shaw dropped his gun.

Her heart dropped with it.

He was surrendering. He was giving up!

Part of her wanted to scream, to beg him to pick

up his gun again, but she knew she had no choice. He couldn't risk the baby being hurt.

The gunman kicked Shaw's weapon under the car, and he took the barrel from her stomach and put it back to her temple. Of course, both she and the baby would die if he shot her point-blank, but she preferred that he keep the gun on her.

But he didn't.

The gunman aimed it at Shaw.

"Inside the car," he ordered, his voice still low and raspy.

This wasn't any better. True, the baby was temporarily safe, but now he had a clean shot of Shaw.

The man kept a tight grip on her, moving his hand from her mouth back to her throat. He squeezed hard and used that pressure to get her moving. He opened the back door of the unmarked car and backed in first so that he was seated. He hauled her next to him, keeping her positioned so that she still couldn't see his face.

Sabrina considered elbowing him in the gut. She was in the perfect position to do just that. But he had that gun pointed right at Shaw. If she did anything, he would fire.

"Shut the door and drive," he ordered Shaw. He tossed the keys onto the front seat.

Shaw stood there a moment, and she could see the argument he was having with himself. She was having the same argument. But it was cut short when the gunman scraped the silencer across her cheek. The pain was instant with the metal digging into her skin. He no doubt drew blood. Sabrina didn't yell out in pain, but it sick-

ened her that this person had total control over her, her
baby and Shaw.

The veins popped out on Shaw's neck and forehead,
and his hands clenched into fists. For a moment, Sabrina
thought he might risk everything and launch himself at
the gunman.

He didn't.

When the gunman started to make another cut on
her cheek, Shaw cursed and hurried around the front of
the car. He glanced at the fallen dispatch officer and no
doubt wanted to call for help. He didn't do that, either.
Shaw threw open the car door, got behind the wheel and
started the engine.

"Where to?" Shaw asked.

He met her gaze in the rearview mirror, and Sabrina
tried her best to look brave and in control. Shaw had
enough on his plate without worrying whether or not she
would panic and make this situation even more dangerous than it already was.

"Just drive," the gunman snarled.

Shaw did. He put the car in gear and drove. He didn't
get far before she saw the security gate. It was tall and
metal, and she thought it might stop them. But the
gunmen pushed the button on the remote control he'd
taken with the keys. The gate slid open.

And Shaw drove through.

"Go left," the gunman instructed.

A left turn would take them away from the front of
the headquarters building and away from the chaos that
was going on there because of the car bombings. There
were so many officers in the area, all of them scrambling amid the smoke and the fires that the bombs had

created. She saw several injured people lying on the street and sidewalks.

But no one seemed to notice them.

Probably because of the heavily tinted windows on the vehicle. Or maybe because they thought she and Shaw were merely evacuating the area as Lieutenant Rico has advised them to do. No one was running to help.

She and Shaw were on their own.

Sabrina turned slightly so she could keep watch behind them, hoping that the car would get someone's attention.

And that's when she saw her attacker's sleeve.

She immediately recognized the shade of blue. And her heart sank even further.

The gunman was a cop.

Chapter Fifteen

Shaw considered a couple of options. None ideal. One was to slam on his brakes and hope the sudden stop would allow him to wrestle the gun away from their would-be kidnapper.

But the guy could still get off a shot.

A shot that could hurt Sabrina.

A second option was to hit another car, preferably a parked one. Or he could run a red light. Anything that would get the attention of his officers. But those weren't risk free, either. Sabrina wasn't wearing a seat belt, and God knew where or how she might land if there was even a light collision.

He couldn't risk it.

And that left only one other option. Somehow, he had to reach over the back of the seat and just grab that gun away from the cop SOB who had it pointed right at Sabrina.

One of his own was responsible for this. Officer Newell was the likely candidate.

Well, maybe.

The guy was wearing a uniform, but Shaw couldn't

see his face because it was covered with a latex super-hero mask. A fake face and maybe a fake uniform.

Or possibly a stolen one.

How the hell had this guy gotten all the way down the hall of police headquarters dressed like that?

He probably hadn't put on the mask until he was out of sight from the other officers and until he'd gotten close enough to the flop room. And with that uniform, he had likely walked right past everyone. With all the commotion going on from the car bombings and the bathroom fire, no one would have noticed an officer in a hurry. Obviously no one had seen him and gotten suspicious.

"Where are we going?" Shaw asked.

He adjusted the rearview mirror so he could get a better look at Sabrina. Other than that scratch on her face, she seemed okay. *Seemed.* She had to be scared out of her mind. And Shaw would make this armed bastard pay for that scratch and for her fear.

"Just drive," the guy growled.

Their captor was trying to disguise his voice, and it was working. Shaw couldn't tell who the heck this was, and it didn't help that their three major suspects were all about the same height and weight.

"Go right," the guy suddenly barked.

Again, Shaw looked for some escape route or some diversion he could use, but unfortunately people were starting to head out for lunch breaks, and the sidewalks were filled with pedestrians. There were also plenty of cars on the street.

Shaw took the right turn a little faster than he nor-mally would have, the tires squealing in protest at the excessive speed, and he watched the gunman shift in the backseat. The mask slipped a little, only enough to see the guy's neck. It certainly didn't provide Shaw with an ID.

Right now, his best hope was that someone had found the wounded dispatch officer and had notified Rico that an unmarked car was missing. If that happened, the car could be tracked since it was equipped with GPS.

But that was a big if.

There was a lot going on at headquarters, and they were short on officers. It might take an hour or more for anyone to figure out what was going on. By then, they could be into the next county.

Or dead.

But Shaw rethought that.

If the gunman had wanted them dead, he would have just shot them in the hall at the headquarters. He wouldn't have orchestrated a very risky kidnapping.

So, this went back to motive.

Someone intended to use Sabrina for leverage to get him to do something illegal. Probably something to do with that missing baby and the DNA that had been destroyed during the hostage standoff.

Of course, it could be something else.

Shaw thought of the false info that the police had leaked about the missing baby's DNA from a pacifier. The leak had also revealed that the police would soon have the DNA extracted from it.

This guy probably thought the leak was real, and if so, he would want Shaw to destroy the so-called evidence. Shaw considered trying to tell him the truth, that there was no pacifier, but the gunman likely wouldn't believe him, and even if he did, then what?

At best, the gunman might just let them go because they hadn't seen his face. But if that happened, it would mean not finding the location of the baby. Maybe it was because Shaw was so close to becoming a father that he knew that couldn't happen. The baby had to be found, but the trick was to do that without endangering Sabrina and his own child.

"Let Sabrina go," Shaw tried. "I'm the one who can help you with whatever this is all about. She'll just be in the way."

The gunman made a *yeah-right* sound that didn't need clarification. Without Sabrina, the guy had nothing to make Shaw cooperate. She and the unborn child were the ultimate bargaining tools, and this bozo knew that.

"Go left," the guy ordered.

Shaw did, and he immediately recognized the area. There was no traffic on this particular side street because most of the buildings were old and abandoned. Including the one at the end of the street. The one still roped off with ragged yellow crime scene tape.

It was the building where the gunmen had taken Sabrina after the hostage situation.

"Stop by the silver car," the gunman added.

There was indeed a silver Ford parked at the side entrance, and Shaw pulled up next to it. He looked inside the vehicle, praying this guy didn't have reinforcements, but the vehicle appeared to be empty.

The guy shoved open the door, and with the gun still pointed at her head, he dragged Sabrina out. Again, he put her right in front of him and led her in the direction of the silver car. Shaw walked in that direction, as well.

"No!" the gunman ordered Shaw. "Get on your knees, hands behind your head."

That put a knot in Shaw's stomach, but he didn't jump to any conclusions just yet. However, the conclusions came anyway when the man opened the car and pushed Sabrina onto the front passenger seat.

"On your knees!" the gunman repeated to Shaw.

Maybe he'd been wrong about the guy's motive. Maybe he didn't want Shaw to do anything illegal after all. Because it was possible the gunman intended to shoot him execution style, right in front of Sabrina. And that left Shaw with a question even more troubling than his possible murder.

What would happen to Sabrina and their baby if he was killed?

With this sick SOB behind the trigger, Shaw didn't like any of the answers that came to mind.

And that's why he had to do something now, before the gunman managed to get away with her.

Shaw put his hands behind his head. Slowly. While he calculated the distance between him and the gunman.

About ten feet.

Sabrina was in the car, certainly not out of the line of fire, but at least she wasn't standing out in the open. However, she did have a gun pointed at her head, and the guy's finger was definitely positioned on the trigger.

Shaw would have one chance to save her.

Just one.

Shaw took a deep breath and started to lower himself as if he were dropping to his knees. But he didn't.

"Get down!" Shaw shouted to Sabrina.

He couldn't risk waiting to see if she could manage to do that. There was no time. It was now or maybe never.

Shaw lowered his head and charged the gunman.

SABRINA HEARD SHAW SHOUT for her to get down, but it took a split second for that to register. In that split second, she saw Shaw run head first toward the gunman.

The gunman fired.

And Sabrina screamed.

It couldn't end this way. She couldn't lose Shaw now, not after everything they'd managed to survive.

Shaw rammed his body into the gunman, and they landed against the car door. It slammed shut, and because she was already precariously perched on the seat, the momentum threw her off balance and her hip rammed into the gear shift.

She quickly tried to right herself so she could help, but the two were in a fierce battle for the gun. Shaw had clamped on to the gunman's right wrist and had both his hand and gun smashed against the window.

Frantically, she looked for any sign of blood or injury, but she couldn't tell if Shaw had been shot. And she wasn't sure about the best way to help him.

She searched the car, shoving aside newspapers and a fast-food bag. No cell phone. No gun. Nothing she could use as a weapon. But she couldn't just sit there, either, with Shaw in a fight for their lives.

Sabrina crawled over the gear shift and into the driver's seat. No keys. But there was a horn, and she jammed her hand against it. The sound blared, and she didn't let up. Maybe someone would hear the noise and call the police. Of course, this wasn't the best area of the city so it was possible something like a car horn would be ignored.

There was a hard thump against the passenger-side window, and her breath froze. Because it sounded like another shot. She tried to pick through the tangle of the two bodies so she could determine what was happening.

The men were still locked in a fierce battle, and the weapon was still pointed upward, thanks to Shaw's unrelenting grip. But the gunman was using his left fist to pound Shaw in his midsection. With each blow, the gunman's elbow rammed into the glass. Neither was giving up.

But she wouldn't, either.

"Run, Sabrina!" Shaw yelled. He wanted her to try to get away, but she didn't want to leave him like this.

Still, she could try to go for help, especially since the horn didn't seem to be drawing anyone's attention. She threw open the door and climbed out.

Just as there was another shot.

She ducked down, putting her hands over her belly to protect the baby.

The shot went through the passenger window and into the front windshield, shattering both. If she'd stayed put inside the car, she would have almost certainly been hit.

That both terrified her and infuriated her.

She didn't care what their kidnapper's motives were, but she was sick and tired of his total disregard for Shaw's life and the life she carried inside her.

The anger shot through her, and Sabrina looked around. Not for an escape route. But for a rock or a fallen tree limb, anything she could use to hit the guy.

Sabrina quickly spotted several small stones. They weren't much bigger than silver dollars, but she gathered them up, drew back her hand and threw them with as much force as she could. They smacked the gunman in the back of the neck.

It wasn't much of a blow, but it caused him to react by jerking his head to the side. Shaw took full advantage of that slight maneuver and bashed the gunman's hand against the metal rim of the door.

The gun went flying.

And Sabrina didn't waste any time running after it.

She made her way around the front of the car, all the while looking on the ground to see where the weapon had landed. She finally spotted it next to the unmarked car the gunman had used to kidnap them.

She raced toward it.

But didn't get far.

The gunman made a loud, feral-sounding growl. And he shoved Shaw backward—right toward her.

Sabrina barely got out of the way in time.

Shaw fell to the ground, his back just a few inches from the weapon. Sabrina tried to tell him that, but she didn't get the chance. The gunman dove at Shaw and landed on him with his full weight.

Sabrina heard Shaw gasp for breath, and she prayed he wasn't injured. She still couldn't see if he'd been shot, but he did have blood on his face, possibly from a blow the gunman had managed to land.

She reached for the gun again, but the men shifted, rolling toward her, and trapping the gun beneath them.

The fight continued with the sounds of muscle and bone slamming against muscle and bone. Drops of blood and sweat spewed in every direction, some of them landing on her.

Sabrina maneuvered herself around them, hoping she'd have an opportunity to get that gun. Once she had it, she and Shaw could gain control of the situation.

Well, maybe.

And maybe the guy would force her to shoot him. She would. She would do whatever it took to get Shaw and their baby out of this alive.

The men rolled around, jockeying for position, and the fight continued, each of them slamming their fists into the other.

Finally, she saw the gun and reached for it. But the gunman must have seen what she was trying to do, because he threw out his fist, slamming it into her leg.

The pain shot through her, and she gave a loud groan, but she didn't give up.

Neither did Shaw.

That punch the gunman had delivered to her leg seemed to give Shaw a new burst of adrenaline. The muscles in his face turned to iron, and he drew back his fist and slammed it, hard, into the gunman's jaw.

Shaw didn't stop there. He drew back his hand and delivered another punch. And another. Until the gunman dropped his head back on the ground. He appeared to be unconscious. But maybe he was just pretending to be so that they'd let down their guard.

Sabrina wasn't letting anything down. She grabbed the gun and tossed it to Shaw. His hands were cut and bleeding, but he snatched it in midair and jammed it right against the gunman's throat.

"Move and you die," Shaw growled, though she had no idea how he spoke with his teeth clenched that tightly. "Personally, I hope you choose to move."

The threat was clear and real, and the gunman must have realized that because his hands dropped limply to his sides.

Shaw used his left hand to take out his cell phone, and he passed it to Sabrina. "Call for backup," he instructed.

Her hand was shaking, but she took the phone and pressed in nine-one-one.

"What's your emergency?" the dispatcher immediately answered.

Sabrina fought with her ragged breath so she could answer, so she could give the dispatcher enough information to get backup on the way.

She watched as Shaw reached for the guy's latex mask, and he pulled it off with a fierce jerk.

And Sabrina finally saw the gunman's face.

Chapter Sixteen

Shaw stared down into the gunman's eyes, and he prayed the guy would move so he'd have an excuse to beat him senseless.

Or worse.

He had to rein in his anger because it was obvious that merely catching the gunman wasn't going to solve this investigation.

Gavin Cunningham stared back at him, not with fear in his eyes. Definitely no remorse, either. But there was some defiance, and despite Gavin's bruised and bloody face, he managed a dry smile.

"Backup's on the way," Sabrina relayed to him.

While he kept the gun point-blank on Gavin, Shaw glanced at her. Despite everything that had just happened, she looked amazingly well. She certainly wasn't cowering in fear, but like him, she was glaring at Gavin. She had a right to glare. Gavin had manhandled her, kidnapped her and would have done God knows what else if he'd managed to escape with her.

Later, Shaw would hold her and tell her how thankful he was that she and the baby were okay. But for now, there was something more pressing.

The missing baby.

Shaw moved back a little, to put an arm's length between Gavin and him, and he got to work. "I'm guessing you did all this to cover up the fact that you murdered a young woman and stole the child that you'd conceived with her. I figure you hired Burney and his brother to steal the DNA file. You also hired one or both to kill her. They did, but then a lot of things started to go wrong."

Gavin shook his head. "I'm not confessing to anything."

"You don't have to. The DNA from the baby's pacifier will tell us everything we need to know," he lied. Because there was no DNA from the baby to compare to Gavin's. Still, Gavin didn't know that. "So, here's the deal, tell me where you hid your son, and I'll tell the DA you cooperated."

"Right." Gavin's tone was cocky, and Shaw had to fight his rage again.

He really wanted to pound this moron to dust.

"Right," Shaw repeated, trying to put all that rage inside him into a calm, smug veneer. He was a veteran cop, and he had to shove the personal stuff aside so he could get this bastard.

"I guess you don't mind getting the death penalty," Shaw commented. Now, he smiled. "Ever watched someone get a needle shoved in their arm? Contrary to popular belief, it isn't painless. It's a slow agonizing death."

Gavin just stared at him.

"Tell me where the baby is," Shaw demanded.

Gavin chuckled. "No way. A trial could last for years. And a lot could happen to a baby in all that time."

Sabrina made a sound of outrage. "Give me the gun," she demanded. "You're a cop and you're bound by the badge not to shoot him, but I will."

She would, too. Shaw could tell from that steely look that she wasn't bluffing.

Gavin volleyed glances between her and Shaw, and by degrees his smile faded. It faded even more when there was the sound of sirens approaching. It wouldn't be long, mere minutes, before backup arrived.

"Get up," Shaw ordered the man.

Gavin's eyes widened. "Why?"

"Because you're resisting arrest, that's why." Shaw lifted the gun gripped in his hand. "And I'm going to shoot you for resisting."

"You wouldn't do that," Gavin spat out.

"Yes. I. Would." And Shaw left no doubt that he was telling the truth. And it was the truth. It would cost him his badge, but by God he was going to find that missing baby before it was too late. "Get up!"

Gavin struggled to get to his feet. His eyes were wild and wide now, and he looked around as he expected someone to come to his aid.

Shaw aimed the gun at Gavin's left shoulder. "Last chance, where's the baby?"

Gavin lifted his hands, palm out. "You'll shoot an unarmed man?"

"In a heartbeat." Shaw tightened his finger on the trigger and got ready to fire.

"Stop!" Gavin yelled. "You're crazy, you know that?"

Shaw fired a shot over Gavin's shoulder and lowered

the gun so the next bullet would hit the intended target. "Where's the baby?" Shaw didn't change his tone or his body language, because he was already sending the message he wanted to send.

"Okay," Gavin mumbled. And there was no cockiness in that. "Take the death penalty off the table, and I'll tell you where the kid is."

Shaw thought about it a second. "I'll take the death penalty off the table."

Gavin nodded, blew out several short breaths. "The baby's at one-one-two St. Martin's Street, just two blocks from here. He's safe. He wasn't hurt when Burney and Danny took him from his mother. Right now, he's with a nanny I hired. Her name is Peggy Watford."

Shaw heard the backup officers take the turn onto the street. He kept the gun aimed at Gavin. "Give me your phone." And Shaw knew he had one because it was clipped to the man's belt. Gavin removed it, gave it to Shaw, and he passed it to Sabrina.

"What's the phone number of the place where the nanny has the baby?" Shaw demanded. "Sabrina's going to call and make sure you aren't lying. If you are, one bullet will go in your shoulder. The other in your leg. I haven't decided yet where the third bullet will go."

Gavin's voice was a tangle of nerves when he rattled off the number. Sabrina quickly dialed it, just as the cruiser with the backup officers came to a stop.

"Don't tell her who you are," Shaw instructed Sabrina. "Once you hear her voice, hang up."

Sabrina nodded and put the call on speaker.

It seemed to take forever for the call to connect. Shaw

waited, knowing he wasn't leaving this scene until he had confirmed the whereabouts of the child.

"Get officers to one-one-two St. Martin's Street," Shaw ordered his backup, just in case. "I want confirmation ASAP that a newborn baby is there. Call me as soon as you know something."

"Mr. Cunningham," a woman finally answered. She'd obviously seen Gavin's number on her caller ID. "I didn't expect you to phone until later. The baby's fine, though. He's sleeping. And I'll have him ready tonight for the trip, just like you wanted."

Shaw motioned for Sabrina to click off the phone, and she did.

"I told you the kid was all right," Gavin insisted. "I wouldn't hurt a baby, even if his mother was nothing but trash."

Shaw didn't believe that because, after all, Gavin hadn't cared a lick about Sabrina's baby.

"What do you plan to do with him?" Sabrina asked.

The backup officers moved in, and Shaw motioned for them to cuff Gavin. One of the cops also read the man his rights. However, that didn't stop Gavin from answering Sabrina's question.

"A friend of a friend has an adoption agency. I'd made arrangements for the kid to be picked up tonight. He was going to a good family."

Maybe. Or maybe Gavin planned to sell the child. "Why did you think you'd get away with it?"

Gavin lifted his shoulder as the cuffs snapped shut, locking his hands behind him. Apparently, Gavin didn't intend to add anything to his meager confession.

But Shaw figured he knew the rest. "My guess is you were trying to set up Wilson Rouse, to make it look as if he's the one who killed the woman and took the child." Too bad Gavin's sick plan had come close to succeeding. "Rouse probably isn't even your biological father."

The corner of Gavin's mouth lifted. "But he is. That's the kicker. He really is my dear dad, thanks to a roll between the sheets with the hired help thirty years ago."

Oh, yeah. Then the plan would have indeed worked.

Gavin could have claimed that Rouse not only wanted to get rid of his illegitimate son but his less than worthy grandson, as well. Rouse would have fought the charges, might have even won, but his name and reputation would have been ruined. And Gavin would have been long gone or the evidence destroyed so that no one could ever connect him to the dead woman.

"I won't spend my life in prison," Gavin insisted. Some of the cockiness had returned. "I'm a good lawyer, and I have people on my side."

"Don't be so sure of that," Shaw countered. "Your uptown law partners won't like the scandal, either. I'm betting they dump you hard and fast."

Shaw walked to Sabrina, slipped his arm around her waist and pulled her to him. He looked down at her, deep into her eyes. "Are you okay?"

She nodded. "You?"

He tried to keep things light. "I'm too old to get in fistfights."

But his attempt failed because the tears sprang to her eyes. "You could have been killed." Her voice broke, and she buried her face against his shoulder.

"How touching," Gavin called out, and the officers led him to the cruiser. "You can come and visit me in jail while I'm appealing my life sentence."

Shaw glanced at the man. "I took the death penalty off the table, but the DA didn't. It's his call, and I'm betting with the murders at the hospitals and the havoc you've caused, the death penalty is guaranteed. I know I'll do everything to make sure that happens."

Gavin looked as if the breath had been knocked out of him.

Good.

It was a small matter of satisfaction, but Shaw knew it wouldn't stop the nightmares. He might never be able to forget what Gavin had put Sabrina through.

"I'm in love with you," he heard Sabrina say.

He was so deep in his thoughts that it took Shaw a moment to realize what she said.

"It's true," she added before he could speak. "I realized it when Gavin fired the shot, and I didn't know if it'd hit you or not." She sniffed, wiped away tears. "I knew then that I'm in love with you. And it doesn't have anything to do with carrying your child. Or the great sex. That only makes me love you more, but it's not the reason I'm in love with you."

She opened her mouth, probably to continue to convince him that what she felt was the real thing. But Shaw didn't need to be convinced. He could see the love in her eyes.

So, he kissed her.

There were bits of grass and dirt on his mouth, and he pulled back to wipe it off, but Sabrina grabbed a fistful of his shirt and yanked him back to her to continue the kiss anyway. She didn't stop until she had to breathe, and when she broke the kiss, she gasped for air.

"I'm in love with you because..." She stopped, blinked back more tears. "Because you're you."

Shaw was sure he blinked, too. It was a simple reason. The best of reasons.

Now, it was his turn to kiss her.

"Sir?" one of the officers called out. "You want us to wait until a unit arrives to pick up you and Ms. Carr to take you to headquarters?"

Sabrina looked at him, then at the officer who'd asked the question. "Is it safe to go back to headquarters?" Shaw wanted to know.

"Yes. The fire's out. It was more smoke than anything."

Smoke. No doubt to create the diversion. A diversion that had worked.

Well, temporarily.

"Don't wait," Shaw instructed. "Get Mr. Cunningham to the jail for processing. And have someone call me the second you have news about the missing baby."

"Yes, sir," the officer assured him. He got into the cruiser where Gavin was locked into the backseat, and he drove away.

Shaw doubted it would be long before their ride arrived, so he decided to make this quick. Once they did return to headquarters, he'd be swamped with the tail end of this investigation.

First though, he wanted to clear up some things with Sabrina.

"It's okay," she continued while he was trying

to gather his thoughts. "You don't have to say or do anything. I just wanted you to know."

He kissed her again, hoping to use the time to find the right words. It was a bad decision. The kiss turned hot and deep, and it clouded his mind even more.

Finally, Shaw just put an end to the kissing and caught her shoulders. "I'm in love with you, too, Sabrina."

She stood there. Staring. And she looked as stunned as Gavin had when the officers had hauled him away.

"You're in love with me?" she challenged.

"Yeah. And the only reason I have is the same as yours. Because you're you. Because you're a good, decent, kind, caring woman who'd do anything in the world for me, including giving me this precious child."

He slid his hand over her belly.

Her tears started again, and she launched herself at him. Shaw pulled her as close as the baby would allow, and he kissed her again. This time, he kept it short so it wouldn't numb his mind, and he geared up to finish what he'd started.

"Fay—" he said.

But Sabrina pressed her fingers to his mouth. "You don't have to tell me. I know you'll always love Fay. I don't expect you to feel the same way about me as you did about her."

Surprised, he blinked. "Well, you should. Because I love you as much as I loved her when she was alive. But she's not alive anymore, and we are. We're both here, in love with each other, and I can't help but believe that's exactly what Fay would have wanted."

Sabrina stopped, drew in her breath, and she finally nodded. "It is what she would have wanted. She loved us both."

"And we both loved her," Shaw finished. "But Sabrina, you don't deserve anything less than my whole heart, and that's what I'm offering you."

"Ohhhh." She moved her hand to her own mouth to press back a sob. Thankfully, it sounded like a happy sob. "But how can you truly forgive me for Fay's death?"

She had mentally skirted around this for days, but he already knew the answer. "Easy. I blamed you. Myself. But I was wrong. Neither of us is responsible for what happened." He leaned in and kissed her. "Fay is the one who brought us together. She's the one who wanted us to raise this baby, and I'll always be thankful to her for that, for giving me you."

Sabrina's breath trembled from her tears, and she reached out to him.

But then, his phone buzzed.

He glanced down at the caller ID and saw that it was Lieutenant Rico. Shaw cursed and answered it.

"We have the baby, and he's okay," Rico said, obviously not bothering with a greeting. Shaw didn't want one. That was the best news he could have gotten.

"Thanks. I'll be back in a few minutes."

Shaw hung up and hoped those few minutes were enough. "The baby's safe," he relayed to Sabrina.

The relief flooded through her, and he could feel it in every part of her body when she hugged him. Shaw was just as relieved as she was, but he cut the celebration short.

"I want to get married," he blurted out, and winced at his abrupt tone. Sheez. He'd negotiated hostage standoffs that hadn't given him this much trouble.

"Let me try that again," Shaw corrected. "Will you marry me?"

He braced himself for another of her shocked looks, maybe even some hesitation, but her hug got harder, and she found his mouth with hers.

"Yes," she said, a split second before she kissed him.

Yes.

That part registered in Shaw's brain, but the kiss even managed to fog that up a little.

"That was a yes?" he questioned, pulling back just a little.

He kept his mouth right over hers so he could take in her taste with each breath. It was a taste he knew he would want for the rest of his life.

"A definite yes." But now, she hesitated. "I have a condition, though."

He thought maybe his heart stopped. She couldn't back out. He wouldn't let her. Sabrina was his.

"What?" he asked cautiously. He was willing to agree to anything.

"Marry me before the baby comes. I want us to be a real family."

He hadn't realized he'd been holding his breath until it swooshed out of him. "Deal. The wedding before the baby. But the last condition isn't really a condition."

"Why?"

He shrugged. That was the easiest question he'd ever had to answer. "Because we're already a family."

And to prove it, Shaw kissed her so that neither of them would ever forget it.

Chapter Seventeen

Two Weeks Later

Sabrina clamped her teeth over her bottom lip to stop herself from screaming. She'd read all the books about the pain management. She'd prepared herself.

Or so she'd thought.

But nothing could have prepared her for this.

"It's okay," Shaw told her. But his strained voice and expression didn't exactly convey that all was okay.

He looked scared spitless.

Sabrina wasn't scared. She was in too much pain to feel anything but the contractions that had hold of her stomach. Mercy. It was relentless.

"Push," Dr. Nicholson instructed.

The delivery bed was angled high enough so that Sabrina could see the doctor, but Dr. Nicholson had her attention focused on the birth.

Sabrina pushed, and dug her shoes into the stirrups so she could bear down. The ivory peep-toe heels looked absurd against the metal stirrups. For that matter, she probably looked absurd since she was still wearing her lacy cream-colored wedding dress.

Shaw still had on his tux, even though the tie was off and God knew where. It'd been a crazy, frantic ride from the church to the hospital. Things hadn't settled down after their arrival, either. Once Dr. Nicholson checked Sabrina, she had her rushed to the delivery room.

There'd been no time for prep. No time to change into a hospital gown.

No time for anything but the pain.

"Okay, stop pushing," the doctor told her. "We need to wait for the next contraction, but it won't be long."

No doubt. The contractions were only seconds apart, and Sabrina barely had time to catch her breath in between them.

"I'm sorry," Shaw said, shaking his head.

He was right next to her, gripping her left hand. A position he'd taken the instant they'd been ushered into the delivery room.

"Sorry for what?" Sabrina asked while she fought with her breath.

"I didn't know you'd hurt this much." Well, he certainly wasn't the calm, collected police captain now. His nerves were right there on the surface. "I'm so sorry. I wish I could do something. Anything."

"You've done enough," she joked.

Even though Sabrina had no idea how she managed to attempt humor. This didn't feel funny.

She had to bite her lip again to stop herself from yelling. Or cursing. Sheez, how did women go through this multiple times?

"Push," the doctor ordered.

Unlike Shaw, Dr. Nicholson sounded totally in control. And looked it, too. It made Sabrina glad that they had mended fences after Gavin's arrest. She wouldn't have wanted another doctor for this because Dr. Nicholson had been there with her from the beginning.

Thankfully, Shaw had mended his own fences with Officer Newell, and everything was back to normal at headquarters.

Sabrina pressed her peep-toes against the stirrups again and pushed as hard as she could. The pain was blinding, and she used every bit of her energy to fight to maintain the push that the doctor had ordered.

"You're doing great, Sabrina," Dr. Nicholson told her. "Keep it up."

Sabrina cursed in spite of her attempts not to. She wasn't doing great. She was hurting!

But just like that, the pain stopped. Something inside her seemed to give way. The pressure was gone. The contraction ended.

And then Sabrina heard the cry.

It was a sound that touched every part of her body, and she looked in stunned amazement as Dr. Nicholson lifted the baby so she could see.

"It's a boy," the doctor announced.

A boy.

She and Shaw had a son.

"Well, despite being two weeks early, he has healthy lungs," Dr. Nicholson added over the baby's loud cries. "Have you guys picked out a name?"

She and Shaw had chosen the names Elizabeth Sabrina Tolbert for a girl or Jacob Shaw Tolbert for a boy.

So, this was Jacob.

But Sabrina couldn't speak. She looked at Shaw, who seemed as dumbfounded as she was.

"Okay, you can tell me the name later. Captain Dad, it's time to cut the umbilical cord." Dr. Nicholson put the baby on Sabrina's stomach and handed Shaw the scissors.

Shaw took the scissors. Sabrina saw that part, but then she zoomed in on that tiny precious crying face. It was wrinkled and red, but it was the most beautiful face she'd ever seen.

Jacob Shaw Tolbert had his daddy's dark hair. Shaw's chin and mouth, too. But Sabrina could see the shape of her own eyes in him.

The love was instant. Powerful. Unconditional. And it became complete when the doctor wrapped Jacob in a blanket and put him in her arms.

"Are you still in pain?" Shaw asked. He kissed her cheek. Her forehead. And then he kissed the baby. The nervous flurry of kisses continued.

Sabrina definitely wasn't hurting. In fact, had there been pain? She was no longer sure. Her body was humming now, and she felt higher than the moon and stars.

She smiled. "No pain," she assured him.

Because Shaw still looked terrified, she leaned over and kissed him on the mouth.

He kissed her right back.

"I need to borrow this little guy for a second so I can weigh him," the attending nurse said. She took the baby and placed him on a table not too far from the delivery bed.

The doctor finished up with Sabrina and pulled off

her gloves. "You did great. All three of you. I'll arrange to have you taken to a private room, but from the looks of things, you won't have to stay more than a day."

"Thank you," Sabrina and Shaw said in unison.

"For everything," Sabrina added.

The doctor smiled, nodded, and Sabrina saw her blink away some happy tears.

"He's six pounds, fourteen ounces," the nurse relayed. "Twenty-one inches long. And he just peed on me." The nurse laughed.

So did Shaw and Sabrina.

Every little detail was amazing. So were his cries. And the little foot kicks. The hand flails. Even the peeing incident.

Sabrina remembered to count the fingers and toes.

Everything was there.

Everything was perfect.

"Your baby's birthday is September ninth," the nurse continued. "And the delivery time was 1:36 p.m."

Shaw smiled, and Sabrina knew why. Their son had been born on his parents' wedding day, less than an hour after they'd said, "I Do."

"We made it," Sabrina whispered.

"We made it," Shaw whispered back. "I love you, Sabrina Tolbert."

"Good. Because I love you, too, Shaw Tolbert."

And there was no doubt in her mind about that. He was her hot cop now, and he always would be.

Shaw sneaked in another kiss and then moved back slightly so the nurse could place the baby back in Sabrina's arms. But she moved, too, maneuvering Jacob between them so that Shaw was holding him, as well.

Just like that, the baby stopped crying.

Jacob blinked. And he looked at her. His tiny forehead scrunched up, as if he might want to accuse her of something. Then, he looked at Shaw and gave him the same look before his face relaxed. He didn't smile. He just looked at them and seemed to say, "Okay, what's next?"

Shaw laughed, and Sabrina smiled through her own happy tears, which were streaming down her cheeks.

So, this was what a miracle felt like.

Now she knew.

And these miracles were hers for a lifetime.

* * * * *

DADDY DEVASTATING

BY

DELORES FOSSEN

All the characters in this book have no existence outside the imagination of
the author, and have no relation whatsoever to anyone bearing the same name
or names. They are not even distantly inspired by any individual known or
unknown to the author, and all the incidents are pure invention.

First published in Great Britain 2011
Harlequin Mills & Boon Limited,
Eton House, 18-24 Paradise Road, Richmond, Surrey TW9 1SR

DADDY DEVASTATING © Delores Fossen 2010

ISBN: 978 0 263 88506 4

46-0211

Harlequin Mills & Boon policy is to use papers that are natural, renewable
and recyclable products and made from wood grown in sustainable forests.
The logging and manufacturing processes conform to the legal environmental
regulations of the country of origin.

Printed and bound in Spain
by Litografia Rosés S.A., Barcelona

Chapter One

San Saba, Texas

Russ Gentry cursed under his breath when the brunette stepped through the doors of the Silver Dollar bar.

Hell.

She'd followed him.

He had spotted her about fifteen minutes earlier on the walk from his hotel to the bar. She had trailed along behind him in her car, inching up the street, as if he were too stupid or blind to notice her or her sleek silver Jaguar. He had decided to ignore her for the time being anyway, because he'd hoped she was lost.

Obviously not.

Now, he had two questions—who was she? And was this about to turn even more dangerous than it already was?

He watched her from over the top of the bottle of Lone Star beer that the bartender had just served him. She was tall—five-nine, or better—and she was clutching a key ring that had a small can of pepper spray hooked onto it. There was a thin, gold-colored purse tucked beneath her arm, but it didn't have any telltale bulges of a weapon, and her snug blue dress skimmed over her curvy body, so that carrying concealed would have been next to impossible.

Heck, in that dress concealing a paper-thin nicotine patch would have been a challenge. It was a garment obviously meant to keep her cool on a scalding-hot Texas day.

It did the opposite of making him cool.

Under different circumstances, Russ might have taken the time to savor the view, and he might have even made an attempt to hit on her.

But this wasn't different circumstances.

He'd learned the hard way that even a momentary lapse of concentration could have deadly results. As a reminder of that, he rubbed his fingers over the scar just to the left of his heart. The reminder, however, didn't help when the woman made eye contact.

With Willie Nelson blaring from the jukebox, she wended her way through the customers seated at the mismatched tables scattered around the room. The neon sign on the wall that advertised tequila flashed an assortment of tawdry colors over her.

Without taking her gaze from him, she stopped only a few inches away. Close enough for Russ to catch her scent. She smelled high priced and looked high maintenance.

"We need to talk," she said, and slid onto the bar-stool next to him, her silky dress whispering against the leather seat.

Oh, man. Keeping her here would hardly encourage his informant to make contact. Hell, the only thing her presence would do was create problems for him.

"I'm not interested, darlin'," Russ grumbled, hoping that his surly attitude would cause her to leave.

It didn't.

"Well, I'm interested in you," she said, her voice much louder than Willie's.

In fact, she was loud enough to attract the few customers who hadn't already noticed her when she walked in. Of course, with her sex-against-the-bathroom-wall body, Russ figured she'd likely caught the attention of every one of the male patrons.

He eased his beer down onto the bar and turned slightly, so he could look her in the eyes. "Back off," he warned, under his breath.

"I can't."

Okay. He hadn't expected her to say that or ignore his warning.

Her clothes, the sleek sable-colored hair that tumbled onto her shoulders and even her tone might have screamed that she was confident about what she was doing, or about to do, but just beneath those ice-blue eyes was deeply rooted concern. And fear.

That put Russ on full alert.

"Look," he whispered. "This is no place for you. Leave."

She huffed and took the purse from beneath her arm. When she reached inside, Russ caught onto her hand. And got an uneasy thought.

"You can't be Milo," he mumbled. Because from what he'd been told about the would-be contact, Milo was a forty-something-year-old male. Of course, his source could have been wrong.

She stiffened slightly, looked more than a little confused, but it lasted just seconds, before she pushed off his grip. "I'm Julia Howell."

The name sounded vaguely familiar, but he couldn't

press her for more information. If she was Milo, or Milo's replacement, Russ would find out soon enough. And then he could get this show started. But he didn't like the bad feeling that was settling in his gut.

She placed her purse next to his beer, but held on to the pepper-spray keychain. "You didn't introduce yourself, but I know you're Russell James Gentry."

Hell.

Russ looked around to make sure no one had heard her use his real name. It was possible. The body-builder bartender seemed to be trying a little too hard not to look their way. Ditto for the middle-aged guy near the door. And the dark haired man in the corner. Unlike the bartender and the one by the door, Russ was positive this dark haired guy had been following him for days, and Russ had let him keep on following him because he had wanted to send Milo a message—that he had nothing to hide.

Which was a lie, of course.

Russ had plenty to hide.

"You're mistaken," Russ insisted. "I'm Jimmy Marquez."

"I'm not mistaken." She obviously wasn't picking up on any of his nonverbal cues to stay quiet. "I have proof you're Russell James Gentry," she said, and reached for her purse again.

He didn't have any idea what she had in that gold bag to prove his identity, and he didn't really care. He had to do something to get her to turn tail and run.

Russ swiveled his bar stool toward her, and in the same motion he slapped his left palm on her thigh. This would get her out of there in record time. He snared her gaze and tried to give her one hell of a nonverbal warning before he ran his hand straight up to her silk panties.

No, make that lace.

But she still didn't run. She gasped, her eyes narrowed and she drew back her perfectly manicured hand, no doubt ready to slap him into the middle of next week. And she would have, too, if Russ hadn't snagged her wrist.

When she tried to use her other hand to slug him, he had to give up the panty ploy so he could restrain her.

Russ put his mouth right against her ear. "We're leaving now. Get up."

Because her mouth was on his cheek, he felt the word "no" start to form on her peach-tinged lips. Judging from the way the muscles tightened in her arms and legs, she was gearing up for an all-out fight with him.

Gutsy.

But stupid.

He was a good six inches taller than she was, and he had her by at least seventy pounds. Still, he preferred not to have to wrestle her out of there, but he would if it meant saving her lace-pantied butt.

"If you know what's good for you," Russ whispered to her, "you'll do as I say. Or else you can die right here. Your choice, lady."

But he didn't give her a choice. He couldn't. Russ shoved the purse back under her arm, grabbed the pepper-spray keychain and used brute force to wrench her off the barstool. He started in the direction of the door.

Their sudden exit drew some attention, especially from the bartender and the bald guy, but no one made a move to interfere. Thankfully, the bar wasn't the kind of place where people thought about doing their civic duty and assisting a possible damsel in distress.

Julia Howell squirmed and struggled all the way to the door. "I won't let you hurt me," she spat out. "I won't ever let anyone hurt me again."

That sounded like the voice of old baggage, but Russ wasn't interested.

He got her outside, finally. It was dusk, still way too hot for early September, and the sidewalks weren't exactly empty. No cops, but there were two "working girls" making their way past the bar. They stopped and stared, but Russ shot them a *back-off* glare. He was good at glares, too, and he wasn't surprised when the women scurried away, their stilettos tapping against the concrete.

"How did you know my name?" Russ asked. "What so-called proof do you have?"

He didn't look directly at Julia Howell. Too risky. He kept watch all around them. And he shoved her into the narrow, dark alley that separated the bar from a transmission repair shop that had already closed for the day. He moved away from the sidewalk, about twenty feet, until he was in the dark of the alley.

"I won't let you hurt me," she repeated, and tried to knee him in the groin. She missed. Her rock-hard kneecap slammed into his thigh instead, and had him seeing stars and cursing a blue streak.

Tired of the fight and the lack of answers to his simple questions, Russ put her against the brick wall. He wasn't gentle, either, and he used his body to hold her in place. "Tell me how you know my name."

Julia didn't stop struggling, and she continued to ram herself into him. It only took her a few moments to realize that that wasn't a good idea—her breasts thrusting against his chest. Her sex pounding in the general vicinity of his.

She groaned in frustration and dropped the back of her head against the wall. Her breathing also revved up. And now that the fight had apparently gone out of her, the panic was starting to set in. Her chest began to pump as if starved for air, and he could see the pulse hammer in her throat. Sweat popped out above her upper lip.

"Calm down," he warned. "You can't answer my questions if you're hyperventilating."

That earned him a glare, and like him, she was good at them, too. It took her a moment to get her breathing under control so she could speak. "I used facial-recognition software to learn who you are."

"Excuse me?"

"I found you through facial-recognition software," she repeated, through gusts of breath. "I know you're Russell James Gentry."

Russ stared at her, trying to make sense of this, but her explanation wasn't helping much. He shifted her keys in his hand so he could grab her purse. There wasn't much room in the bag, and it was crammed with photos and a cell phone, but he quickly spotted what he was looking for.

Her driver's license.

It was there tucked behind a clear sleeve attached to the inside of the bag. The name and photo matched what she'd told him, but Russ wasn't about to take any chances.

While keeping her restrained, he shoved her purse back under her arm and took out his cell from his front jeans pocket. He pressed the first name in his list of contacts, and as expected, Silas Duran answered on the first ring.

Russ didn't say the man's name aloud, nor his own, and he didn't even offer a greeting. He wanted this done quickly and hoped it would be. Silas was a new partner. A replacement. And Russ wasn't sure how good Silas would be when thrown a monkey wrench.

Like now.

"Julia Elise Howell," Russ stated. "Run a quick check on her."

He immediately heard Silas making clicks on a keyboard. He waited, with Julia staring holes in him and with her breath gusting. He wouldn't be able to contain her for long. Well, he could physically, but that wouldn't be a smart thing to do in public. Someone might eventually call the cops.

"She's a San Antonio heiress who manages a charity foundation," Silas said. "Her father was a well-known real-estate developer. Both parents are dead. She's single. Twenty-nine. Says here she's considered a recluse, and that makes sense, because the only pictures that popped up were ones from over a decade ago. She's worth about fifty million. Why?"

None of that info explained why she had walked into the bar and plopped down next to him. "She's here. In San Saba. About an inch away from my face."

"Why?" Silas repeated. "Is she connected to the meeting with Milo?"

"I'm about to ask the same thing. She has a cell phone in her purse, probably in her own name. Check and make sure this really is Julia Howell in front of me."

A minute or so passed before Silas said, "She's there.

Well, her phone is anyway. Should I send someone to take care of her?"

"Not yet." Russ slapped his cell shut and crammed it back into his pocket.

Well, at least Julia was who she said she was. That was something at least.

Maybe.

Russ stared at her. "Why and how exactly did you find me?" he asked. "Not the facial-recognition software. I got that part. I want to know how you made the match and why."

She tipped her head to her left breast, and it took him a moment to realize she was motioning toward her purse and not the body contact between them. "Your picture is in there. A friend owns a security company, and he fed your photo through the software and came up with a match."

"Impossible." His records were buried under layers and layers of false information. Of course, his face wasn't buried. But any info about him was.

"Not impossible. My friend is very good at what he does, and he had access to security cameras all over the state. He ran the facial-recognition software twenty-four/seven, until he finally spotted you at a bank in San Antonio. Then he asked around, offered money." She hesitantly added, "And one of the bank employees gave us your name."

Russ wanted to punch the brick wall. He'd covered all bases, or so he thought. Yes, he had gone to the San Antonio bank to take care of some family business, but he hadn't counted on a chatty employee ratting him out. Nor had he counted on anyone digging this deep to find him.

"Even after we had your name, we couldn't find out anything about you," she continued. "Finally, one of the P.I.s who works for my friend spotted your face on a traffic-camera feed and was able to do the match. That's how I knew you were in San Saba. The P.I. came down here, followed you for several days and found out where you were staying."

That was a P.I.? Russ had thought it was one of Milo's men following him and checking him out. That's why he hadn't done anything about the tail. Mercy. And now that mistake had come back to bite him in the butt.

"The P.I. wanted to approach you, but I thought it best if I did it myself," she added. "Because it is such a personal matter."

Her explanation prompted more profanity and a dozen more questions, but Russ started with a simple one. "Why go through the trouble to look for me?"

"Because of Lissa," she said, as if the answer were obvious. "Lissa gave me your photograph."

Russ was sure he looked as pole-axed as he felt. "Who the hell is Lissa?"

For the first time since they'd started this little wrestling match and confusing conversation, Julia relaxed. At least, she went limp, as if she'd huffed all the breath right out of her. "My first cousin, Lissa McIntyre." Then her eyes narrowed. "Are you saying you don't remember her?"

"Yeah, that's exactly what I'm saying," Russ answered, honestly.

Her muscles went stiff again, and the remainder of the fear faded from her expression. It was replaced by a healthy dose of anger. "Let me refresh your memory. San Antonio. Last December. You met Lissa at a downtown bar, and after a night of drinking you went into one of those photo booths on the Riverwalk and had your picture taken."

Russ went through the past months. Yeah, it was possible he'd met a woman in a bar. But he certainly didn't remember anybody named Lissa, and he absolutely didn't remember taking a picture in a photo booth.

"Why are you here?" he asked, pressing her further.

"Because Lissa wanted me to find you." Julia took a deep breath. "She's dead. She was injured in the hostage standoff at the San Antonio Maternity Hospital two weeks ago. The doctors tried to save her but couldn't." Her voice broke, and tears sprang into her blue eyes. "She used her dying breath to ask me to find you."

He'd heard about the hostage situation, of course, it'd been all over the news. And he was also aware there'd been several deaths. But that had nothing to do with him.

"I'm sorry for your loss," Russ said, because he didn't know what else to say. This still wasn't making any sense. "But why the hell would your cousin want you to find me?"

She stared at him. "You don't remember?"

"Remember what?"

There was some movement at the back end of the alley. A shadow maybe. Maybe something worse. So Russ eased his hand into the slide holster in the back waistband of his jeans.

She snatched the purse from beneath her arm and practically ripped the bag open. "Look, I know Lissa was probably a one-night stand, but you have to remember her."

Julia pulled out a photo of an attractive brunette and practically stuck it in his face. Russ glanced at it, just a glance, and he turned his attention back to that damn shadow.

Was it Milo?

Or had one of the working girls grown a conscience and called the cops?

Those were the best-case scenarios. But Russ had a feeling this wasn't a best-case scenario kind of moment. He took out his gun and kept it behind his back.

"Well?" Julia demanded. If she noticed the gun, she didn't have a reaction—which meant she almost certainly hadn't seen it. "Do you remember Lissa?"

That was an easy answer. "No. Why should I?"

She made a sound, not of anger but outrage, and grabbed another photo from her purse. Russ glanced at it, too, and saw the baby. A newborn, swaddled in a pink blanket.

He froze.

Oh, this was suddenly getting a lot clearer. Or was it? Was this hot brunette really a black-market baby seller? If so, she certainly didn't look the part.

"Did Milo send you?" he snarled. "Is this the kid the seller's offering? Because it's not supposed to be a girl."

Julia went still again. Very still. And Russ risked looking at her so he could see what was going on in her eyes.

"Seller?" she repeated. There was a lot of emotion in that one word. Confusion, fear and a boatload of concern. "No. The newborn in the picture is Lissa's."

"I don't understand." Was she trying to sell her own cousin's kid?

"Well, you *should* understand, because you're the baby's father."

What?! It felt as if someone had slugged him in the gut. "Father?" Russ managed to say, though it didn't have any sound to it.

Ah, hell.

Russ's stomach dropped to the cracked dirty concrete, but that was the only reaction he managed. There certainly wasn't time to question Julia about what she'd just said about him being a father.

The movement at the back of the alley grabbed his full attention. Because the shadow moved.

So did Russ.

He shoved the photos back into her purse and gave Julia the keychain with the pepper spray. She might need it. He hooked his left arm around her, pushing her behind him.

"What's wrong?" she asked. Julia looked around, and no doubt saw the figure dressed in dark clothes and wearing a ski mask.

Russ took aim.

But it was too late.

Another man stepped into the alley from the front sidewalk. He lifted his gun. So did the ski mask wearing man.

They were trapped.

Chapter Two

Julia clamped her teeth over her bottom lip to choke back a scream. What was happening?

"Lower your gun," the man at the front of the alley warned Russell. "Keep your hands where I can see them and don't make any sudden moves."

The man giving the orders was tall and lanky and wore jeans and a scruffy t-shirt—unlike his comrade at the other end of the alley who wasn't wearing a ski mask. And that frightened Julia even more, because it meant Russell and she could identify him.

And that meant the man might kill them for that reason alone.

Of course, he might have already had killing on his mind before he stepped into that alley.

Julia cursed herself. How could she have gotten herself into this situation again? She didn't have the answer for that yet, but she wouldn't just stand around and whimper about this, and she wouldn't give up without a fight.

She cleared her throat so her voice would have some sound. "What's going on?" she asked Russell.

Not that she expected him to tell her. So far, he hadn't volunteered much, and she didn't trust him any further than she could throw him. Still, Russell had stepped in front of her when the men first appeared, and he appeared to be trying to protect her.

For all the good it'd do.

They literally had two guns aimed right at them.

Julia felt the jolt of panic and tried to get it under control before it snowballed. Not easy to do. Everything inside her was telling her to run for her life.

"Keep quiet," Russell growled. "Stay calm. And slow down your breathing." He glanced back at her, his coffee-brown eyes narrowed and intense. His gaze slashed from one end of the alley to the other, and he finally lifted his hands in surrender.

"Who are you?" Russell asked the man.

The ski-masked gunman stayed put, but the other one walked closer. He was dressed better than his partner. His crisp khakis and pale blue shirt made him look more like a preppy college professor than a criminal, and there were some threads of gray in his dark hair. But there was no doubt in Julia's mind that this man was up to no good.

"Who are *you?*" the preppy guy echoed, aiming his stare at Russell.

"Jimmy Marquez," Russell replied.

Julia hoped she didn't look surprised that he'd given them that name—the same one he'd used in the bar when she had first approached him. It wasn't his real name, she was sure of that. She'd paid Sentron Securities too much money for them to make a mistake like that.

"And who the hell are you?" Russell added, staring at the approaching man.

"Milo."

She felt the muscles in Russell's arm relax. Why, she didn't know.

"Well, it's about damn time you showed up," Russell snarled. "You should have been here yesterday. I waited in that bar half the night for you."

Milo offered no apology, no explanation. He merely lifted his shoulder and tipped his head to the ski-masked guy.

Both men lowered their weapons.

That didn't make Julia breathe any easier. Something dangerous and probably illegal was likely about to happen, and she had no idea if she could rely on Russell. Thankfully, he kept his gun gripped in his hand.

She held on to the pepper spray.

Lissa had been stupid, or duped, to get involved with a man like Russell Gentry. Julia should have ignored Lissa's deathbed request that she personally find the father of Lissa's child. There was no way Julia would hand over the baby to the likes of him, and it didn't matter that she would be violating Lissa's dying wish.

"Who's the woman?" Milo asked, staring holes into Julia.

As much as she distrusted Russell, Julia distrusted this one even more.

"Julia Howell," Russell said.

Mercy, he'd used her real name. Not that it would matter who she was to these men. But she preferred that criminals not know who she was.

"She's a *friend,*" Russell added, "and she was just leaving." He nudged Julia in the direction of the front of the alley, and that was the only invitation Julia needed to get moving. She turned.

But didn't get far.

Milo stepped in front of her, calmly reached out and took her purse. Did he intend to rob her? Julia didn't care. She only wanted out of there. But he blocked her again when she tried to move.

"She's not carrying a weapon," Russell said.

But Milo didn't take his word for it. The man dug through her purse and pulled out the three pictures inside. He glanced at the first two, shoved them back inside, but the third picture he held up.

It was the one of Lissa's baby.

Julia could feel her pulse thicken and throb. The throbbing got worse, and she tried to snatch the photo from his hand. Milo held on and aimed his stony gaze at Russell.

"Is this one of the babies you've acquired?" Milo asked.

Julia started to speak up, to tell them that the child was her cousin's, but then she remembered something Russell had asked before the goons showed up.

"Is this the kid the seller's offering?"

Sweet heaven. What was going on here? Were these men involved with black-marketing babies? If so, they weren't going to get their hands on Emily. She would kill them before she let that happen.

"No. It's my kid," Russell said. "Julia came here to tell me that I'm a daddy. Fate can sure be a kick in the butt, huh?"

Milo volleyed glances between the photo and Russell. "This is your child?"

There was skepticism in his tone, but Julia figured Milo had to see the resemblance. Baby Emily had the shape of her daddy's mouth and his sandy brown hair. Of course, Emily looked sweet and innocent, whereas her father, well, he just looked dangerous. That'd been Julia's first impression of him anyway, and he wasn't doing anything to change that.

Russell turned, angling his body, so he could slip his arm around her waist. The corner of his mouth hitched into a cocky smile that only he and a rock star could have managed to pull off, and those dark brown eyes that'd been so intense just a second earlier, softened.

It was an act.

"Yeah, that's my kid," Russell said to Milo, but the fake smile was directed at her. "Julia and I have got some things to work out, but the old feelings are still there," he added, all slow and sexy.

Then he leaned in. Too close. Julia was certain she stiffened and looked stunned. Because she did. But that didn't stop Russell. He caught onto the back of her neck and hauled her to him.

He kissed her!

She didn't fight him, though she considered it, but decided to wait and see where this was going. However, she got her pepper spray ready just in case.

He moved his mouth over hers as if this were something they did every day. He was good at the facade. Very good. And for just a split second Julia's body reacted to the man who was doling out that one, hot kiss.

And, sadly, he was hot, too.

In that split second, she understood the attraction that had no doubt drawn Lissa to him. She hated it, especially since she was feeling it herself. But she understood it. Russell Gentry, with his butt-hugging jeans, cowboy boots and too-long hair, was the kind of man who reminded a woman that she was indeed a woman.

A reminder she never wanted to feel again.

She slapped her hand on his chest, pushed him away and glared at him. But Russell only chuckled.

"Julia's upset that I missed the birth of our little one." Russell stared at her when he spoke. His tone was all light, but the facade didn't make it to his eyes. He was giving her a warning to stay quiet. "But she understands how important my work is. She knows I need to make a living. That's why she'll head out while we talk business."

Milo made a grunting sound that could have meant anything, and he didn't say a word for several moments. Julia felt every one of those moments in her held breath and racing heart.

"I have a better idea," Milo finally responded, and there was sarcasm in both his tone and body language. "You spend the evening with your girlfriend and baby, and I'll call you about another meeting."

"This meeting is important," Russell snapped. He was staring at Milo now, so she couldn't see his face, but Julia didn't need to see his expression to know Russell wasn't pleased. Whatever this meeting was supposed to be about, it was obvious he didn't want it postponed.

But she did.

Julia wanted out of there so she could get some answers and then call the police. It was entirely possible that Emily's father would be arrested before the night was over.

"The meeting can wait," Milo insisted. He motioned toward the ski-masked guy, who then darted out of sight. Milo turned to leave, as well, but Russell caught onto his arm with this left hand. The gun was still ready in his right.

Russell shook his head. "It can't wait. I have people already onboard for this deal, and they aren't into waiting. They want this to go down in the next twenty-four hours, or else they'll pull out. All that money will be gone, including your sizeable cut."

Milo looked down at the grip Russell had on his arm, and he didn't say anything until Russell released it. "I'll be in touch." And with that calmly spoken exit line, Milo turned and strolled away.

Russell cursed, stared at her, and then cursed some more. "Lady, you have no idea what you've just done."

Though he was furious and she didn't know if he would act on that fury or not, Julia still hiked up her chin and met him eye-to-eye. "Oh, I have an idea. I stopped something illegal from happening."

The stare turned to a glare, and he grabbed her arm. "Come on. Did you leave your silver Jag in the bar parking lot?"

Julia blinked but didn't ask how he knew about her vehicle. He'd obviously noticed her earlier, when she was following him. Strange, he hadn't given any indication that he'd known.

"Why do you ask about my car?" she demanded.

"Because we're going to get in it, that's why, and then we can have a serious chat about how you just screwed up everything I've worked so damn hard to put together."

She didn't even have to think about that proposal. "No, we're not doing that. And I don't care a rat's you-know-what about screwing up any of your plans. I'm also not getting in a car with you, but we *are* going to get some things straight right here, right now."

But where should she start? There were so many questions. So many concerns and fears. Julia started with the most recent one.

"You told that man, Milo, who I was. Why? Why not just give him a fake name the way *you* did? Now he knows who I am, and I would have preferred someone like that to not have any personal info about me."

Russell continued to volley cautious glances at both ends of the alley, but he also huffed to let her know he wasn't pleased about her not budging. "Milo saw your driver's license in your purse."

Of course. It was right there. Russ had looked at it himself, just minutes earlier. That took a little of the fight out of her.

"Unnecessary lies cause unnecessary suspicion," he added. "Trust me, you don't want to make a man like Milo more suspicious."

He glanced at the sidewalk again and eased his gun into the waistband of his jeans. "And you don't want to hang around in this alley. I'll walk you to your car, and then I'll watch you drive out of town. We can have the rest of this conversation over the phone."

Russell Gentry expected her to leave. And what she wanted was nothing more than to get away from this man and whatever was happening—but not before she had the answers she'd come for.

"Did Lissa know you were a criminal when she slept with you?" she asked angrily.

This was supposed to be a quick trip to turn over custody of Emily, but Julia had no idea what to do now.

This might end up in a custody battle, though she seriously doubted that Russell had a burning desire to raise a newborn.

He used the grip he had on her to get her moving, much as he'd done in the bar. "I told you I don't remember your cousin, so I have no idea what she knew or didn't know about me. Other than Lissa's word on her deathbed, what proof do you have the baby is mine?"

"DNA proof," she snapped.

That stopped him, and even though they were now on the sidewalk where Milo and his henchman would see them if they returned, Russell stared at her. "Impossible."

She was too scared and angry to be smug. "No. The P.I. who followed you around San Saba took a coffee cup you used, and the lab compared it to Emily's. There's a ninety-nine-point-nine percent chance that you're Emily's biological father. And I stress the biological part, because anyone, including the likes of you, can father a child."

He blew out a slow breath, and even though he didn't dispute her claim, he didn't jump to announce that he was indeed the birth father. There wasn't just doubt in his eyes, there was total disbelief.

"Look, I don't know if you're trying to scam me, or what," he said, his voice low and somewhat threatening. "And at this point, I really don't care, other than to warn you that scamming me isn't a good idea."

"Why would I lie about something like this?" she asked, not waiting for an answer. "No one with any common sense would want you to be an innocent newborn's father. If I had any doubts whatsoever about that,

I don't have them now. I know what you are, and I don't want you anywhere near Emily or me."

He stayed in deep thought for several moments. His forehead bunched up. His mouth slightly tightened. "Is the baby here in San Saba?"

Baby Emily was with a temporary nanny in Julia's hotel room, but she had no intention of revealing that to Russell. It'd been a mistake to bring Emily. But Julia hadn't known she would be walking into a vipers' nest.

"She *is* here," he insisted. And he cursed, the words even more vicious than before. "The baby is here in San Saba." He kicked at a piece of broken beer bottle on the sidewalk, and he got her moving again in the direction of the bar—and the parking lot that was on the other side.

"It doesn't matter where Emily is, you're not going to see her," Julia informed him. "You're a criminal, and I'll fight you with every breath in my body to stop you from getting anywhere near her."

Of course, she hadn't actually counted on becoming a permanent guardian to the child, but at the moment Julia didn't think there was another option. Not for her, and definitely not for Emily. She could return to her San Antonio estate with Emily and lock them both away from Russell and his cohorts. With her money and connections, she could be sure to keep him away.

She hoped.

He didn't say a word. Not when they passed the bar. Not when he hauled her into the parking lot and toward her car, which she'd parked directly beneath the lone security light. While they walked across the cracked concrete of the parking lot, he used the remote button on her keys to open the car door. He maneuvered her inside behind the wheel and shoved the key into the ignition.

She considered just driving away as fast as she could, but Julia first wanted to get something crystal clear. "You won't challenge me for custody. Because no judge would give a baby to a criminal like you."

The muscles in his jaw stirred. He opened his mouth, but before he could answer, something caught his attention. It caught Julia's attention, too. It was a slow moving black car creeping past the parking lot. Because of the darkly tinted windows and the poor lighting on the street, Julia couldn't see the driver, but she got a bad feeling that Milo or the ski-masked guy had returned.

"They're watching you," Russell mumbled, more to himself than her. And then he repeated it in the same tone as his profanity.

"What does that mean?" Julia was afraid of the answer.

He scrubbed his hand over his face and groaned. "It means Milo is suspicious."

She didn't think it was her imagination that he was carefully choosing his words and having a mental debate about what to say next. An angry mental debate.

"What I'm about to tell you," he finally said, "you have to keep secret, and if you do tell anyone, you'll be arrested for obstruction of justice. Got that?"

No. She didn't get that. Julia shook her head. "What's going on?"

"I'm not a criminal." Another pause, and she could see the mental debate continue. "I'm Special Agent Russ Gentry, FBI."

Julia's mouth dropped open. "What—"

He reached inside and used the central latch on her door to unlock the passenger's side. Before she could stop him he got inside.

"You just walked into the middle of a dangerous undercover investigation," he snarled.

He pressed the control pad on her key chain, and the locks on the doors snapped shut. "You'll be lucky, damn lucky, if I can get you out of this alive."

Chapter Three

Russ watched the chain of emotions slide across her face. First total, undeniable skepticism. She didn't believe him. Then, her eyebrows drew together. She eased her gaping mouth shut.

And then reached for her phone.

Russ would have bet a month's paycheck that she would either do that or try to slap him again. The latter still might happen if she didn't get the answers she wanted to this paternity issue. Russ wanted those answers, too but right now, both their butts were on the line. God knows who Milo had alerted about this wrinkle in their plan.

"If you tell anyone who I am," he reminded her, "I'll arrest you."

She pushed his pointing finger aside. "And you can't expect me to blindly accept what you're saying without confirmation. I'm calling Sentron Securities. The owner will be discrete."

Maybe. Maybe not. Russ knew *of* the owner, Burke Dennison. And Sentron seemed to be an above board operation. But he sure as hell didn't want his cover blown.

He had to establish his identity so he could force

Julia to cooperate. He could probably force her anyway, but it would take time and cause a scene. Julia was an heiress, and he couldn't very well force her into protective custody without someone asking the wrong questions.

"Make your call to Burke Dennison," Russ conceded, but he shot her another warning glare. "But put it on speaker and be very careful about what you say."

She pressed some buttons on the cell, waited and stared hard at him.

"Burke, it's Julia Howell," she said, to the person who answered. She placed her purse on the console between them. "I need a favor, but this has to stay between us."

"Absolutely." The man's voice was clear over the speaker. "What is it?"

"Russell Gentry might be a government employee. Could you check?"

"Contact Silas Duran at the FBI," Russ said, in a loud-enough voice for Burke to hear. "He'll brief you, then debrief you, and if you give the information you learn about me to anyone but Julia Howell, expect a full-scale investigation that will land your butt and Sentron in scalding hot water. Got that, Dennison?"

There was a pause, or more likely a hesitation from Dennison. "Give me a minute." Finally, he said "I'll call you back."

"Start driving to your hotel," Russ told Julia. He reached over to turn the key in the ignition. Not the brightest idea, since she batted his hand away and in doing so, his arm grazed her breast.

That earned him a glare. And it would have been better if she'd let out an outraged gasp, rather than that breathy feminine sound similar to the one she'd made after he kissed her.

That kiss had been a stupid idea, too.

Even though Julia Howell was perhaps a liar and a boatload of trouble, she was attractive, and damn it, his body wouldn't let him forget that. She was making him hot. Well, she and the Texas heat. He could feel the sweat trickling down his back. Julia wasn't immune to it, either, because she blotted the perspiration from her face.

Since they appeared to be staying put for a while, Russ got started on more damage control. "Who knew that you picked up Lissa's baby from the San Antonio Maternity Hospital?"

She pulled back her shoulders. "Why?"

Man, she doesn't give an inch. "Don't make everything hard. Just answer the question. Who knew?"

Her shoulders went back even more, and she continued to glare at him. "SAPD, of course. And several members of the medical staff."

Russ groaned. "Reporters?"

"No. I paid a lot of money to keep the details of Lissa's story quiet. Her death was initially reported, and her name was listed in the newspapers, but I asked everyone to hold off mentioning the baby."

"And they cooperated?" he asked, stunned.

"Yes. I told them I didn't want you to learn you were a father by hearing it on the news. I wanted to tell you in person."

Well that was something, at least. Half the state didn't know the truth about the baby, and that meant Russ could slant the info in his favor.

Russ took out his own phone to make another call

to FBI headquarters in San Antonio. He asked to speak to a computer tech, and it didn't take long for Denny Lord to come on the line. "I need you to doctor some files for Julia Elise Howell."

"What?" she snarled.

Russ ignored her. "People will be digging into her background, and I need you to plant information that she recently gave birth to a baby girl. Keep all details vague, as if she tried to keep the pregnancy hush-hush. Doctor a photo if necessary. Oh, and let me know if anyone does any deep searches on her."

"What was that about?" she demanded, the moment he was off the phone.

"It was about making the story I told in the alley mesh with what Milo's people will learn about you." He only hoped it was enough. "By the way, it's not a good idea for us to be sitting in this parking lot."

"And I don't think it's a good idea to be driving to a hotel with you. I don't trust you," Julia snapped.

"I don't trust you, either, since I think you're trying to scam me. Or kill me from dehydration. Turn on the AC."

"If I do that, it'll only encourage you to stay. I don't want you to stay. I want you to get out." She blotted her upper lip again.

"Well, I'm staying until I get some clarification about why you chose me for this…well, whatever the hell it is."

However, Russ rethought that. Julia had money, so why would she come after him with this ridiculous daddy claim? "But right now the scam is on the back burner. First we deal with the fallout from the meeting in the alley."

"No. First we deal with your identity."

"I'm an FBI agent," Russ repeated, "and you're messing with an investigation that's taken me a long time to put together." And it could all be in the toilet, thanks to a prissy San Antonio heiress and her baby charades.

"Does your investigation have to do with black-market infants?" she asked.

He laughed, but not with humor. The woman had nerve…or something. "I'm not discussing one detail of my investigation with you. You've already overheard way too much."

"Or maybe I've overheard the dealings of two criminals meeting in an alley to discuss selling a baby." She swiveled around and faced him. "Do you have a badge?"

It took him a moment to answer, because when she swiveled, her dress slid up a little, and he got a visual reminder of her great thighs.

"Not with me. It's generally not a good idea to carry a badge while undercover. Bad guys tend to kill you if they find out you're an FBI agent. Imagine that." He didn't bother to tone down the sarcasm.

With a mighty effort, he forced his attention off her thighs.

She tipped her head to the ceiling and groaned softly. Finally she started the car. She turned on the AC, but didn't put the car into gear. "If you're lying to me, somehow I will make you pay."

Russ leaned into the AC vent and let the cold air spill over him. "Ditto, darlin'. Except, there is no *if* in what you're saying. It's a lie. I didn't sleep with your cousin and I'm not her baby's father."

Julia put her face closer to her vent, as well. "The DNA says otherwise."

Yeah? It did? Well, it did if she was telling the truth about that. Of course, that went back to motive. Why would she lie about something like that? He wasn't rich, and he had no prospects of getting rich anytime soon.

And then it hit him.

Russ snapped back from the AC vent. "You said something about using my photo for facial recognition software. Where is that picture?"

"In my purse." She tipped her head toward it.

He couldn't get to it fast enough. Russ rifled through the gold bag and came up with three photos. One was of the baby, which he'd already seen. The other was a young twenty-something brunette who resembled Julia. Cousin Lissa, no doubt. But it was the final picture that grabbed his attention and sucker-punched him.

Suddenly, all of this became crystal clear.

"Let me guess," Russ said. Though he wondered how he could speak with his jaw suddenly so tight. "Lissa called her baby's daddy 'RJ'?"

She shrugged. "Yes. So?"

Russ started to groan, curse and hit his fist against the console, but he knew none of those things would undo what had apparently happened nine months ago.

"RJ, as in Russell James," Julia interjected. "As in *you*."

"As in *Robert Jason* Gentry." Those words had been even harder to speak than the others, and despite all the anger and frustration, he couldn't help but feel the pain, too. It'd been months, and it was still there. Fresh and raw.

Russ figured it always would be.

"Who's Robert Jason?" Julia asked, suddenly looking as dumbfounded as Russ felt.

He reached in his pocket and took out his wallet so he could extract the only photo he carried. It wasn't standard procedure to carry personal photos while in a deep cover situation, but Russ hadn't had the heart to take it out. He did now, and passed it to Julia.

She studied it, but Russ already knew every little detail. It'd been taken nearly two years ago, on a rare fishing trip they'd managed to schedule.

It was the last time he'd seen RJ.

"You have a twin brother," Julia mumbled.

"Identical twin." Which explained the match in the DNA. Identical twins didn't have the same fingerprints, but the standard DNA test couldn't distinguish one from the other.

She shook her head. "But your brother didn't come up during Sentron's search."

"He wouldn't have. RJ is…*was* black ops for the CIA. It would have taken more than Sentron or a traffic camera to find anything on him. All of his real records were sealed years ago."

Her gaze slashed to his. *"Was?"*

"Was," Russ repeated. And he repeated it again to give himself time to clear the lump in his throat. "He was killed on assignment nine months ago, probably just days after he met your cousin. He's the reason I was in San Antonio at that bank. I was the beneficiary of his estate, and I had some paperwork to sign."

"He's dead," Julia mumbled. But she continued to volley glances between the photo and him. "And you really are who you said you are—Russell Gentry?"

"Russ," he said, automatically making the correction. Russell had been his dad's name, and he wasn't comfortable calling himself that.

The answer had no sooner left his mouth when her cell rang, and in the dimly lit car, he saw Sentron Securities flash on her caller ID screen.

Russ merely motioned for her to answer it.

"Burke," she said, placing the call on speaker. "You have something for me?"

"Julia, he's telling you the truth. Russell Gentry is an FBI agent."

She pulled in a hard breath. "Thank you, Burke."

"I'm sorry about this, Julia. We dug as deep as we could go, and we didn't find his FBI records."

Russ cut off what sounded like just the beginning of an apologetic explanation. "Silas Duran will clear up loose ends with you," Russ informed the security specialist, and he reached over, took her phone and clicked it off.

"I'm sorry—" Julia began.

But he cut her off, too. "Sorry won't help. The only thing that will help is damage control, and that's about to get started."

Julia nodded and handed him back the picture. "What can I do?"

"For now, you can go back to your hotel, take the baby and return to San Antonio. Did you fly or drive here?"

"I drove. Emily's only two weeks old. She's too young to fly."

Well, in some ways that made it easier. No trip to and from the airport, but that meant she had to go about a hundred and fifty miles to get home safely.

"You have some kind of security system, I assume?" he asked.

Another nod, but her eyes widened with alarm. "You think Emily could be in danger?"

She shoved the car in gear and darted out of the parking lot. The tires squealed and kicked up bits of rock that spattered against the car. She didn't stop there. She grabbed her cell and made another call.

"I need to speak to the nanny. Don't worry. I won't mention you," she explained. "Zoey," she said, when the nanny answered. "I need you to make sure the door is locked. Don't let anyone in until I get there."

Julia ended the call, but she continued to mumble to herself.

Russ actually welcomed this high level of concern. It might get her to cooperate. "The baby's probably not in danger...*probably*," he emphasized. "But I don't want to take any chances." He carefully placed the photo back in his wallet and put it in his pocket. "After all, she's my niece."

Russ mentally repeated that. He was an uncle.

Later, he'd come to terms with that and the fact that RJ had fathered a child he'd never seen, never even known about. But that had to wait.

"I have a security system," Julia explained. "Supposedly, it's the best money can buy. And I can hire bodyguards. I'll do whatever it takes to keep Emily safe."

Russ nodded. "I'll arrange to have an agent or a cop follow you home. And once I've wrapped up things down here, I'll contact you."

She had a white-knuckle grip on the steering wheel. "Milo can't hurt her."

She was taking his warning very seriously, but there was no reason for Milo to go after Emily.

Because she looked ready to lose it, Russ reached over and skimmed his hand down her arm. Why, he didn't know. After everything she'd just learned about him, his touch probably wasn't very comforting.

"How badly did I mess up your investigation?" Julia asked. She stopped when the light turned red and drummed her fingers impatiently until it turned green. She gunned the engine.

"I can salvage it," he assured her.

But Russ wasn't certain of that at all. Still, he had no choice but to try.

Julia pulled to a quick stop in the parking lot of the Wainwright Hotel. Even though it had three floors, it was a fairly small building and only had about two dozen rooms. He'd already guessed that that was where she'd be staying, since it was the nicest hotel in a town that was seriously lacking nice things. The outskirts of the town were okay—more family oriented; and more likely than not, if you were in downtown San Saba, you were looking for trouble.

"Let me call my partner, Silas Duran," he told her. "He can make the arrangements for a security escort, and I can wait with you until everything is in place, so you can leave."

"You trust this Silas?" she asked.

Russ nearly gave her an automatic yes—but stopped. He settled for a nod.

Silas was a fellow agent and probably well trained. But Russ didn't like that Silas had only been on this case for a couple of days. He also didn't like that Silas might have pulled strings to get the assignment. That's the way it seemed to Russ, anyway. But that was a problem for him to mull over when he had more time.

She opened her door and looked at him. She nibbled lightly on her bottom lip, caught it between her teeth for several seconds. "I suppose you want to see Emily?"

He did. But the timing was all wrong.

Or was it?

Russ didn't know how long it would take to get this investigation back on track, and he couldn't leave San Saba until Milo put him in touch with the head honcho—the slimeball only identified as Z. Russ wanted to find Z and lock him away for a long, long time for what he'd done. If it took him weeks or longer to do that, it would be weeks before he first got to see his niece.

"Yeah," Russ heard himself say. "I'd like to see her. I won't stay long."

He had to pay an uncle's tribute to his dead brother's child and give Julia a promise that he would be back as soon as he could.

Since Julia was obviously too anxious to stay put any longer, Russ took out his phone and called Silas while they made their way into the hotel. He also kept watch around them, and breathed a little easier, once they made it into the lobby.

"Russ," Silas answered, "I was just about to call you."

Oh, no. Even though he'd only been working with Silas a short time, he knew that tone, and this wasn't good news.

"Where are you now?" Silas asked.

"With Julia Howell." Ahead of him, Julia made it to the elevator and jabbed the up button. "She's about to leave for her estate, but I need to request a security detail for her."

"We have a problem. She can't leave," Silas said.

Russ hoped he'd misunderstood. "What do you mean?"

"I mean she can't leave. If she does, this investigation is over, and you get to start it from scratch."

Because he might lose signal in the elevator, Russ clamped onto Julia's arm to stop her from stepping into it.

"I need to check on Emily," she insisted.

Russ pulled her to the side so he could continue this conversation, a discussion that he was positive he wasn't going to like.

"Explain," Russ told Silas.

"Milo just called his contact to set up another meeting for tomorrow afternoon. We can choose the exact time and the location."

Russ relaxed a little. Maybe the investigation hadn't been ruined. Maybe he could rescue that baby after all. "Well, that's good. The meeting's critical." And it was critical they control the location so they could set up security.

"No, it's not good." Silas said, cursing. A first. He had never heard Silas use even mild profanity before.

Russ listened to Silas's news. Yep, it was bad all right. And a few moments later, he was doing his own cursing. "Can we change Milo's mind?" Russ asked.

"No. Believe me, I tried, but he was adamant. We can take extra precautions. We can even bring in a few more agents. So the question is, do you think you can talk Julia Howell into cooperating?"

Russ looked over her at and saw the nerves right

there at the surface. He could possibly convince her to do what Milo wanted. *Possibly.* But even if they controlled the security and the meeting place, it didn't mean something wouldn't go wrong. Julia could ultimately be in more danger than she already was.

If that was possible.

Milo would dig to find out who she was, and then he'd wonder why an heiress worth fifty million would get involved with a lowlife like Jimmy Marquez. By doctoring her records, they could make it work.

Well, maybe…if they could convince Milo that Julia had a thing for slumming or bad boys.

"The stakes are too high to fail," Silas reminded him.

Yeah. And that was the real bottom line.

One way or another, even if he had to resort to begging, even if he had to put her in more danger, Russ had to bring Julia deeper into this.

Because a baby's life depended on it.

Chapter Four

The moment Russ ended his call, Julia got them into the elevator. Everything inside her was starting to spin. Her breathing was too fast. Her thoughts were going a mile a minute.

She tried to make herself slow down, so she could think this through, but the only thing that kept going through her mind was the importance of keeping Emily safe. Later, she'd berate herself for coming here to San Saba before she had thoroughly assessed the dangers. Julia had been in such a hurry to carry out Lissa's dying wish that she hadn't considered that some dying wishes just couldn't be fulfilled.

This was obviously one of them.

She had to grab Emily and leave the minute Russ had a security escort in place.

When the elevator door finally opened, Julia rushed out. She fished her keycard from her purse and slid it into the lock as soon as she reached the door. Then she hesitated—looked back at Russ, who was right on her heels.

"What?" he asked. After a moment of studying her face, he cocked his eyebrow. "Trust me, I'm having second thoughts about being here with you, too. But unless you got a time machine in that purse, we can't go back to the bar and undo what happened."

True, but Julia still didn't open the door. "Just how much are things messed up?"

"They're messed up," he answered. Now it was his turn to hesitate. "But I swear I'll do everything humanly possible to keep Emily safe."

Julia nodded. That was something at least. "You should know, I don't handle danger well. Old wounds." She added "Literally." Out of breath, she knew she had to get control of herself.

He touched his fingers to his chest. "Does this mean you're about to have a panic attack or something?"

"No," she snapped.

That wasn't exactly the truth. She might have one. It wouldn't be the first.

"I'm not sure what it means. I just thought you should know that alley meetings and having guns pointed at me aren't things I can handle."

"You already have," he reminded her.

"Things I can't handle *again*," she said. "*Or* after the fact. I usually don't break during the heat of the moment, but afterward, all bets are off."

Russ stared at her, and that stare reminded her of how close they were. Not as close as in the alley of course, but still close enough. He was a disturbingly attractive man, and the sooner she got him out of her life the better.

He huffed, cursed under his breath and reached out to touch her arm, as he had earlier. A sort of gentle rub, with just the tips of his fingers. It had worked then. A small miracle. But she was too close to the edge for it to work now. Still, she didn't move away from him.

"When I was seventeen I was attacked." Her words rushed out with her breath, and she felt her heart pounding. Her chest began to hurt. And she had no idea why she was telling him any of this. "A date went wrong. My parents had warned me that the guy was bad news. I didn't listen. I thought I knew more than they did. And when the guy tried to rape me, and he couldn't, uh, perform, he stabbed me three times and left me to die in the trunk of my car."

The tears came, and she cursed, used the profanity to quell the building anger. She wasn't that naïve girl anymore. It wasn't worth crying or panicking over now. She'd been rescued twelve years ago, and was still alive.

"Shhh," Russ said, his voice so calm. He put his arm around her and eased her closer. Not quite a hug, but almost. "Want to show me your scars, and I'll show you mine?"

She went stiff and eased back a little so she could make eye contact. But he was busy lifting his chest-hugging black T-shirt. She got a good look at his toned and tanned chest, his tight abs and the scar just to the left of his heart.

"I know a little bit about being left for dead…and staying alive." He lowered his T-shirt. "So do you. That's good, Julia. Because I need you to be a survivor."

She smeared the tears off her face and narrowed her eyes. "What do you mean?"

He opened his mouth as if he were about to answer, but then he shook his head. "Let me meet my niece first, and then we'll talk."

She just continued to stare at him so, he reached around her and opened the door. Or rather, he tried to do that. The nanny had obviously put on the safety latch and chain.

"It's me," Julia called to Zoey.

"Julia, thank God you're here. You scared me with that phone call." Zoey opened the door, but she stopped when she spotted Russ. Probably because Russ looked... well, dangerous.

And was.

"Everything's okay," Julia said, trying to assure the woman. "I might have overreacted." She hoped she had, anyway. Julia motioned toward Russ and shut the door. "This is Russ Gentry, Emily's *uncle*."

Zoey's dark brown eyes widened, and she looked him over from head to toe. "What happened to the birth father?"

"My brother was killed," Russ replied, as he double-locked the door.

"Oh." The young woman probably didn't realize that her mouth had dropped open. She stayed that way for several moments. "Well, I'm sorry. And I'm sorry for Emily. She's barely two weeks old and already an orphan."

Yes. She was. The poor thing. Julia would soon have to figure out what to do about that orphan status. She'd need to contact her attorney and see what the process was to become Emily's permanent legal guardian.

Julia thought of her old baggage. The old wounds. They were the reason she'd given up the idea of having children of her own. She hadn't wanted to bring a child into her world of panic attacks, nightmares and fear. A "recluse," the press called her. Well, while that might be good enough for her, she couldn't raise a child in a vacuum.

The idea caused her to take a deep breath.

"Emily's still asleep," Zoey explained, stepping to the side. "She hasn't woken up since you gave her the bottle before you went out to talk with Mr. Gentry."

That wasn't a surprise. Emily slept a lot, and when she wasn't sleeping she was eating, fussing and requiring a diaper change. Still, with all that work involved, Julia hadn't expected to find the baby to be so enthralling. She had tried not to let herself get attached, but there was nothing to hold her back now.

"This way," Julia told Russ, and she led him through the small living area, in the direction of one of the bedrooms in their three-room suite. Julia had had the crib moved into her own room so she could stay up nights with Emily. Zoey was using the other.

The door was already open, and the lamp was on, so she had no trouble gazing fondly at Emily in the crib. Julia automatically smiled—and she was glad for that reason to smile. With the incident in the alley, she needed something to bring her back to normal, and Emily had a unique way of doing that.

With Russ right next to her, she tiptoed closer and stared down at the baby. She was so precious, with her light brown curls and pink cheeks.

"Her eyes are brown," Julia whispered to him. Like Russ's eyes, and no doubt, his twin brother's. Now that they were side-by-side, Julia could see the resemblance even more. Emily definitely had the Gentry DNA.

"Despite the circumstances of her birth, she's very healthy." Julia gave the pink blanket an adjustment that it didn't really need. She just needed to touch the baby. "She weighed seven pounds, three ounces when she was born, but she's already gained nearly a pound."

When Russ didn't say anything, she looked at him. But he didn't seem to notice that she was even in the room. His attention was focused on Emily.

"She's beautiful," he whispered. He touched Emily's hand lightly, and she closed her fingers over his thumb. He sucked in his breath. "She's like a tiny angel."

There was so much emotion in his voice, Julia had to do a double take to make sure Russ Gentry had spoken those words.

He had.

This was the man who had stared down gunmen in the alley?

He was turning into a marshmallow right before her eyes.

"Oh, man," he mumbled. The smile started in the corner of his mouth and spread until it was a full grin. "I didn't expect this."

Julia didn't need clarification. She'd had the same reaction when she first saw the child.

"The love," he said. "It's instant. I mean, it's like my blood knows that she's my niece."

She understood that, too, but she suddenly became very uncomfortable.

She thought Russ would do a quick peek and head back to the sitting room so they could have that talk he'd mentioned. But this was no quick peek.

He drew back his hand so he could scrub it over his face. He groaned softly. "Okay. I can deal with this. I can make it work."

"Make what work?" Julia asked.

He tipped his head to Emily. "I was due to move to a supervisor's job in the next year anyway, but this will just speed things up. I'll get out of undercover work when I'm done with this case."

"What do you mean?" Julia said that a little louder than expected.

He shrugged, as if the answer was obvious. "A desk job in the San Antonio office will give me regular work hours. And it'll be safer. I can have a more normal life. And I can finally get a haircut," he added, shoving the strands of hair away from his face.

Julia put all those things together. *Oh, no! He couldn't mean* that. "Are you saying you want to raise Emily?"

He gave another shrug. "Of course. She's RJ's daughter. My niece. I'm her next of kin. Who else would be raising her?"

"Me," Julia blurted out.

That erased any trace of Russ's goofy smile. "You're her cousin. I'm her uncle, and her father was my identical twin brother. That's a closer bloodline than you have with her. Besides, if Lissa had wanted you to raise her, she would have said so."

It felt as if someone were squeezing a fist around Julia's heart.

"Lissa said that because she thought Emily's father was alive. And because she probably thought I didn't want children. She was wrong. Besides, need I remind you that you're in the middle of a dangerous investigation?"

"An investigation that'll end soon." He stared at her. "You want to raise her yourself?"

Julia managed an indignant nod. "Well, I am the natural choice."

That was far from the truth, but Julia wasn't speaking with her head. This was a *heart* thing.

"Why? Because you're a woman? Because you're rich?" he asked, challenging her. "I can feed her a bottle and buy her clothes just as well as you can."

Since this was obviously about to turn into a nasty argument, Julia gave Emily's blanket another adjustment and caught onto Russ's arm so she could lead him out of the room.

Zoey was there, apparently waiting for an update, but it would have to wait. "Could you excuse us?" Julia asked her, then waited until Zoey was in her room before she continued.

"What makes you think you'd be a good father?" Julia demanded.

"Maybe the same thing that makes you think you'd be a good mother," he countered. "I love Emily. It doesn't matter that I just saw her for the first time, I love her."

"And I don't suppose it matters that the dangerous elements of your job could follow you from undercover work to a desk?"

"The FBI makes it a priority to protect the families of their agents."

She was about to launch into the next wave of the argument, but he lifted his hand in a stop-right-there gesture. "Look, this isn't a good time to go at each other about custody. We can work that out later."

"Can we?" she snapped.

"We can," he calmly assured her. Russ glanced around the room, and his attention landed on the minibar. Next to it was the small microwave she'd had brought in so she could heat up Emily's formula.

"Do you have any hard liquor?" Russ asked.

Julia was still in a fit of temper, and that trivial-sounding question didn't help. "Help yourself."

"It's not for me. It's for you." He went to the bar, selected a bottle of bourbon and poured some into a glass. He brought it back to her and motioned for her to sit on the sofa.

Because Julia's legs were still wobbly, she did. She also took the drink and had a sip, despite the fact that she hated bourbon. As expected, it watered her eyes.

Russ eased down on the sofa next to her. Not on the other side. But practically hip-to-hip with her. So close that she could see the trouble brewing in his eyes.

"This drink is to help pave the way for what you need to tell me," she said.

He nodded and combed his gaze over her. "I'm physically attracted to you. That'll be a problem—"

"What?" The remark was such a surprise that it took her a moment to continue. "This is what you needed to tell me?"

"No. It's just FYI. I keep thinking about your lace panties. I keep thinking about kissing you. That'll be a problem because I'm a guy, and in my mind, that attraction will get all screwed up, and I'll have this overwhelming need to protect you. I can't have that now, because there's someone else I have to think about."

Julia had another sip of the bourbon and was disgusted that she needed it. "Am I supposed to understand that?"

"Yeah. Because I'm pretty sure you're attracted to me, too."

She tried to deny it. Tried hard. But the lie wouldn't make it past her throat. "I won't get involved with you."

No lie there. It was the truth. Julia didn't get involved with anyone—ever.

"Good." He didn't seem insulted. More like *relieved.* "Because I need to ask you to do something, and I don't want sex, lace panties or attraction to have any part in your answer."

She stared at him. "You're not making sense."

"I will, soon." He took the drink from her and finished it. "Milo, the gunman from the alley, contacted my partner to set up another meeting."

"Good." She nodded. "You said the meeting was important."

"It's more than important. And Milo won't go through with it unless I bring you with me."

Julia felt her heart skip a very big beat. "W-what?"

"Normally, I wouldn't have even considered it, but the stakes are astronomical. Besides, if I don't bring you, Milo will be even more suspicious. He might panic and do something stupid. Something that could set things back worse than they already are."

Oh, God. Julia wished she'd finished that drink after all. Her heart started racing. She could feel the adrenaline flash through her. The anxiety hit her like a ton of bricks. She was racing toward a full-blown panic attack.

"Just take a deep breath," Russ said, as if knew exactly what she was experiencing. He caught onto her chin. "Don't make me put my hand up your dress again."

"What?" She pushed him away from her.

"That's right. Get mad. Slap me if it'll help. Hell, kiss me. Do whatever you need to do to stop that response. It's old garbage, and you're stronger than you think, Julia. I watched you in that alley, and if I thought for one minute that you couldn't handle this, I wouldn't be asking."

She blinked. No one had ever accused her of being strong. And much to her surprise, it worked. She felt her heart rate ease back to normal.

"That's good," Russ mumbled. "And for the record, I've never threatened to put my hand up a woman's dress before. Well, not unless it involved mutual foreplay."

A nervous laugh escaped before she could stop it. But she had nothing to laugh about. *Nothing.* Russ had just told her he wanted her to meet with a dangerous criminal.

"What's at stake at this meeting?" she asked.

He met her eye to eye before he answered. "A baby's life."

Russ said it so softly that it took a moment to sink in. Julia gasped. "A baby?"

He nodded. "A child just a little older than Emily." Russ took a deep breath. "I'm at the tail end of an investigation. Milo thinks I'm a black-market baby buyer, and that my client is someone rich, but who doesn't have the credentials or the background for a legal adoption. Milo's boss is the seller, a man whose identity I need to know so I can stop him from doing this again. Or it's entirely possible that Milo is working alone. Either way, he has the baby."

"Then why not just arrest Milo and make him tell you where the baby is?"

"Because he'll just deny it. And if he's put in jail, he'll have his hired guns take the baby, go in to deep hiding, and we'll never see the child again."

She touched her fingers to her lips to stop them from trembling. "Where did they get the baby?"

"They stole him from his parents, Aaron and Tracy Richardson. And they left a note, warning the parents not to go to the authorities or the baby would be harmed. Thankfully, the Richardsons called the cops and the FBI anyway, because we learned that Milo or his boss intended to sell the child all along—probably by pitting the buyer he thinks he has waiting against what the parents will shell out. The baby will go to whoever pays the most."

Julia hadn't thought this day could get any worse, but she'd obviously been wrong. "My God."

"Yes, I've been saying that a lot lately myself. People are messed up, Julia, and they do disgusting things. If I don't complete this sale and get the baby, then Milo will find another buyer, and the little boy will end up being sold. Maybe he'll get lucky and get good parents. Maybe he won't. We know from past deals that Milo has been very careful about the buyers he chooses."

Julia didn't feel a panic attack, but her heart broke at the thought of an innocent child being bought and sold. "And if I don't go…"

"The meeting won't happen." He lifted his shoulder. "Not unless I can somehow reason with Milo."

She'd already seen him fail to do that in the alley, when Milo had cancelled the meeting. A cancellation that'd happened because she was there. If she hadn't chosen this night to approach Russ about Emily, then the stolen baby might have been rescued and on the way back to his parents.

"How safe will this meeting be?" she asked.

Russ took a deep breath. "We can set up security in

the area to take out any of Milo's men if they make a wrong move. I don't think they will. This is about the money. Milo wants the huge middleman fee, and I think he'll play nice to get his hands on the cash."

Julia stayed quiet a moment and gave that some thought. "And what would I have to do?"

"Maybe just stand there and look beautiful. Which won't be a stretch," he added, in a mumble.

She hated that she felt flattered with that ill-timed compliment. "Then why does Milo want me there if I'm just to be your arm dressing?"

Now it was Russ's turn to have a few moments of silent thought. "Could be several possibilities. He might already know you're a rich heiress. He might think you're the actual buyer instead of Silas Duran, the agent we have in place for that. Or he might just want you there because he believes it'll be safer for him."

"Safer how?"

"If Milo suspects this is a sting operation, then he could see you as a shield of sorts. The FBI wouldn't go in with guns blazing if you're in the line of fire."

"This is a lot to put on you," Russ continued. "I'll understand if you say no."

If she said no, Julia couldn't live with herself, but if she said yes, she might not make it through the meeting without a panic attack. Still, she would be there. She would fulfill Milo's demand, and if she had an attack, so what? It would be humiliating for her, but it might speed things along with Milo. Besides, there really wasn't a choice here. Julia knew what had to happen.

"I'll do it," she heard herself say. "Just tell me where I have to go and what I have to do."

Russ didn't seem surprised that she agreed. He

simply nodded and gave her another of those arm rubs.

"We'll know the details of the meeting in the morning," Russ explained. "For tonight, there'll be an agent outside your room. I won't leave until he arrives."

"Where's the stolen baby right now?"

Russ shrugged. "We don't know. But I'm sure he's fine. The deal is to deliver a healthy baby boy to the buyer."

That was something at least.

Julia heard the soft sound. It was barely audible, but it got her to her feet so she could go to the bedroom. Emily was stirring in her crib.

Russ got up, too, and followed her. "She's awake."

When Julia reached the crib, she saw those big brown eyes staring up at her. The baby looked first at Julia, then at Russ.

"Hi, princess," Russ said, before Julia could say anything.

But he didn't stop with just a greeting. Russ reached down into the crib and picked her up. He didn't hesitate, and he didn't say something clichéd about being afraid she'd break. He eased Emily right into his arms, cradling her protectively against him, and he rocked her as if he'd done this a thousand times.

"What?" he said, defensively, when he glanced at Julia, who was staring at him.

She had several questions she was trying to ask at once. "Do you have children of your own?"

"No. And I'm not married, either. Never have been. But I love kids. Always have."

Obviously. "This isn't your first time holding a baby, is it?"

"Hardly. Most of my coworkers and friends have kids. I'm godfather to three of them. All boys." He leaned down and gently kissed Emily's forehead. "What about you? Do you have much experience with kids?"

"Plenty," she lied. Truth was, Emily was the first and only baby she'd ever held.

He chuckled when Emily puckered her lips. "I rescued a little boy not much older than her just three months ago, and I held him for hours before we could get him back to his parents. He was a cute kid all right, but nothing like the little angel here."

Rescued? So, the stolen baby wasn't his first. She supposed that made Russ a hero of sorts. And he certainly seemed to be a natural with Emily.

My God. She could actually lose custody of Emily to him. Yes, she had more money than Russ. Well, maybe. But she had also been in therapy for twelve years. She had panic attacks. And the final blow—Lissa hadn't asked her to raise Emily. She'd wanted Julia to merely be the locator, and Lissa had murmured that dying wish in front of several members of the medical staff and a cop.

None of that would be in Julia's favor.

Still, she had to fight; and her first step was to put some distance between Russ and her. Between Russ and Emily. Out of sight, out of mind might help him realize that he didn't want to give up his undercover life after all.

"You're breathing fast again," Russ pointed out. But he didn't look at Julia when he spoke. He kept his attention on Emily and made cooing sounds.

Cooing!

"I was thinking about Lissa," Julia mumbled, and forced herself to breathe normally.

"You were close to her?" He didn't wait for an answer, as he announced "The angel just smiled."

Julia looked at the baby, who did indeed seem to have the right corner of her mouth lifted into a pseudo-smile. Her first. And she'd smiled for Russ, not for her.

"Lissa and I weren't close," Julia admitted. "But we used to be."

"Before the attack," Russ added when she didn't say more.

A cooing hero with ESP. Great. This wouldn't be a custody battle, it would be a custody war.

"Yes," she finally answered. "It was Lissa who set me up with the guy who stabbed me. He was a friend of hers." A friend from the wrong side of town, her parents had said. Lissa had been from the wrong part, too. That's what had drawn Julia to her. And look how that had turned out.

Russ pulled his attention from Emily and looked at her. "You blame Lissa for what happened to you?"

"No. But she blamed herself. We weren't close after that, and I was too broken to try to mend things between us." Uncomfortable with yet another personal wound that she hadn't intended to reveal, she reached out and took Emily. "It's probably time for a diaper change."

Now, that should send Russ running, Julia thought. But it didn't. "I can do it," he said, when Julia placed the baby in the crib. "With my godsons, diapering can be a challenge. I've gotten hosed down more than once."

He reached into the bag next to the crib and pulled

out the wipes and a diaper, but he had barely gotten started when his phone rang. The sound shot through the room and startled Emily. Julia picked her up again before she could break into a full-fledged cry.

Russ glanced at the caller ID on his phone. "I have to take this." And he stepped back into the sitting room.

While Julia finished up the diaper changing, she tried to hear Russ's conversation. But she couldn't tell anything from his monosyllabic answers. It was possibly about the security guard who would be assigned duty outside her door. Or maybe it was about the meeting with Milo.

The meeting she hoped she wouldn't regret.

Of course, she would have regretted not trying to save the stolen baby even more.

"I understand," Russ said. He ended the call and came back into the room.

"Is the security guard here?" she asked.

"He is." Russ reached down and ran his fingers over Emily's toes. "But there's a problem."

Her head whipped up, and she met his gaze. "Not the baby?"

"No. Not the baby. My partner, Silas, just informed me that Milo has one of his men staked out near the hotel."

Her heart dropped. "You don't think his man will try to get in here?"

"No reason for him to do that. He's watching us with an infrared thermal device."

"A what?"

"It means he can see us. Not complete images, but the heat that our bodies are generating." Russ turned and slipped his arm around her waist. He eased her closer. "It means Milo is trying to figure out if you really are my fiancée."

Sweet heaven. Her first instinct was to jump back from Russ, because it made her skin crawl to think that someone was spying on them. But Russ held on to her.

"What do we do?" she asked.

"I stay here tonight." He tipped his head to the bed. "There. With you."

Chapter Five

Russ stared at the laptop and tried not to break the screen.

Silas had sent him the reports and pictures on Julia's computer, since Russ didn't have his own with him. And the FBI hadn't wanted to risk having one delivered to the hotel, in case it would make Milo even more suspicious. If that was possible.

Russ wasn't feeling good about Milo's meeting. But then, he was feeling even worse about the pictures in front of him.

They were photos of Julia's attack.

Everything had been documented by the San Antonio police and used to convict the SOB who'd done this to her. There it all was—the details of the assault with a deadly weapon, the position of each stab wound, every bruise and scrape.

She'd been damn lucky to survive, because any one of the stab wounds could have hit a vital organ. Added to that, she'd nearly bled to death in the trunk of her car. A passerby, out walking his dog, had heard her moaning and rescued her. It'd been cold that night, close to freezing, and the low temperatures had slowed her bleeding.

Julia was alive because of a freak cold spell and a dog who needed a midnight walk.

In other words, blind luck.

Russ wasn't able to hold back his feelings any longer, and he mumbled some profanity. Her attacker had gotten a life sentence, but that didn't seem nearly harsh enough for what he'd done.

Beside him, Julia stirred a bit, pulling the cover to her chin, but she went back to sleep. Good thing, too. They'd been up and down most of the night, with Emily feeding every four hours. Julia had taken the midnight shift, and after he watched how she prepared the formula, he did bottle duty at 4:00 a.m. Since it was going on seven, it wouldn't be long before Emily woke up for the morning round. She might be a little angel, but she ate like a lumberjack.

He smiled at that thought. It'd be like having daily miracles, just watching her grow up.

Russ closed down the files on Julia's stabbing, and then deleted them from her computer. He didn't want her coming across them accidentally, even though she probably remembered every single detail in those reports. He certainly remembered the bullet that had landed him in a hospital bed for over a week; but as an undercover agent, bullets were a possible job hazard. Julia had been attacked on a date. Big difference.

Julia stirred again, moving from her side to her back, and shifting the comforter in the process. That shift exposed her breasts. She was wearing a gown and a robe, but the robe had opened, and he could see the outline of her nipples.

Too bad Milo's infrared couldn't read Russ's dirty thoughts. There would have been no doubts about Julia being his fiancée. Well, Milo wouldn't have had doubts about the attraction being real, anyway.

Oh, it was real, all right.

And the bed sharing hadn't helped. It also hadn't helped that he'd slept on top of the covers so there wouldn't be any skin-to-skin contact between them. All through the night, Russ's body hadn't let him forget that he was in bed with an attractive woman.

Thankfully, Russ didn't have to pretend to have sex with her. Since Milo thought Julia had given birth just two weeks ago, that gave Russ and her an excuse not to take the pretense to the next level.

Russ saw her eyes open. There was that sleepy flash of ice blue, before she gasped and tried to scramble away from him. She obviously wasn't accustomed to waking up in bed next to a man.

He didn't say anything, just gave her a few moments to pull out of the sleepy haze.

"Oh," she murmured, and she swiveled around so she could see Emily.

"She's still asleep," Russ whispered.

Julia made a small sound of relief and sat up, her robe shifting again. He caught a glimpse of the scar at the top of her right breast.

She looked at his damp hair and his bare chest. "You showered already?"

He nodded. "About an hour ago. I washed out my shirt, since I don't have a change of clothes." He'd been as quiet as possible, so he wouldn't wake anyone. And then he'd gotten some work done on her laptop. "I figured, with only one bathroom, I'd better get in and out before Zoey or you needed it."

He glanced at her breast again and bit back a groan.

"Any news about the meeting?" she asked. Was it his imagination, or did she dodge looking at his chest, as well?

"No. Silas should call soon." He paused and tried not to look at her. "Are you having second thoughts?"

"Yes," she admitted, "but I'm going through with it anyway."

"You're a brave woman," Russ said.

"Right. Remind me of that when it looks as if I want to turn and run."

Oh, he would. But what he couldn't seem to do was keep his mind off her breasts.

Julia's gaze dropped down to her partially exposed breast, and she gasped again. She tried to cover it up, but Russ caught onto her hand.

"It's okay," he said, keeping his voice emotionless.

She shook her head and her eyes watered. She obviously wasn't used to anyone seeing her old wounds.

Russ didn't think. He just leaned over and dropped a kiss on the scar. The moment his lips touched her warm, musk-scented skin, he knew it was a whopper of a mistake. His sympathetic brain was trying to assure Julia that she was beautiful, with or without scars, but that stupid, brainless part of him below the waist assumed this was foreplay.

He got rock hard.

And he waited for Julia to slap some sense back into him.

But she didn't.

She caught onto his face with both hands. Maybe to stop him from kissing her again, but she didn't push him away, and she kept her touch gentle. She stared at him with those now-hot-blue eyes.

"I can't," Julia whispered. "I mean, I haven't. I won't…and I can't."

Russ tried to process that semibabble—was she saying she was a virgin? It would fit. The attack had left her with physical and emotional scars. But the virginity didn't fit with the rest of her. She was beautiful by anyone's standards, and certainly, after twelve years, some guy had to have been able to help her get past the wounds and make love to her.

"Never," she added.

Or maybe not.

"Oh, man. You've obviously crossed paths with your share of…jerks." Though that was mild, compared to what he wanted to call them. "Never?"

"Never," she snapped. "It's no big deal. I've never wanted to have sex. Not since the attack, anyway."

Maybe she didn't want to, but she had admitted she was attracted to him.

She pushed him away and tightened the robe back around her. That was his cue to drop the subject—and to ice down the hot blood he had for her. She certainly didn't need a man with his track record. He was thirty-three and hadn't dated a woman for more than two months at a time.

"Change the subject," she insisted.

"Okay."

Russ moved the laptop to the nightstand and looked at her—at the white terry-cloth robe she was gripping like a full-body chastity belt. And he knew he should just back off and leave this alone. But then he thought of Milo's man watching them. Except, that was more of an excuse than anything, because mainly, he just thought about kissing that not-wanting-to-have-sex lie right off Julia's mouth.

He leaned in and their breath met. Julia got that deer-caught-in-the-headlights look, but she didn't move away. So he got even closer, until his mouth hovered over hers.

And he waited her out.

"All right," she snarled. She slapped her hand on his chest and pushed him away. But not nearly far enough. Besides, with her hand on his bare skin, it only made things more intense. "Maybe I do want you. But because I want something, it doesn't mean it'll happen. You're not my type."

"You're not mine, either."

Though it seemed true for both of them, he was still hard—and she seemed to be going softer, hotter and breathier with each passing moment. Everything kicked up another notch when her fingers moved. Just a little. But enough to glide through his chest hair. Maybe she wasn't even aware of the touching, but he certainly was.

His phone rang, the sound shattering the insane moment. Russ fumbled to get his phone from his pocket so he could answer it before it woke Emily. But he wasn't successful, because Emily immediately started to cry.

Julia sprang from the bed to get the baby, and Russ answered the call, because he knew it would be from Silas and therefore important. He only hoped he didn't sound as out of breath or aroused as he actually was.

Damn, he'd let Julia get under his skin.

"How's baby-and-heiress duty?" Silas greeted,

probably because he heard Emily fussing. But Russ didn't care for the man's tone.

"It's all right. Better than I thought it'd be." And much to Russ's surprise, that was the truth. He hadn't minded the short sleep time in between feedings.

Julia was another story. If he had to sleep next to her again, it would require multiple cold showers and maybe a big rock that he could use to hit himself in the head.

"Well, I hope you're rested," Silas continued, "because its shaping up to be a full day. The meeting with Milo is all set at the state park at two p.m. I won't be on the park grounds, because I want to stay out of sight, but I'll be nearby, in case you can close the deal."

So it was on schedule as planned. If Milo agreed to the one-million-dollar offer for the baby sale, then Silas was to arrive on the scene as the buyer. The next step was to get Milo to agree to a time and a place for the exchange. Silas would get the baby, and Russ would follow Milo or his henchmen back to his boss, Z. If there was no Z, and Milo was the sole person responsible for taking the baby, then Milo would be arrested.

With luck, they could have the baby by nightfall. And Julia and Emily would be safely on their way back to her estate. After that, Russ could, well, he could get his own head on straight so he could figure out how to approach the whole custody issue.

"So, is Julia Howell onboard for the meeting?" Silas asked.

"She is," he said, though he was beginning to have more doubts about it all. "Please don't tell me Milo's made any other crazy requests."

"No. Not so far. But there has been a hitch. I'm in the lobby of the hotel where you're staying."

"Why?" Russ demanded. "You know Milo has a man watching us."

"I do. And he's still there, parked less than a block up the street. I came in through the back. Neither Milo not his man would recognize me, and I didn't know if you wanted to keep it that way."

"I do." Since Silas was going to pose as the buyer for the infant, Russ didn't want Milo asking questions about why Silas had been at the Wainwright, where Julia was staying. "So why did you come?"

"I had no choice. Twenty minutes ago I got a call about someone else who was already here at the hotel."

"Not Milo?"

"No. The stolen baby's parents, Aaron and Tracy Richardson. I have them waiting in the manager's office, but I don't know how long I can talk them into staying put. The mother is nearly hysterical."

Russ almost dropped the phone. "The parents? How the hell did they end up in the Wainwright Hotel in San Saba?" Russ tried to keep his voice down, but it was hard.

"My fault. They've been calling me for updates every hour, and yesterday I let it slip that we were in San Saba."

"You what?" Russ couldn't help it. He cursed.

"I didn't mean to tell them," Silas insisted, his voice suddenly louder. "It just happened. The mother was crying. The father was yelling. I was just trying to assure them that we were close to finding their baby."

"And you did that by giving away our location," Russ

growled. "Did you also let it slip that *I* was here at the hotel?"

"No. But when they told me they were coming to San Saba, I said I'd meet them. I just went there to calm them down. Russ, they were scared, and I didn't want them going to every hotel in town looking for me. That would have sent plenty of red flags up for Milo's men."

Yeah, it would have, but the parents' arrival at the Wainwright would be a massive red flag on its own.

Russ had to get his teeth unclenched so he could speak. "Please tell me you didn't meet the parents here, when you were trying to calm them down?" One meeting was bad enough, two would be a disaster.

"No. I met them at a café on the other side of town. I was careful, but the parents had someone follow me. And he must have been good, because I didn't make him. He followed me straight to the Wainwright Hotel."

Russ shook his head. "When were you here at the Wainwright?"

"Last night."

Well, that was news to Russ. "Why?"

"I was going to do the security detail to escort Julia Howell, but by the time I arrived, I got the call about Milo and the meeting."

And Silas hadn't told him this, even though it could be a huge problem. "You risked Milo and his men seeing you here twice," Russ pointed out.

"That's why I went in the back. I was careful. But if Milo brings it up, we can just say that since I'm the buyer, I've been meeting with you to discuss the money and the details."

That sounded logical, unless Milo was already suspicious of Silas. "This changes the plans for the meeting. Even if the deal closes today, I don't want you to come waltzing in there while Julia's around. We'll wait until she leaves."

"If Milo agrees to that," Silas said.

Yes. Milo might be a problem, but they were going to have an even bigger problem on their hands if their covers were blown.

"I hope you told the parents they put their baby in more danger by coming here," Russ asked.

"I told them, but they aren't listening. They aren't leaving either. They're demanding to talk to *you* now."

"Why me?"

"Because they believe you're the one who'll be in direct contact with the seller."

That was true. Russ would be in direct contact with Milo. But that didn't mean he should give in to their demands and meet with them.

"My advice?" Silas added. "Listen to what they have to say, because they're claiming they have new information about who has their son."

Chapter Six

Julia changed Emily and started the bottle, but her attention was on the phone call that Russ had gotten. She could tell he was talking to Silas, but the conversation wasn't going well. Something had obviously gone wrong.

Zoey came out of her room, glanced at Russ and then joined Julia. "Is there a problem?" Zoey asked.

"Too many to name," Julia mumbled.

And after the all the danger, one of the biggest problems was Russ. She'd thought their relationship was already complicated enough, but that breast kiss had sent this crazy camaraderie spinning out of control. She needed to attend the meeting with Milo so she could take Emily and get far away from Russ. She couldn't think when he was around.

Russ finally ended the call and walked into the sitting room, but he didn't offer an immediate explanation as to why his forehead was bunched up with worry. Zoey obviously noticed there was a problem, because she took Emily and the bottle into her bedroom.

"Well?" Julia asked Russ, when he still didn't say anything.

"The stolen baby's parents are here at the hotel."

Surprised, she shook her head. "Was that planned?"

"Not even close." And his tone and body language indicated it wasn't just unplanned, it might be a huge complication. He went into the bathroom, and when he came back out, he was putting on his shirt. "I need to talk with them, because they might possibly have some new information about the case, but I want to make it look like a social meeting."

Julia thought about that a moment. "You want me to go with you?"

"I don't want you to go," he said, gritting his teeth, "but I think it's better than any alternative I can come up with. I certainly don't want to meet with them here, with Emily in the next room. And since Milo's man is still watching, I don't want him to get the idea that I'm doing a deal with another seller. That might send him to look for another buyer."

Julia nearly laughed. Not from humor, but from the irony of the situation. Two weeks ago, she'd been closeted away at her estate, only leaving a couple of times a year when it was an absolute necessity. She had even arranged to have her therapy sessions done at the estate.

Now, here she was in the middle of a dangerous FBI investigation. And while she was scared for Emily and herself, she was more frightened of not being able to get the stolen child back to his parents.

"What do you need me to do?" she asked. She sounded far more certain of herself than she was, but Russ likely knew that.

"First, get dressed. I'll give you instructions on the ride down in the elevator."

Julia forced herself to move. She hurried into the

bedroom, grabbed a wine-colored, loose-fitting dress, and sandals from the closet. She wasn't sure what a person was supposed to wear to a clandestine meeting, but she dressed as quickly as she could, put on some makeup and brushed her hair. When she finished, she found Russ talking to Zoey. Specifically, telling her to double lock the door and not let anyone in.

That nearly caused Julia to panic.

"You think Milo's man will try to sneak in here?" she asked and then held her breath.

"No," Russ answered, quickly. "But just in case, there'll be an agent in the hall outside the room. He's posing as a housekeeper."

Good. Julia would help with this investigation, but not at the expense of Emily's safety.

Russ took her by the arm and led her out of the suite, but he didn't leave the door until they heard Zoey engage both locks as Russ had instructed.

"After the two o'clock meeting with Milo, my plan is to get you and Emily out of San Saba," he explained, on the way to the elevator. He nodded to a man wearing a hotel uniform, who was in the room next to the suite changing sheets.

The undercover agent, no doubt.

"You think Milo will agree to me leaving?" she asked.

"He'll have to. One meeting is bad enough. I don't want you involved with this any longer than necessary."

"I don't want to be involved, either, but does that mean you think you'll have the little boy by this afternoon?"

"It's possible, but even if it's not, you and I are going

to stage an argument for Milo." He turned and faced her while they were in the elevator. "I want you to call me all the names you've been thinking about calling me. I want you to say it's not going to work between us, and for me to get out of your life. And then I want you to leave. An agent will keep an eye on you when you go to your car, and someone will make sure you get safely back to the hotel."

That didn't seem difficult, but it left a lot of things unanswered, too. "Then what?"

"The next part will be easy. You'll take Emily and Zoey, and leave for the estate. I'll get the Richardson baby and hand him over to his parents."

That was exactly what she wanted to hear. So, it might all be over by early afternoon. Julia didn't want to think beyond that, but she was certain this wasn't the last she'd see of Russ Gentry.

Once this investigation was over, he would return to San Antonio and challenge her for custody. The anger came with that reminder, and she could already think of some names to call him in front of Milo, when Russ and she had their fake argument.

"As for this meeting with the Richardsons, I'll just introduce you as my fiancée," Russ continued. The elevator doors swung open, but he caught onto her arm to stop her from stepping out. "And don't say too much around my partner, Silas. He's the one who told the Richardsons where we were."

Julia couldn't believe what she'd just heard. "What?"

"Yeah. That was my reaction, too. He's either incompetent or…" But Russ didn't finish the thought. "Don't worry. I've arranged for extra security for you at the meeting. I don't intend to rely on Silas for anything."

Great.

So, she was walking into a meeting with terrified parents and an idiot agent who was possibly dangerous. Julia checked her hands. She wasn't shaking, and she didn't feel a wave of panic. Maybe she'd had so much anxiety dumped on her in the past twenty-four hours that her body was adjusting.

"By the way, you look hot," Russ mumbled to her, a split-second before they walked into the café off the lobby.

"So do you," she mumbled back, and was pleased that it actually caused him to pause a step. She was betting not too many things off-balanced a man like Russ.

Russ smiled at her and ushered her toward the trio seated at a table in the corner. A tall blond woman immediately jumped from her chair.

"Her name is Tracy Richardson," Russ told Julia, in a whisper. "She's the mom, and I want you to greet her as if she were an old friend."

Julia did. She walked to the woman and pulled her into a hug, probably surprising everyone at the table, especially Tracy Richardson.

"We need to look friendly and cozy," Russ whispered to all of them. The other two men stood, as well. "Because we almost certainly have an audience."

Julia glanced around the small café and didn't see anyone suspicious, but that didn't mean Milo's man wasn't using the infrared device to watch them.

"Aaron." Russ greeted the father in a louder voice. They shook hands. "Julia's told me all about you." The thin-faced man was dressed to perfection in a dark blue suit, white shirt and Ivy League tie. He had old money written all over him, and being from old money herself, Julia recognized it.

Since the man in the suit was Aaron Richardson, that meant the other man was Silas Durant. Like Russ, she wouldn't have picked him out of the crowd as an agent, which was probably why he was one.

Silas was around six feet tall and heavily muscled, as if he'd once played football. He was younger that Russ, probably by at least five years, and he wore khakis and a pale blue shirt. Unlike Russ, who still wore jeans and a black T-shirt. His rough haircut and attire was probably the reason he'd wanted her to pretend to be friends with the Richardsons.

"I ordered all of us coffee," Tracy said, her voice shaking.

Everyone sat, but Russ's gaze was firing everywhere. He was keeping watch.

"You said you had information about who might have taken your son?" Russ prompted. He kept his voice low, and held the coffee mug in front of his mouth.

"We think our nanny, Marita Gomez, might have been involved," Tracy said.

Russ exchanged glances with Silas. "But we checked on Ms. Gomez and cleared her as a suspect. Yes, she was with your son when he was taken, but she was also clubbed on the head and had defensive wounds. It seems to us that Marita Gomez did everything within her power to stop your son from being taken."

Aaron shook his head. "Tracy found a note."

Tracy reached into her purse and produced the folded piece of paper. "It's not an actual note. I went through Marita's room and saw this pad of paper on the desk, and I thumbed through it. I didn't see any writing, but I saw these indentations on one of the last pages of paper, so I used a pencil to rub across it."

Russ unfolded the paper, and Julia glanced over and saw the numbers.

"It's a phone number," Aaron explained. "But it's probably for one of those prepaid cells that can't be traced."

"How do you know that?" Russ asked.

"Because I tried to call it, and when no one answered, I phoned directory assistance. They said the account didn't have any minutes remaining, so it was no longer active. Now, why would Marita have been calling someone with a prepaid phone?"

Julia could think of one reason—maybe the nanny was phoning a friend who just happened to have that type of cell service.

"If you thought this was important," Russ said, "you should have turned it in to the FBI office near your home in Houston."

"We couldn't. I had to see you, to show you." Tracy's voice was still a whisper, but the low tone couldn't conceal the emotion.

"Tracy." Julia reached across the table and placed her hand on the woman's. "It'll be okay. They'll find your son."

Tracy stiffened, probably because she didn't care for the intimate gesture offered to her by a stranger, but she finally nodded. "Silas said it could all be over soon. I pray he's right."

From the corner of her eye, Julia saw Russ scowl. Like her, he was probably wondering what else Silas had told them that he shouldn't have.

"Here's what I need you to do." Russ set down his

coffee cup and directed his comments to the Richardsons. "I need you to go home and wait."

"You're not helping by being here," Silas added. "In fact, you could jeopardize the plan for us to rescue your son."

Tracy gasped, and tears instantly sprang to her eyes. Beside her, her husband didn't make a move to comfort her as Julia had done.

"We can put up more money," Aaron told Russ. "When you meet with the buyer, offer him two million."

"Three," Tracy insisted. "Or more. Offer him whatever he wants. I just want Matthew back safely with me."

Aaron didn't immediately jump to agree to that, but he finally nodded. "Offer them whatever's necessary."

"Money might not be an issue if the seller loses trust in me," Russ pointed out. "So, finish your coffee, hug Julia goodbye, and then leave. If anyone asks, you were in town on business and dropped by the hotel to say a quick hello to an old friend. That's it."

Aaron gulped down the coffee and shook his head. "I knew we shouldn't have come. I told Tracy, but she wouldn't listen."

"Because you didn't listen to me," Tracy fired back. "I can't sit around like a block of ice, waiting." She looked at Julia. "I just can't."

Julia could relate, unfortunately. If Emily had been taken, she would have done worse than shown up in the San Saba. She would have P.I.s out searching for the baby, and no one—not even the FBI—could have stopped her.

Tracy took a sip of coffee and seemed to calm down a bit. "I'm sorry. I haven't been myself since Matthew was taken. I shouldn't have had the nanny take him to his pediatric checkup. If I'd been with him, I would have fought to the death to stop them from taking him." Her pale green eyes landed on Russ, then Silas. "You're doing your best. I know that. But please check on the nanny. Make sure she wasn't calling the person who stole Matthew."

"Let's go," Aaron insisted, getting to his feet.

Tracy stood, too, and as Russ had instructed, she gave Julia a hug. "Please," she whispered to Julia. "Bring my baby back to me."

"I'll try," Julia promised. She watched them walk out of the café, and then sank back in her chair next to Russ. "What now?"

But Russ didn't answer. His attention was on Silas. "We'll talk later," Russ said. And it sounded like a warning.

"You have a right to be upset—" Silas started.

"I said we'll talk later," Russ interrupted.

Silas looked ready to argue, but his phone rang. He glanced down at the screen and then excused himself so he could walk to the other side of the room and take the call.

"You don't trust him?" Julia asked, following Russ's suddenly stony gaze that was aimed at his partner.

"I'm not sure." He blew out a weary breath and scrubbed his hand over his face. "But then, I'm not sure I trust the Richardsons. Meeting them was a real eye-opener."

"What do you mean?" she asked.

"I mean they put their son in more danger by coming here. They're not stupid, and they should have known that."

"True, but I think they're working from a purely emotional level. Well, Tracy is anyway. I'm not so sure about Aaron. He seems immune to her tears."

"Yeah. Their marriage doesn't seem to be on solid ground, does it?"

Julia agreed. "This might seem like a callous question, but why are you, as the intended buyer, offering so much money for the child? I mean, won't the large amount make Milo suspicious? Because I suspect someone greedy and resourceful, like your theoretical buyer, could go into a poor neighborhood and buy a child for far less than a million."

Russ nodded. "That happens. But Milo's selling the Richardsons' baby as a blue blood. Solid genes. Good potential. And the other thing Milo's got going for him is that, initially, he had more than one buyer. Or so he said. We think it was a ploy to pump up the price, but he turned down our initial bid. When we upped the price, it was accepted."

"Accepted," Julia mumbled, in disgust. And if Russ had been a real baby broker, then the money would have been exchanged, and the child would be forever lost to his parents.

Julia wasn't in the mood for coffee, but she drank some, and hoped the caffeine would ease the headache she had from lack of sleep. "Will you do more checking on the nanny?"

"I will. And I'll check more on the Richardsons, too…." The last part of that trailed off, because Silas returned to the table.

The man didn't sit, and there were beads of sweat on his upper lip. "We have a problem."

Russ groaned. "Not with Milo."

"Yes, Milo," Silas confirmed. "That was one of his henchmen on the phone. Milo wants to change the time of the meeting."

Julia's stomach clenched. "Not another delay?"

Silas shook his head. "Just the opposite. Milo says the meeting happens now, or it doesn't happen at all. He's giving you fifteen minutes to get to the state park. If you're not there, then the sale is off, and he finds another buyer."

Chapter Seven

Russ pulled Julia's Jaguar into the space at the far end of the parking lot of Mendoza State Park. In the hurried instructions he'd gotten on the drive over, it was where the head of the security detail, Chris Soto, had told him to park. It was a spot where the agents could keep Julia and him under surveillance.

But it was also a spot that left them out in the open.

Russ wasn't sure he liked that. Yes, it would make it easier for security to keep an eye on them, but he felt too exposed. Normally, he would have just accepted it as part of the job, but with Julia there, he didn't want to blindly accept anything.

"The fifteen minutes are nearly up," Julia pointed out. For the entire ride, she had her attention fastened to her watch.

Time was indeed running out, but Russ still took a moment to check their surroundings. He didn't see any agents on the security detail, which was probably a good thing, because that meant they were adequately hidden. But there were people milling about—families using the playground equipment and joggers on the red gravel track that wound through the park.

If Milo was indeed planning some kind of attack here, he'd have to do it in a very public place. Hopefully, Milo wouldn't want to draw that type of attention to himself.

"Here's the one rule you have to remember," Russ told Julia, "if anything—and I mean anything—goes wrong, you run for cover."

She nodded and drew in several shallow breaths. She was pale and trembling, too, but she didn't look to be on the verge of a panic attack. Well not yet, anyway. The meeting hadn't even started.

He checked to make sure his gun was in place in the slide holster at the back of his jeans. It was. Milo might search him and find the weapon, but Milo already believed that Russ was no saint. The man would no doubt expect Russ to be armed. Of course, Milo might also demand that Russ surrender the gun, but that was something he'd deal with if it came up.

Russ opened the car door, and Julia got out with him. Russ waited until she was by his side before they started the short walk to the picnic table that was just off a grassy path. Above the table was a flat, wooden roof, but the sides were wide-open.

Milo was there, sitting at the table and smoking a cigarette. And he wasn't alone. There was a tall, auburn-haired woman with him. Not seated. She appeared to be pacing. She wore a pale blue business suit. Which meant she could be carrying a concealed weapon.

"Who is she?" Julia asked in a whisper.

"I'm not sure."

Russ stopped, even though Milo and the woman had obviously spotted them, and he fired off a text message to Silas asking him for details. He hated to use Silas for this or anything else, but with the rush on the meeting, there hadn't been time to request another agent.

Sylvia Hartman, Silas texted back, *Milo's asst. Not armed.*

Good on the "not armed" part. But it did make Russ wonder why Silas hadn't called him about this possible glitch. Of course, with all the chaos going on to get Julia and him to the location, and arranging for an agent to guard Emily, Silas had likely had his hands full. For this, Russ would give the agent the benefit of the doubt.

"Jimmy," Milo greeted him. He didn't stand, nor did he put out his cigarette. But he did turn his attention to Julia. "So glad you could make it."

"You didn't give me a choice," Julia fired back.

Milo gave a brief, oily smile. "True. I thought your fiancé might want to speed things along if you were with him."

"And what about her?" Russ asked, indicating Sylvia. "Is she here to speed things along, too?"

"Absolutely," the woman insisted. "I'm Sylvia Hartman. I work for Milo."

She took what seemed to be a PDA from her purse, but it wasn't a PDA. Russ knew what was about to happen next.

Sylvia moved closer to them, and without actually touching them, she ran the device first over Russ. Then, Julia.

"They aren't wearing wires," Sylvia said to Milo.

"Are you?" Russ demanded of Milo.

"No need for one," Milo said calmly. "I can relay anything said here to my boss."

To Z, the real buyer behind all of this. And that

meant someone from the FBI would follow Milo from this meeting. So far though, following hadn't helped. Agents had tailed him the night before when he'd left the alley next to the bar, but the man had simply gone home.

"Now that I'm sure we can talk in private," Sylvia continued, "I can tell you that I've been dealing with the details of the *possible* transfer."

"Possible?" Russ demanded, aiming that at Milo and not his assistant.

"Possible," Milo repeated. "Why don't you sit, and we'll discuss it."

"I'd prefer to stand. And I'd prefer to hurry. Julia's anxious to get back."

"I'm sure she is." Milo let that hang in the air for several moments. "What, with her being a new mom and all. Hmmm. You certainly look good for a woman who just had a baby two weeks ago."

Julia shrugged and looked surprisingly calm. "I'll pass that along to my personal trainer."

Russ nearly smiled. Nearly. But he didn't care for the way Milo was studying Julia.

"If we're done with small talk," Russ started, "can we finally get down to business?"

It was Sylvia who answered, not Milo. "Sure. We assume your buyer is still onboard with this?"

Russ nodded. "Absolutely."

"Good. Because the exchange will take place tomorrow night, right here in the park."

Russ was shaking his head before she finished. "Tomorrow night? Why not sooner? The buyer's anxious to get this over with."

"Well, we're anxious, too," Sylvia insisted, "but it

can't happen before tomorrow. Logistics issues. I'm sure you understand."

"No. I don't, and my buyer won't be pleased." Russ didn't know how far he could push this. He wanted the deal to go down sooner than later, but he didn't want to blow it completely by not budging on the final hour.

"Well?" Milo questioned. "Does that mean everything is off?"

Russ took his time answering. Even though Milo seemed beyond calm, he hoped the man was as unsettled about this as Russ was. "Everything's on. What time?"

"Eight p.m.," Sylvia said. "Now, as for payment. The seller has had a change of heart."

Beside him, Russ felt Julia tense. "What the hell does that mean?" Russ asked.

"He no longer wants one million. He wants two."

Russ cursed. "For one kid? Come on. Two million?" Even though the Richardsons had agreed to that and more, Russ didn't want to put more of their money on the table if it wasn't necessary. "The agreement was for one."

Sylvia glanced at Milo, and he was the one to continue. "The seller is aware that the baby's parents might be willing to compensate him more than your buyer."

And this was something Milo would have known right from the start. "So why not just go to the parents?"

Milo gave another of those smiles and put his cigarette out on the table. "Because it's too risky. The parents have probably contacted the authorities, and any exchange might be…scrutinized. We'd rather deal with you and your buyer. The question is, would you rather deal with us?"

Again, Russ hesitated, and he looked at Julia to see how she was handling all of this. She was nibbling on her bottom lip, but there were still no signs of panic.

"I'll contact the buyer," Russ finally said. "But if he agrees to the substantial jump in price, then that's it. That's the bottom line. I don't want you jerking us around."

Milo stood and stared at Russ from the other side of the picnic table. "Ditto."

"Am I supposed to know what that means?" Russ made sure he looked Milo straight in the eyes when he asked that.

But Milo only shrugged. "Tomorrow. Eight p.m." He reached in his pocket and extracted a folded piece of notepaper. "That's the bank where we want the money deposited. Once we've verified the deposit, you'll get the goods."

"Not so fast," Russ tossed back. "Who will be at this meeting?"

"Me, of course. You. And Sylvia. The baby will be nearby."

"*How* nearby?" Russ demanded.

"Within minutes. Don't worry. We have no desire to keep this child any longer than absolutely necessary, and I'm sure your buyers feel the same."

"Buyer," Russ corrected.

But maybe Milo hadn't made a mistake. After all, the Richardsons had come to the hotel, and Milo could have figured out who they were. Milo might even believe the parents hadn't gone to the cops and were now in the running to outbid any other buyer to get their baby back.

"Right," Milo murmured. He walked closer and extended his hand for Russ to shake. Russ did, though he wanted to grab the SOB and beat the information out of him. Maybe before this was over, he'd get the chance to make Milo pay for this.

"Julia," Milo said, in the same tone as a goodbye. But he still took a moment to look her over from head to toe. It wasn't a casual look, but one from a man who was admiring the view.

Russ shot the man a glare. Yet another reason to beat him senseless.

Milo only smiled, turned and walked away. But Sylvia didn't. She stayed put and stared at both of them.

"Nothing can go wrong tomorrow night," Sylvia said, her voice practically a whisper now. And she certainly wasn't as calm as she'd been with Milo around.

Russ decided to push that lack of calmness a bit. "I don't want anything to go wrong, either, but my buyer is only willing to go so far. No more price jumps. No changes on the meeting time and place. This goes down just as we agreed."

She didn't nod, but she did swallow hard and walk closer. "There's a lot at stake here. Milo's anxious." Sylvia looked at Julia. "Mainly because of you. He didn't like that you just showed up here in San Saba when things were all coming to a conclusion."

"I didn't know about this deal," Julia insisted. "I came to tell Jimmy about the baby, that's all. I had no idea about Jimmy's deal with Milo."

"And I don't want her involved in this," Russ added.

"I especially don't want her at the exchange tomorrow night."

"I don't think it'll be possible to exclude Julia," Sylvia said, under her breath. She glanced around, as if to make sure no one was listening. Then, she moved even closer to Julia. "Milo is going to insist you be there."

Ah, hell. Russ was afraid this was going to happen. That's why he'd insisted on knowing who would be at the meeting. "Give me Milo's number. I need to talk to him."

"It won't do any good. As I said, he's anxious. He thinks this could all be a sting operation."

And Russ could perhaps thank the Richardsons for that. Milo might not have known who they were, but anyone's arrival at this point could have given him reason to be alarmed.

"For your sake, I hope it's not a sting," Sylvia continued. "Or anything else, other than a simple sale." She didn't direct that comment to Russ but to Julia.

"Is that some kind of warning?" Julia demanded.

"You bet it is." Sylvia gathered her things from the table. "Because Milo said, if anything goes wrong at the meeting tomorrow night, then he'll retaliate by taking your daughter."

JULIA TRIED NOT TO PANIC, but it was nearly impossible to stay calm. She didn't even wait for Sylvia to leave before starting for her car. She had to get back to the hotel so she could protect Emily.

While they ran, Russ took out his phone and punched in some numbers. "Lock down the Wainwright Hotel," he told the agent who answered. "Milo might try to take the baby from Julia's suite."

"It'll be okay," Russ told Julia, the moment he hung up. "Sylvia said Milo would only go after Emily *if* there was a problem with tomorrow night's meeting. We just have to make sure there won't be any problems."

Well, there was a huge one. Milo wanted her to be there, and Julia wasn't sure she could go through with it now. She wanted desperately to help the Richardsons get their son back, but she couldn't do that at Emily's expense. She had to take Emily and go into hiding, at least until Russ had all of this resolved.

She didn't want to think about how long that might take.

"An agent is outside your room," Russ reminded her when they reached the parking lot. But Julia could hear the concern in his whispered voice, and it was written all over his face.

She wanted to kick herself. Here she'd gone miles out of her comfort zone to keep the deathbed promise to Lissa, and now Emily might have to pay the price. This is what she got for taking a dangerous chance that she shouldn't have taken.

Russ used her keychain to unlock the car doors, and Julia hurried to get inside so they could drive back to the hotel. She wasn't far from the door, only about a yard away, when she heard the sound.

A loud pop.

At first Julia thought it was the sound of a car back-firing, but she thought differently when Russ yelled, "Get down!"

But he didn't just yell. He dove at her and pulled her to the ground. She hit hard, and her elbows and knees scraped against the rough concrete when Russ pushed her against the metal rim of her front tire.

There was another loud sound, and she saw concrete spraying from the pavement. And that's when Julia knew that someone was shooting at them.

She choked back a scream and tried to get up so she could get into the car, but Russ held her in place by crawling over her. He also drew his gun. He was obviously trying to protect her, but she couldn't see how that would help, especially if he got shot.

Or killed.

They could both die here. And *then* what would happen to Emily? Was Milo going after her right now? Was that what this was really all about? Maybe he wanted Russ and her pinned down like this so he could kidnap Emily.

Julia struggled, trying to get to the car, but Russ pushed her right back down until she was pressed against the tire. She couldn't figure out why he wouldn't let her just reach up and grab the door handle so she could jump inside, but she soon figured it out.

The next bullet landed just behind them and to the right, and it kicked up another spray of concrete and dust. Judging from the direction the bullet had come, the shooter was somewhere on the other side of her car.

Maybe *directly* on the other side.

There were other vehicles around hers, but it was hard to see. Worse, there were massive trees that towered over the park and the parking lot. The shooter could be in one of those or even in the two-story office building near the park entrance.

She heard someone yell, and all around were the

sounds of people running and calling for help. Hopefully, no one had been shot, but if the gunman kept firing, there was a possibility of that. Julia remembered all the families and children she'd seen. Every one of them was at risk.

But the shooter only seemed to have Russ and her in his sights.

There was another shot. Then another. Both came too close and stirred up more concrete dust. It was hard to see. And even harder for Russ to return fire. With everyone now running and screaming, he couldn't risk shooting someone who just happened to get in the way.

But they couldn't stay put, either.

"Emily," she reminded him. She glanced over her shoulder at him, but his attention was darting all around the parking lot, including behind them.

"I know." He took out his cell and made another call. "Where is this SOB?" he yelled into the phone.

She was close to both Russ and the phone, but Julia didn't hear the answer because another round of gunfire drowned it out. The shot tore through the windows of her Jag, and pellets of safety glass fell to the ground beside them.

The next bullet came through the hood of the car.

It gashed through the metal and just missed Russ's head. Julia didn't want to know how close it'd come to killing him.

Russ ducked down, thank God, and yelled for backup to respond.

Julia prayed it wouldn't take long for that to happen. After all, backup should have already been in place. Well, if Silas had done his job, it should have been. She suddenly didn't like relying on a man Russ didn't seem to trust.

There was the squeal of tires, and from the corner of her eye, she saw a black car come to a jarring stop at the edge of the parking lot. Her heart dropped.

Was this Milo's men?

But Russ didn't move, and he didn't take aim at the two men who barreled out of the car. Both men were dressed in street clothes and were armed, one with a rifle and the other, a handgun. They took cover behind their vehicle but aimed their weapons in the direction of one of the massive trees. Russ aimed his gun there as well.

The shots stopped.

"The gunman's getting away," Russ spat out, adding a profanity.

He motioned toward the men who had gotten out of the black car, and one of them started to make his way toward Russ and Julia. Not in a straight line. He used some of the other vehicles as cover, and he inched his way across the parking lot until he got to them.

"Guard Julia," Russ told the man. "Get her back to the hotel."

Obviously, this guy was an agent, but she didn't understand Russ's "guard Julia" instructions.

Not until Russ moved away from her.

"I'll join you at the hotel as soon as I can," Russ said to her.

"You're not going after that gunman." She tried to catch onto his arm, but Russ shook off her grip.

"That's exactly what I'm doing."

Chapter Eight

Russ heard Julia beg him not to go, but he tuned her out so he could focus on the gunman. There was no way he was going to let this SOB get away with trying to kill them—even if that meant he'd have to do yet more damage control so he didn't blow his cover with Milo.

If there was anything left of his cover not to blow.

Someone had sent this gunman after Julia and him, and Milo was at the top of Russ's suspect list.

Somehow, he had to end this latest threat and gather all the pieces, so he could put them in place. But for now, his first priority was to stop a would-be killer.

He checked over his shoulder and made sure Julia was getting in the car with one of the agents. She was, but she wasn't going voluntarily. The agent was shoving her into the backseat of the vehicle. The adrenaline had ahold of her now. She was in fight mode, but it wouldn't take her long to remember that she needed to be back at the hotel with Emily. Once that happened, Russ could be sure both of them were as safe as they could possibly be.

It was up to him to make sure they stayed safe.

Ducking behind shrubs and playground equipment,

he looked in the direction of a clump of tall live oak trees. If the gunman was still there, the thick branches and leaves were hiding him; but Russ suspected he was already on the ground, or making his way down that tree as fast as he could.

He kept his gun aimed and ready, and he shouted for the park visitors to evacuate. He certainly didn't need a stray bullet hitting an innocent bystander.

Russ got beneath a tall metal slide so he could take a better look into those trees. But he saw no one.

His phone rang, and while he looked all around him to avoid an ambush, he also glanced at the caller-ID screen. It was Silas. Russ had a five-second debate with himself about answering it, but he knew he had to hear what his partner had to say. Besides, this call might be about Julia or Emily.

"Get out of there now," Silas told him, the moment he came on the line. "Milo had a man watching. He's waiting to see what you'll do."

"What I'm going to do is kill the SOB who fired those shots at Julia."

"You can't. I'm going in pursuit. Yeah, it'll blow my cover as the buyer, but Milo thinks the Richardsons are the real buyers anyway."

No doubt. But that was only one of the issues they'd have to resolve. "What about the agents who took Julia?" Russ asked. "Milo's man saw that happen, too."

"We'll convince him that they were your hired guns." Silas sounded out of breath, as if he had been running, but Russ couldn't see the man anywhere in the park. "We can create fake IDs for them and plant some bogus employment records that'll link them to you. They're waiting at the park entrance for you to get in the car."

His stomach dropped. "Waiting? I told them to get Julia to the hotel."

"I told them to wait for you. It's the only thing that makes sense, Russ. Now, get the hell out of here, or we might end up losing the Richardson kid."

Russ wanted badly to argue. Like Julia, he was primed for a fight, and he didn't want to let this shooter walk. Still, he couldn't blow the investigation.

He couldn't just turn and make a run for the car. Russ had to get out of the park in the same cautious way he'd come in—because it was possible the gunman was still in that tree waiting for an opportunity to shoot him.

Russ hurried. He didn't want Julia waiting out in the open any longer than necessary, and he finally spotted the black sedan parked on the side of the road at the entrance. Other vehicles were speeding away, and the San Saba cops were responding with seemingly every unit they had. The air was filled with the sound of sirens and people shouting.

The back door opened when Russ was just a few feet away, and he got in before he cops could see him. He didn't want to have to explain his gun or his lack of a badge. Especially since Silas had already warned him that one of Milo's men was watching.

Julia was the one who opened the door for him, Russ soon learned. She was there on the backseat, and she grabbed his arm to pull him inside so he could shut the door. The moment he did that, the agent behind the wheel drove away. Not speeding. He didn't want to do anything to draw attention to them so they'd be stopped. Russ's supervisor and Silas would be the ones to fill in the local police on what was happening.

"You're okay," she said, her voice filled with breath and nerves.

Was he? Maybe physically he was, but inside he felt as if he were battling a hurricane. He looked at the scrapes on her knees and cursed. "You're hurt."

She shook her head. "Just worried. I called Zoey. Emily and she are okay. For now."

That was good. But Julia was indeed hurt. He'd have to tend to those scrapes and check for anything more serious.

Unlike at the meeting, she looked on the verge of losing it. Russ hooked his arm around her and pulled her to him. "It'll be okay," he promised. But it was a promise he wasn't sure he could keep. Still, he would try, no matter the cost.

"We need to get to the Wainwright Hotel," Russ reminded the agents.

He knew both of them—Kevin Lopez and Chris Soto—and knew he could trust them. If they'd been available at the beginning of his investigation, he would have requested either of them for a partner.

"Silas," Russ mumbled.

"What about him?" Julia asked.

"He went after the shooter." Perhaps without FBI backup, since the two security detail agents were with Russ. But maybe Silas would get lucky and be able to apprehend the guy and haul him in for questioning. Russ had a dozen things he wanted to ask, including first and foremost—who had ordered him to fire those shots?

Unless Milo was the shooter.

That thought caused him to rethink his hired gun theory. Milo had left in plenty of time to get up in that tree. If he had a rifle already planted there, he could have been the one to take the shots. And if it was him, Russ would make him pay. As soon as the Richardson baby was safe, that is.

"Emily has to be all right," Julia whispered.

"She will be. But I have to move her to a safe house. You know that, right?"

There were tears in her eyes when she pulled back a little and met his gaze. "I know."

"Just hang on," he told her, and tightened his grip. All he could do was sit there and hold her.

Russ wanted to punch himself for allowing this to happen to her. Julia didn't need this in her head, not with all the other nightmares she already had to manage. Unfortunately, this new nightmare wasn't close to being over.

"Get started on the arrangements for the safe house and try to find some place local, so the move can happen ASAP," Russ told the agents, when they pulled to a stop in front of the hotel. "I also want any surveillance disks from the park. I saw some security cameras, so let's hope they were on and working."

"Anything else?" Chris Soto asked.

"Yeah. I need to speak with Milo. Find a way for that to happen. I don't have a number, because he uses only prepaid cells, but you might be able to reach him through his assistant, Sylvia Hartman."

The agents assured him they would get right on his requests, and Russ didn't waste any more time. He got Julia out of the car and into the hotel. The lobby had several people milling around, all of whom suddenly looked suspicious. Hell, everything was suspect right now and would be until he had answers.

There was a guard outside Julia's suite door, but Russ didn't dismiss him. He ordered him to stay put while he knocked and told Zoey to open the door. The woman did, and like Julia, she looked worried. Julia rushed past her and into the bedroom suite. Russ was right behind her, and they both saw Emily sleeping in her crib.

"You haven't had any visitors or calls, have you?" Russ whispered to Zoey.

"Just the call from Julia. Are we in danger?"

Because he didn't want to wake the baby, he took Zoey out into the sitting room. "No," he lied. "But as a precaution, I'm moving all of you to an FBI safe house. Don't call anyone. Don't tell anyone what's going on. I just need you to pack your things and get ready. Then wait in your room with the door locked and the curtains closed," he added.

Zoey gave a shaky nod and hurried toward her room. Russ then turned his full attention to Julia, who was no doubt ready for a panic attack. But he did a double take. Yes, there were the remnants of tears in her eyes, but she didn't have the pale, clammy look as she'd had after the alley meeting with Milo.

"I can't go to the safe house," Julia insisted.

"Excuse me?" Because Russ was sure he'd understood her.

She lifted her hands, which were scratched, and then quickly hid them behind her back when she noticed the damage. "If I'm not there for the meeting, Milo said it wouldn't take place."

He just stared at her. "After what just happened, I

don't intend to trust Milo about anything, much less a meeting that involves you being just inches away from him."

"Then what about the baby?" she asked.

Yeah. That was the two-million-dollar question. "If the shooter isn't Milo, then my next step is to call him. To tell him I don't trust him. I want his boss, Z, to find someone else to use as a go-between. Sylvia, maybe." Even though he didn't trust Milo's assistant, either. Sylvia might have given them the warning about Emily, but the woman was dirty by association, because no one legal and above-board would voluntarily work for a man like Milo.

"All I'm saying is I need to be available," Julia explained. Her voice broke on the last word. "And I can't be available if I'm shut away in a safe house. What if Milo wants another meeting in fifteen minutes? What if I'm not there and he finds another buyer?"

Russ was about to argue, even if the argument he had in mind made no sense, but Julia reached out and put her hand around the back of his neck. She pulled him down to her and kissed him.

In the back of his mind, Russ considered that she was kissing him to get him to shut up. He considered it. Accepted it.

And because he needed to feel her in his arms, he kissed her right back. The mouth-to-mouth contact didn't soothe him exactly, but it helped when he felt Julia's muscles relax a little.

The taste of her went right through him, turning his anger and rage into something warm. Something that felt too damn right for something so wrong.

He pulled back not because he wanted the kiss to

stop, but because he knew it shouldn't continue. He needed to check her for injuries, and it didn't take him long to find them. In addition to the scratches on her knees, there were some on her elbows, as well.

Russ double-locked the front room door and took her by the arm. "Come with me."

He had her sit on the bed, and he went to the bathroom to get a wet washcloth. The curtains were also closed tight, so he shut the bedroom door, too, and locked it. Double precaution since Emily was in the room with them. If he could figure out a triple one, he'd take it, too.

Russ knelt in front of her and got to work, trying to be as gentle as he could. Still, Julia winced.

"Sorry," he mumbled.

"It's all right. It has to be done." She kept her voice soft and low, probably so she wouldn't wake Emily. "I didn't have a panic attack."

"I noticed." He pressed the cloth to her right knee and looked up at her. "Want to have one now? There's time."

The corner of her mouth lifted, but it didn't stay there long. "When the bullets were coming at us, all I could think about was Emily. I was terrified something bad would happen to her."

"Yeah. I know." Russ had had those same fears. But not just for Emily. For Julia, too. He wouldn't have been able to forgive himself if something worse had happened to her in that parking lot.

"I realized just how important Emily is to me," Julia continued. "And how I would feel if someone took her."

Hell.

Russ knew where this was leading. "Julia, no one

expects you to help with an FBI investigation. Better yet, I don't want you to help. I want you to be safe."

She touched his cheek with her fingertips. "I will be, because you'll be with me."

"Right," he growled, moving her hand away. He recognized that maneuver. She was trying to soothe him. The woman sure learned fast. "You noticed what a good job I did of protecting you today," he mumbled, in disgust.

"Actually, I did notice." Unlike him, there was no sarcasm in her voice. "You shielded me with your own body. You put yourself in the line of fire for me."

Russ wasn't comfortable with her gratitude. He damn well didn't deserve any credit for reacting *after* the danger was right on them. If he'd done things right, if he'd anticipated better, he might have been able to get her out of there before the bullets started.

She caught onto his face again, this time with both hands. "You can't put me ahead of the Richardson baby," she whispered. "And I can't put my fears ahead of him, either."

He stared at her and thought of a lot of things he could say. Russ settled for probably the dumbest one of the bunch. "Who the hell *are* you? Are you the same woman I met in the bar yesterday?"

"I'm Julia Howell, recluse heiress and occasional neurotic. Who the hell are you? Are you the same cocky guy who put his hand up my dress?"

"Absolutely. I haven't changed a bit."

"Liar," she said, and her mouth came to his again.

Unlike the other kiss, there was no desperation in this one. No unspoken need for comfort.

Man, he was a goner.

The air left the room. It left his lungs too, but he didn't need air to feel. One kiss from her, one touch of his tongue to hers, and Russ was already thinking about stripping off her clothes and having sex.

But it couldn't happen.

For one thing, Emily was sleeping just yards away. *Sleeping,* his body reminded him. On the other side of the room. Far away. With her head turned in the opposite direction. Not that she could see them from that far away anyway.

Zoey was in the next room. *The door is locked,* his body reminded him. Besides, Zoey was packing, and he'd told her to stay in her room.

A third argument came to mind—and it was a biggie—Julia was a virgin. If they ever did have sex, it couldn't be something quick and dirty. Well, not the first time anyway.

But the point was, they couldn't have sex right here, right now. Even if his idiot erection had a different take on things.

He started to get up from his kneeling position, but Julia apparently had other ideas, too. It didn't help matters when she moved closer, her knees sliding against his lower chest. Her dress slid too, right up her thighs, but she didn't stop until he was against the bed. And between her legs.

The kiss got hotter. Deeper. He shaped her lips with his, the pressure much harder than he figured it should be. But Russ just kept on, and did his own share of making matters worse when he hooked his arm around and moved her closer still.

With her dress hiked up, it didn't take much effort

for Russ to ease his hand into the back of her panties. Over her bare bottom.

The woman had some curves.

He was playing with fire, but Russ was quickly reaching the point where he didn't care if he burned to death.

He spotted more curves when she leaned down further, and he got a look down her dress. *Mercy.* He fumbled with the tiny buttons on the front and got enough of them undone so he could unclip her bra.

Russ was sure he'd died and gone to heaven when her breasts spilled into his hands.

He looked up at her to make sure she wasn't about to panic, then he rolled his eyes. No panic. Just the face of a hot woman silently saying *take me*. Russ didn't think that was his erection talking, either. Julia was sending out some serious sex vibes.

"We can't," he reminded her. Russ wet his fingers with his mouth and brushed them over her left nipple. She moaned. What a sound. So Russ did it again, just so he could hear her. And then he pleasured both her and himself by taking that already damp nipple into his mouth.

"We can't," she repeated. Her hands raced over him, as if she didn't know what part of him to pull closer, and she wrapped her legs around him.

"I'm not panicking," Julia mumbled, sounding stunned and completely aroused. "I should be. I always do."

"Well, you'd better start panicking soon," Russ countered, "because neither of us is listening to that 'we can't' logic. And we really can't have sex with the baby in the room."

That stopped her. Her breath was gusting, her breasts reacting to those gusts and tempting his mouth with each little movement. Russ had to close his eyes to keep from pulling her back to him.

"You're right," she conceded.

But Russ didn't celebrate the victory of finally getting one of them to back off. It didn't feel like a victory when he could barely walk, but he did manage to get himself off the floor. Once he'd accomplished that, he fixed her bra and buttoned her dress. He then pushed her legs back together so he couldn't see her lacy panties.

"You think this was a danger response?" she asked. "Maybe because we came so close to dying, we needed to feel a human connection?"

Russ wanted to agree with her, but he didn't want to lie. "No. I think we just have the hots for each other. It doesn't make sense. Everything about my investigation is going to hell in a hand basket, and I keep thinking about getting you into bed."

"I keep thinking about that, too," she mumbled.

He gave her a flat response. "That didn't help."

Because this had to end now, Russ took out his phone and went into the sitting room so he could get some updates. He scrolled through his contacts and found the one labeled Pizza Delivery, and he called it.

"Cheesy Jack's Pizza," the man answered. It was Special Agent Chris Soto, the man who'd driven them to the hotel. All the numbers in Russ's phone were coded in case someone like Milo got their hands on it, and the security detail's number had been listed as a pizza place.

"It's me, Russ." He gave them a code word to prove who he was. "Tell me you have good news."

"Some good, some bad. Some very bad."

Russ mentally cursed and tried to brace himself for the "very bad" news.

"No luck getting in touch with Milo," Soto explained, "but the safe house is nearly ready, and we're using a place that's local, just on the edge of town. We just have to put a few more things in place. Oh, and the surveillance disks from the park are on the way over. We don't know if they'll have anything on them, but as soon as they arrive, I'll figure out a way to get them to you."

"Deliver them in a pizza box," Russ suggested. "And what about the shooter?"

Soto's hesitation said it all. Russ groaned. Was this the bad news? "He got away?"

"For now. But we have a description, and we know which direction he was headed when he got into a dark green compact car. The description doesn't match Milo or anyone else who's been involved in this case, so we believe it might have been a hired gun."

That was not what Russ wanted to hear. He wanted the man in custody so they could get some answers.

"Silas lost him," Russ mumbled.

"Maybe." And that was all Soto said for several seconds. "But maybe not. You know that very bad news I mentioned? Well, it's about Silas."

Chapter Nine

Julia sank down onto the foot of the bed to watch and wait as Russ finished his call. She could tell from Russ's side of the conversation that he was talking to a fellow agent. She could also tell that he'd just learned something disturbing. He cursed and stared up at the ceiling for a moment, before coming back into the room with her.

"Silas Durant is missing," Russ told her.

Julia had braced herself for him to say that Silas was dead, that the shooter had killed him; or even worse, that the shooter was on the way to the hotel, but this was news she hadn't expected.

"Missing?" she questioned. "You're sure he's not dead?"

"We're not sure of anything except that he's not answering his phone, and no one has seen him since he went in pursuit of the gunman. No shots were heard after Silas left the park area on foot. An eyewitness saw the gunman drive away and was able to give us a description, but the witness didn't see anyone, including Silas, anywhere near the guy."

Julia shook her head. "Maybe the gunman had a partner? Or Milo took Silas?"

Russ eased down on the bed next to her. "Well, we know Milo wasn't the shooter, so there really wouldn't be a logical reason for Milo to take Silas, even if he'd learned that Silas was a federal agent. If Milo knew that, he'd simply leave. After all, his boss and he have the ultimate bargaining tool—the baby. Kidnapping an agent would be a complication neither would want."

That made sense, but then it still didn't explain why Silas was missing. Russ hadn't completely trusted the man, so therefore, neither had she; but she hoped he wasn't injured, or worse, and was lying somewhere just waiting to be found.

Russ's phone rang again, and Julia immediately glanced at the crib, figuring the sound would wake Emily. The baby stirred but went right back to sleep. Still, Julia got up so she could check on her. It was amazing, but just looking at the little girl could tamp down Julia's nerves. Right now, she needed all the help she could get.

Thanks to the Milo situation—and Russ.

She considered berating herself for the kissing session on the bed. Here she'd hung on to her virginity like some deep, ugly scar that wouldn't fade, and now she seemed more than willing to surrender herself to a man she barely knew.

Except, she did know him. She'd learned a lot about Russ when he'd insisted on raising his dead brother's child. Many men would have just stepped back rather than stepped up. He'd stepped up all right, and was willing to change his life for the baby. She wasn't sure she'd ever met anyone like that.

And she was falling for him.

Julia wanted to dismiss her feelings as pure sexual

attraction, but unfortunately it was deeper than that. Maybe it was their crazy, dangerous circumstances that had created this bond between them. Maybe it was Emily. Either way, the bond was there, and when this investigation was over, Julia was going to have to decide what to do about it.

"The safe house is ready," Russ told her, when he ended the call. "It won't be too far away, so that when this ends, you'll be able to see Emily almost right away."

"But what about Milo's man, the one who was watching the hotel? It won't be safe for Emily to leave if he's still out there."

"He won't be out there much longer. Someone from the San Saba PD is about to arrest him. The charge will be bogus, of course, but it'll get him away from the hotel long enough, and there shouldn't be enough time for Milo to get another man in place."

"Good." That was something, at least. She wanted every possible advantage for Emily.

"The agents are on their way up to get Zoey and Emily," Russ explained. "You, too, if you've changed your mind."

"I haven't changed my mind." Though she wanted to. She didn't want to be away from Emily for even a few hours, much less days. But this was something she had to do.

Russ just stared at her a moment, as if he might try to change her mind, but he didn't. He picked up Emily's diaper bag from the nightstand and began to pack it with the spare diapers and wipes that were next to it.

"You need to get Zoey," Russ let her know.

Julia nodded, gave Emily one last look and went

to Zoey's room. The nanny was already packed and waiting at the door. "Remember," Julia reminded her, "don't tell anyone where you're going."

"I won't. You're not coming with us?"

"No." Julia didn't get into her reasons why. The less Zoey knew about the missing baby, the better. "Just take care of Emily, please, and I'll get to you as soon as I can."

There were tears in Zoey's eyes, probably because the young woman was scared out of her mind. Julia had thoroughly screened Zoey when she'd employed her, and according to the nanny agency, she was supposedly one of the best. But Zoey certainly hadn't counted on the job that included staying at an FBI safe house.

When Julia went back into the bedroom, Russ had already picked up Emily from the crib. The baby was awake, her forehead wrinkled as if objecting to the abrupt end to her nap. Russ kissed both her cheeks, whispered something to her and then passed the baby to Julia. Just as there was a knock at the door.

Julia's heart dropped. She didn't think this was another threat, and she was right. It was the two agents who'd driven them back to the hotel. One was a thin Asian man, and the other was heavily muscled, with blond hair. They were dressed in casual clothes but wore baseball caps with Cheesy Jack's Pizza stamped on them.

One of them handed Russ three large pizza boxes while the other set two thick cardboard carriers filled with cups of soft drinks on the floor. The pair of agents had apparently brought along such a big order to help maintain their cover. It was enough food that it would definitely take two people to deliver it.

"We'll do this fast," the Asian man said. "There's a car waiting at the service entrance at the back of the hotel. There are two decoy cars, too, because we don't want anyone to know which vehicle the baby will be in." He motioned for Zoey to take Emily, and she did, but not before Julia grabbed a quick kiss.

"Keep her safe," Julia whispered to Zoey.

"I will," the nanny promised.

And just like that, before Julia could get another kiss or add anything else, they were out the door and gone.

Russ stood there for several moments with the pizza boxes perched on his left palm, and he blew out a long breath. "The agents are experienced," he told her. "They do this sort of thing all the time. And I trust them."

Those were all the right things to say, but it didn't stop the tears. Julia tried to wipe them away but more came. When Russ spotted them, he locked the door and slid his arm around her.

"I can't believe this," Julia mumbled. "Emily's only been with me two weeks, and I feel as if my heart just walked out that door."

"Yeah." And while the one-word response might have been simple, it was laced with emotion.

Russ gave her a kiss on each cheek, as he'd done with Emily, and tipped his head to the pizza boxes. "You should eat something."

She eyed the boxes. "There's really pizza in there?"

"Smells like it." He set the bottom boxes on the floor and the top one on the coffee table. He opened it. "Cheese, sausage and black olives," he said. "It's probably not your usual breakfast."

No, it wasn't; and she wasn't hungry, despite the fact she hadn't eaten anything for the past eighteen hours. Still, it wouldn't help Emily or the Richardsons' baby if she starved herself. So she got some napkins from the bar area and joined Russ on the sofa. He grabbed a slice, took a huge bite and then lifted the pizza and the foil it was sitting on to extract something beneath.

It was a thick, padded envelope.

"A CD from the park's security system," Russ explained, taking it from the envelope. "This is a copy, and the San Saba PD and the FBI are likely already reviewing it, but I wanted to see if I could spot the shooter myself—or Milo, after he left the meeting."

Yes, she was interested in that, too.

"I need to use your laptop," he said, and headed to the bedroom to get it while Julia ate her pizza. She still wasn't hungry, but her stomach was growling.

Russ ate, too, as he loaded the CD into her laptop and started to go through the images that appeared on the screen. There were apparently multiple cameras, but Russ finally managed to locate the one at the picnic table. He saw Milo, Sylvia, Julia and himself.

He sped up the surveillance, but slowed it again when Milo made his exit from the meeting. Russ adjusted the feed so that it followed the man. Milo took out his phone, made a short call and headed for his vehicle—a black Mercedes that was parked not far from Julia's own vehicle. He drove away.

"You think that call was to alert the shooter?" Julia asked.

"Could be. The lab at Quantico can try to enhance it to see if they can figure out the number he called. We might get lucky."

They watched until Milo was out of surveillance range, then Russ reversed the action on the disk. Next, he changed the camera shots to the one in the area near the trees.

Both of them automatically moved closer, and their arms bumped into each other. Even though they were involved in something that could be critical, Julia wasn't able to ignore the little jolt she felt.

Russ must have felt it, too, because he gave her one of those smiles that made her feel as if she were melting. *Oh, mercy*. She was *so* in trouble.

"Yeah," he whispered. "We'll work all that out later. Promise."

She stiffened. "Am I that easy to read?" she asked, wanting very much to know.

"Sometimes. Don't worry. I don't have you all worked out and understood in my mind. Truth is, you're driving me crazy. I can usually peg people, put them in the right category or box. But I'm not sure where to put you, Julia."

Unfortunately, she understood what he meant. "Maybe the attraction is because of Emily. Because subconsciously we're trying to be parents to her."

Sheez, it sounded worse when said out loud than it had when it was stumbling around in her head. "Or maybe not," she amended.

While volleying glances between the screen and her, he leaned in and gave her a quick kiss. Quick and hot. It was a reminder that the attraction between them had nothing to do with Emily.

However, his smile faded when he spotted something on the screen. "Silas," he said, pointing to the man who was near those trees where the shooter was likely hidden. Silas appeared to be hiding, too.

"He shouldn't have been there," Russ said.

She didn't take the bite of pizza that was already on the way to her mouth. "Where should he have been?"

"Nowhere in the park itself. He was backup, and was assigned to be at one of the park entrances. He certainly shouldn't have put himself in a position where Milo could have seen him. Remember, Silas was supposed to pose as the buyer."

Julia gave that some thought, hoping that it didn't blow the meeting. "So why was he there?"

"I'll ask him as soon as he's found."

A few moments later, the CD showed Silas ducking out of sight. More time passed, and she could see the images of when the shooting started.

Russ panned around, and even though it seemed as if the shots were coming from the trees, Julia couldn't be certain of that.

"Is it possible Silas was the one shooting at us?" she asked.

"I don't know, but he's got some serious explaining to do when he gets back."

If he gets back, Julia silently amended. If Silas was the shooter, if he'd gone rogue, then it was possible the person who'd hired him had already killed him. That could be the real reason he was missing.

Russ's phone rang, and he set aside the rest of his pizza so he could take the call. He glanced at the caller ID, frowned, and when he answered it, he didn't say his name. He only said, "Hello."

"Sylvia," he said, a moment later, and he put the call on speaker.

Good. Because Julia wanted to hear what the woman had to say. It was because of Milo's threat and the shooting that Emily had to be rushed away to a safe house, and Sylvia probably had answers about what was going on. Of course, the question was, would Milo's assistant share those answers?

"How did you get my number?" Russ asked.

"Someone contacted me. A friend of yours, he said. And he wanted me to call you."

Julia hoped that friend was an agent, and she remembered Russ telling the Asian man in the car to try to get in touch with Milo or Sylvia.

"Who tried to kill Julia and me?" Russ demanded.

"We thought you might be able to tell us that," Sylvia countered.

"Why would I know?"

"Because the man who did the shooting was the same person who arrived at the Wainwright Hotel this morning. He went inside and stayed for over a half hour."

She was talking about Silas and the meeting with the Richardsons. It didn't surprise Julia that Milo knew about that, but she wondered how he'd interpreted that meeting. Had he been so suspicious that he'd ordered those shots to be fired?

"What makes you think my visitor had anything to do with the shooting?" Russ wanted to know.

"Because I saw him in the area after you left. Milo saw him, too."

"Maybe because Milo hired him to fire those shots?"

"Impossible," Sylvia insisted. "Milo has no reason to want Julia Howell or you dead. This is simply a business deal, and fired shots and a police investigation would only delay things."

"Does that mean this business deal is still on?" Russ asked.

"It is if you still have a buyer," she replied.

"I do," Russ assured her.

Sylvia didn't respond immediately, and Julia heard someone else talking in the background. "Could you hold on until I step outside?" Sylvia asked. "There's something I need to tell you, and I don't want an audience."

Julia looked at Russ to see if he knew what this was all about, but he only shook his head. They waited for what seemed an eternity, but Sylvia finally came back on the line.

"Look, Milo wants the deal to be completed at noon tomorrow at the city golf course," the woman continued. "He wants both Julia and you there. You provide him proof that the money is in the offshore account, and he'll give you the location of the baby."

"I don't want Julia at the meeting," Russ countered.

"That's not negotiable."

Russ mumbled some profanity. "Everything's negotiable. Just tell him. While you're at it, tell him that he'll only get half the account number for the deposit. And one more thing—I want the meeting to take place here in the lobby of the Wainwright Hotel. No more outdoor venues where people can be in trees to shoot at us."

Sylvia hesitated. "I'll tell Milo what you've requested and I'll get back to you." More hesitation. "Just how much do really know about what's going on here?"

Russ pulled back his shoulders. "What do you mean?"

"I mean we should talk. Face-to-face. Just you, Julia and me."

"Right," Russ mumbled. "Is that because you want a second chance at trying to kill us?"

"I didn't try to kill you!" she practically shouted. "I didn't try to kill anyone." When she continued, her voice was considerably softer. "Look, this is just a job, and I didn't sign up to be an accessory to murder. That's why we have to talk. There's something I have to show you before you walk into that meeting with Milo."

He glanced at Julia and shook his head. "How do I know this isn't some kind of trick?" Russ asked.

"You don't. But I'm willing to meet with you at the police station. I'd be stupid to try to kill you there."

Russ stayed quiet a moment. "Are you a cop?"

"Hardly." Sylvia's answer was fast and loaded with disbelief that he would even suggest it. "I'm just someone who's concerned about Milo and what's going on. Be at the police station in one hour, and maybe what I show you will help keep us all alive."

Chapter Ten

Russ hoped Sylvia's meeting wasn't a ploy to draw Julia and him out of the hotel. That's why he arranged to have a security detail follow them in the unmarked car that had been delivered to the hotel for him to use.

Still, even with a security detail, there was the possibility that something could go wrong.

Julia was obviously concerned as well, because she kept a white-knuckled grip on the arm rest, and she spent the entire ten-minute drive glancing all around them. Russ wanted to reassure her that they were safe, but he knew that wasn't true. If the person who'd tried to kill them wanted to make another attempt, the only thing that would keep Julia out of harm's way was to send her off to the safe house.

Russ was going to work on that.

He could find an agent to guard her while he had the big meeting with Milo. But if the meeting didn't go as planned for, on the following day with Milo, then he had no choice but to get Julia out of San Saba. Hell, he should get her out immediately, but he was positive she wouldn't go, despite the drained color on her face and her raw, exposed nerves.

"What do you think Sylvia wants to show us?" Julia asked.

"I don't have a clue." And he didn't.

This meeting had come out of the blue, and Russ didn't know if that meant Sylvia was getting cold feet about the deal, or if she had something else in mind. It was that something else that put a knot in Russ's gut. He didn't want Julia in any more danger, but he hadn't wanted to leave her at the hotel either, because no one would go as far as he would to protect her. And it didn't seem to matter if he didn't want to feel that way about her.

"You okay?" he asked her, as they pulled in to the parking lot.

"Don't worry. I'm not about to have a panic attack."

He caught onto her arm and turned her to face him. "That wasn't what I asked. Are you *okay?*"

She moistened her lips, pushed a wisp of hair from her cheek. "I just want this to be over so I can be with Emily."

He wanted the same thing, and he wanted it sooner than later.

Because Russ thought it might help them both, he leaned into her and gave her a quick kiss. It felt comfortable, as if quick, reassuring kisses were part of their normal lives instead of something he'd just started to experience.

"You're not going to put your hand up my dress to stop me from going nuts, are you?" she asked.

Russ thought she was only partly serious, so he kissed her again, and he wished that they were at a place and time where he could figure out where the hell they were going with the dirty thoughts and long, lingering looks.

"Maybe later," he told her, but it wasn't as much of a joke as he wanted it to be.

"Let's get inside," he said. "And make it as fast as you can." The parking lot seemed secure, and there were two uniformed officers milling around outside on what appeared to be a smoke break, but Russ didn't want to take any unnecessary chances.

San Saba wasn't a big city, and neither was the police station. It was a single-story, yellow brick building with a covered walkway across the front.

"I don't see Sylvia," Julia said.

Neither did Russ, and that tightened the knot in his stomach even more.

He'd had his badge delivered with the car, and he stuck it in his back pocket, just in case someone inside questioned him. He locked his weapon in the glove compartment because it would never make it through the metal detector. The trick would be to keep Julia safe and meet with Sylvia without letting her suspect that he was a federal agent.

Julia and he walked past the two smoking officers. Russ made eye contact with him and nodded a greeting before he ushered Julia inside. As expected, there was a metal detector just steps past the door, and they walked through it, thankful they didn't set anything off.

Sylvia was there in the waiting area across from reception. The reception desk was manned by a female uniformed officer, and when she gave him a questioning look, Russ tipped his head to Sylvia.

"I'm here to pick her up," Russ lied.

That seemed to satisfy the officer, and Julia and he

made their way to Sylvia. Russ took the seat directly next to the woman, and Julia sat beside him.

"This had better be worth my time," Russ told her, right off the bat.

"It will be." But Sylvia didn't make a move to show him anything—other than her nerves. The woman's hands were trembling, and her eyes were red—she'd obviously been crying or had somehow faked the look— and she was gripping her purse as if were a lifeline.

"Well?" Russ demanded.

"First of all, I'm in love with Milo, and this meeting is a last resort for me." Her voice was barely audible. "I've tried to reason with him, to talk him out of this deal, but he won't listen. He insists on going through with it, even though I think it's dangerous."

"It *is* dangerous," Russ told her. And he thought about how he should phrase this. "But we can bypass Milo if you know where the baby is."

"I don't." She met his gaze. "But I don't think it's safe for anyone to carry out this deal." Sylvia pulled in a weary breath and opened her purse. "I don't know what's going on, but I hope you can find out."

Julia moved to the edge of her seat, probably so she could see what Sylvia was taking from her purse.

Photos.

She handed them to Russ.

There were two of them, both black-and-white. Grainy shots, obviously taken from a long distance, and perhaps only seconds apart. Two people were in both photos and Russ immediately recognized one of them.

Milo.

Julia's soft gasp let him know that she recognized the other person, as well.

Sylvia stood. "My advice? Before you show up at that meeting tomorrow, you find out why those two are together."

Russ intended to do just that.

Because the second person in the photos was none other than Tracy Richardson, the "stolen" baby's mother.

"I WANT SYLVIA HARTMAN FOLLOWED," Julia heard Russ say to the agent he'd phoned the moment that Sylvia was out of sight. "And have someone call me with the financials on Aaron and Tracy Richardson."

Russ was talking to the agent who'd accompanied them to the police station, and while Julia didn't like the idea of driving to the hotel without backup, she didn't want Sylvia to get away. Not after what the woman had just given them.

She glanced at the photos again before Russ folded them and slid them into his pocket.

"You think they're real?" Julia asked, in a whisper. "Or did Sylvia doctor them?"

"I don't know, but I intend to find out."

Julia only hoped that it was possible before the meeting. She hadn't exactly felt comfortable about going another round with Milo, but this would make things even more questionable. And perhaps more dangerous.

"How long will it take you to get the financial information on the Richardsons?" she asked.

"Not long."

Good, because that might give them some important pieces to this puzzle.

"Is there a place in here to get some coffee?" Russ asked the officer at the reception desk. "Our friend had to run a quick errand, and we need to wait for her to get back," he lied.

She pointed toward a side hall. "It's from a vending machine and tastes like sludge. There's a café across the street if you want something better."

"Sludge is fine," Russ mumbled, and he didn't say anything else until Julia and he were out of earshot. "I want us to hang around here until another security detail arrives."

Julia was thankful for the precaution and equally thankful that the small room with several vending machines was vacant. She had a dozen things she wanted to ask Russ, and she didn't want anyone around to listen in.

While keeping watch around them, he threaded several one-dollar bills into the machine and got them each a cup of coffee. The officer was right. It did taste like sludge.

"So what's going on?" Julia asked. "Why do you think Sylvia really wanted us to meet her?"

"Could be several things." There were four metal chairs lined up across from the machines, and she and Russ sat.

"The pictures could be a hoax. Milo's man could have seen Tracy Richardson at the hotel, followed her and then orchestrated the photos to make it look as if she knows Milo. Heck, Milo and Tracy might have never even met."

"But why doctor the photos to make us think that?"

"Milo could have done it to see how we'd react. This could all be some kind of sick test just to see what we'll do. He might think we'll panic and do something stupid."

Julia couldn't rule that out. "But Tracy could actually know Milo. And that means he could also know that she's the baby's mother."

Russ nodded. "Milo could have figured that out. Or maybe he just suspects she's involved with us. If that's true, it goes without saying that he'll be more suspicious of us."

Yes, he would. And it could be worse than that. "Milo might know you're an agent. Tracy could have told him."

"She could have," Russ readily admitted. "But if she did, I think Milo would have already confronted me about it. He's not shy about saying what's on his mind."

True, but Julia didn't like the possibilities. Sylvia could be playing her own game, maybe so she could turn Russ and her against Milo and then somehow collect the money for herself. Or it could be Milo or Tracy playing a game. A dangerous one.

Russ sipped the coffee and grimaced at the taste. He tossed the cup into the garbage can beside them. "We have to wait and see what all of this means. Maybe Milo wants us off kilter when and if we walk into that meeting. Hell, he might even have Tracy show up so she can get in a bidding war with my *buyer*."

"That's assuming Milo still believes you *have* a buyer," Julia pointed out. "Since Sylvia knew Silas had shown up at the hotel this morning, Milo and she probably also know the Richardsons dropped by for a visit, too. So maybe they now assume that the Richardsons are the ones behind the two-million-dollar offer."

"Entirely possible."

Julia thought of something else. "If Milo knew he could get this much money from the Richardsons, then why didn't he just hold their baby for ransom?"

"Good question, and I don't know the answer. Maybe he thought the buying process would keep him safer, one step away from the authorities. He can definitely control this situation better than he could if he risked going to the birth parents. Hell, maybe there is no actual Z, and *he's* the real seller." He checked his watch and settled deeper into the chair, as if this might be a long wait.

And it just might be.

Even though she grimaced, too, at the coffee taste, she continued to sip it. She needed the caffeine to stay alert, since the fatigue was starting to catch up with her. "You said *if* we walk into the meeting with Milo. I thought we'd gotten past your argument that I shouldn't be there."

"We haven't gotten past it." He leaned his head against the wall and looked at her. "I don't want you there. I want you safe."

"That's your libido talking. You need me there. The Richardsons' baby needs me there."

He blew out an audible breath. "And if something goes wrong? If you're hurt?"

She tried to shrug. "It'd be worth it if the baby was safe."

Russ cursed. "The baby might not be safe because his own mother put him in danger." Since he hadn't exactly said that in a whisper, he looked around to make sure he hadn't drawn any attention. They still had the room to themselves.

"I've been trained to do this kind of thing," Russ said, continuing, his voice quieter but definitely not calmer. "You haven't been. And you shouldn't have to take the risk. I'll just tell Milo that you're sick. Or indisposed. Or that you refused to come. He'll have no choice but to back off about you being there."

Julia wasn't at all sure that would work. Milo was calling the shots, and he could continue to do that as long as he had the baby.

She stared into the cup and wondered if she should even bring this up. The timing was wrong, but then it might not be right for a while. "What are we going to do?" she asked.

"About Emily?" Russ didn't wait for her to answer. "We'll work out an arrangement. Maybe split custody, or something."

"Wow." She took a moment to let that sink in. "You've had a change of heart. Just yesterday, you were reminding me that you were the best choice to raise her."

"I was wrong," he readily admitted. "Emily has to come first. Even if you and I are as different as night and day, we can put our differences aside and do what's best for her."

Julia made a sound of agreement. Partial agreement, anyway. "We're not that different, Russ."

He raised his eyebrows and gave her a dry smile.

She only shrugged. "Maybe our bank accounts are different, but I inherited my money. Not much accomplishment in that. And until I got that call about Emily, I'd closed down. The press called me a recluse. That's a kind word. I would go months without leaving the safe little world I created at my estate."

"But that safe little world *was* safe," he reminded her.

"*Safe* isn't necessarily the way to live your whole life. What about you?" she asked. "Why did you close down and get lost in your job? Does it have something to do with that scar you showed me?"

He rubbed his fingers against it. "Yeah." That was all he said for several moments. He checked his watch again, then his phone. "Three years ago I got sexually involved with a woman in my protective custody." Russ met her eye-to-eye. "She was killed. It was my fault," he added.

"I doubt that."

"Then you're the only one," he mumbled.

So he'd been punishing himself all this time. "You were in love with her?" Julia asked.

"No." There was no hesitation in his answer. "But that didn't make it easier."

"I suspect not. And I suspect you're thinking that this situation with me might be history repeating itself."

"Aren't *you?*" he fired back. "The last time you got involved with a dangerous man, you nearly died."

Yes, and even though there was a huge difference between Russ and her attacker, Julia couldn't completely tamp down the fear. Part of her wanted to take Emily and go running back to her estate; but if she did that, she would never be able to forget the child she could have saved.

Russ's phone rang, and he seemed relieved. Maybe because he wouldn't have to continue this too personal conversation. As usual, he didn't identify himself when he answered, but a moment later she heard him say "Soto."

That grabbed her attention, because he was the agent taking Emily to the safe house.

"They'll be at the location soon," Russ relayed to her.

"Soon? But I thought it wouldn't take them so long to get there?"

"They can't just drive there. They have to make sure no one is following them, so they take what we call a circuitous route. They're doing this by the book. And everything is okay, going just as planned."

Julia released the breath she'd been holding and said a quick prayer of thanks. Emily was away from Milo, and she was safe. Now she had to see what she could do so the Richardson baby was, as well.

Russ stayed on the line, listening to whatever Soto was telling him. He asked about Silas. And about Milo. By the time he ended the call, Julia was anxious for answers.

"What about Silas?" she asked.

"Still no sign of him, but they did locate his phone. It was in a trash bin at the park."

Where he'd last been seen. That could mean Silas had been kidnapped. Or maybe he was setting all of this up so it would appear that way.

Or maybe Silas was dead.

"And Milo?"

Russ shook his head. "He's staying put at his office. He's had no visitors, so if he's been in contact with his boss, then it hasn't been in person."

Russ had no sooner put his phone away when it rang again. Julia hoped this would be the call to tell them that another security detail was in place. She didn't mind being in the police station, but the longer they stayed, the more it might alert Milo that something was wrong.

Again, Julia tried to make sense of what part of the conversation she could hear, but Russ didn't give much away—except for his expression. The muscles in his jaw turned to iron.

"Repeat that," Russ asked the caller.

Julia moved closer and waited.

"I want them brought to the Wainwright Hotel ASAP," Russ insisted. "Keep it quiet, but if they won't come, arrest them. Do whatever you need to do to get them there."

He hung up but continued to stare at the phone. "That was Special Agent Toby Kaplan. He's the one who followed Sylvia. She left here and went straight to another meeting."

"With Milo?" Julia questioned.

"No. With the stolen baby's father, Aaron Richardson."

"What?" Julia was stunned. First, Milo had met with the child's mother, and now Sylvia had met with the father? "Why would Aaron be meeting with Milo's assistant?" Julia asked.

"I don't know, but Toby's bringing the Richardsons to the hotel, and they won't be leaving until they tell us exactly what the hell is going on."

Chapter Eleven

Russ mentally went over the details.

He wanted answers, but he didn't want them at the expense of Julia's safety or blowing the case completely. That's why he'd gotten another room to do the interview with the stolen child's parents. Thankfully, the hotel had very few guests, and other than Julia, none were on the third floor, which was made up entirely of suites. So they'd have privacy, and Russ would better be able to control security.

Of course, nothing was foolproof. But at least this way the Richardsons wouldn't be in Julia's room.

Russ hoped that would be enough.

He had the photos of Tracy's meeting with Milo, and thanks to a fax from Agent Toby Kaplan, Russ now had pictures of Aaron's meeting with Sylvia. It would be interesting to see how the Richardsons reacted when they saw the images. And just in case that reaction turned ugly, Toby would be in the bedroom of the suite, so he could respond.

Of course, the Richardsons could be innocent in all of this. Those photos with Sylvia and Milo could be fake. They could be Milo's attempt at muddying the waters. Or they could be snapshots of desperate parents who'd do anything to get their child back. Still, it was too big of a risk to trust them completely. That desperation could have spurred either Tracy, Aaron or both to cut their own deal with Milo. A deal that involved betraying the FBI and sacrificing Russ and Julia. The Richardsons could have worked things out so they would get the baby, and Milo would get the money—and dibs at killing a federal agent who was trying to bring him down.

The bottom line was that Russ had to be ready for anything.

"It's been nearly an hour," Julia pointed out. She was pacing in the new suite and kept glancing out the window. When she wasn't doing that, she was checking her phone in the hopes that Zoey would call her with an update about Emily.

"They're on their way," Russ answered, though time did seem to be crawling by.

He hadn't realized just how on edge he was, until his phone rang, and he nearly jumped. From the caller ID, he could tell it wasn't Toby, but someone at FBI headquarters. The number was encrypted and listed as unknown. It was yet another precaution, in case he got such a call in front of one of the suspects.

"Yes?" Russ answered.

"It's Denny Lord." Denny was the tech who'd already helped Russ out several times during this investigation. "I have the financials you asked for on the Richardsons. I found a few new things that I didn't find in our initial background check."

Probably because the initial check had been just that—initial. Something to rule them out as obvious suspects in the disappearance of their child.

"The couple has about ten million in assets, mainly from Aaron's trust fund and the business he owns. But I did some checking and found out that Tracy Richardson has some debts in her maiden name. She made some bad investments with her own trust fund and lost nearly everything. I don't think her husband knows about the losses, because he listed her trust as an asset on a recent application for a loan."

"Interesting. What kind of loan?" Russ asked.

"One to make improvements to his business. Or maybe a better word would be to salvage it. He's had some stock market losses, too, and he drained the business profits to cover them."

"Does his wife know?"

"Hard to tell. The loan wasn't made through a bank, but rather, through one of Aaron Richardson's friends who owns an investment company. It's not off the books, but it's not a traditional loan, either. In fact, the money they're using to put up for payment to Milo is from this same source."

So, the Richardsons were having money flow problems and were borrowing to get back their child. That wasn't unreasonable. Unless the Richardsons had actually had their own baby kidnapped so they could play the sympathy card with their money-lending friend. The friend could be in the dark and not have any way of knowing that the payoff money was really a payoff to the Richardsons' debts.

There was a knock at the door. "It's me, Toby," the person said, from the other side.

"Finally," Julia mumbled.

Russ ended the call so he could check the peephole viewer and make sure the agent wasn't being held at gunpoint or something. But everything looked normal for Toby. Not for the Richardsons though. They looked as if they were about to face a firing squad.

Russ opened the door and ushered them in. "Anyone see you?" he asked Toby.

Toby shook his head and lowered his voice so that the others wouldn't be able to hear. "Milo's man is still being held. The guy had an outstanding warrant for writing hot checks. We got lucky."

And luckier still that Milo hadn't sent a replacement. Or maybe he had. Maybe one of the Richardsons was working for him, and that's why Milo hadn't felt it necessary to send in another henchman.

"Sit," Russ instructed the couple. He took out the photos and dropped them on the coffee table in front of them. "And explain these."

Neither Aaron nor Tracy touched them, but they both leaned forward and had a long look. When Tracy saw the one with her husband and Sylvia, her hand flew to her mouth, as if to mask her gasp. Aaron kept his reaction more concealed. He picked up the photo of his wife with Milo and stared at it.

"I met with Sylvia Hartman because I thought she could help me find my son," Aaron offered.

"What made you think that?" Tracy demanded.

Aaron dodged her gaze. "Because I learned that Sylvia works for the man whom I believe has our child. Milo. But obviously, you already know him."

Tracy didn't make another gasp, but it was close. "I can't believe this—"

Aaron held up the picture, cutting off whatever else she'd been about to say. "You didn't tell me about this meeting, either. Why did you see this monster?"

Tracy grabbed the other photo of Aaron and Sylvia and pushed it closer to his face. "The same reason you met with this monster."

"And how did you know they were *monsters?*" Julia asked, taking the words out of Russ's mouth. She wasn't detached from this, either. Judging from the anger in her voice, she didn't think the Richardsons were innocent.

Aaron looked at Tracy. She looked at him. And he shook his head. "The P.I. I hired to follow you also had Milo followed, after he left Julia and you in the alley at the Silver Dollar bar. When he left there, he went to Sylvia, and that's how I learned she worked for him." He glanced at his wife again. "I didn't tell Tracy that part," he explained to Russ.

"Because he knew how I would react," Tracy clarified. "Is Sylvia the woman you've been seeing?"

Russ decided it was a good time to stand there and listen.

"I'm not seeing another woman," Aaron spat out. "I'd never met Sylvia Hartman until I learned she worked for Milo. That's why I went to see her. I thought I could reason with her."

"And you didn't bother to tell me any of this," Tracy fired back at him.

Aaron only waved the photo again, to remind her that she'd done the same with Milo.

"I met with him because I didn't think you were doing enough to save Matthew." She turned her teary eyes toward Julia. "You're a mother. Certainly you understand I was desperate to get back my child."

Julia shook her head. "Desperation I understand.

But you didn't think you were putting Matthew in more danger by meeting with a man like Milo?"

"No," Tracy answered, readily. "I thought I could plead with him or offer him money. But I was wrong. He said he didn't know anything about my son, that I was mistaken, and I should go to the police."

Milo might have indeed said that, because Tracy had already been to the police and still didn't have her son back.

"You offered him money?" Russ wanted to know.

"I did. But he just kept saying he didn't know anything about my son." More tears came, and she buried her face in her hands.

"And you?" Russ said, looking at Aaron. "Did you offer Sylvia money?"

"No. She denied knowing anything about Matthew's kidnapping so I didn't see any reason to offer her anything."

"You should have offered her the money!" Tracy practically shouted. "What, were you trying to save a dollar or two, Aaron? Is that it? You're too cheap to give these people what they want so we can get Matthew back?"

"I want him back." Aaron didn't shout, but there seemed to be a storm brewing behind his dust-gray eyes. "But I'm not convinced either Milo or Sylvia has him. If they did, they would be willing to deal with the source, *with me*, rather than trying to sell him to someone else."

"Maybe this is Milo's way of trying to get a higher price," Russ replied, and Julia nodded. "The longer he waits, the more desperate you become."

"The more desperate *I* become," Tracy mumbled.

"What do you mean by that?" Aaron tossed right back at her.

"It means I don't think you're all that interested in getting our son back."

Aaron didn't answer that—not verbally, anyway. But he silently hurled daggers at his wife. Tracy's tears started to flow again, and Julia crossed the room and caught onto the woman's arm.

"Why don't you come with me," Julia said, softly. "You can freshen up in the bathroom."

Good move. Russ didn't think Julia had freshening up on her mind. Maybe Tracy would spill more with some girl talk. In the meantime, Russ concentrated on Aaron.

"You're having an affair?" he asked Aaron, point-blank.

"No." Aaron paused. "But I've had them in the past. Tracy doesn't trust me."

"Can you blame her?" Russ poured the man a Scotch from the minibar and took it to him.

"She's had affairs, too," Aaron practically whispered, and he downed the drink in one gulp.

Russ sat down next to the man. "Do your former trysts have anything to do with your missing son?"

"No." He didn't hesitate, either. "I think the person who took him is greedy and sick. This is about money, not about my personal life."

"Money and personal lives often cross paths," Russ reminded him.

"Not in this case." Aaron met him eye-to-eye. "I didn't have anything to do with my son's disappearance. I love him, and despite what my wife says, I want him back. I've sold stocks and cashed in investments. I've even borrowed from friends to get the money to pay whatever Milo asks. Would I do that if I didn't love him?"

"I don't know. Would you?" Russ couldn't think of a good reason why he would, unless this was some bizarre way of getting his friends to cough up money.

"I won't continue this conversation without my attorney present." He stood. "I love my wife, too, but I don't think she believes that."

"That might have something to do with your affairs." Russ stood, as well.

Aaron lifted his shoulder. "Those were a long time ago, on my part, anyway. I don't think Tracy can say the same." He paused only long enough to draw a quick breath. "As I said, this interrogation is over, and I'm going to my car. Tell my wife I'll be waiting for her."

Russ didn't stop Aaron when he walked out the door, mainly because he didn't think the man would add more to his story, or change it. Maybe because he was telling the truth.

Or maybe because he'd rehearsed the lies so well that it just sounded that way.

"Do some checking," Russ whispered to Toby, "and see if Aaron told the truth about his affairs being old news. I want to know if he's sleeping with Sylvia."

Toby nodded but didn't say anything, because Julia and Tracy came back into the room. Tracy looked around but didn't seem surprised that her husband wasn't there.

"He's in the car," Russ informed her.

"Of course. Aaron has trouble handling emotional situations. My crying embarrassed him." Tracy turned to Julia. "Thank you for listening."

"Anytime." She gave Tracy a brief hug and walked with the woman to the door. "Remember, call me if you want to talk."

Julia shut the door behind Tracy and waited, no doubt to give the woman some time to get down the hall and completely out of hearing range.

"Will someone follow them?" Julia asked.

"There's an agent posted outside the hotel who'll do that," Russ explained. "I want both of them in our sights until this meeting with Milo is over." He stared at Julia. "So, what did you learn from your chat with Tracy?"

"This isn't exactly a news flash, but the Richardsons are on the verge of a divorce. According to Tracy, she already hired an attorney, and was about to serve Aaron papers when their son went missing."

Russ gave that some thought. If Aaron was telling the truth about loving his wife, then maybe this was his extreme way of trying to hang on to her. It had certainly delayed the divorce.

Toby checked his watch. "I'll get started on the things you wanted me to check," he told Russ. "I have a laptop and some other equipment down in the lobby." Then the agent glanced around. "Should I use this room, or Ms. Howell's suite?"

"This one," Russ decided. If the Richardsons were the real bad guys in all of this, then he didn't want Julia to stay in the suite where the Richardsons had last seen her. It might be an unnecessary precaution, but there was so little he could do right now, that he wanted to take advantage of anything he had.

Russ led Julia back down the hall to her suite, and he made sure no one saw them enter. He locked the doors and turned to see how she was really holding up, but his phone rang.

"It's Soto," he relayed to her.

Russ caught a glimpse of the terror that shot through her eyes. It shot through him, too. Because a call from Agent Soto could be bad news about Emily.

"Is Emily all right?" Russ said, the moment he answered the call.

"She's fine. We're at the safe house. We're only about five miles from you. This is a secure location, with a security system that can monitor the entire area surrounding the house."

"Thanks," Russ told him.

"Don't thank me yet," Soto warned. And Russ braced himself for the news that Soto had obviously not wanted to deliver.

"Is something wrong with Emily?" Julia asked, the moment Russ was off the phone. She had gone pale and had her hand pressed to her heart.

"She's fine. They're at the safe house, and all is well." With Emily, anyway.

Because Julia knew something was wrong, and because she still looked ready to lose it, Russ crossed the room and went to her. "They found the shooter."

She swallowed hard. "And?"

Russ couldn't figure out an easy way to say this, so he just tossed it out there. "He's dead. A single gunshot wound to the head. Could be suicide. Could be an execution."

Her hand dropped away from her chest. "So we don't know who hired him?"

"No."

And they might never learn. A dead man wasn't

going to give them many answers. It didn't mean this was over, either, because the person who'd hired the gunman could turn around and hire someone else.

Russ leaned down a little so he'd be at eye level with Julia. "I don't see any sign of panic."

"Look closer," she mumbled. But she waved him off and scrubbed her hands up and down her arms. "I think I'm past the panic stage, and I've moved on to whatever's next."

"Anger," Russ suggested.

After a moment, she gave a crisp nod. "Yes, I'm angry that I can't be with Emily. I'm angry someone tried to kill us. And I'm also really angry at the possibility that maybe Aaron or Tracy might be responsible for having their child kidnapped. If they're behind this, I want to throttle both of them."

Russ smiled. For a very brief moment, anyway. This new-and-improved version of Julia was going to be trouble. He was a sucker for a damsel in distress, but what really got him revved up was a strong, confident woman. Too bad, because Julia already had him revved up before she'd learned how to cope with the anxiety.

He was about to remind himself why kissing her would be a bad idea, but he gave up. Julia was a lost cause anyway. When this was over, she'd return to her estate and maybe battle with him over the custody arrangement with Emily. She'd probably start dating—someone of her own kind, someone rich, successful and in the old social circle she used to haunt before her attack.

Hell, now *he* was angry. He didn't want her dating anyone else. He didn't want her thinking about any other man. So Russ latched onto the back of her neck and yanked her to him so he could kiss her.

He wasn't sure what he hoped to accomplish. Maybe nothing more than to remind himself of what he'd be missing when this was over.

And he got a reminder all right.

Julia might not have a lot of recent kissing experience, but that little, silky sound of pleasure she made in her throat made up for everything. So did the way she wound her arms around him, slipping her fingers into his hair.

She was the one who deepened the kiss. She was also the one who made it French. But Russ knew he was responsible for upping the stakes when he cupped her breast.

Man, he was out of control.

He should be thinking about the case, but here he was pinching her nipples and wondering if there was enough time to strip that dress off her and taste her the way she deserved to be tasted.

Russ had almost convinced himself to back away, but Julia held on. The kiss just kept on going. So did the touching, and she moved her own hand to his chest to do some touching of her own.

Those chest rubs, and the sex-to-sex body contact, overrode any chance of common sense coming into this. He kissed Julia harder and pushed her against the wall so he could do something about getting her dress undone.

But then he stopped. Pulled back and met her gaze. "Am I being too rough?"

She rolled her eyes, latched onto his hair and pulled him right back to her.

So roughness wasn't an issue. Then what was? Russ decided to do some test touching.

He ran his hand up the back of her thigh, pushing her dress up. She moved into his touch while the searing kiss only got hotter. Hot enough for him to think *to hell with test touching*. He pushed her dress up to her waist and slid his fingers in the direction of her panties.

The scar stopped him.

He felt the raised skin and glanced at it. There was the old wound, right there on her belly.

Julia snagged him by the wrist. "Can we do this with the lights off?"

A loaded question. He was aroused to the point of pain, and part of him was ready to agree to anything— including lights off. But that *"lights off"* was a big red flag he needed to address.

"No," he told her.

Julia blinked. "No?"

"Your scars don't bother me," he let her know. "Well, not like you think. They bother me because of what you went through, but they're reminders you survived. They certainly don't cool this heat that's between us."

She blinked again. And judging from her expression, she probably would have argued, but then he heard a sound. A loud pop.

Before he could react, his phone rang again.

"It's Toby," the caller said, the moment Russ answered. With just those two words, Russ could hear the agent's frantic tone.

"What's wrong?" Russ asked.

There was another of those loud popping noises, and Russ knew it hadn't been caused by a car. He drew his weapon and checked to make sure the door was locked. It was.

"I just got a call from the agent who's been tailing the Richardsons. There's gunfire," Toby explained, his words rushed together. "Just a block up from the hotel."

Russ didn't like the sound of that, or the third shot he heard. "Get down," he told Julia. But she was already headed toward the floor anyway. She pulled her dress back in place and dropped to the thick carpet.

Russ headed to the window. "Are the Richardsons involved?" he asked Toby.

"Not that I've heard. The agent said he followed them to a café, and while he was waiting outside, he saw a man running up the sidewalk with a gun."

Russ glanced out the window but didn't see anyone. "Milo?" he questioned.

"No, the missing agent, Silas Duran. It looks like he's the one firing those shots, and he's coming straight for the hotel."

Chapter Twelve

"Get down here so you can guard Julia," she heard Russ say to the caller.

Julia looked up at Russ so she could try to figure out what was happening, but he was at the window with his back to her. "What's going on?" she asked.

"Silas." And that was all he said for several moments. "He might be the person firing shots."

Silas? So the agent obviously wasn't dead after all. "But why?"

"I don't know."

There was a knock at the door, and Russ hurried across the room so he could peek out through the tiny viewer. A moment later he opened it, and she spotted Toby.

"Toby's going to stay here and guard you," Russ explained.

Julia shook her head. "You're going after Silas?"

"He's my partner. I have to go." That was apparently the only explanation she was going to get, because Russ raced away.

Toby tried to give her a reassuring look, but he failed. Probably because he was standing there, gun drawn, while he kept watching the hall.

"Maybe you should go in the bedroom," he advised. "And lock the door."

That didn't make her feel any safer. "Sweet heaven. You think Silas is on his way here to come after Russ or me?"

"We just don't know. Silas might not even be the one shooting. This is a precaution."

It didn't feel like a precaution. The danger felt as if it were closing in fast. A federal agent had possibly gone berserk, and Russ was out there with him, all because the man was his partner. It sickened her to think that Russ could be facing down bullets while she was tucked away in a hotel room.

Julia stayed crouched down and made her way to the bedroom. She locked the door, as Toby had suggested, and she sank onto the foot of the bed.

She thought of Emily and prayed her little girl was far safer than Julia felt at the moment.

Her little girl, she mentally repeated.

It probably wasn't a good idea to stake an emotional claim on Lissa's daughter, at least not until Julia had worked out the custody arrangements with Russ. Still, she couldn't help it. She couldn't possibly have loved the child any more if Emily were her own, by birth.

She heard another of those loud pops. Another shot, no doubt. And Julia put her hands over her ears to block out the sounds. Without Russ there with her, to anchor her with his wry humor and well-timed touches, she felt the old panic return.

Her heart started to race. Her breathing became thin.

But she forced herself to remember what Russ had threatened to do—to put his hand up her dress.

That gave her a brief reprieve, and made her smile. A smile that quickly faded.

That's because she also thought of the latest kissing session they'd had, a session that seemed to take them one step closer to landing in bed. She wasn't completely certain she was ready for that, but those doubts seemed to evaporate whenever she was in Russ's arms.

Julia lay back on the bed, took the pillows and pressed them against the sides of her head. Finally, it was quiet.

Even though thoughts of Russ were flying at warp speed through her head, Julia focused on her breathing. On staying calm. On slowing her heartbeat. It wouldn't help the situation if she had a full-blown panic attack.

Because she had blocked out the sound, she didn't actually hear anything, but something alerted her. She snapped to a sitting position so she could try to figure out what was going on.

The door burst open.

Her first thought was that it was Russ. It wasn't. The man who'd kicked in the door had dark brown hair.

And a gun.

He shoved something into his back pocket and came right at her.

Julia didn't scream. She couldn't. Her throat clamped shut, and in the back of her mind she wondered if Toby was about to come in and try to save her. But she couldn't wait for Toby to do that. She knew that look in the man's cold, green eyes.

She knew it because she'd seen that look before.

In the eyes on the man who'd tried to kill her twelve years ago.

Julia scrambled across the bed and grabbed the first thing she could reach, the clock. She jerked the cord from the wall and tossed it at the man. It hit his chest, but it didn't stop him. He still came after her.

She knocked the corded phone off the hook, hoping that it would automatically call the front desk or alert someone. Then, she tossed a notepad at her attacker and latched onto the ink pen. It wasn't much against the man's bulky size and his gun, but it was all she had.

She drew the pen back like a knife, and braced herself for him to shoot her.

But he didn't. He came rushing around the bed toward her again. That told her a lot about this situation. He likely hadn't been sent to kill her, but to kidnap her. Or maybe he just wanted to prolong this attack.

Julia stabbed at his beefy arm with the pen and connected, the end of the pen actually scraping into his flesh. He made a sound of pain and paused just a second. That pause was enough for her to try to get to the bathroom. She made it three steps before he latched onto her hair.

The panic returned with a vengeance. Images of the other attack came at her like bullets. The slash of metal on her skin. The pain. The blood.

She felt each stab of the knife again and each inch he'd dragged her over, to the trunk of her car.

This man dragged her, too, toward him, but Julia didn't cooperate with whatever he had in mind. She kicked at him and slapped at him, trying to dig her nails into his wrist. Still, he used his brute strength and pulled her closer and closer. Julia waited until he was right against her, his chest on her back.

She remembered other images, especially those

from her self-defense class. She wasn't helpless, and she wouldn't be a victim again. Julia drew back her elbow, ramming it as hard as she could into his stomach. She didn't stop there. She stomped on his foot, and then pivoted, smacking him in the eyes with the heels of her hands.

He cursed and howled in pain. But he let go of her.

Julia bolted for the bathroom door.

It was open, thank God, and she raced into the small room and slammed the door. Or rather that's what she tried to do. But the man got to her before she could fully close and lock it.

He rammed his heavy weight against the door, and she was no match for his size. Julia flew backwards, her body slamming into the tiled wall between the toilet and the bath.

"You're gonna pay for that," the man growled. He shoved his gun in the back waistband of his pants.

And he came at Julia again.

"STAY INSIDE!" RUSS YELLED to the trio of people in the hotel lobby.

He didn't flash his badge, something he normally would have done, because he didn't want to take the chance that one of Milo's men would see him. He wanted to hang on to his cover, even if there was a chance there was nothing left to hang on to.

Russ stepped through the hotel door, and using the building for protection, he glanced around. There was another shot, and that helped him pinpoint the location of the shooter.

Just to his left.

There was no one on the sidewalks. Thank God.

They'd probably already taken cover or run. Either was fine by him. Russ didn't want an audience, or innocent bystanders getting hurt.

"It's me, Jimmy Marquez," Russ called out, just in case Silas was in earshot. Silas would recognize Russ's undercover name, but the question was—would that cause Silas to shoot? Or would it just give him a direction in which to aim? Because it was entirely possible that Silas was out to kill him.

There was another shot.

This one came from his right, but it hadn't been aimed at the building. Russ crouched down and made his way to the edge of the hotel so he could have a better look.

Another shot.

But this time he saw the gunman—the guy was against the adjacent building and was standing next to a car. It could be Silas. The man was wearing dark pants and a hoodie. And he was indeed armed. Then Russ saw the direction in which the gun was pointed.

His heart went to his knees.

The man had the gun pointed straight up toward the sky. And it wasn't Silas. There was a resemblance, and Russ didn't believe that had been by accident. That's because the shots were a diversion.

Cursing, Russ turned and raced back inside. The shooter would likely get away, but Russ didn't care. Right now, he had to make sure the diversion hadn't been created so that someone could get to Julia.

He jabbed the elevator button, but when it didn't come immediately, he headed for the stairs. He took them two and three at a time. With his heart pounding and a death grip on his gun, he went as fast as he could, because he knew that Julia's life might depend on it.

When he reached the stairwell door of the third floor, he eased it open and looked around to make sure he wasn't about to be ambushed. There was no one lurking around—and that included Toby.

The last time Russ had seen him, the agent had been standing in the doorway of Julia's suite. Russ prayed he'd gone inside.

Russ made his way up the hall toward the suite, and he silently cursed again when he saw the door slightly ajar. Still no sign of Toby, but that all changed when Russ elbowed open the door and saw the agent lying on the floor. Judging from the marks on his neck, someone had used a stun gun on him.

He heard the sounds of the struggle then.

Julia!

He didn't yell out her name, though he had to fight his instincts to do just that. Instead, Russ hurried to the bedroom and took aim.

She wasn't there.

His gaze slashed to the adjoining bathroom, and he heard a loud thump. Maybe a punch. Maybe something much worse.

Russ knew he should try to sneak up on whoever was attacking Julia, but he raced toward the bathroom instead. What he saw confirmed his worst fears.

Julia was on the floor, kicking and struggling. She was trying to break free of the goon looming over her who had a hand locked on her arm. The man reached for something in his back pocket.

A stun gun.

Russ lurched forward and used the butt of his gun to bash the man in the back of his head.

It stopped the guy from getting that stun gun, but he whirled around, and he reached for the handgun that Russ had seen tucked in the back waistband of his pants.

"Please go for it," Russ insisted, though he wasn't sure how he managed to speak. He wanted to kill this guy. Something slow and painful. But he'd settle for a quick kill if he drew that gun. "Give me a reason to put some bullets in you."

The man froze, and Russ's expression must have conveyed that he would have no hesitation pulling the trigger. A moment later, the guy lifted his hands in the air, surrendering.

Russ couldn't see Julia. The room was small, and the big goon was blocking his view, but he did know she was on the floor. And she wasn't moving.

"Julia, are you hurt?" Russ called out to her, without taking his attention off her attacker. Part of him was still hoping her attacker would make one wrong move so this would end right here.

"I'm okay," she said.

But she wasn't. Russ could hear the fear in her voice. "Stay put for just a second," he instructed, and he motioned for the guy to follow him, as he backed out and into the bedroom.

"Facedown on the floor," Russ ordered. "Put your hands on the back of your head." The moment the goon complied, Russ took the guy's weapon and did a quick pat down to make sure there wasn't a backup gun.

Then Russ glanced over his shoulder at Julia. He was scared of what he might see.

She was ghostly pale, as he'd expected, and her chest was pumping as if starved for air. Thankfully, he didn't see any injuries. But mentally, the injuries were there. She had no doubt just relived the attack that had nearly killed her all those years ago.

Julia caught onto the bathtub to steady herself. She got up from the floor, but not easily. Her legs were obviously wobbly, but she finally managed to stand. Russ motioned for her to wait in the bathroom doorway while he called for backup.

Because the guy on the bedroom floor might be wired so that someone, like Milo, could be listening in, Russ didn't identify himself as an agent. He made the call to headquarters and asked for help. Russ had no idea how long it would take someone to respond, especially since the local police were likely tied up with the bogus shooter. He didn't want the locals anyway. This was almost certainly connected to the Richardson baby, and Russ wanted to keep it in-house, if possible.

He thought of Toby and considered having Julia check on the agent, but it was too big a risk. Having the door unlocked was a risk, too. The shooter who had created the diversion could double back to help his comrade.

"Follow me, Julia," Russ told her.

He kept her at his side, with his gun aimed at the attacker on the floor. Once he was in the doorway of the bedroom, he could see Toby. Thankfully, the man was starting to move.

"Lock the door," he told Julia. And Russ kept an eye on her until that was done. She went to Toby to help him. That freed up Russ to get started with the goon he still wanted to kill.

"Who are you?" Russ asked.

When he didn't answer, Russ gave the guy another whack on the head with his gun. "Who are you?" Russ repeated.

"I'll answer questions when the cops get here," he snarled.

"There won't be any cops," Russ informed him.

"Feds, then. Like you."

Russ almost cursed, but he hadn't missed the tinge of doubt in the man's tone.

"What makes you think I'm a fed?"

He made a sound to indicate the answer was obvious. "You were at the police station. I know all the local cops, including the guys they have undercover, and you're not one of them. That means you're probably a fed."

"I'm not a fed. And there won't be anybody coming to arrest you." He jammed his gun against the man's head. "This is between you and me."

Because he was watching him so closely, he saw the sweat pop out on the man's forehead. "You're lying," the guy said.

Since that seemed an open invitation to prove him wrong, Russ whacked the guy upside the head again, and he made sure it was harder than the others. "I'm not lying. And I'm not lying either when I say I'll kill you. After all, you just tried to hurt my woman. I'm not very happy about that, and if you're not willing to give me answers, then I might was well finish you off right now and get to work disposing of your body."

The man angled his eyes at Russ. "You wouldn't."

Russ focused in on the image of Julia fighting for her life against this moron. "Oh yeah, I would."

More sweat popped out on the guy's face, and the seconds crawled by. "All right," he finally mumbled. "I work for Milo."

Of course he did. That also meant Milo must have someone watching the police station after all. That's what had likely prompted this attack. "Tell me something I don't know. Why did Milo send you?"

When the man started to shake his head, Russ rammed the gun even harder against his temple. He winced in pain.

"Milo wanted your woman," the man said, still grimacing.

Russ didn't ease up on the pressure he was delivering to the guy's head. "Why?"

"I don't know. That's the truth," he quickly added, when Russ dug the gun in even deeper. "If you want to know why, then you need to ask Milo."

Good advice.

Russ grabbed the guy's cell phone that was partially sticking out of his pocket. "Call Milo for me," Russ ordered. *"Now."*

Chapter Thirteen

Julia caught onto Toby's arm and helped him to his feet. He was shaky, just as she still was, but he didn't seem injured. He took out his gun and made his way to the bedroom. Julia followed him and spotted Russ crouched down next to the man who'd attacked her. Russ had his gun jammed against the man's head, and Toby took aim at the man as well.

She had an instant of panic when she saw her attacker's face. Hardly more than a flash, before she felt the rage. How dare this monster try to hurt them.

Russ looked back at her, and a dozen unspoken things passed between them. He was worried about her. She was worried about him, too. But he was staying in character, being Jimmy Marquez, the black-market baby broker.

"I'm sorry," Toby told her. And then Russ. "He came at me with a stun gun, and I didn't have time to stop him before he popped me with it."

"Don't worry," Julia assured him. "It wasn't your fault."

Russ nodded, as if to say ditto, but he kept his attention on her attacker. "Bozo here says that Milo sent him," Russ explained to Toby and Julia.

That didn't surprise her, but it did surprise her that the man was frantically pressing in numbers on his cell phone. He then handed the cell to Russ.

"Milo," Russ greeted. "I'd like to know why you sent one of your dogs after Julia."

She wanted to know the same thing, and inched closer. However, Toby nudged her back, probably because he didn't want her too close to the man on the floor.

"Really?" Russ said, with thick sarcasm dripping from his voice. "And you thought the best way to make sure I cooperated with you was to piss me off?" The intense anger merged with his sarcasm.

As upset as Julia was about the attack, she prayed it wouldn't affect the Richardson baby's rescue. In fact, she was even more convinced that Russ and she had to do whatever was necessary to save the child, because Milo was a dangerous man.

"You thought the reason Julia and I were at the police station was because I'm a fed?" Russ questioned.

Julia hoped Russ could convince Milo that it wasn't true.

"Well, you were wrong again. I'm not a fed, and we weren't talking to the police," Russ continued. "We were there because that's where Sylvia asked us to meet her." He paused, obviously listening to what Milo had to say. "Why don't you ask *her* why she wanted to meet us? Are you losing control of your people, Milo? You might want to keep your assistant on a shorter leash."

It was risky, telling Milo about Sylvia, and could ultimately put the woman in danger. On the other hand, this might rid Milo of some suspicions about Russ and

Julia; and after all, Sylvia worked for Milo, so she obviously knew what kind of man he was.

"Julia won't be at the meeting," Russ insisted. "No. That's not negotiable." Another pause. "Fine, then go ahead and get another buyer who'll cough up two million dollars."

Her heart nearly stopped. But Russ just stayed silently on the line.

"I thought you'd see the light," Russ said, a faint smile of celebration shaping his mouth. "Having Julia there would only complicate things."

So she wouldn't be at the meeting. That was good. Well, it was, as long as the deal closed as planned and the Richardson baby was returned.

"No. You're not getting your gunman back," Russ added, a moment later.

The guy on the floor cursed and probably thought he was about to die.

"I'll release him when and if this deal is closed," Russ said. "The meeting happens tomorrow morning, at nine o'clock. Without Julia. Just me, you and the baby. I'll call you with a location. In the meantime, make sure all your hired guns stay far away from me and what's mine."

Russ slapped the phone shut and put it in his pocket—perhaps so he could send it to the FBI for analysis; or maybe he just didn't want her attacker to be able to use it.

Toby went to the man and used the guy's own leather belt to create a hand restraint. He caught onto the back of his shirt and hauled him to his feet. "I'll take care of him. You'll be okay?"

It took Julia a moment to realize Toby was talking to

her. She settled for a nod. No, she wouldn't be okay any-time soon, but she wasn't about to fall apart, either.

Toby led the man out of the suite, and Russ caught onto her arm to lead her out as well. When he pulled the keycard from his pocket, that's when she knew they were going back to the suite where they'd met with the Richardsons.

"We'll be safe there?" she asked.

"As safe as I can make it. Once Toby's taken care of that piece of slime, I'll have him set up a decoy. I want Milo or anyone else watching to think we've left."

"And what about the thermal equipment?"

"The police confiscated it when they picked up Milo's man. They haven't released the equipment, and they won't—not until the FBI clears them to do that."

That didn't mean Milo couldn't use new equipment, but no need to borrow trouble. "Did Silas really fire those shots?"

Russ shook his head. "I don't think so. I believe Milo hired a gunman who looks like Silas to set up a diversion."

She heard the doubt in his explanation. She saw it, too, in his eyes. So Silas might still turn out to be a problem for them.

Russ got her into the suite, shut the door and double-locked it. He spun around and faced her. "If you want to hit me, go ahead."

Surprised, Julia just stared at him. "Hit you for what?"

"For nearly getting you killed."

Okay. So, that's where this conversation was going. Russ was about to take a guilt trip, and this particular journey wouldn't help either of them.

"Milo did this. Not you," she reminded him. "I'm not hurt, and you got to me in time, before that man could kidnap me."

He shook his head. "It wasn't enough. I've added another nightmare to your dreams."

Hardly. If anything, he'd taken some of those nightmares away. And that's when she realized what she had to do. It wasn't even a tough decision. In fact, it would be a relief on many levels.

Julia went to Russ, pulled him into her arms and kissed him.

RUSS WASN'T EXACTLY SURPRISED by the kiss. If Julia hadn't come to him at that exact moment, he would have been heading in her direction. She just saved them a few steps and moments.

And suddenly every moment seemed to count.

The kiss started hot and hard, and it only got more intense. Russ knew it would, but first he had to give Julia an out. He had to be sure this was what she really wanted, even if it was going to hurt if she put an end to this with just some kisses.

He tore his mouth from hers and looked her straight in the eyes. "This could be about panic. You could be—"

She stopped him with a kiss, and it was a doozie. Julia thrust her body against his, pushing him back against the door. She didn't stop there. She curved her arm around his neck and tightened the embrace.

The need shot through him, consuming him, and Russ figured he only had one more try before both Julia and he were beyond stopping.

He pulled back and held her in place, so that she

couldn't go back for round three. "You don't know me that well—"

"I know you." And she brushed against him and nearly caused his eyes to cross.

Best just to cut to the chase. "Think this through. This is sex, Julia."

She gave a crisp nod. "Good."

Russ groaned. "Sex that you've never had before. And I don't have a condom."

That stopped her all right. She stared at him and blinked. "I'm on the pill to regulate my periods. But I'm pretty sure that covers sex."

"Physically, maybe. But how about emotionally?"

"You want to talk about feelings?" she asked, but she didn't wait for his answer. "Well, here's what I feel. I want you. I've never wanted a man as much as I want you. Now, is that enough for you?"

Hell. It had to be enough, even if he had doubts. There was no way he could turn away from her. Still, sex against the door probably wasn't the way to go here. So he kissed her until she was gasping for breath, scooped her up and headed for the bedroom.

She lit some more fires along the way by kissing his neck and touching his chest. By the time he eased her onto the mattress, he was primed and ready. But Russ forced himself to slow down.

He grabbed both of her wrists in one hand and pinned them to the bed so she couldn't do any more of those maddening caresses. He kissed her again, letting the slow heat slide right through them. It was enough for a moment, but she soon began lifting her hips to meet his.

To hell with slow. It was a lost cause anyway.

Russ unbuttoned her dress and went after her breasts. He already knew how that particular part of her tasted, but he had seconds. And thirds. He kissed every inch of her and then took her right nipple into his mouth.

Julia didn't say anything coherent, and she ground herself against him to let him know what she wanted. *Him.* She wiggled one of her hands out of his grip and pulled up her dress until it was at her waist. She tried to lower his zipper, too, but he was huge and hard, and that didn't make her task easy. Plus, all that groping against his erection wasn't doing much for his willpower.

"Can you cut the foreplay?" she asked, hooking her fingers onto her panties and pulling them off. "I've waited long enough."

Russ couldn't argue with that. Hell, his body would have laughed at him if he'd tried. So he just took what Julia was offering him. Later, he'd deal with the emotional aftermath, and he was pretty sure there'd be one.

He didn't take off his pants, because every second suddenly seemed to matter. Everything was racing. His heart. Julia's caresses. The needy kisses and urgent whispers. He got his jeans unzipped—how he managed that, he didn't know—but it was Julia who took his sex from his shorts.

She guided him to her and lifted her hips. Russ tried to hold back, but she would have no part of gentleness. She wrapped her legs around him and thrust him forward, so that he slid right into her.

There was a flash of pain on her face. Russ cursed and tried to pull out. But she wouldn't have any part of that, either.

"Finish," she insisted.

As if he could have done anything else.

Russ moved inside her, keeping the strokes easy and slow. At first, anyway. Julia soon picked up the pace, and Russ put his hand between their sweat-slick bodies, so he could touch the sensitive flesh at the top of her sex.

He got the reaction he wanted. Julia tossed back her head and dug her fingernails into his back. Russ kept moving. Kept touching. And he watched her face.

Her eyes widened, and her expression said it all. *Ahhh. So that's what all the fuss is about.*

She came in a flash, her body pulling him deeper into hers. The sound of his name repeated on her lips.

She wound her arms and legs tighter around him, and for a moment, Russ got so caught up in watching her that he almost forgot that he was on the receiving end of this, too. Julia's climax was what pulled him back. That, and that look on her face. That look was something he would remember for the rest of his life.

Russ buried his face against her neck and let Julia do the rest.

Chapter Fourteen

Russ was naked right in front of her. He probably didn't know that this, too, was a first for her. She was only an arm's length away from a hot man with no clothes.

How much her life had changed in such a short time. Here, she'd come to this small Texas town to find Emily's father and had also found the man of her dreams.

Well, almost.

Russ was rough around the edges, and perhaps a little dangerous, but he had a way of making her remember that she alive. Like now, for instance.

She idly thumbed one of the iridescent bubbles in her bath. The water was warm and perfect. It soothed what little soreness she had from making love with Russ. And his naked body made her all hot again.

After they'd napped and had eaten the food an agent delivered, Russ had undressed to join her in the large tub, but then he'd gotten a call, an update about the investigation. It was because of that call she'd gotten the nice view of seeing him pace across the bathroom.

He certainly had some interesting parts.

"Yeah, I got that," he said to the caller. He sandwiched the phone between his ear and shoulder while he wrote down something on a piece of paper. He folded the paper and placed it on top of his gun, which was on the vanity.

"Good news," Russ said to her, when he ended the call. "Toby did the decoy departure, so it'll look as if we've left the hotel. I have the number for the account, and the money is in place. We should have the Richardson boy back in…" he checked his watch, "…about twelve hours."

That meant it was around 9:00 p.m. She should be exhausted, what with the adrenaline-spiked day she'd had, and the little sleep the night before, but her body was humming.

"What about the man Toby took away?" she asked.

"He's at the FBI's regional office. Don't worry, he won't be leaving. He'll be charged with a long list of crimes."

Russ frowned, as if he regretted bringing up the attack, so Julia decided to make him forget all about it—something she was trying hard to do. So she smiled and popped more of the bubbles around her breasts so that she could flash him.

Still, it was a paltry effort, considering that Russ was buck naked.

He chuckled, a sound all smoky and thick, and he practically jumped into the tub. The water and the bubbles splashed all over them and the tiled floor. He scooped her up, and she had the pleasure of kissing a soapy, slick, smiling man.

So this was what it was like to have an intimate partner. No wonder people were so anxious to fall in love.

Julia froze at that thought.

Russ noticed, because he pulled back and stared at her. "Everything okay?" he asked.

She wanted to curse herself for ruining the moment. She might not get many of these, and she'd wanted to savor every one.

"Everything's fine," she assured him, and was surprised that it was as true as it had been for her in years. Strange, considering that, hours earlier, someone had tried to kidnap her. Before that, someone had fired shots at her. Yet, here she was, panic free.

And aroused.

She leaned in and took pleasure in a long, slow taste of Russ's mouth. A taste cut way too short because Russ's phone rang.

He cursed but got up from the water, the suds streaming off his rock-hard body. Julia knew he couldn't just ignore the call, because it might be related to the investigation, but she hoped it wouldn't take him too long to handle whatever it was.

Russ grabbed a towel, wound it around his waist and grabbed his phone. He glanced at the screen and frowned.

"Yes?" Russ said. A moment later, he added, "Silas?"

That grabbed her attention, and Julia sat up so she could listen. Thankfully, Russ put it on speaker while he dried off.

"Someone tried to kill me," Silas insisted. His words were rushed, and his voice was anxious.

"Where are you?" Russ ignored the bombshell Silas had just delivered.

"I'm here, at the service entrance to the hotel. Russ, you have to let me in."

Sweet heaven, Julia thought. *What else could go wrong?* But she immediately rethought that. Silas might not be telling the truth. Obviously, Russ had his doubts, too. After all, the man had gone missing only minutes after someone had fired those shots in the park, and Silas was implicated again in the ruse shooting.

"What hotel?" Russ questioned.

"The Wainwright, of course, where Julia and you are staying."

Russ's jaw tightened. "Who says we're still there?"

"I paid one of the maids to check. I paid her to use her phone, too, because I lost mine when I was chasing the shooter at the park. You have to let me in, Russ. I'm hurt, and I need some help."

"Hurt how?" Russ asked.

Russ continued to dry off and then reached for his clothes. Since Russ might have to leave the room to help Silas, Julia got out of the tub so she could dress as well. So much for her humming body and those extra kisses she'd been anticipating.

"I can't get into that now," Silas insisted. "Didn't you hear me? Someone tried to kill me."

"I heard. The problem is, I'm not sure I believe you."

"What?" Silas howled. "But you have to believe me. I'm your partner, Russ."

Russ groaned. He was obviously torn between whether he should help Silas or not. "I know who you say you are." Russ let that hang between them for several seconds. "What happened to you? Why did you disappear from the park?"

Silas cursed. "I was in pursuit of the shooter when someone came up from behind me and hit me with a stun gun. I lost consciousness, and when I came to, I was tied up in the backseat of a car. The driver took me out into the sticks and dumped me."

Russ pulled on his jeans and zipped them. He also stuffed the folded piece of paper in his front pocket. "Describe the guy."

"Dark brown hair. Green eyes." Silas didn't hesitate, and Julia immediately realized that was a similar description to the man who'd attacked her.

Still, it didn't mean Silas was innocent. Maybe her attacker and Silas were working together.

"You have to let me in," Silas repeated.

Russ shook his head and finished dressing. "No, I don't. And I won't. I can't risk putting Julia in any more danger. Besides, we're not at the Wainwright. The maid you paid off was mistaken."

"Julia?" Silas spat out. "You won't help me because of her? You're putting her ahead of me?"

"Absolutely," Russ said, not hesitating. "I know she's innocent, but I'm not so sure about you. And until I'm sure, here's what I want you to do. Call Toby."

"I don't have his number. Hell, I don't have anyone's number, because I'm not using my own phone. Yours was the only number I remembered. That's why I called you. That, and because I was sure you'd help."

Russ's jaw muscles continued to stir, and he rattled off some numbers to Silas. "That's Toby's cell. Tell him where you are and he'll come and get you immediately. He won't be alone," Russ warned.

"So Toby suspects me, too?" Silas asked. In addition to the anxiety, now there was anger.

"It's just a precaution," Russ explained. "If you're

innocent, then I'll owe you a huge apology." He paused. "How bad are you hurt?"

"I'll live." Silas mumbled something she couldn't understand, but it was clear that the man wasn't happy about Russ's decision. "It's just a broken arm. It happened when my kidnapper dumped me from the car."

"Any idea why the guy didn't just kill you?" Russ asked.

Silas hesitated. "I don't know. Maybe he kept me alive so I'd look guilty. But I'm not."

"I hope you're right. Call Toby," Russ told him, and he gave Silas the number again before he hung up.

"Could Silas be telling the truth?" Julia immediately asked. She hurriedly put on her dress and finger-combed her wet hair.

"I hope to hell he is. But I don't like that he's here at the hotel. At the very least, it's suspicious. But it could be far worse than that. We need to leave."

That sent her heart racing. "Right now? With Silas still nearby? Remember, you tried to convince him that we were at another hotel. If we try to leave, he might see us."

"We won't leave until I'm sure Silas has contacted Toby." Russ shoved his gun into the slide holster of his jeans. "We'll give Toby a couple of minutes to respond, and once he has Silas away from here and on the way to the hospital, then we'll use the unmarked car in the parking lot to leave."

Julia thought through all those steps they'd have to take. "Will we be safe?"

He looked at her and planted a quick kiss on her lips. "Safer than we will be here. I don't think Silas believed we were anywhere other than at the Wainwright. And if Silas is working for Milo, then this could be the start of another attempt to kidnap you."

That made the danger crystal clear. Milo could still want to use her as leverage, so that Russ would fully cooperate at the meeting. She would be Milo's insurance policy. And his hostage.

Julia nodded and slipped into her shoes. "Just let me grab my purse and we can go."

With Russ right behind her, Julia hurried to the bedroom, but she only took a few steps, when the lights went out, plunging the room into total darkness.

RUSS DREW HIS GUN, because he didn't believe this was a coincidence. Only a few minutes after he'd refused to help Silas, the power had gone out in the hotel. Either Silas was responsible, or Milo just wanted to make the agent look guilty. There wasn't time to figure out which.

Russ took out his phone. Thank God for the backlit keypad, because his eyes hadn't had time to adjust to the darkness. The drapes were all closed, and it was possible the street lights would help illuminate the room; but he didn't want to take the risk of someone watching for him to open the curtains.

He pressed in Toby's number, and waited.

Toby didn't answer. On the seventh ring, Russ gave up and slapped his phone shut. This couldn't be good. Even if Toby was helping a wounded Silas, the man still should have been able to answer his phone. Unless someone—or something—was preventing Toby from answering.

"What do we do?" Julia asked.

Her breathing was already too fast, so Russ pulled

her to him. He couldn't take long to comfort her, because he had to call headquarters for backup.

The sound stopped him. Someone was pounding on several of the doors. Russ didn't answer. He put his fingers to Julia's lips so she'd stay quiet, as well. But he was praying it was Toby out in the hall.

"It's me," someone called out. "The lights went out when I was coming up the stairs. I can't see my hand in front of my face out here."

Not Toby.

Silas.

"Russ, if you're in one of these suites, you have to let me in," Silas demanded. "Toby didn't answer his phone, and I've got no way to protect myself. And we have to protect ourselves. There's some guy in the parking lot, and I'm sure he's got some thermal imaging equipment. I think he's looking for us."

Oh, man. That wasn't something he wanted to hear. "Don't answer him," Russ whispered to Julia.

Silas knocked again, and it sounded as if he were at the door across the hall from them. "Russ, are you in there? The maid told me you were probably in one of the suites on this floor. I'm in pain, and I need help. *Please.*"

Russ waited, his breath held. Beside him, Julia did the same. He hated not responding, but he couldn't take the risk. He only hoped Silas would understand, if he turned out to be innocent in all of this.

Silas moved to their door, and he started to hit his fists against it. Russ hoped the locks wouldn't give way. Just in case, he aimed his gun in that direction. He wasn't happy about the possibility of having to shoot a fellow agent, but if Silas came through that door, Russ couldn't let him get to Julia.

"I'm going to the front desk to ask them to call for an ambulance," Silas said, his voice way too loud. Even if he was completely innocent, he had to be drawing some attention. The wrong attention, no doubt.

The pounding and shouting stopped. Russ waited, listening, and stayed quiet. He wanted to call headquarters, but Silas was possibly still lurking outside the door.

He brushed his fingers along Julia's arm again and hoped it would keep her calm. This had to be scaring her to death. It was scaring him, too, and he hoped he could get her safely out of there.

The seconds crawled by, each one ticking off in his head. Russ thought of Toby, of reasons why the man wouldn't be answering his phone, but none of those reasons were good. Maybe, just maybe, Toby was still alive.

Russ took out his phone again to call headquarters. It wasn't his first choice of ways to handle this incident, because if agents had to come into the hotel for a full scale rescue, it might blow his cover. That couldn't happen with him so close to getting the Richardsons' baby back.

Russ had barely opened his phone when he heard the sound.

A crash.

Russ automatically pushed Julia to the floor, and he crawled over her to protect her with his own body. He glanced around, trying to pick through the darkness to see what had happened. The door was still closed, so Silas, or someone, hadn't broken through it.

He spotted the glass then. Shards of it glistened on the floor. And Russ knew why. There was a hole in the drapes, and light from the outside was pouring through the tiny opening.

What the hell had happened? But he soon knew.

There was another crash, more of a soft pop, followed by the sound of breaking glass. And that's when Russ realized that someone was shooting at them with a gun rigged with a silencer.

Chapter Fifteen

Julia felt something smack into her leg, and she glanced behind her to see what it was. A shard of glass. Something had broken through the window and sent the glass flying.

Was someone shooting at them again?

If so, there hadn't been a loud bang like the shots in the park, or the ones fired earlier, outside the hotel.

"Let's go into the bathroom," Russ told her. He helped her get into a crouching position so they could get moving. But there was another swooshing sound.

The bullet, or whatever it was, tore through the thick drapes and sent more glass onto the floor.

That got Russ moving even faster. He practically pushed her to the floor and took out his phone. She waited and prayed, while he called for backup, but he only cursed.

"Someone's jammed the lines," Russ told her.

Her heart dropped. *No. This couldn't be happening.*

"Go into the bathroom," he said.

There were no windows in that room, so Julia was about to run in that direction, but the next sound was considerably louder than the others.

Not a bullet coming through glass.

This was much louder and more of a crashing sound. Light rushed through the sitting room, spraying out from the window, and she soon knew why.

Someone had actually broken through the window.

But how? They were on the top floor of the three-story hotel. That meant that someone had gotten to the roof and climbed out onto the ledge outside the window. It wouldn't have been difficult to do.

"Get down!" Russ shouted to her.

Julia dropped to the floor, and it wasn't a second too soon. One of those silenced shots came flying into the bedroom. Not at Russ, but at her.

The bullet slammed into the thick down comforter and sent feathers swirling around like confetti.

Russ returned fire. Unlike their attacker, his shot wasn't muffled through a silencer. It was a loud blast that echoed in the room.

She caught a glimpse of the shooter diving to the side of the sofa. Russ took cover, as well, behind the slightly ajar bedroom door. But Julia knew that wouldn't be much protection. Bullets could easily go through wood.

Julia wanted to yell for Russ to slam the door and get down, but she couldn't risk giving away their exact locations. Especially hers. The gunman had fired at her.

Why?

Earlier, Milo had tried to kidnap her, but now it appeared that Milo, or someone else, didn't care if she was killed. Did that mean they no longer needed her for leverage, or did this have something to do with Silas?

Another shot came her way and hit the pillows that were stacked against the headboard. Julia flattened her body on the floor and covered her head.

She considered trying to get into the bathroom, but it was too dangerous for her to move now. There was more than enough light coming from the broken windows for their attacker to see them and take aim right at her.

The next shot tore into the nightstand, just inches above her. She heard Russ curse, and he came out of cover with his gun pointed.

"No!" she shouted. He could be killed, and all because he was protecting her.

But that didn't stop him. Russ fired a shot, then another.

The next sound she heard was something or someone falling to the floor. A loud thud, like deadweight crashing against the carpet.

For a moment Julia lost sight of Russ, and that sent her into a near panic. He wasn't be hurt. That sound couldn't have been him falling.

But then she heard footsteps and followed their sound. Russ was still there. Standing. And he didn't appear to be injured. He had his weapon and was inching into the sitting room.

"Is he dead?" she asked.

Russ didn't answer. She saw him shake his head, and he disappeared into the other room.

Julia started praying. She hated that she wished someone dead, but better their attacker than Russ or her.

She forced herself to slow her breathing. Not easy to do. But she formed an image of Russ and Emily in her mind. She didn't let that image waver, and she drew much needed strength from it. She had to get through this for them. Emily needed her, and Russ would go through a bad guilt trip if she went crazy on him.

"He's dead," she heard Russ say.

The relief was immediate, and she jumped to her feet so she could see for herself. But Russ was there in the doorway, and he turned her away from the dead man.

"He has a thermal monitor on him," Russ explained. "This is the guy that Silas saw in the parking lot."

No doubt. And he'd used that equipment to pinpoint them for an attack.

"My phone isn't working," Russ added. "But someone probably heard those shots. I'm thinking we'll wait here until the cops arrive."

Julia nodded, and then went willingly when he pulled her into his arms.

"Why did he want me dead?" she managed to ask. "It doesn't make sense. Milo probably thinks I'm the buyer. He likely believes I'm the one who'll be giving him access to the money. So why would he risk killing me?"

"I don't know." Russ brushed a kiss on her cheek. "But I intend to find out."

Yes, but that would take time. "What about tomorrow morning's meeting?"

"I'll go with backup," he said.

Backup suddenly didn't seem nearly enough. Still, what other choice did Russ have? They couldn't let the Richardson baby be sold to someone else.

She stood there in his arms, while she listened for the sound of sirens. But she didn't hear any. Maybe because it was too soon. Maybe the cops were on the way but still out of earshot. She didn't want to think of the alternative—that Russ's bullets had been dismissed as a car backfiring.

"How long do we wait?" she whispered.

"As long as it takes."

But the words had no sooner left Russ's mouth when Julia finally heard something. It wasn't what she wanted to hear.

It was coming from the hallway.

There was another of those deadly swishing sounds. And this time, she knew exactly what it was.

Someone had fired a shot just outside their suite.

NOT AGAIN.

That was Russ's first thought, quickly followed by a trained response that he had to do something, anything, to protect Julia. For whatever reason, someone was out to kill her tonight.

The dead guy on the floor had certainly tried. And failed, thank God. Russ had wanted to find out who he was, and better yet, who had sent him. But those questions would obviously have to wait.

Round two had begun.

There was another shot in the hall. It also came from a gun rigged with a silencer.

Apparently, someone didn't want to be detected. Too bad Russ couldn't just start firing shots at the ceiling, so that it would alert someone to call the police, but he couldn't waste the ammunition. He didn't have any extra magazines with him, or a backup weapon. Since he was using a smaller, more compact handgun, suited for undercover work, he'd only started with fifteen rounds—two of which he'd spent on the dead guy.

Thirteen better turn out to be a lucky number,

because that wouldn't be enough firepower if he got into a long gunfight.

Russ caught onto Julia's arm and positioned her behind the bar. It wasn't an ideal location, since it wasn't that far from the now gaping window where the gunman had entered. But the bathroom was out, since it was on the same side of the wall as the hall. In fact, that could have been where the last shot went. Anyone with any experience in attacks would have known that Russ would have sent Julia into the bathroom.

And he'd nearly succeeded in getting her there. But blind luck again had kept her remaining safe. Later, he'd kick himself for not getting her out of town. She should be at the safe house with Emily. But instead she'd stayed behind, and was now in danger because of it.

Russ stayed in front of her and tried to keep watch on all sides. If someone tried to break down the door, he'd have time to fire, but he couldn't cover both the door and the window. If the assault came from both sides, they were in trouble.

There was another shot. And it confirmed what Russ had already suspected. Someone had fired into the bathroom. This wasn't just an ordinary attack. It was a mission of murder.

Now the question was why?

He checked his phone again: still blocked. He picked up the house phone, but it was dead as well. Though maybe, just maybe, help was on the way.

Just in case this turned ugly, Russ took the folded piece of paper from his front pocket and stuffed it in between the foil-bagged nuts on the bar. Leaving it there was a gamble, but it would be an even bigger gamble to keep it on him.

There was a thump at the door. Not exactly the sound of a kick, but close. Russ aimed his gun in that direction and braced himself for another attack.

He didn't have to wait long.

The second attempt was a hard kick to the door. The locks held. Until the person fired a shot into the lock. Not one, but three. Each rough gust was followed by the sound of metal slashing through metal.

Russ's heart was in his throat, and he had no doubt that Julia was about to lose it. She didn't have his training. But she damn sure had the experience with violent situations. This was no doubt causing an avalanche of flashbacks.

"Stay down," Russ warned her, in a whisper.

Another bullet went into the lock, and it was followed by a hard kick. Russ got ready. His finger tightened on the trigger, and he tried to get the best aim he could. He had no idea who or what was coming through the door, but he might have only one shot to save Julia.

The door burst open, and Russ was within a split-second of firing when he saw the man's face.

Silas.

But he wasn't armed, and he didn't look as if he had the strength to kick down a door. There was blood on his forehead and on the sleeve of his shirt. He was holding on to his left arm.

"I'm sorry," Silas said. He hadn't said it clearly, either. He slurred the two words.

Russ wanted to ask "sorry for what?" But he soon realized Silas wasn't alone.

Someone was standing directly behind him.

Russ couldn't see the person's other face, but he had no trouble seeing that a gun was aimed at Silas's head.

That put a knot in Russ's stomach. He hadn't trusted Silas when he'd called out earlier, and maybe because of that lack of trust, Silas was now in danger. Still, Russ hadn't had a choice. The agent's behavior had been too erratic for Russ to believe him and let him anywhere near Julia.

"I depended on the wrong person," Silas mumbled, and that remark caused the individual behind him to jam the gun harder against his head.

Russ pushed aside Silas's comment. Later, there'd be time to question his partner as to what he meant by that. Right now, Russ had to deal with what was essentially a hostage situation. And Julia was right in the middle of all this.

"Who are you?" Russ demanded of the gunman. He kept his gun aimed, but he knew he couldn't fire. Silas was literally a human shield.

The person didn't answer for several seconds. "It's me."

Russ had no trouble recognizing that voice. It was Milo.

Apparently, Julia recognized his voice, too, because she made a soft groan.

This latest incident shouldn't have surprised Russ— he knew the man was a criminal—but what he couldn't figure out was why this was happening. The meeting had been scheduled. He had the number for the offshore account. Within a matter of hours, the baby deal would have been closed, and in theory, Milo would have a lot of money for his part in the illegal transaction.

So what had happened to make Milo resort to this?

Maybe Milo had objected to Russ's insistence that Julia not be at the meeting. Or maybe he had just gotten suspicious. Something had certainly set him off, if he was holding a hostage at gunpoint.

"What do you want?" Russ demanded.

Again, Milo took his time answering. Russ shifted a little so he could see him, and Milo was glancing all around the hall, as if he expected someone to jump out and attack him.

Good. That probably meant Milo didn't have backup, either. Maybe because his backup was supposed to have been the dead guy now lying on the floor.

"I want Julia," Milo finally answered.

Everything inside Russ went still. Hell. He didn't hear any reaction from Julia. He didn't have to. Russ knew she had to be terrified at the thought of being held captive by this monster.

"Why do you want Julia?" Russ asked the man.

"Because if I have her, then I can make sure you cooperate."

That didn't make sense. "You already had my cooperation before you decided to pull this stunt."

"No. I had the façade of your cooperation. I know who you are, Special Agent Russ Gentry. And I know this is a sting operation to bring me down."

Russ tried not to react to that. He had to stay calm. And he prayed Silas did the same. The agent was sweating like crazy, and he was grimacing in pain.

"If you believe I'm an agent out to get you, then why do you want Julia?" Russ wanted to know.

"Because I still need the money, and I can be sure that you'll give it to me if I have her."

Russ chose his words carefully. "The deal can still happen. You give me the baby, and I'll give you the number for the offshore account."

Milo laughed. "Not without some insurance. Julia is that insurance."

Milo was obviously lying. Just a few minutes ago, the dead gunman had tried to kill her. And then someone, probably Milo, had fired shots into the bathroom, the most likely place for her to be. This was more than just Milo wanting some kind of insurance. He wanted Julia dead.

Why?

The reason didn't matter; Russ wasn't going to let Milo get the chance.

"You don't want Julia," Russ tried again. "Make a call. Get the baby here, and I'll give you the number of the offshore account so you can get that money. Everybody will be happy, and no one else gets killed."

"No," Milo answered.

"No to which part?" Russ asked, holding his breath. This couldn't fall apart now.

"To all of it," Milo calmly said. "If Julia doesn't come with me, there'll be no exchange. And you won't get your hands on the baby. In fact, if I don't make a call within fifteen minutes, the baby will be taken out of the country, and neither his parents nor you will ever see him again."

Russ took a deep breath and got ready to go another round with Milo. He had to make this deal happen. But before he could say anything else, he heard movement behind him. He also saw Silas shaking his head. It didn't last long, because Silas's eyelids fluttered down, and the man appeared to lose consciousness. At least Russ hoped that was all it was. It was possible that he was close to death, because Russ had no idea how serious his injuries were.

Despite Silas going limp, Milo hung on to him and continued to use him like a shield.

"I'll go with you, Milo," Russ heard Julia say.

Despite the fact that he wouldn't take his eyes off Milo and Silas, her words caused Russ to look at Julia. She had her hands lifted in the air.

Surrendering.

Russ cursed. "Get back," he ordered.

"No," she answered. Her voice wasn't nearly as calm and assured as Milo's, but that didn't stop her from moving away from the bar, and closer to Milo.

She looked at Russ, and he saw the determination in her eyes. "I'm not going to lose the baby," she insisted.

"Smart woman," Milo proclaimed.

Russ wanted to shoot Milo for encouraging her and putting her in this position. "This isn't smart," Russ told her. "He wants to kill you."

But that didn't stop Julia.

Russ tried to latch onto her and pull her back, but she walked straight toward Milo.

Chapter Sixteen

Julia forced herself not to think beyond the moment. She didn't want to put herself in harm's way, but she also didn't want the Richardson baby to be taken out of the country.

She thought of her own precious Emily—of how horrible it would be to have her stolen from her, never to be seen again.

Julia also thought of Russ. He definitely didn't approve of what she was doing. He was the protector, and he wanted her safe.

But sometimes being safe wasn't the right thing to do.

Russ reached out to grab her again, but that caused Milo to dig the barrel of his gun into Silas's head. "You want him dead?" Milo taunted. "Because that's what will happen if you don't stop."

Julia glanced at Russ and tried to reassure him that this was the only option they had, but he only shook his head and demanded that she back up.

She didn't. When she was within just a foot or so of Milo, he shoved Silas forward, nearly pushing him straight into Julia. When she stepped to the side to avoid the impact, Milo latched onto her and pulled her in front of him.

Now *she* was Milo's hostage.

"Let her go," Russ demanded. He glanced at Silas, probably to make sure the man was okay, but then he nailed his attention on Milo and Julia.

"See?" Milo said in a sappy sweet, mocking tone. "You're already in a more cooperative mood. No more demands from you. No more lies."

Russ's eyes narrowed, and the muscles in his jaw went stiff. "What do you want?"

"The number of the offshore account."

Julia had expected him to say that, and she also expected Russ to start bargaining. She didn't have to wait long.

"I only have half the numbers," Russ told him. Julia knew that was a lie. "The other half is with the buyer."

"Then you'd better get those numbers now or I'll kill Julia," Milo insisted.

Russ lifted his shoulder. "Julia's my ex-lover. Nothing more. She doesn't mean anything to me."

Julia knew this was a ploy, but she couldn't believe how convincing Russ was. Or how much it hurt to hear him say that. He certainly meant a lot to her. Too much, maybe.

She was in love with him.

It wasn't the best time for her heart to announce that to her head, so she pushed it aside. Later—if there *was* a later—she would deal with her feelings. Right now, she had to stay alive and stop Milo from hurting anyone else, especially Russ and the baby.

"Just your ex-lover, huh?" Milo asked. "You don't expect me to believe that."

"It's true," Russ fired back.

Because Milo's chest was against her back, Julia felt Milo go stiff. His tone might be all calm and cool, but he was getting agitated. He had counted on Russ being willing to do anything to protect her. Maybe that's what the shots had been about. If one of those bullets had seriously injured her, Russ would have handed over the account numbers to save her life. And in doing so, Milo would have likely killed them both.

From the corners of her eyes, Julia looked down the hall, in case she needed an escape route. It was dark because the electricity was still off, but there was a window at the opposite end of the suite entrance, and some light trickled in. Enough for her to see that there was no one else around.

But the door immediately next to her suite was ajar.

Mercy. Russ had already told her that there weren't any other guests staying on the third floor, that the all-suites floor didn't get much use at the Wainwright, but that didn't mean someone couldn't have sneaked up there. She hoped Milo didn't have one of his hired guns in there, waiting to step in and help.

"Here's what happens now," Milo said. The calmness faded. "You give me *all* the numbers of the offshore account number, and once I've verified that the money's there, I'll take Julia out to the parking lot, where I'll give her the baby."

Julia wanted that to be true, but she knew she couldn't trust him. Once Milo had the full account number, there was no reason to keep any of them alive.

Russ didn't look at her. He kept his attention trained on Milo. "The buyer won't give me the other half of the account until I have proof that we have the baby."

"Then we're at a stalemate," Milo said, his voice a threat now. "You'd better hope my finger doesn't tense, or the bullet will go right into Julia. And despite what you said about her being your ex-lover, I'm betting you still feel enough for her that you can't let her die this way."

Russ didn't flinch. Didn't react. But Julia had to bite her lip to keep from making a sound.

"A stalemate's not going to do either of us any good," Russ said.

"You got a better idea?" Milo asked.

"I think I do. You and I can go to the parking lot together. Just the two of us. And after we both put down our guns, I can call the buyer for the second half of the account at the exact moment that you put the baby in my arms."

She braced herself for Milo to laugh or say an out-right *no,* but he didn't.

"All right," Milo agreed. "But we keep the guns. For now. And Julia goes with us."

"No," Russ barked, angrily disagreeing. "She'd only be in the way."

"Maybe she'll be in *your* way, but not mine. I'd prefer not to be shot by a sniper when I walk out of this hotel."

Julia waited, holding her breath. She held it for so long that her lungs began to ache.

Russ finally nodded. "Let's finish this."

Julia didn't feel any relief. They still had a long way to go, and too many things could go wrong. But maybe this was a start. Still, she had to be ready to escape, because all of this could be a trick.

Milo moved slightly, so he could turn her to face the hall. "You first," he told Russ.

Russ hesitated. "We go side-by-side," he insisted.

Probably because he was concerned that Milo would shoot him in the back. And he just might try to do that. But Julia figured Russ was safe, at least until Milo got those account numbers he wanted.

With his gun still aimed and ready, Russ mumbled something to Silas, and he stepped out into the hall with Milo and Julia. She was ahead of them, but glanced over her shoulder at Russ.

Julia tried to read what was going on in his mind, but then Milo pushed her forward to get her into position. She adjusted her stance, and Milo curved his left arm around her throat so that she wouldn't be able to get too far ahead of him. And so he could keep his gun pressed to her head.

Russ stayed on Milo's right, and together the three of them started up the hall.

They'd only made it a few steps when Julia saw the movement. It'd come from the room next to her suite.

The room with the open door.

Julia started to call out to Russ, to warn him, but it was already too late.

RUSS SAW THE FLASH of movement to his right.

He automatically pulled back and turned his weapon in that direction, but he found himself gun-to-gun with the person just inside the dark doorway.

"Shoot and Julia dies," Milo reminded Russ.

Russ held back on pulling the trigger, and he tried to

focus on the person across from him. Unfortunately, the light wasn't cooperating. He could see some things in the hall, thanks to a small window and the street lights outside it, but the rays didn't extend to the open suite.

This was obviously Milo's backup. Or maybe it was his boss, Z.

That got Russ's heart pumping, but not just because he might finally come face-to-face with the baby seller, but because he didn't like two guns aimed anywhere near Julia.

Somehow, he had to get her out of this situation. Unfortunately, now that he was outgunned, he might need a miracle for that to happen.

"There's been a change of plans," Milo said. Minutes earlier, his nerves had started to show, but, he seemed back in control now.

Russ couldn't say the same for Julia. Her eyes were wide, and her breath was gusting.

"Just hang on," he whispered to her. She was stronger than she thought and could get through this, but he hated that she'd been put in this position again.

"What change of plans?" Russ asked Milo. Though he was pretty sure he already knew the answer. Milo only wanted one thing—the money.

"You give us the complete account number, and I'll let Julia live."

Russ looked him straight in the eye and knew that Milo was lying. Once he had the money, that would be it.

"For now though, I'll just make a few cuts," Milo continued. He kept the gun pointed at Julia, but used his left hand to take something from his pocket.

A switchblade.

Milo clicked it open, and the gleaming silver blade snapped up and caught the light. "I read all about Julia's attack, and I figured she'd have a particular distaste for knives. I'll keep cutting her until you drop the gun."

Hell!

Without the gun, Russ would have no way to protect Julia or himself. But he couldn't stand there and let Milo cut her to pieces, either.

Julia had her eyes fixed on the blade. She didn't struggle. She froze. Unable to break free without risking Russ's and her lives, she could no doubt see what was coming next.

This was the return of her worst nightmare.

Russ knew she wouldn't be able to handle this for long. Neither would he. He couldn't stand what this was doing to her. Even though he had no idea how to stop this, Russ did the only thing he could.

He dropped his gun.

Julia's gaze met his, and he saw the momentary relief when Milo pulled back the knife. But it was only momentary. Because like Russ, she knew that without the gun, they were in deep trouble.

"He'll have the account number on him," Milo told the person inside the room.

And then the person in the dark room stepped out.

Russ realized why he hadn't been able to make out any of the person's features. That's because Milo's henchman was dressed head-to-toe in all black, and that included a mesh cover over the face.

"Search him," Milo ordered.

The mysterious person checked Russ's pockets. Russ considered just grabbing the SOB and using him as a shield, the way Milo was using Julia. But there was a huge difference in their situations. Milo probably wouldn't care if Russ killed his accomplice.

Russ didn't want Julia harmed.

She was the ultimate bargaining tool, and Milo knew it.

Russ cursed. He'd been here before, with someone he cared about who was in danger, and it hadn't turned out so well the last time.

"It's not in his pockets?" Milo snapped.

His assistant shook his head.

Now, it was Milo who cursed. "Don't make me take out the knife again," Milo said to Russ. "Where's the account number?"

Russ debated what he should do, and finally said, "It's in the suite on the bar."

It was a huge risk, because he still wasn't sure if he could trust Silas, but maybe if Russ could split up these two goons, then he might be able to wrestle the gun away from Milo.

Milo tipped his head to his partner, and the person headed back to Julia's suite. Even in the dark, it wouldn't take long to see the white piece of paper that Russ had put amid the packs of nuts. He had a minute, maybe two, at the most.

Russ kept his attention fastened on Milo. And he counted down the seconds. Milo finally did what Russ had been waiting for him to do.

Milo glanced behind him at Julia's suite.

It was just a glance, a fraction of a second, but it was more than enough.

"Get down!" Russ shouted to Julia.

But he didn't wait for her to do that. Knowing he had only one shot at this, Russ dove right at Milo.

Chapter Seventeen

Julia didn't have time to get down before Russ launched himself at Milo. Russ plowed right into them, and all three of them went to the floor. Julia hit hard, nearly knocking the breath out of her, but she still tried to do whatever she could to help.

She rammed her arm against Milo to put some distance between them. It worked, even though Milo latched onto her hair and didn't let go.

Russ didn't let go of Milo either. He bashed his forehead against Milo's, and in the same motion Russ knocked the gun from Milo's hand.

The gun went flying across the hall and landed on the carpet.

Julia tried to go after it, but Milo wouldn't let go of her hair. He pulled hard, dragging her back toward him. The pain was excruciating, but she didn't scream. She concentrated all her energy on one thing: getting to that gun.

She couldn't let Milo or his partner get to it first because they would almost certainly use it on Russ and her. Russ continued to pound at Milo, trying to break the fierce grip he had on her.

Julia sensed some movement behind them, and she

glanced back to see Milo's partner. The sounds of the struggle had obviously made it into the suite, and the man had come running to help.

That couldn't happen. Because, unlike Milo, his hired gun was still in control of a weapon. Gathering as much strength as she could, Julia swung her body around so she could kick the gunman. She managed to connect with the person's shin, but the impact didn't dislodge his weapon.

Worse, he pointed the gun at Julia.

Julia had no doubt he would kill her on the spot, so she took drastic action. She dove back into the fracas with Russ and Milo. She barely dodged getting smacked in the head with Russ's fist. The blow hit Milo instead, but that didn't stop him from curving his arm around her neck.

Milo put her in a choke hold.

"I'll kill her!" Milo yelled to Russ.

Russ's answer was another fist to the man's face.

Julia fought with Milo's grip, and she fought to breathe. She couldn't let him win this. Nor could she let his hired gun get in a position to take a clean shot at Russ and her. As long as the three of them were wound around each other and fighting, the hired gun would have to wait to get a clear shot.

"Shoot them!" Milo told his comrade.

Julia didn't brace herself for the gunfire. She glanced back at the gunman, but she focused her energy on helping Russ get control of Milo. She bit and kicked and hit, all while trying to keep Milo between Russ and her.

The gunman waved his weapon, aiming and reaiming, obviously trying to take a shot that wouldn't hit Milo.

Without warning, Milo let go of her, and Julia fell backward, landing several feet away from Russ and Milo. She tried to scramble back into position so Milo's body would shield her, but it was too late.

The gunman fired.

The bullet came through a silencer, so there was no loud blast. Just the deadly swishing sound that Julia had heard when this latest attack began. The bullet didn't hit her, she realized. It slammed into the wall next to her. But it created just enough distraction for Russ to look her way.

"Julia!" Russ called out, as if pleading with her to get out of the line of fire.

And she tried to do that. She scrambled to the side so she could retrieve Milo's gun. However, the next shot was just the distraction Milo needed, because he latched onto her again and shoved her right in front of him.

"Move and she dies," Milo warned Russ.

Since the gunman was pointing his weapon at her and was less than three feet away, Julia didn't think she had much of a chance of dodging a bullet. The last time she'd gotten lucky, but she didn't think anyone could miss at this short range.

She went still—and waited.

Russ stopped struggling, as well, and they all looked at each other, as if trying to decide what to do next. The only sounds were their rough breaths.

With the quiet closing in around them and the gun pointed at her, Julia felt the old fears return. She wondered if she'd ever get to see Emily or Russ again.

Was this how it would all end?

But then she saw something that pushed away her thoughts of panic and death. She stared at the gunman dressed all in black. He even had on black gloves. And wore a net mask that curtained down from the black baseball cap.

There was something familiar about him.

Not so much anything visual about the person, but Julia caught the scent in the air. The scent that was cutting right though the sweat and humidity.

The scent was perfume.

Since she wasn't wearing any, that probably meant Milo's hired gun was a woman.

Was it Sylvia?

Julia wouldn't be surprised. The woman had tried to convince them she wanted to help by showing them those photographs, but Julia hadn't trusted her then. And she didn't trust her now.

"I know who you are," Julia told her.

The woman went stiff, and even though Julia couldn't see her eyes, she knew she was staring at her.

"Just kill her," Milo snarled. "Hell, what are you waiting for?"

But Russ didn't wait. He came off the floor and dove at the woman, crashing into her before she could get off a shot.

Julia didn't wait either. She went after Milo's gun. Unfortunately, Milo had the same idea. She barely managed to touch the weapon, when Milo jerked her away from it. He didn't stop there. Milo caught onto her and flung her against the wall.

Julia didn't have enough time to better position her body to take the impact, so her head slammed against a framed picture that'd been hung at eye level. She didn't even catch her breath before Milo came at her again.

She fought, punching at him and using her feet to keep him away. Next to her, just inches away, Russ was having his own battle, but she couldn't tell what was going on, because of the poor lighting and the way Milo was tossing her around like a rag doll.

"Run, Julia!" Russ told her.

She tried—she tried hard. But Milo just wouldn't let go.

From the corner of her eye, she saw Russ grab the woman and put the gun to her neck. He had control of the accomplice, but unless Julia could get away from Milo, the advantage would do them no good.

"I'll break her neck," Milo threatened. And he tightened his hands around her throat.

"Stop or I'll shoot," Russ threatened, right back. He jammed the gun against the woman and gave her hat and face covering a fierce jerk to remove it.

Julia froze, because it wasn't Sylvia. It was Tracy Richardson.

Maybe because she was no longer struggling, Milo stopped, too, and he looked back at Russ and Tracy.

"You should have shot them when you had the chance," Milo told her.

"Easy for you to say." Tracy didn't look nearly as composed as Milo. Her eyes were wild, and it was clear she was way out of her league here. "You're a killer. I'm not."

"What exactly are you?" Julia asked, hearing the anger in her own voice.

Tracy just gave an indignant stare.

"Tell them," Milo taunted. "If I'm the killer, then

you're a mother who arranged to have her own baby kidnapped. She's also the idiot who hired someone to fire shots at Julia and you in the park. And because that wasn't enough screwing up for one person, she hired the other moron to break into your suite."

"Why?" Russ wanted to know.

Milo didn't seem to mind telling all. "Because she got scared. I had the meeting all set up for tomorrow, and she decided she couldn't wait a few more hours. Amateur," he added, in a mumble.

Russ cursed, and if Julia hadn't gotten her teeth unclenched, she might have done the same. "You had your baby stolen?" Julia wanted to know.

Tracy gave an indignant nod. "So what if I did."

That didn't help the anger that was slowly building into a rage inside Julia. "You put him in danger."

"He was never in danger. Not really."

That wasn't true. Any association with Milo was a dangerous one, and Tracy had put her son right in the line of fire. She'd apparently done the same to Russ and Julia, since Tracy hadn't denied it when Milo had accused her of hiring a hit man to fire those shots in the park.

"You did this for the money," Russ mumbled, his tone as enraged as Julia's.

"For *my* money," Tracy snapped. "I deserved it after putting up with Aaron's affairs for seven years. *Seven years!* But I was young and stupid when I married, and I signed a pre-nup. I wouldn't have gotten a penny in the divorce, so this was my way of making sure my son and I had a good future."

"It was your way of staying rich," Julia corrected.

Tracy glared at her. "I don't have to take this from

you. Break her neck, Milo. Agent Gentry won't kill an unarmed woman."

"The hell I won't." Russ jammed the gun to her face.

"Stop!" Milo yelled. "Even with Tracy's impatience and penchant for messing everything up, we can all get what we want here. I need the numbers for that offshore account, and you two can still get to rescue the baby. Everyone lives, and the only one who's out anything is Aaron Richardson."

None of that soothed Julia's anger. She wanted both of these monsters to pay for what they'd done.

"What about the hurt agent on the floor?" Russ asked. "What about your own hired guns? Two people are dead, Milo."

"All Tracy's fault. The agent on the floor had been drugged. You can thank her for that, too. None of this, including the hired guns, can be traced back to me. She knows, if this all goes wrong she'll take the blame. I'll just walk away."

Tracy mumbled something under her breath. She obviously wasn't happy that Milo was ready to throw her under a bus. What could she have expected? She was dealing with a hard-core criminal.

Julia glanced down at her hands. She wasn't shaking. And she wasn't on the verge of a panic attack. But she hated that Russ and she were still in danger, and it might not end anytime soon. One thing was for sure. She didn't intend to stay in Milo's grip.

She drew back her elbow and rammed it into his stomach. In the same motion, she bolted forward and snatched up the gun from the floor. It took everything in her to stop herself from firing at the man who'd made their lives a living hell, and had sent Emily into hiding.

"You know where the Richardson baby is?" Russ asked, tipping his head to Milo.

"I do. He's…nearby. Why?"

"Because I'll make a deal with you. Who's Z?"

She couldn't see Milo's expression, but she thought he might have smiled. "I am. Z is the name I give to the sellers who get in touch with me. Most people respond better if they think they're dealing with a team, rather than an individual."

Well, that was one riddle solved.

"Mind you, that's not a confession to any crime," Milo explained. "People just seem to think the worst of me, and assume I can find them buyers for the children they've acquired through illegal means."

"Can't imagine why," Russ snarled. "So, here's what we'll do. First, you put that knife on the floor."

Milo hesitated, as if giving that some thought, but he finally took it from his pocket, and tossed it so that it landed near Julia's feet. She tried not to react, but she couldn't suppress a shiver. She kicked the switchblade to the side.

"I'll give you the offshore account numbers, and you give me the baby," Russ told Milo. "I'll let you walk. Tracy here, however, will get to spend the rest of her life in prison."

"What?" Tracy yelled.

Milo seemed to relax. "Sounds like a good deal to me. Let's start for the parking lot, while you give me the first half of the account number."

"This isn't going to happen," Tracy shouted.

"You're wrong," Russ informed her. He shoved her, to get her moving.

They began walking. Not quickly, and Tracy didn't exactly break any speed records. She loped along, all the while cursing her former partner.

All of them continued to fire glances at each other. Since Russ kept his gun aimed at Tracy, Julia concentrated on Milo. She wasn't even sure she could shoot straight, but if the man made one wrong move, she would stop him.

"Six, four, eight, eight, three," Russ said, but Julia had no idea if that was a correct set of numbers or not.

While they continued to make their way down the hall, Milo reached for his phone, causing Russ to aim the gun at him.

"It's just my cell. I want to verify that there is indeed an account that starts with those numbers."

Russ hesitated a moment, then motioned for him to continue. That brought a sound of outrage from Tracy.

"I can't believe you're letting him do this." Tracy stopped, but Russ just ground the gun against her and shoved her forward.

Milo led them to the stairs, and Julia was thankful for the emergency lighting. She could actually see the steps, and she could also see that no one was lurking there, ready to ambush them.

"Confirmed," Milo said, a moment later. He held onto his phone, probably so he'd have quick access when and if Russ gave him the other numbers.

"Open the door," Russ instructed Milo, when they reached the exit. "And Julia, you stay behind him. Shoot him if he does anything that makes you uncomfortable."

She nodded and made brief eye contact with Russ, to see how he was doing. He had his attention on the task. Good thing, too. She didn't want his concern for her to cause him to lose focus.

The moment Milo opened the door, the heat and humidity rushed in and engulfed them. It was night, but the parking lot was actually better lit than the hotel. And there was the sound of sirens. Finally, the police were responding. The problem was, they might see the guns and start firing. That meant Russ and she had to move fast.

"The baby's in one of the vehicles," Milo insisted.

Julia looked around at the half-dozen cars parked in the back lot.

"Which one?" Russ demanded.

Milo shook his head.

"I'll look in all of them," Julia volunteered.

"If you do that, the nanny has instructions to drive away," Milo explained. "The only way she'll stay put is if I tell her, with a call."

"Nine, four, three," Russ said, giving Milo more of the numbers.

"Don't do this!" Tracy yelled. She was crying now, the tears streaming down her cheeks, and she sounded beyond hysterical. "Make the deal with me. Not him. That's my baby. All Milo wants is the money."

The men ignored her, and Milo looked at Julia. "Start walking to that dark blue van at the back of the parking lot."

"It's not the blue van," Tracy insisted. "It's the white

car." She glared at Milo. "I'll be damned if I let you take my money and stick me in jail."

"She's lying," Milo insisted.

"I don't think so," Russ mumbled, and Julia agreed. "Why don't we all have a look?"

Russ used his gun to get Milo and Tracy walking in the direction of the white car. Julia held her breath, hoping Milo was wrong about the driver taking off if she didn't get the phone call.

"Keep Milo in front of you, Julia," Russ instructed. She did, even though she prayed shooting him wouldn't be necessary. Julia didn't want shots fired with the baby around.

She approached the car.

And she saw the driver. It was a young woman with a death grip on the steering wheel. She was obviously terrified. Then Julia saw something else.

There was a sleeping baby in a carrier on the back-seat.

"That's the Richardson boy," Russ confirmed, prob-ably because he'd seen photos in his investigation.

Julia opened the car door and motioned for the nanny-driver to get out. She did, and the woman began to rattle off something in Spanish while she cried un-controllably. Julia reached for the keys to take them out of the ignition. Her back was turned for just a second when she heard the sound.

She whirled around, gun and keys in hand, and saw Milo dive toward Russ. Her heart dropped. *No, this couldn't happen.* They were so close to bringing this to an end.

Tracy managed to get out of the way, but Russ took the full impact of Milo's body crashing into his. Both men went to the pavement, and Russ's gun flew out of his hand.

The fight began all over again, fists flying, their bodies twisting around, so that it made it impossible for Julia to take aim. She couldn't risk shooting Russ, or having a bullet ricochet and hit the baby.

The nanny started to run, but Julia didn't go after her. She had to stay and try to help Russ.

Milo delivered a hard punch to Russ's jaw, but it didn't seem to faze him. However, Julia felt it, it seemed as if the pain shot through her.

Russ was operating on pure, raw adrenaline and had no fear of dying or being beaten. Julia had enough fear for both of them. She didn't want either of them to die before she'd had a chance to tell him that she was in love with him.

"Don't," Julia warned Tracy, when the woman started after the gun.

Tracy stopped. Thank God. Julia didn't want to risk firing a shot at her, either.

Russ brought back his fist and slammed it into Milo's face.

"But I have to leave," Tracy begged, glancing back at the struggle that was about to end. "As a mother, you must understand. If I go to jail, I won't be able to see my baby."

Julia looked her straight in the eyes. "You don't deserve to see him."

Tracy's face tightened and she let out a feral howl. She came at Julia and pushed her away from the car. Julia still couldn't fire, for fear of hitting Russ or the baby. But she also had no intentions of letting Tracy get anywhere near the son she'd had stolen for money.

Julia put all of her anger and emotions into the hard grip she had on Tracy's shoulder. She slammed the woman against the car and pinned her there.

"If I have to, I will kill you," Julia warned her.

Tracy stared at her, and Julia could see the debate in her eyes. It didn't last long. Tracy went limp and started to sob again.

Julia didn't take the gun off the woman, but she took her eyes off her just for a second so she could check on Russ.

Just a second.

She saw the gun, not in Russ's hand, but in Milo's.

And then the shot rang out.

Chapter Eighteen

Everything seemed to freeze.

One moment Milo and Russ were in a fight to gain control of the gun. The next moment, Russ heard the shot. He looked around and tried to figure out what had happened. And in those moments, he had a horrible thought: that the bullet had hit Julia.

He heard her scream, except it wasn't a scream, exactly. She was calling out his name. Her voice was filled with panic, and it merged with the piercing sounds of the sirens and the frantic shouts from the police who were approaching the scene.

Russ felt the gun that was between him and Milo. Both of them had their hands gripped around it.

It was Milo's finger on the trigger.

Hell, has Milo shot me? Russ wondered.

Russ looked at the man whose face was only a few inches from his own. Everything still felt frozen, except for Julia's screams. He had to check on her. He had to make sure she was all right, but he couldn't move, because Milo's weight was pinning him in place.

Dead weight.

Russ saw his lifeless eyes, then he looked between their bodies. Milo had indeed pulled the trigger, but the gun had been aimed at his own chest. He'd killed himself.

Russ was betting that it was an accident, because men like Milo didn't commit suicide.

"I'm all right," Russ tried to tell Julia, but he wasn't sure she heard him.

He threw Milo off him, and in case this attack wasn't over, he wrenched the gun from the dead man's hand.

Julia came racing toward him but stopped a few feet away. She had no color in her face, and she stared at him with her fingers pressed to her mouth.

"I'm okay," Russ said again.

But she shook her head and pointed to his chest.

Russ looked down, wondering if he had been shot after all, and he saw the blood. Now he understood.

"It's Milo's, not mine," he told her. He got to his feet and went to her as quickly as he could. He pulled her into his arms.

"Milo's," she mumbled. "Not yours. You're alive."

"Yeah." But it was obvious that Julia was about to fall apart. He didn't blame her. She'd been through hell and back tonight.

Behind them, Tracy latched onto the car door as if she were going to open it. "Don't," Russ warned her, and he pointed his gun at her. "It's over."

He had to let go of Julia so he could get a better aim and remove his badge from his back pocket. From the corner of his eye, he saw the uniformed officers approach the scene. Silas and Toby were with them, and Silas was being helped into an ambulance.

Later, he would apologize to Silas for not trusting him. But for now, he needed to get the Richardson baby out of here and tend to Julia.

Russ lifted his badge so the officers could see it. "Special Agent Russ Gentry," he let them know.

"I love you," Julia blurted out.

Even though there was pure chaos going on around them, that still grabbed every bit of Russ's attention. "Excuse me?" Because he was sure he'd misheard her.

"I love you." She gave a shaky, confirming nod. "I wanted you to know."

It was hardly the appropriate time, but Russ kissed her—and then eased her away from him. "Hold that thought," he whispered.

Russ went to Toby, who was barking out orders to the uniformed officers. Thankfully, he'd filled them in on what was happening, because one of the cops rushed to take Tracy Richardson into custody. The woman continued to sob, and she pled for a deal.

"The baby's father is on the way," Toby let Russ know. "Sorry I was late getting here. I was at the police station, questioning Sylvia."

"Sylvia? What did she have to say?"

"A lot. Apparently, she learned the love of her life, Milo, had been sleeping with Tracy Richardson. That didn't sit well with her, so she's spilling her guts."

Good. That might insure that Tracy would receive

a maximum sentence. As for Milo, well, he'd already gotten what he deserved.

"I didn't know what was going on here at the hotel, until I heard on the monitor that the local police were responding to sounds of gunshots," Toby added.

"I think Milo jammed the phone lines and cut the power," Russ said, nodding his head toward the lifeless man. One of the uniforms was checking him out.

Despite the fact that his full attention should be on what was happening, Russ's gaze went back to Julia. She'd opened the back door of the car and was trying to comfort the baby. Obviously, the shouts and the gunfire had woken him, and he was crying at the top of his lungs.

"Is Julia okay?" Toby asked.

"I think so." *Well...except that she'd just told me that she loved me.*

Had that been the adrenaline talking?

It made him a little sick to think that it might have been. Russ wasn't exactly surprised that he wanted it to be real. He'd wanted a lot of things from Julia, from the first moment he'd laid eyes on her.

First, he'd wanted sex. Then, more. The question was—how much more?

"I found Silas staggering out the front door of the hotel," Toby continued. "He'd been drugged, but was able to tell me some of what was going on. He said Tracy had him kidnapped so he'd look guilty." It'd worked.

"How is he?"

"He'll be fine. He has a broken arm and he's dehydrated, but I'm sure the medics will fix him up."

So that was one less thing on Russ's plate to worry about. Of course, there were still gaps he needed to fill in.

"There's a dead gunman on the floor of Julia's suite. According to Milo, Tracy hired him because she knew I was a federal agent. She also hired the other gunman in the park."

Toby nodded. "She obviously wanted you out of the way, and maybe Julia, too. She probably thought you were getting too close to figuring out that she's the one who had her son stolen."

"Can you make a call?" Russ asked Toby. "I think it'd help Julia and me if Emily were on her way back to us."

Toby studied him, probably because there was way too much emotion in his voice, but the agent finally nodded. "I'll get right on that. It'll be the first call I make." And the agent proceeded to do just that.

Russ took a deep breath and looked back at Julia. She had the baby in her arms and was rocking him back and forth, trying to soothe him. Russ had faced down gunmen recently, but he hadn't been this nervous.

But then, he'd never had this much at stake.

Once Toby had made the call, Russ finished up the briefing. He needed to give the agent some of the details of what had happened, so the reports could get started. Tracy would need to be interrogated as well. The nanny who'd run from the car would have to be found. Sylvia would have to be questioned further, so the FBI could determine what exactly she knew about Milo's baby-selling activities.

So many details. However, Russ was going to leave those details to someone else.

After he'd finished with Toby, Russ made his way across the parking lot toward Julia. She looked up, snared his gaze. He thought for a moment that she might smile, but then her attention dropped to his shirt.

Specifically, to the blood.

"How's the baby?" he asked, to give himself time to gather his thoughts.

"He's okay. Not a scratch." As if he knew he was now the topic of discussion, the baby stopped crying and volleyed glances at them. "His mother will go to jail, but he still has his father."

Yeah. That was more than Emily had. But then, Emily had Julia and him.

"Come on," Russ said, taking her by the arm. "Let's go in the hotel lobby."

He didn't want her to have to keep looking at Milo's body—and his bloody shirt. He stripped it off and gave it to one of the agents who was at the back entrance of the hotel.

"You should probably bag this," Russ told him. It almost certainly wouldn't be needed, but he wanted it out of Julia's sight. Besides, Emily would arrive soon, and he didn't want the baby around it, either.

The agent was wearing a button-down shirt over a tee, so he took off the outer shirt and handed it to Russ. Russ thanked him and put it on.

Julia gave a nod of approval. "I'm glad Milo's dead," she whispered. "If he'd gotten away—"

"He didn't," Russ reminded her. "And neither did Tracy. It's all over, Julia. We're safe now."

She gave another shaky nod, and even though she didn't seem ready to panic, Russ was still worried about her. Even more, he was worried about how to say the things he needed to say.

They took their time walking inside, probably because Julia was drained, and seemed to pause with each step. Russ felt the fatigue, too, but more than that, he felt relief that they'd all come through this unscathed.

When the baby started to fuss again, Julia placed him against her chest and patted his back. A female uniformed officer stepped forward. "Want me to take him? His father just arrived."

Julia kissed the little boy on the cheek and handed him over. The officer had no sooner taken the baby when Russ spotted Aaron Richardson coming in through the front lobby doors. No slow steps for him. The man practically ran to his son, and gathered him into his arms.

If Russ had any doubts about Aaron's love for his son, he didn't have them after witnessing that encounter.

"Thank you," Aaron told them, and he just kept repeating it while he kissed his baby. The man started to cry.

Several officers and an agent converged on Aaron, probably to fill him in on the details of what had happened to his wife. Russ decided those were not details

Julia needed to relive, so he led her into the reception area and had her sit on one of the sofas with him.

"It's okay," she reassured him. "I'm not about to fall apart."

He examined her face and realized that it was true. She was shaky of course, but it would have been unnatural if she hadn't been.

She examined his face, too, and nibbled on her bottom lip. "About what I said in the parking lot—"

"You can't take it back," Russ said, interrupting her.

Julia stopped nibbling and stared at him. "I don't want to take it back."

"Really?"

"Really," she assured him. "I just wanted to apologize for blurting it out there, when you had so much else on your mind."

That eased the knot in his stomach, but he knew something else would ease it more. Russ put his hand around the back of her neck and drew her to him for a kiss. Not a quick peck of reassurance. He put his heart and soul into this one.

When he pulled back, Julia made a silky sigh. "Good," she whispered.

Yes, it was; but he wanted better. He wanted *more*.

"I'm in love with you, too," he told her.

Julia's eyes widened and she froze. For one terrifying moment, Russ thought she was about to say that she didn't want him to be in love with her, that it wouldn't work out between them, but a smile curved her beautiful mouth.

"Are you just saying that because we nearly died?" she asked, cautiously.

"No. I'm saying that because it's true."

She seemed to be holding her breath. "You're sure?"

"A million percent. I don't need months or years to sort out my feelings for you. I love you, plain and simple. And I love Emily, too. I want us to adopt her—together. I want her to have the Gentry name, because I think that would have pleased R.J. and Lissa."

Tears filled her eyes, but since she was still smiling, Russ thought this was better. He gathered his breath, and his courage, and he went in for the big prize.

"Marry me?" Russ asked.

"Can we get married?" Julia said at the same moment.

Both of them stared at each other. And despite the investigation going on around them, they laughed.

They were still laughing when the lobby doors swung open and in came Agent Soto, Zoey and Emily.

Russ and Julia jumped up from the sofa and hurried toward the baby. Russ got there first, but he stepped back so that Julia could scoop Emily into her arms.

The baby was sleeping, but she lifted one eye to check out what was happening. Emily must not have deemed this big enough to warrant waking up from her nap.

Julia kissed the baby and passed her to Russ. The gesture felt as natural as anything he'd ever experienced. This was right, and he knew exactly what he had to do to make the rightness stay that way.

"Could you excuse us a minute?" Russ asked Zoey and Soto. With Emily still cradled in his arm, he led

Julia back into the reception area. "I believe we owe each other an answer. I asked you to marry me, and you did the same."

He paused a heartbeat.

"The answer is yes," they said together.

The energy between them seemed electric, as it always did when they were together. It was even more special because Emily was there.

Russ put his arm around Julia and stole another kiss. He made it long, hot and special—because it was the first kiss of their new life together with their daughter, Emily.

* * * * *

2 FREE BOOKS
AND A SURPRISE GIFT

We would like to take this opportunity to thank you for reading this Mills & Boon® book by offering you the chance to take TWO more specially selected books from the Intrigue series absolutely FREE! We're also making this offer to introduce you to the benefits of the Mills & Boon® Book Club™—

- **FREE home delivery**
- **FREE gifts and competitions**
- **FREE monthly Newsletter**
- **Exclusive Mills & Boon Book Club offers**
- **Books available before they're in the shops**

Accepting these FREE books and gift places you under no obligation to buy, you may cancel at any time, even after receiving your free books. Simply complete your details below and return the entire page to the address below. You don't even need a stamp!

YES Please send me 2 free Intrigue books and a surprise gift. I understand that unless you hear from me, I will receive 5 superb new stories every month, including two 2-in-1 books priced at £5.30 each and a single book priced at £3.30, postage and packing free. I am under no obligation to purchase any books and may cancel my subscription at any time. The free books and gift will be mine to keep in any case.

Ms/Mrs/Miss/Mr _____ Initials _____

_____

Surname _____
Address _____

_____

_____ Postcode _____
E-mail _____

Send this whole page to: Mills & Boon Book Club, Free Book Offer, FREEPOST NAT 10298, Richmond, TW9 1BR